A SWORD INTO DARKNESS

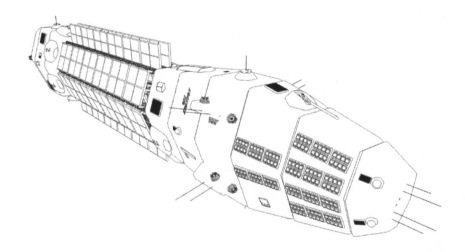

"*Solid adventure, intrigue and speculative space-tech, from a rising star in military science fiction.*"

— **DAVID BRIN**, Hugo and Nebula Award-winning author of
'*EXISTENCE*,' '*THE POSTMAN*,' and '*STARTIDE RISING*'

"*There are brilliant first contact stories, great space combat stories, and amazing stories of technological discovery. Rarely do you find all three in the same novel. Remember the name Thomas A. Mays. You're going to be seeing it on the bestseller list.*"

— **JEFF EDWARDS,** Award-winning author of '*SEA OF SHADOWS*,' and '*THE SEVENTH ANGEL*'

"*Sharply written, suspenseful and tightly plotted, A SWORD INTO DARKNESS reads like the best Tom Clancy novels, with a science fiction heart provided by Arthur C. Clark. Can't wait to read more from Thomas Mays!*"

— **GRAHAM BROWN**, #1 New York Times Bestselling author of
'*ZERO HOUR*,' '*BLACK RAIN*,' and '*THE EDEN PROPHECY*'

A SWORD INTO DARKNESS

Thomas A. Mays

STEALTH BOOKS

A SWORD INTO DARKNESS

Copyright © 2013 by Thomas A. Mays

Stealth Books

www.stealthbooks.com

www.improbableauthor.com

ISBN-13: 978-1-939398-08-6

Printed in the United States of America

DEDICATION

To my lovely wife, Jen. She's not a big sci-fi reader, but
hopefully she makes it far enough in to see this.

I love you, Babe!

ACKNOWLEDGMENTS

This book would not have been possible without the massive assistance I've received from a great many people across this wonderful nation of ours. All the good things about it came out of close collaboration with these fine folks and groups. Any bit of awful science, military strategy, or prose that remains is entirely my fault. Special thanks to:

The United States Navy and all my shipmates from USS STETHEM (DDG 63), USS LASSEN (DDG 82), USS BONHOMME RICHARD (LHD 6), COMDESRON 26, Naval Postgraduate School, Surface Warfare Officers' School, Pacific Missile Range Facility, and US Fleet Forces Command

Jeff Edwards (who goes above and beyond the call)

Winchell Chung and his amazing site, Atomic Rockets

Mark and Melissa Ellis, and the whole Newport Roundtable

Baen's Bar and the Barflies, especially Edith Maor, Sam Hidaka,

Gray Rinehart, and Gary Cuba

Nathaniel Torson

Charles Lakey

Chris Ross Leong

Maria Edwards

The Kevins (Henson, Csubak, and Allison)

Joe, Iris, and Daniel Peace

All of those who followed me over from SciFi-Meshes.com

the entire First Readers Group (you know who you are!)

and lastly, but most importantly, my family: Mom, Dad, the Brothers, Jen, Isabel, Gabrielle, Dylan, and Kona. Without you, I wouldn't be who I am and I wouldn't write how I write. Love y'all.

BOOK ONE: "FORGED"

1: "TURNAROUND"

April 3, 2023; NASA Headquarters; Washington DC

There was nothing quite like the District in springtime. Gentle sunlight bathed the cityscape with warmth, banishing the last vestiges of winter's gloom and filling the idealistic and the unscrupulous alike with hope for the coming year. Fragrant, flowering ramparts of lilacs, forsythia, and cherry blossoms bordered sidewalks, providing tourists, politicos, and drivers an almost idyllic setting for navigating the nation's capitol. Not even thoughts of the inevitable scandals, gang violence, and traffic congestion—which were certain to come with summer—could spoil Washington's upbeat mood.

That mood was not shared by all, however.

A side door to the National Aeronautic and Space Administration's DC headquarters burst open and released a furious, embarrassed Gordon Elliot Lee upon the city. He stormed out of the building, muttering to himself and glaring at the knots of ill-attired tourists walking along E street. Gordon strode forward with purpose, his own dark mood unrelieved by the joyful colors and pleasantly fragrant air everyone else seemed to bask in. He brushed past stupefied Washingtonians and stalked toward the nearest garbage can he could find, right at the intersection of E and 3rd. Reaching the can, he ripped open his slim briefcase.

As Gordon began to stuff page after page from his briefcase into the brown steel mouth of the can, the door to NASA's concrete and glass offices burst open again. Lydia Russ scanned up and down E street and blanched when she saw what he was doing. She hurried as fast as her stylish pumps would allow her, and reached Gordon just as he ran out of paper and began to sort through the golden rainbow of data disks he had brought with him. She drew to a halt and tried to catch her breath, crying out, "Gordon! Stop this right now!"

He looked back at her and frowned. Apparently deciding the garbage can was no longer worthy of his offerings, he instead flung the disks outward into the four lanes of traffic heading up and down E street. The BlueROMs made excellent Frisbees and they shone and flashed beautifully

1

as they bounced off cars and up from the blacktop. The drivers were somewhat less appreciative of his thoughtful gift, however. Everyone heard the familiar dissonance of screeching brakes, squealing tires, blaring horns, and one final movement of crunching metal.

Gordon grimaced and looked back to Lydia. His fine-boned, vaguely Amer-Asian features appeared unreadable, lost in a tumult of emotion. "Looks like my reputation's not the only thing I've wrecked today."

She approached and snatched the briefcase from him. Looking inside, she saw the only things left were some pens, flash drives, and Gordon's ultra-expensive, ultra-thin business tablet. She wondered if his tantrum would have extended to throwing that into the street.

Raised voices and slamming car doors rose above the din of traffic resuming. Lydia saw the two drivers whose Lexus-on-Mercedes ballet had ended so abruptly. Each gentleman gestured wildly to the other, intent on fixing blame upon their obviously guilty counterpart. Then one picked up a battered BlueROM and they both began scanning up and down the street. Lydia took Gordon's arm and pulled him away, hurrying down 3rd street, away from the accident.

He followed her lead only grudgingly, still in a huff over whatever had precipitated his fit. She glared at him. "Gordon, what the hell were you thinking?"

He looked at Lydia, remembering when they had been much more than industry associates. Her shoulder length, light brown hair whipped around her face in the building spawned wind, and he felt an unexpected pang of regret cutting through his pique. They had parted ways so long ago, but he thought their reunion had gone well until this. He had burned many bridges in the intervening years in order to make his mark in the world, yet he had to admit to himself that it hurt to think he had burned his final one to her. "I figured if I couldn't even get you to listen, then all my work belonged in the garbage. The disk thing may have been a bit much, but it's not like I didn't have provocation."

"That's not what I'm talking about. What were you thinking, going to the NASA with … that?"

He pulled his arm free of her grasp and stopped on the sidewalk, his anger resurging anew. "I've earned the right to tell NASA anything I damn well please! I'm Gordon-god-damn-Lee, not some wacko in a tinfoil hat. Who did you come to when you lost your little satellite constellation? And when Samuels threatened to drag you in front of the Senate for that thruster explosion, who did you get to explain it all away? Me! Every time me, so I think that entitles me to a little benefit of the friggin' doubt."

Lydia looked back to the street. One of the drivers stood on the sidewalk now, looking at the knots of tourists and business people for his quarry's face. She turned back to Gordon and motioned for them to continue walking. He followed alongside and she hissed in a stage whisper, "You're right. You've earned at least a fair hearing, but all benefit of the doubt is forfeit when you start talking about alien invasions. We get too many crackpot ideas pitched at us to not be a little sick of that sort of thing."

His face grew hot as his fury was joined by a twinge of embarrassment. "I never said anything about invasions! That was that little toad with the narrow glasses—Evenrude, or Evensly, or—"

"Evanston," she sighed. "The Associate Deputy Administrator for Policy and Planning. You also had the deputy directors from Ames, Marshall, and Goddard in there, but Evanston's the one guy you really needed to convince if you wanted to get any real support from us."

"Yeah," he said, the heat in his voice sheepishly dampened. "Evanston. Damn it, Lydia, how can they look at everything I showed them and just refuse to see it for what it is? It's damn near irrefutable!"

"No, it's not. It's preliminary: neither refuted nor vetted. You only have five months of data from a single, non-NASA observatory. That's barely enough to get decent parallax, so that throws your distance calculations into question. Your velocity estimates are extremely tentative, and calling your acceleration figures a fair guess would be pure charity on my part. Your spectral analysis is questionable, and your conclusions, well, I believe I've already mentioned the word 'crackpot', right?"

Gordon grimaced and spun about, searching the bright lip of the horizon. Finding his bearings, he jabbed an accusing finger due south. "Someone or something is coming, Lydia, and griping about the quality of my data isn't going to change that! I only have five months of data because the light only showed up five months ago, which is more or less what has me so damned concerned in the first place. It's a turnaround!"

Her face showed her confusion, and that only made him more exasperated. "A turnaround flip! Kinematics! Newton's damned laws! Weren't you listening?"

"Do not yell at me, Gordon! I'm your friend, not your employee."

He visibly tried to restrain his emotions. "Okay, I'm sorry, but listen to me now. Delta Pavonis is 19.9 light-years away. Call it even twenty, and now that little yellow sun—a sun just like our own—has started turning blue. But stars don't just turn blue. No, there's something else there, some bright blue light in front of the star, covering it up a bit, a bright blue light which is ten rather than twenty light-years away and on a direct line to us. Essentially, the light's shown up at the exact halfway point between Delta Pavonis and our solar system, and if my blue-shift guesstimate is to be believed, it's moving at 46% the speed of light. That means only one thing to me."

She shook her head. "It leads me to any number of possibilities, of which 'turnaround' is the least likely."

"You keep denying what's so obvious, and you're going to cut yourself on Occam's Razor. We're dumb monkeys, barely out of the trees. When we go to space, we do these high thrust, low efficiency, short burn Hohmann transfers. It's all we have the technology for, but it's slow— deadly slow. We could never reach another solar system that way.

"If you're an advanced, space-going culture, on the other hand, then the fastest way to get from one star to another—without cheating with a wormhole—is to apply thrust the whole way. You point your exhaust towards home for half the journey, accelerating to some ungodly speed, and then flip around and accelerate in the opposite direction until you match speed with your target system. It's called a brachistocrone trajectory and it's only possible with something that can thrust for a long, long time. And using this super-rocket, you wouldn't see any engine flare until it was at the half-way point, exactly what we are seeing."

She smiled softly. "Listen to yourself, Gordon. You're talking about an alien rocketship. Even if I accepted your data, there're still too many holes. What are the odds of our closest, truly compatible star having a decent solar system? And if it could support life, what are the odds they would be technologically advanced enough to notice us and come for a visit, a visit that would take nearly a century of continuous thrust if I'm doing the numbers right? How could they possibly carry enough reaction mass to make the engine work from there to here? And why wouldn't they just send a message? That would only take 40 years round-trip."

"Precisely! There's no good reason for them to come here physically. If they were benign, they would call. If they wanted to just kill us, they wouldn't ever have bothered to turn around. They could have cracked the planet in half with velocity alone and we'd never see them in time. So why are they coming here? That's the big question. That's NASA's mission."

She ran a hand through her hair, brushing its billowing strands from her face in her own matching frustration. "No, it's not. It's not because there is no alien ship coming here. You wonder why you got put in the crackpot category? Because the crackpots are the ones who'd rather believe in the unbelievable than consider things with a skeptical eye."

"Damn it, Lydia! Where's the imagination and wonder you used to dazzle me with? You and NASA have the exact same problem these days. You're all so worried about conservative budgets and little missions, about appearing respectable and professional to the world at large, that you reject anything that has the air of the fantastic or unusual. God forbid the agency that makes science fiction fact take a cue from science fiction. Find me a scientist in there who's read the "Mote in God's Eye" and I'll show you the person who should be backing me up."

Lydia crossed her arms and regarded him quietly. She gave a glance to the sidewalk along E street and saw that the angry driver was gone. Shaking her head, she began to walk back toward the headquarters entrance, speaking loudly enough for him to hear as she left him behind. "I've read Niven and Pournelle, and a host of others. The thing you don't seem to understand is that comparing your speculative observations to some whiz-bang space opera doesn't make your case more believable. It makes you look like a fanatic who's lost his touch with reality."

Gordon looked at her in dismay, but hurried forward to join her. He locked eyes with Lydia for a brief moment, finally catching sight of the pity she now viewed him with. He wanted to yell at her, to tell her how and why she was wrong, but it was pointless. She was closed to him, his last bridge burned. "Is it as bad as all that?"

"Well," she smiled. "You're an idle-rich tech wizard with an over-funded amateur astronomy bug, so some eccentricity has to be expected, I guess. The tantrums are a bit much, though. Listen, Gordon, it's just too crazy, too ambiguous, and too soon. No one's going to worry about something ten light-years away and forty years down the calendar right now. But, if it happens, you may reserve the right to say 'I told you so,' and I'll owe you a beer or something." She held out his briefcase to him.

He took it and closed the top. This was goodbye. "Actually, I figure you'll be proven wrong in about 33 years, what with 43 years to slow down and ten years for the light from the half-way point to get here."

They reached the sidewalk along E street. Lydia came close and gave him a gentle squeeze on his arm. "Thirty three years then. Plenty of time."

Gordon smiled tightly. He looked over at the two cars that had kissed fenders when he had thrown out the BlueROMs. The drivers stood by the side of the road, exchanging information and casting baleful glances in his direction. "No, not nearly enough time, Lydia. I don't know why they're coming, but if it's to do us harm, we haven't got a chance in hell of stopping them, not without the government's support anyway. To face what's coming on any sort of equal footing, we need to play catch-up in a big way. A single generation is way too short to do that, not without a little faith and a whole lotta luck."

"I'm sorry, Gordon."

He smiled back, the anger and frustration supplanted by melancholy in his eyes. "It's all right. If the Air Force won't have me, and NASA won't have me, and you won't have me, I can go it alone. It won't be the first time. Take care of yourself, all right?"

Lydia Russ nodded and watched him as he walked away. He did not get far before his car drove up to meet him. The driver opened his door, and Gordon gave one last long look to her and the building behind her, then he entered and the sleek black car drove away. She turned slowly about, taking in the city, the flowers, the trees, and steadily increasing throngs of tourists and travelers.

Gordon's car turned the corner and she smiled, her frustration and wistful regret fading away. It was hard to stay worried about so distant a threat as Gordon Lee and his alien rocket. After all, it was springtime in Washington DC.

2: "DEATH FROM BELOW"

March 29, 2031; USS Rivero (DDG 1004); Sea of Japan, 150 nm from North Korean coast, STLAM Launch Basket S2

In the dusking skies of evening above *USS Rivero*, the sharp boundary of the eastern horizon had already merged with the night, while to the west a wash of orange and red still set the water afire. The deep blue waters around the destroyer were empty, livened only by the occasional flash of a whitecap blown into spray by the chill, rising wind.

Lieutenant Nathaniel Robert Kelley, *Rivero*'s Weapons Officer, or Weps, nodded and turned the forward and aft cameras away from the scene and back toward their respective missile decks. Nathan, who sat in the hot seat as Tactical Action Officer in *Rivero*'s Combat Information Center (CIC), keyed his microphone. "Bridge, TAO. Captain, line 26 and 27 complete, no surface or air tracks within safety range and clear visually. Line 28 also complete, forward and aft VLS visually clear. Pass the word, 'All hands remain within the skin of the ship while launching missiles.'"

"Tac, Captain. Bridge concurs. Passing the word," came his CO's tinny voice. A moment later, the announcement was made all over the lethal, elongated pyramid shape of the *Zumwalt*-class destroyer. Between the announcement, the internal net he listened to in one ear, the radio circuit to the Strike Group TAO he guarded in the other ear, another three radio circuits he listened for on speakers, the checklist he was completing, and the different tactical chat rooms he was involved with, Nathan was dividing his attentions between ten different, equally vital conversations, not including the internal debate on the impending strike package he also worried over. His ability to multitask was stretched just about as far as was humanly possible.

But that did not stop Senior Chief David Edwards from adding his own sidebar to the jumbled mess. "'DDM', Weps. What the hell does that mean?"

"I have no idea, Senior." Nathan keyed his mike. "Strike, TAO. Lines 29 through 32 complete." He flipped the page of his StealthHawk launch checklist.

Across the space, and in his ear, Nathan heard the young Strike Officer respond, "Strike, aye. Five minutes until primary package launch." The CIC was one of the largest non-engineering spaces within *Rivero*. Fitted out with the standard light blue and gray bulkheads, a multitude of pipes and cableways leapfrogging one another through the overhead, and dark gray false decking, the space's most striking features were the tightly packed ranks of bulky, militarized computer consoles through which the combat watchstanders interacted with the destroyer's weapon systems and the world outside the ship. The dim lighting left only the monitors and large screen displays to provide their ghostly illumination upon the grim faces of the sailors, who were all dressed in either coveralls or Navy digital-patterned camouflage utilities. Each person was identically bundled in a thick blue jacket as proof against the cold, conditioned air, the temperature at which the combat computer system worked most efficiently.

Senior Chief Edwards, Nathan's Combat Systems Coordinator, punched a few keys on his console, updated his own checklist and then turned back toward his TAO. "It's gotta mean something if they're going to go to all the trouble of re-designating every one of the *Zumwalts*. DDM ... Dreadnought Destroyer Miniature?"

Nathan shook his head. Edwards was too damn cheerful to get mad at, and he knew the Senior Chief's off-topic question was a ploy to keep Nathan from considering any of the ethical ambiguities associated with launching strikes into North Korea. "We're 600 feet long, Senior. That's not so miniature. I think it stands for multi-mission destroyer, since we do so much more than just shoot guided missiles. Apparently DDG no longer suffices."

"I think some admiral just wanted himself another star, so he makes a Navy-wide change that doesn't actually change anything. It's just another example of our grand traditions, sir. Dreaded Destructive Marsupial?"

Nathan grinned at that. "How about Devilish Dancehall Morons?"

Edwards' own smile broadened and he nodded. "Daffy Duckish Militants?"

Nathan's sudden, barking laugh caused everyone in CIC to look around. He and the Senior Chief instantly became engrossed in their checklists and displays, each turning a different shade of red. All eyes soon turned back to their own consoles in the darkened space, and the two top surface warriors in CIC devolved into a fit of restrained giggles.

Their reverie was broken by the Captain's sobering voice on the net. "TAO, Captain. Batteries release."

"TAO, aye. Combat, TAO. We have batteries release. Shifting

forward and aft VLS to launch. Break, Strike." Nathan reached up and turned the rarely-seen launcher keys from Standby to Launch. A fresh wave of butterflies hit his stomach. Some were no doubt due to the concern he had over what their missiles would do when they reached their targets in the Democratic People's Republic of Korea.

Would their missiles be effective? How many innocent lives, "collateral", would be lost? How would China respond? Would the strikes give the newly aggressive North Korea pause and make them pull back out from the DMZ, or would they drive them to use any nukes that escaped destruction?

Aside from the larger, national concerns, most of his worry was about more mundane things. He worried about his men and women. Would all their training and preparation pay off? Would they become the tip of the sword they yearned to be? Would they be able to hold their heads high when they remembered the destruction they had wrought?

Ensign Blake sounded even younger than his short 23 years. "Strike, aye. Launchers show ready. StealthHawks one through thirty are green for primary package launch. StealthHawks thirty-one through forty-five are green for backup launch. Primary package launch in thirty seconds."

"TAO, aye." All was quiet throughout the ship, sailors from the Commanding Officer to the junior engineering security rover holding their breath without realizing it. Fifteen seconds later, the VLS sirens sounded, their high-pitched wail at a volume that would drive any foolhardy sailor either back inside the ship or over the side. Ten seconds after that, the first pair of Vertical Launch System hatches opened up, the forward-most cells on the port and starboard sides of the ship.

Five seconds later, at precisely 1900 local, twin blooms of fire boiled upward out of the VLS exhaust, casting the young night back into day. The sharp roar of the rocket motors could be heard throughout the ship, and Nathan could feel the white noise through the soles of his boots. Instants after, a pair of dark shapes slid up as one from the open hatches, leaping into the sky on columns of liquid flame. The missiles screamed higher and higher, twin stars whose radiance was quickly lost on the waters below. Their fiery trajectories tipped over, arcing toward the distant, unseen land. Seconds after going horizontal, the rockets burned out and broke apart, their thick cylindrical tails falling away while smaller, sleeker shapes jetted forward on much more modest tongues of fire.

Then the departing StealthHawks were lost from view as another pair of VLS hatches sprang open, disgorging another pair of missiles in nearly identical fashion. The gray on black contrail of this twosome angled slightly off from the first pair, seeking fresh air through which to climb, and new gaps in the armor that was the North Korean air defense net. In the distance, flares of light could be seen from other ships: destroyers, cruisers, and submerged submarines, the world's last blue water navy projecting the power that had always proved so decisive in the past.

Aboard *USS Rivero*, the process was repeated thirteen more times in the next six and a half minutes, until there was nothing left but the final hush of closing VLS hatches, the lap of the waves, and the muted whine of her gas turbines. The dull haze gray sides of the ship were now blackened in spots from the toxic, acidic fires of the StealthHawks' solid rocket boosters, but even that was lost in the smoky gloom of night on the open sea. The sudden fury had gone and peace settled over the water once again.

"TAO, Strike. All missiles have transitioned to cruise, datalink sat, crypto sat. StealthHawks one through thirty handed off to Strike East. No backup missions for ownship. Request permission to spin down StealthHawks thirty-one through forty-five and secure from Condition Two Strike."

"Strike, TAO. Roger. Forward and aft VLS placed in Standby. Spin down all remaining birds and conduct post-fire checks. Secure from Condition Two Strike with exception of key watchstanders." Nathan blew a slow whistle in relief and pulled his headphones down to the back of his neck. He turned in his seat and spoke loud enough for all in CIC to hear. "Good work, people. The world asks and you deliver. Now let's clean up and turn this bitch over. The near-beer is on me, cigars you can scrounge up your own damn self."

There were a couple of chuckles, and several grins, but no applause and never a cheer. You might cheer the defeat of an enemy in combat, but this was strike, not battle. The targets here were nameless, faceless, and too often innocent of any other crime than being strategically necessary. They felt pride in a job done well, professionally, but any man who found joy in this work was a man few would care to associate with.

Nathan put his headphones back on and began updating the interminable situation reports in chat. Out of the corner of his eye, he saw Edwards' hand sticking out. Nathan allowed himself a small smile and took the offered hand in a slow, strong shake. Edwards squinted slightly at him. "How you doin', Weps?"

"I'm good, Senior Chief. It's the first time I've done it for real is all."

Edwards nodded. "I've shot missiles into Iraq, I've shot 'em into Syria, and I've shot 'em in Iran. Now I've done it in North Korea. I'm hoping to get a matched set of 'Axis of Evil' commemorative plates for the 'I Love Me' wall at home, but that would probably be in poor taste."

Nathan just shook his head. The older enlisted man knew exactly which buttons to push on his department head in order to interrupt his spiraling chain of thoughts. Nathan punched a few buttons of his own and took a look at the air picture on his console. Where before there had been only a few commercial airliners moving down their precise air corridors, there were now literally hundreds of individual beaconed tracks blossoming, radiating out from the Surface Strike Group and the Carrier Strike Group.

At first one by one, and then by the dozens, the low-flying contacts disappeared, as they shut off their ID beacons and passed below the SPY-3 radar's horizon. Within twenty minutes they would all be gone, and all the ships would have to show for their end of the offensive against North Korea would be a bunch of empty STLAM canisters. The strikes would continue for days, but with Coalition Air Force bombers and naval aviation in the lead, winding up with what was hoped would be a very limited ground push to secure South Korea's border and take out the North's ability to threaten them further. Either way, from this point on the wet Navy was largely relegated to a supporting role, there being no real opposing navy to engage.

"TAO, Bridge. The Skipper's on his way down to Combat. Good shooting, Weps."

Nathan half stood in front of his console and stretched. "Roger that, Bridge. You might want to have your Quartermaster update PIM. We'll be leaving the launch baskets pretty soon and rejoining formation to screen the ESG. Work with the CIC Watch Supe and give me your best bet so I can info the Old Man."

"Bridge, aye. Already on it, sir."

Nathan settled back down to his seat and began reading his own post-fire checklist when a shrill voice on his tactical net almost popped his eardrum. "All stations, Sonar! I have two passive broadband contacts with matching narrowband tonals off the bow and starboard bow, bearing 263 and 340. No corresponding surface tracks on those lines of bearing. Evaluate both as possible sub, confidence high! Request permission to go active."

Two acoustic lines of bearing speared out from the circle on the display that represented the *Rivero*, one to the west and one toward the north. Nathan's mind spun and everyone returned to their consoles, punching keys and bringing up displays. He shook his head in dismay.

They had sanitized this area for three days prior to beginning the strike package, for the sole purpose of ensuring that something like this would not happen. And it had. "Sonar, TAO. Go active and stand by on countermeasure activation. Break, Surface, TAO. Inform Victor Zulu and request ASW pouncer from *Chafee*. Break, Bridge, TAO. Set flight quarters for Firescout launch and come up to full power. Set Condition Two AS Gold."

The acknowledgements came, and announcements issued from the speaker over his head and all around the ship. CIC, which had just begun to wind down, became a flurry of activity as the strike technicians going off watch jockeyed for seating with those anti-submarine warfare watchstanders taking over. Back aft, the hangar doors folded upward and sailors in blue/white/gray digi-cammies and brightly colored flight deck jerseys rolled out and prepared a small helicopter UAV for launch. The Firescout-II itself was nearly dwarfed by the pair of sonobouy launchers and the single mini torpedo it mounted. Amidships, the muted whine of the destroyer's gas turbines changed in pitch as another pair of Rolls Royce engines came online, ready to propel the *Rivero*'s electric drive to her full 35+ knots.

Back in CIC, Nathan was forced to wait in the dark as status reports rolled in, praying the whole time that it was a false alarm. Submariners liked to kid surface warriors that there were two kinds of ships in the world: submarines and targets. On any normal day, Nathan would dispute that. The Navy had let their ASW know-how atrophy for decades, but the last 12 years had seen a resurgence of anti-submarine pride. He would have bet that the *Rivero* and her destroyer squadron could hunt subs almost as well as another submarine or a P-8 Maritime Patrol Aircraft squadron, given enough warning. But having a pair of hostile subs show up in your back yard without the usual aviation screen, tracking data, or defense in depth was a recipe for disaster. Destroyer sailors knew that anytime you seriously contemplated using the short-range, ship mounted torpedo tubes, you had already failed the ASW problem.

"TAO, ASWE. I'm online, conferring with Sonar and going active. Port and starboard mounts are trained to forty-five degrees offset, torpedo firing checks in progress. Firescout launch in about seven minutes." That was LTJG Calhoun, the ship's ASW Officer. There was no telling where he had been, but he was alert and on the job now.

"TAO, aye." A figure appeared off to one side of Nathan's elbow without a sound, causing him to look behind him. Commander Anthony Jones, *Rivero*'s Commanding Officer, stood behind him, looking over the tactical picture on Nathan's console and nodding his head. He caught Nathan's eye and gestured for him to turn back around. Nathan did so immediately and continued changing the system data displayed on his status boards.

Captain Jones was a quiet, reserved man who usually liked to let his people do as they trained. He was not afraid to correct someone and step in when they required it, and the blistering heat of those corrections were not soon forgotten, but he believed in his crew fighting the ship, not himself. If they all relied upon his decisions before making their own, they would be doomed if he became unavailable. In Nathan's case, he was more than happy to leave the Weapons Officer in charge. For the moment, anyway.

Numerous, disparate flows of information streamed around Nathan, but he stayed atop the flood. He turned slightly to Senior Chief Edwards at his console. "How the hell could a pair of subs sneak by us? We spent three days combing this whole area."

Edwards shrugged. "Could have been a million ways. It depends on who's down there. Might our intel be wrong and not all the North Korean Kilos are in port? Could they own some diesel boats we don't know about? Did they sneak in or were they already here, bottomed out and quiet?"

"I doubt anyone could have snuck by us with all the buoys and dippers we used, and there's no way they could just happen to bottom out right where we put our launch basket."

Edwards looked thoughtful and then turned back to his screen. "Might be a pair of midget boats. We never have had good numbers on them. Maybe those two fishing boats we saw yesterday had more on their mind than fishing. Attach a couple of North Korean midget subs to your keel, and you'll chug along like you have a hold full of fish whether you caught any or not. We'd be none the wiser, even if we'd been allowed to board and inspect them."

Nathan shook his head in dismay. "A two billion dollar destroyer ambushed by a pair of fake fishing boats and a couple of communist-crafted midget subs? If you're right, then it's wrong on so many levels."

"Well, sir, if we survive this, it's open season on fishermen, I'm tellin' you."

"TAO, ASWE! I have active sonar contacts bearing 265 at 6200 yards and 342 at 5600 yards. Corresponds to previous lines of bearing, probable subs. Tracks 04012 and 04013 refer. Request permission to engage with over-the-side shots!"

"Bridge, TAO. Go to General Quarters. Come to 14 knots, course 120. Break, ASWE, TAO. Negative. Hold your fire." Edwards looked at him sharply. The war was on and their rules of engagement covered this, so they were justified in shooting, but Nathan simply held up his hand. "ASWE, maintain track quality and torps at ready. Report status of the pouncer."

The staccato shriek of the GQ alarm sounded, and people all over the ship rushed purposefully about, manning repair stations and additional watches, battening down hatches and scuttles, and making *USS Rivero* as watertight and survivable as possible. In CIC, there was yet another shuffling of personnel as watches changed out for their Condition One positions. *Rivero* herself sped up to a moderate speed, but came about languidly, cruising away from the two submarines as if they were scarcely a concern. Some might have turned to attack, others might have run away at flank speed, but Nathan had a different plan in mind.

"TAO, ASWE. *USS Chafee* was hot-pumping her helo when we called. Anticipate ten minutes before pouncer can be on station." The squadron's always at the ready SH-60R Seahawk dipping sonar ASW helicopter was in the midst of refueling, another note of either bad luck or excellent timing on the part of the North Koreans. Their own Firescout UAV would be up before the other destroyer's helicopter could assist them.

"TAO, aye." He turned back to Edwards and the Captain, the question still in the Senior Chief's eyes. "Those subs are too damn close to us. If we shoot, they'll shoot, and the odds are we'll be screwed. If they let us put a little distance between us and them, and maybe even get a couple of helos in the air, the odds shift in our favor. So we turn away, keep track on them, and try to set ourselves up for a better engagement while not making ourselves into even more of a target than we already are."

"But what if the only reason they haven't fired yet is that they're firming up their weapons solution? If we fire first and force them to evade, we can wreck their targeting."

Both Nathan and Edwards pointedly refused to look at the CO, and he, just as stubbornly, said nothing, seeing how his two warfighters would hash it out. "Those subs are so close, they could put their fish on circle search without any targeting, and they'd still get us. No, Senior. We crawl away. We'll shoot if forced and fight with helos and P-8's if they'll let us." He left unsaid whether or not it was likely the North Koreans would allow them to complete their escape. Captain Jones simply nodded and squeezed both men on the shoulder in silent, unquestioning support as they turned back to their consoles.

Their enemy then rendered the argument pointless.

"All stations, Sonar! I have launch transients from both subs!"

"Bridge, TAO! Flank speed! Conduct Hargrove turn and launch countermeasures. ASWE, TAO! Counterfire! Shoot—shoot—shoot!"

The dark triangular bulk of the ship sounded a higher pitched whine as her gas turbines ramped up, and her electrically driven, twin controllable pitch screws chewed deeper and faster through the sea, churning the water astern into white foam. The *Rivero* began to loop around in a tight turn to cross her own wake, while noisemakers and bubble generators launched themselves from the bridge wings and disrupted the water further, all in an attempt to confuse the enemy torpedoes and hide the relatively slow moving bulk of the destroyer. From both sides of the ship, a pair of torpedoes popped out and slid into the water, coming to life and seeking out the enemy like a pod of orcas hunting a couple of whales. Astern, the men manning the miniature anti-torpedo torpedo rails kept aim on where sonar held the enemy weapons, through the blue-white rooster tail kicking up from the stern, ready to shoot when they came in range.

As bad as the situation was, the *Rivero* still had a chance. Their countermeasures were as good as the lopsided physics of the situation could make them, and their own Mk-54B torpedoes would ensure that there would not be more than one additional salvo coming for them. It was an accepted part of modern naval warfare that vessels rarely engaged one another directly. Instead, they lunged and parried by proxy, their smart weapons doing the lion's share of the seeking and destroying. It was the ship's responsibility to position those weapons and set them up for success. In this, Nathan Kelley and his combat team excelled, but the enemy could not always be counted on to play fair.

It did not seem possible, but the sonar operator grew even more shrill. "Combat, Sonar! Flying Fish! Flying Fish! Enemy torpedoes are super-cavs!"

"Shit. Bridge, TAO! Cancel Hargrove. Steady on 090 and standby for hard turn to 180." Nathan suddenly found it hard to hear the nets over the pounding of his own heart, but the bridge heard him and he felt the ship heel over as it reversed its maneuver and settled onto its new course due east. Everything vibrated as the destroyer clawed at the water in her bid to escape.

Supercavitation. Torpedoes already had a speed advantage over nearly any kind of ship, 50 to 60 knots versus 25 to 30. The engagements still moved at a snail's pace compared to aerial battles or duels with cruise missiles, however. Supercavitating torpedoes, super-cavs, blurred that distinction. By using a rocket motor rather than screws or propulsors, and by encasing the body of the torpedo in a drag-free layer of continuously generated steam, the torpedo left the viscous confines of the ocean and acted like an underwater missile. Now rather than a twenty or thirty knot advantage, the enemy weapons had a two hundred knot advantage. Fired from only a few miles away, there was no time for countermeasures, no time for maneuvers, and almost no time to think.

Nathan's and *Rivero*'s sole advantage was that super-cavs, or "Flying Fish", were nearly blind and could barely maneuver even if they could see beyond their enveloping sheath of gas. Newer Flying Fish had sensors and spars that extended out of the gas bubble, allowing them to both see and turn. He bet that, surprised as he had been by the North Koreans having super-cavs at all, they probably would not have the latest model. If he could coax the torpedoes to commit to full speed on one line of bearing, it might be possible to turn the ship at the last instant to offset the blast. But he also knew that the North Koreans would be aware of their weapons' limitations and would likely have accounted for them.

He watched the ten subsurface tracks held on sonar. Four were his, en route to the two tracks furthest out, the enemy subs. The last four formed a staggered line, showing up as question marks rather than the usual symbology since they were not behaving according to the normal kinematics of submerged contacts. The whole world paused as they began to merge with *Rivero*'s symbol at the center of the display.

"Bridge, TAO! Turn!"

USS Rivero tilted over toward the outside of her desperate course change to starboard. The stern of the ship nearly skipped through the water as she came about at 34 knots with a hard rudder angle. From the ASW Countermeasures compartment at her fantail, Torpedomen began to fire countertorp after countertorp down into the path of the Flying Fish.

The first torpedo streaked past *Rivero*, detonating 100 yards off her port side, turning the water into a globe of pure white that imploded and then erupted in a column of spray hundreds of feet high. The destroyer was rung like a bell, pushed laterally by over ten feet. Loose gear rocketed through the air, along with anyone not secured in a seat. Captain Jones, who was braced for shock but not strapped down, was thrown over a row of consoles and down to the deck. Sparks exploded from some of the panels and the lights actually brightened as the normal, dim sources in CIC went out and the emergency supplies to all the lights came on.

The second torpedo went far afield, detonating 500 yards away. The third fell victim to the swarm of anti-torpedo torpedoes, with four of the miniscule devices detonating in its path. The supercavitating torpedo's gas bubble was ripped away and a combination of shaped charge jets and a water hammer moving at 240 knots ripped the torpedo apart. It never detonated.

The fourth torpedo slid beneath *Rivero*'s violently maneuvering stern as if destiny had willed it there. The underwater rocket detonated, blowing a spherical hollow in the water below the destroyer's aft keel. The screws sped up into a blur, freed from their watery prison, followed immediately by the buckling of both shafts. Thousands of tons of mass, now unsupported by the buoyant ocean, sagged down amidships and snapped the ship's spine.

Then, even above the sound of screeching steel and screaming men, there came the roar of water rushing back into the void. Hydrodynamics coalesced the collapsing sphere of liquid into a beautiful, terrible lance of pure, incompressible force. The lance speared the already broken back of the ship and erupted upwards through deck upon deck, emerging in a fountain of destructive energy from the middle of *Rivero*'s hangar.

Rivero collapsed back into the water, her after third shorn away in a blast of twisted, torn, burning metal. The stern of the ship sank in less than a minute, greedily claiming everyone stationed inside. The bodies of the flight deck crew and wrecked hulk of the autonomous Firescout-II helo were launched several hundred yards. None of them survived intact.

The forward two thirds of the *Rivero* wallowed in relative peace. The hangar crew and the engineers who had faced the blast directly were no longer even recognizable as bodies. Water flooded into open spaces, past sprung doors and hatches and into the forward half of the ship, even as oil and sewage spilled back out into the sea. Throughout the ship, the few survivors who remained conscious set about organizing themselves to make it out to the life rafts and to evacuate everyone they could. They stopped any real attempt at damage control once they realized there was no way to stop the ship from going down, nor could they tell if it was going down in five minutes or fifty.

Unseen by any aboard, either because they were unconscious, dead, or too busy to worry about being attacked again, there was a sequence of four more explosions a couple of miles away to the north and to the west. These eruptions were followed by a pair of spreading oil slicks, some debris, and nothing more. The dark, wind tossed sea returned to a state of calm without further attacks upon the doomed destroyer.

Five minutes later, *Chafee*'s helicopter hovered into view to face a scene sailors had only regarded in nightmares since the end of the Second World

War. Pitifully few of the *Rivero*'s bright orange inflatable life rafts floated around her rolling, sinking wreckage. It was another twenty minutes before *USS Chafee* herself arrived, with *Halsey* and *Port Royal* showing up to render aid soon thereafter.

LT Nathaniel Robert Kelley, Weapons Officer of the former *USS Rivero*, kept his haunted eyes upon her grave long after she slipped beneath the waves.

3: "ZINGER"

Looking up at the redwood shrouded main house, Nathan Kelley realized this had to go down as the weirdest damned job interview in history. If he had known the process would be quite this ... complicated, he doubted he would have ever responded to Windward Technologies' invitation to that first meeting.

That initial interview had been almost painfully normal. The Windward representative had come out to Boston as part of a larger science and technology job fair along with a score of other companies like Lockheed, Raytheon, and Orbital Sciences. Nathan—like a few hundred other prospective candidates—was finishing up his Master's degree at MIT, ready to begin the next chapter of his life. Having come from a now aborted career in the Navy, he had been older than his competition and not a perpetual student.

His Windward meet-and-greet had been utterly typical interview fodder, blending in with his dozen or so other attempts to sell himself to corporate America that day:

"What are your goals, Mr. Kelley?"

"What are your best and worst qualities, Mr. Kelley?"

"Why should Windward hire you, Mr. Kelley?"

Nathan had left the job fair less than hopeful about the possibility of Windward calling him back, so he had gone back to school and finished the final draft of his thesis. There were no nibbles from Windward Technologies, so he had moved on to other applications, other prospects, targeting résumés to every tech-firm that might remotely be hiring.

It was so different from the Navy, where your career path was often laid out in stone. That regimented military existence had proved his undoing, however, a discordant note of calm in the white noise of life following the sinking. He had simply been unable to go back to the routine of service stateside, and the war would not keep him as damaged goods. The reason they gave for medically discharging him was post traumatic stress disorder, but Nathan knew there were other reasons as well. They were the reasons that went unsaid, the reasons related to the furtive, accusatory stares of doubt other officers gave him when they thought he could not see them, stares that would continue for the rest of his career, cleared by a board of inquiry or not.

So he had given it all up, and after a brief respite in his Pennsylvania hometown, he had sought a new existence as a student and engineer, essentially rebooting his life at the not insignificant age of 30 years old. Leaving was a big change, an unanticipated change, but a welcome one. It did necessitate some adjustment. Life in the civilian sector could be so much more uncertain, precarious even.

But in the civilian world, no one shattered your whole world in a single act of cold anger and your ambiguous split-second decisions did not lead to the deaths of 103 subordinates, shipmates, and friends. In the civilian world, perhaps he would no longer wake up in a clammy sweat, shaking from half-remembered dreams of rending steel and screaming, faceless men.

Precarious. He was fine with precarious.

On the day after graduation, while packing up his small office at the university, a welcome—though unexpected—call had come, starting him upon an extremely odd journey into the world of corporate job-seeking: "Mr. Kelley, would you mind traveling to Windward's New York office for a second interview?"

That interview, like his first, had been deceptively normal, just the corporate machine getting to know one of their potential cogs a little better. Nathan had smiled and nodded, answering their questions as best he could and trying his utmost to exude an air of professional competence. The New York office Human Resources director had smiled back, clearly impressed. "That was very good, Mr. Kelley. Would you mind taking a short written exam?"

Again, not too unusual. Nathan supposed that many companies wanted to test their candidates to find out if their degrees were more than just sheets of paper. The test had covered a gamut of topics: physics, biology, math, chemistry, systems engineering, politics, sociology, and finance. It was not terribly difficult, but it had stretched his limited academic background. He figured it might have been a great deal harder for someone else, someone whose life experience before MIT had not been so diverse.

"Excellent job, Mr. Kelley! How about flying down to our Dallas offices for another interview?" They also put up the offer of per diem compensation for all his time, so Nathan shrugged and agreed, still happy to have gotten past the first interview, the second interview, and then the test. And now another interview in another city, for what was for all intents and purposes a relatively entry-level position in Windward Technologies engineering management program. It was then that the first pangs of doubt and anxious bewilderment hit him.

Did everyone go through such a rigorous process?

The meeting in Dallas had been more than odd. There, he met Windward's Dallas VP, and the interview had gone far afield in both scope and location. They met in the VP's corner office downtown and covered much of the same interview territory that had been asked in the first and second interviews. Then they had gone for lunch in the West End and the interview shifted to Nathan's personal life: Thirty-two, small town boy, single, never married, no kids, but wants the full package later, looking for the right girl, in no hurry, love to fish, love baseball, love movies, love reading, love science fiction.

"Science fiction?" Nathan's inadvertent admission had led to a literary discussion that lasted throughout the afternoon as they walked around downtown Dallas, down past the JFK memorial, and back up into the financial district. At times, it seemed as if the poor executive was simply starved for attention, keeping Nathan talking just so he would not have to go back to his dreary office. It ended in a somewhat awkward silence, almost like the end of a blind date, and Nathan was unsure what to do or say as the sun began to set. The VP finally turned to him and broke the silence with, "What would you think of going down to Pensacola for some physical exams?"

As long as Windward footed the bill, Nathan was game. Thus he had gone to Pensacola to be poked and prodded, but it did not end there. Then it was back to Dallas for a series of much more in depth written and oral exams, then back to New York for a polygraph, a psychological battery, and a security screening which made his Naval background investigation appear narrow in comparison. Then there was yet another interview, this time in Washington DC and mainly concerned with his military background. That one had made him the most uncomfortable, but, thankfully, they had largely avoided any discussion of the *Rivero* or the war with North Korea.

And now this. If this was not the final interview, Nathan knew he was done. He was either hired today, or he would finally walk away from the whole process. Of course, this was probably the last step regardless. How many more hurdles could there be after an interview at the CEO's own home?

Gordon Elliot Lee, the founder and Chief Executive Officer of Windward Technologies Incorporated, lived in a large two-story home of cedar, stone, and glass. It was bigger than a house, but too small for a mansion, fitting into its own category as the perfect size for a single California billionaire entrepreneur. The main house led a phalanx of other buildings: a pair of guest houses on either side of the main house, barns, garages, greenhouses, and what appeared to be a large domed observatory, all of which cut into a rocky hillside of coastal redwoods and seemingly natural drifts of yellow, purple, and white flowers. At the very edge of perception, identified by the smells of salt and sea in the air, Nathan could hear the crash of waves upon rocks, from a beach no doubt beyond the house and estate.

He parked the rental hybrid next to a battered truck that he doubted could ever pass California's emission and fuel efficiency standards. The gravel of the drive gave way to a landscaped walk lined with manicured plots of floral excess and a slate-walled porch. Taking a deep breath to settle nerves that had once again been set afire with anxiety, Nathan knocked loudly upon the front door. A blurred image soon appeared beyond the door's translucent stained glass and it opened to reveal a smiling Gordon Lee, wiping his hands on a faded, threadbare apron.

Lee was wiry, and fit in a way that seemed to have come from work rather than working out. His features gave a hint of his Asian heritage, making it hard to discern his exact age, while his balding head and graying hair belied his nearly sixty years—a lifetime which had seen Lee's sharp business and technical acumen turn Windward from a garage sideline into a Fortune 100 corporation.

"Nathan Kelley?" Lee stuck out a hand.

Nathan gave it a firm shake, self-consciously debating with himself just how much of a grip to use. Though he had tired of the interview process, Nathan still wanted the job, so he nervously worried over how he could make himself appear neither nervous nor worried. "It's an honor to meet you, Mr. Lee. You have no idea how big a deal it is to meet the man behind Windward Tech."

Lee grinned. "Of course I do. I pay people a lot of money to make me seem as impressive as I am. If you weren't in complete and utter awe of me, I'd have to fire a whole department of minions. Come on in. Lunch is almost ready."

Nathan followed him in and through the house as Lee walked quickly toward the back. The interior was a mix of blonde and pale red woods, with walls of pastel green striped paper and creamy white plaster. It was a simple, elegant look, and well appointed with an assortment of lively abstract paintings and comfortable, overstuffed furnishings. It appeared inviting, lived-in, and fabulously expensive. The only incongruous element was in the foyer, where an oversized terra cotta warrior of gigantic proportions dominated the entrance, standing ready for battle, in defiance of the homey interior. Nathan felt sure it was the only decoration that Lee had chosen himself.

There had been stories, concerns in the past ten years about some of Lee's eccentricities, but those did not bother Nathan at the moment. He was here to secure a job, and he would not have cared if Lee had answered the door painted blue and wearing just a cape and underwear. As it was, he appeared to be nothing if not kind, lucid, and rational. Nathan relaxed the slightest bit.

Exiting out the back, the two men emerged onto a stained cedar deck, where a large brick grill provided the focal point for a wrought iron and red lacquered wood dining set. Behind the house, past the deck, was a meticulously managed Oriental garden. Nathan wondered if Lee maintained it himself or if there were invisible servants waiting in the wings of this elaborate stage of tranquility.

Lee raised the cover of the grill, releasing a cloud of fragrant wood smoke and the smell of pleasantly charring meat. "Ribs or chicken breast, Nathan?"

"That depends, sir. If it's lunch, I'll go for the ribs, that being a secret personal weakness of mine. But if this is business, I'll have the chicken, which I'm sure I could eat with a bit more couth. I'll just need to know, is this lunch or is this the interview?"

"Yes."

Nathan shook his head, reached up, and loosened his necktie and shirt collar. "Ribs then, if you please, sir." He removed his blazer, deciding his casual interview attire was not quite casual enough in the face of the oncoming heat of the day and the apparent mood of their meeting.

Lee served up two plates of ribs, along with half a chicken breast each, and added healthy portions of potato salad and cups of frijoles rancheros. As both men sat, Lee also passed Nathan a freshly opened bottle of beer and held it up in a silent toast.

Nathan clinked the proffered bottle with his own and took a swig, letting the ice-cold brew wash away some of his own anxiety and confusion. "I've got to tell you, sir. This is not what I expected. Then again, almost every step of this process has defied my expectations."

Lee nodded and had a spoonful of the spicy bean soup. "And what do you think of the process, thus far I mean?"

"It's been frustrating, Mr. Lee. I haven't exactly known why I've been doing what I've been doing. I've had five interviews, physical exams, background checks, psych tests, IQ tests, knowledge exams, and just about everything else, and it all seems a bit much for a simple systems engineering management position."

Lee laughed. "Of course it is. You're absolutely right. No company would spend this amount of time and expense on hiring some faceless engineer ... but it makes a lot more sense when you consider the job you were actually interviewing for."

"Pardon me?"

"Oh, yeah. You had the Systems Engineer job after the second interview. We kept the process going for *you*, though. It was partly out of a sadistic desire to watch you squirm, but mostly, or almost mostly, it was because we had to see if you were qualified for a far more important job."

Nathan was quiet for a long measure as he considered the implications. He had hoped, and feared, for something like this. He took a bite of the succulent, sweet ribs, and wiped his mouth. "I don't know whether to be flattered or pissed."

"Too early for either, I'd say. After all, we've already filled that Systems Engineering position with someone else and you haven't gotten this other job yet. You still have more than enough opportunity to screw things up, and then you can be both flattered and pissed. How's that sound?"

Nathan took another bite of his meat and a swig of his beer. "Sounds like this is the best barbecue man has ever put to plate. And have I mentioned how handsome and youthful you are in person, sir?"

Gordon Lee laughed harder that time and touched his bottle to Nathan's. "Funny! Clever boy. I have indeed hired some obsequious morons in the past, and it was always a mistake. But you've got a genuine sense of humor on you, Nathan, even if it does tend toward the smartass end of the scale. So why don't I ask you what I brought you here to ask?"

"Suits me, sir, but I think I've already been asked and answered every possible question in the book."

"I doubt that, but here it is. Ready?"

"Absolutely."

"Mr. Kelley, how would you go about stopping an alien invasion?"

Nathan almost giggled, but stopped himself with a supreme effort. He took a bite of potato salad to cover any further inclination to laugh, though he could not stop an incredulous smirk as he thought about Lee's question.

Eventually, after a long pull on his bottle, he cocked his beer toward his potential boss in a quasi-salute. "That's quite the zinger."

"A zinger? What's a zinger?"

"You know. A zinger's the big 'out-of-the-box' question you get during the interview: If you were a plant, what kind of plant would you be? It's the question that's designed to show how innovative you can be, to show how you think: a zinger."

Lee leaned back and nodded. "Quite the zinger indeed, Nathan. So, how about it? How would you stop an alien invasion?"

Nathan frowned as he thought about Lee's odd question, and how the entire last few weeks could hinge upon his answer. He stood up and began to pace slightly. Nathan never could understand people who could think sitting down. "Okay, an alien invasion is pretty vague, but defeating any other kind of invasion depends on establishing the parameters of the battlespace. How are these aliens getting here exactly?"

"They're flying here in a giant rocket or rocket-like contraption from a distant star. They turned around at the halfway point and are decelerating toward Earth, which they will reach in a little over 22 years."

"My, my, how specific."

Lee had a drink. "You did say exactly."

"Well, from what you're saying, several methods present themselves, but are we even sure this is an invasion?"

"No, we aren't. Let us say that this hypothetical alien visitor has made no attempt to contact us by signals, or at least there has been no attempt that we have recognized. Also, the distances are so great that there is no way for us to have yet received a response to our own attempts at communication. And since we can think of no reason for this unknown alien species to physically come to us other than for invasion, we are proceeding upon a worst-case scenario."

Nathan's pacing was now more rapid, purposeful. "But they are an alien race, correct? So ascribing our own reasoning on them is an uncertain proposition, wouldn't you think?"

"Of course. Alien race equals alien reasoning. Perhaps they are coming here just to say hello, or to plant poppy seeds and welcome us to the inter-galactic love fest. But why not just contact us with a radio signal? Radio signals are undoubtedly how they discovered we were even here in this universe, so our common sense would seem to suggest that if their intentions were benign they would have called before stopping by for a visit.

"Now, that common sense is really just the laws of motion and thermodynamics expressing themselves in our everyday reasoning, laws that the aliens are also bounded by. If their intentions are benign and they wanted to avoid conflict, it makes sense to make initial contact through signals. Signals move at the speed of light, and are transmitted at a relatively low power level. For a species forced to travel below that speed, think of all the time wasted, all the energy wasted in coming here physically. Signaling us is safer, faster, and cheaper."

Nathan stopped and looked at Lee. "All right, it's your game. If you contend that their worries about time and energy expenditure are identical to ours, then their reasoning might be similar to ours as well. So, the only reason for them to come here is that they need something physical from us, like our resources or our women—Mars always needs women, after all. And because they didn't call first or yet, we have to assume their intentions are hostile."

"That's right, but you're dancing around the question, Mr. Kelley. How do you stop the potential invasion?"

Nathan started to walk back and forth again. "Well, since we've established how they're getting here and confirmed their intentions, the next step is to know the enemy. We have to conduct reconnaissance at the earliest opportunity. How far away are these aliens who are taking 22 years to get here?"

"Let's say they are about three light-years away now, though they appear four light-years away due to the light speed lag. They would have slowed from 46% the speed of light to only about a quarter c."

Nathan shook his head with a grin. "You've put a lot of thought into this, sir. Okay. Am I assuming we have a magic space drive or current technology only?"

"I am not aware of any magic space drive. Yet."

"Fine. With current technology, there's virtually no chance we can field a mission to the enemy within the next 22 years. Chemical rockets have high thrust, but are too bulky and have abysmal specific impulse. Ion engines approach the right efficiency and specific impulse but lack any real thrust or payload capability, and they have the same problem as chemical rockets with endurance. They simply can't carry enough reaction mass.

"It's the rocket equation. Since you have to carry your fuel with you, and you have to accelerate your own reaction mass at the same time as you boost your payload, there's an upper limit to the velocities you can achieve, not to mention that 99% of your ship will be fuel and sacrificial mass. A laser driven lightsail or an Orion-style nuclear pulse detonation engine might work, but that's still theoretical—not exactly current technology.

The furthest we might get within the next 22 years with current rockets, ion engines, gravity assists, et cetera, would be the Kuiper Belt and that's practically in our own back yard."

"I would agree, unfortunately. So that's out."

Nathan shook a finger at him. "No, sir, not out. It's just of limited utility, but information is information, even if it's of the last-minute variety. I would send a spy probe out yesterday with current technology and hope I come up with something better within the next couple of decades. At the same time, I'd invest in some at-home recon. Maybe I could get some time on the Earth based telescope networks, or accelerate development of the SSBA. That baby would make something a couple of light-years away look like something orbiting Mars from an Earth-based scope." The SSBA, or Solar System Baseline Array, was a system of space-based optical telescopes which would be orbiting throughout the entire solar system in a few years. By spreading the telescopes out and combining their images electronically through interferometry, they would become a virtual telescope with a primary lens the width of the solar system from Earth to Saturn. It would be immeasurably powerful, capable of resolving terrestrial planets in nearby solar systems with ease. It was also obscenely expensive, delayed and opposed as a boondoggle at every turn.

Gordon Lee took to his feet as well. There was a strange sparkle in his eyes as he began to get caught up in Nathan's speculations. "Yes. All right, we send out probes and we use the most powerful, most capable telescopes we can. What next?"

"Next depends on the recon. Everything depends upon what we know or don't know about the aliens. It's impossible to say much now, without any observational data, but there are a few assumptions we can make about the enemy just because of the way it moves."

"Go on."

"They're traveling here in a rocket—a magic rocket with an inexhaustible source of fuel, but a rocket nonetheless. That would seem to indicate that they don't have any sort of warp drive or wormhole jumps or reactionless, inertialess, Roswell alien sort of spaceships. Right?"

Lee tipped back his beer and fetched another pair of bottles as he actually seemed to consider Nathan's supposition. Nathan finished his own beer and took the fresh bottle the other man held out to him. Eventually, Lee nodded. "I think you may have over-extended your assumptions, but I'll go along with it."

"Okay. They have high technology but not supernatural, magical technology. They are bound by inertia the same as we are, so the simplest way to attack them would be to put something in their way. A kinetic missile strike would ruin their day, and given the velocities involved, it would be fairly simple to achieve. On the same mission that sends out the recon probe, you can seed the outer solar system with mines. When the big bad aliens show up, the mines rocket toward them and no more invasion."

Lee sat down, looking vaguely disappointed. "Mr. Kelley, these aliens have come here from nearly twenty light-years away and have traveled at nearly half the speed of light. Given the amount of damage a single grain of sand could do at those velocities, not to mention the radiation involved, don't you think the aliens would have come up with some method of clearing their path? I doubt simply throwing a rock in their way to trip them up would be the best defense for the planet."

Nathan nodded slowly and grinned in a way that was more adversarial than friendly. He would either confirm or end his chances at this mysterious job, depending upon how he responded to Lee's criticism. Agree or disagree with the boss, both choices were dangerous. "Sir, I said that was the simplest method of attack, not the best. And while they probably do have some sort of deflector shield or clearance beam or relativistic dust-buster, it's a completely different proposition to deflect a coordinated strike with hardened, militarized weapons than it is to annihilate some micrometeors."

Lee's eyes had narrowed and his mouth was set in a grim line. "Very well."

"The best ways to defeat any defensive system is with depth, diversity, mass, and maneuver. Depth is layers upon layers of weapons. Diversity is in types of weapons. You hit them with every type of attack that might even remotely be effective: lasers, nukes, bomb-pumped lasers, particle beams, kinetic strikes, logic bombs, and more. Hell, if you can put a rocket underneath the kitchen sink, you use that too.

"Mass is the density of attacks in each layer. Every defense has a threshold, a limit to what it can take. You give me enough of the right kind of weapons, I can storm the gates of heaven. And maneuver, well, we've already said they're bound by inertia. If you make your weapons agile enough, set them up on just the right bearing, at just the right offset and velocity, throw in some countermeasures perhaps, then you can slip past almost any defense short of a force field. And defeating a force field just brings us back to mass. You want to defeat an alien invasion, that's how you do it."

"And what is the most important part of our defensive plan?" Lee's voice was quiet, almost too quiet to hear, and absolutely too quiet to determine if his hush was in disappointment or admiration.

"Time and distance. The most important thing, sir, is to keep the aliens from reaching Earth. If they make it to the planet, it's all over. All they have to do is turn the exhaust of their magic space drive toward us and the planet would be roasted like a marshmallow. Or, if they favor things up close and personal, put them in orbit at the top of our deep gravity well so the energy balance is on their side. They can just rain down strike after strike until not even the cockroaches are left."

Lee just stared at him. Nathan took a long drink, nervously finishing most of the bottle. When he looked back down, Gordon Lee was walking away. Nathan grimaced and said under his breath, "Damn it."

Lee came back with a tablet computer in his hand and gave it over to Nathan. It automatically scrolled through a series of astronomy slides. The first picture was of a particular night sky. An unfamiliar constellation drew itself around a set of stars, and a number of Greek symbols popped up next to the most prominent stars.

"Mr. Kelley, what you are looking at is the constellation Pavo, the Peacock. It's only visible in the southern hemisphere. The fourth brightest star in Pavo is Delta Pavonis, and it's a G-type star much like our own. In fact, of all the nearby stars capable of supporting life as we know it, Delta Pavonis has long been considered one of the best candidates for an alien intelligence, even though it is a bit old and in its declining years. All the other G-type yellow suns in our vicinity are binary pairs, and it is thought that the interactions of the sister stars would interrupt the regular orbits and seasons of a terrestrial planet, making life almost impossible. But Delta Pavonis is alone in the heavens, 19.9 light-years away, and free to develop life, much as we did."

"Why are you telling me this, sir?"

Lee tapped the tablet's screen and another series of slides popped up. It focused in on the fuzzy yellow circle/dot of Delta Pavonis. In the next slide, a blue pinprick dominated one side of the star. In successive slides the pinprick drifted across the face of the yellow dot and back again, getting ever brighter and wider, and drifting further and further over the dot in the background.

"In the 1930's, radio was truly born. It went from a laboratory and military oddity to a worldwide tool, a tool which would help drive empires and wars, and a tool which cast out its beacon into the night sky. Much of it was of too low a power to penetrate the ionosphere in any sort of intelligible fashion, but it is apparent that something did. Whatever the reason, nineteen point nine years later, someone around Delta Pavonis noticed us, and they sent out a magic rocket without any sort of warning or courtesy call to the people they're coming to visit. Forty three years later, they turned around and began to slow down, because they intend on staying a while, it seems. Ten years after that, in 2023, I saw it and began my preparations. And now, here we are, with uninvited guests en route, and no way to turn them back at the door."

Nathan had no idea what to say. Some of the rumors he had heard about Lee now seemed to be a little closer to fact. He sat the tablet down upon the table and stared at the garden. "So, that question wasn't a zinger. It was an actual question."

"It was a question and a job offer, Mr. Kelley. I've spent the last ten years planting the seeds of our defense. Not including a few notable exceptions, people able to see beyond their own preconceived notions of what's out there, I've done it all myself. Because of the nature of this new truth, it unfortunately seems like almost all of the people I can convince I'm serious are the crackpots who have the least to offer me. And don't even ask about government support."

Nathan turned back to Lee, whose eyes burned intensely, but whether it was in madness or determination, Nathan could not tell. "Okay. I won't ask."

"I've sown the seeds, but now I need someone to reap the results. I don't ask that you believe me, or believe the data, but I do ask that you approach this task seriously. You have a unique skill set. I've read military sci-fi, but I need someone with some actual tactical and strategic skills to *do* military sci-fi, to make the possibilities real. I need you to lead my Special Projects branch, consolidating the results of the various research initiatives I've funded in order to develop a defense of the planet. I need an engineer, a manager, a leader, and a seasoned, bloodied naval warrior. You're all of that in a single package."

Nathan finished his beer, but his mouth was still bone-dry. He turned away from Lee and began pacing again, running a hand through his hair. "When you say 'bloodied naval warrior', I assume you're referring to the *Rivero*."

"Yes."

"I *sank* the *Rivero*, Mr. Lee!"

"The enemy sank your ship, Nathan, and two other ships that day as well. You were all sucker punched, but out of every battle of that day, you were the only one to sink your attackers in return. You defeated the enemy and blunted the ferocity of his attack, saving over a hundred and fifty members of your crew."

"And killing 103 of them, including the Captain who put me in charge."

"I've read the proceedings from your board of inquiry. The board endorsed your actions and awarded you the Navy Cross in return."

"Medals and boards don't stop the looks of doubt every officer has when they first meet you, every officer who *knows* they could have done it better if they had been in that situation instead. They also don't stop the looks you give yourself in the mirror every morning either."

Lee spread his hands and smiled. "Look at me, Nathan. I don't doubt you. I'm not second-guessing you. You're who I need. Be the architect of Earth's first space navy. Accept the most important calling in history: the defense of the whole planet. What do you say?"

Nathan turned and stared at him, shaking his head in disbelief. This was the weirdest damn job interview in history, but nowhere nearly as weird as the job itself.

4: "MATTERS OF STATE"

May 27, 2038; Allied Composites, Inc.; Norfolk, VA

Nathan lifted the enormous I-beam slowly and carefully under the apprehensive gaze of Dr. Emil Korso. Nathan looked back at him with a grin and tossed the beam up, catching it with ease. He flipped it over, examining its length closely. The surface was rippled, striated, and gleamed with a dull gray sheen. Nathan set the structural member down and turned back to Korso. "It's everything you promised. And so light!"

"Foamed alloy of aluminum, molybdenum, titanium, and a dozen other trace elements, encasing a three dimensional weave of graphene and carbon nanotubes—one fiftieth the density of steel, and over a hundred times its structural strength per unit volume. And that doesn't include the shear strength, which is so far off the charts, we had to come up with a new chart. I have the full specifications available if you, Mr. Lee, or your materials staff would like to examine them."

"Absolutely. How's the performance of test units under environmental test conditions? Shake it, bake it, freeze it, and nuke it? How does it hold together then?"

"Well, we haven't been able to test full-sized mock-ups in every condition. We simply don't have a freezer, kiln, or radiation chamber quite big enough. If the low end tests we've done are directly scaleable, though, it looks promising. Thermal properties are as expected and it's withstood neutron embrittlement very well, in addition to a full gamma series. We're going to need more time for better data, though."

"Sure, sure. That's understandable. I'll tell you what, Doctor, flash me the specs and we'll have our own testers do some independent validation and verification, but I doubt there will be any problems. We've been following Allied pretty closely. Out of all of our research projects, this one has been the biggest outright success."

Korso smiled sheepishly and smoothed nonexistent wrinkles from his suit coat. "It pleases me to hear you say that, Nathan. We never could have expanded the way we did without Windward's patronage, and we might have even closed down. As it is now, once we've fulfilled our contract with you we'll be able to start marketing Allocarbium to the world. I foresee a very lucrative future in naval and aviation circles." There was a new, greedy look in the scientist's usually unassuming expression.

Nathan shook his head slightly at that. "No doubt, but we're going to be taking every bit of your projected output for the foreseeable future, Doctor. Until you fill our order, you're not to do *any* marketing of our material to outside interests: no samples, no flashes, and no personal tours." Nathan's voice took on a rather darker tone. "Allocarbium belongs to Windward until we say otherwise. Understood?"

"Certainly!" Korso responded nervously, as the gleam of avarice in his eyes faded.

"I'll be sending you a list of required parts to be formed. Nothing too fancy—just beams, frames, plates, decking, equipment mounts, that sort of thing. I'll need a breakdown by part type and size on when you can have it fabricated. And you'd also mentioned some issue about welding?"

Korso nodded, back to his blandly professional self. "Oh, yes. Any welders or post-fabrication people you use are going to have to be trained to work with Allocarbium. You can't simply weld two pieces together. If you did, you'd end up with a fairly weak bond between the two foamed alloys. Welding does nothing for the graphene/nanotube substrate, so instead of welding we do joining. That's an argon environment thermal bonding for the foamed metals and a microscopic interweaving for the carbon mesh underlayer-joining."

Nathan frowned. "Sounds time consuming. And expensive."

Korso held up placating hands. "It is what it is, Nathan, but what you get in return is a join which is indistinguishable from a prefabricated part. It's just as strong as that I-beam and basically turns your structure into one big piece with no weak spots. Speaking of structure, I'd love to know what you're building. There's a pretty high stakes pool going over what it is. Any hints?"

"Well, when the pool makes it to a cool million, let me know and you and I can come to some fair arrangement, say a 90 - 10 split in my favor?" Nathan flashed a grin.

"I think I'd rather guess on my own. A mystery it remains then, but whatever it is, it will be the strongest whatever ever made."

They exchanged suite addresses for the flashes of the technical specs and the fabrication order, said a brief goodbye, and Nathan left. Once outside Allied Composites' offices, in the bright warmth of the Virginia sunshine, he pulled out his suite and called the first number in the memory, a number he called ten times as often as he called his family or the girl-of-the-moment. Before he could dwell on just how depressing that was, Gordon Lee answered.

"This is Lee. What do you want?" His employer's voice out of the earpiece sounded tense, angry.

Nathan grinned. "Temper, temper, boss. If you trash your office again, Melinda's going to quit on you."

"I haven't tossed the place yet, but if you hadn't called, I was probably going to."

"Something wrong?"

"Yeah. Well, no, nothing you should have to worry about. Overseas procurement issues, but nothing connected to your end of things. Forget it. Hey, was there a reason for this call?"

Nathan reached his car, opened the door to the BMW hybrid turbine coupe, and climbed in. "I'm all done at Allied. The Allocarbium fits the bill for our structural material. The only bad news is construction is going to take longer than planned. The stuff has to be welded or joined in a special way. It should all be in their spec flash."

Settling himself behind the wheel, Nathan extended the seven inch flat screen rolled within his cellular smart-suite and scrolled through his e-mail app's received files. The flash download from Korso was the most recent. He opened it and the screen filled with complex metallurgical jargon and equations. Halfway through, there were some attached animations showing the forming process, testing, and joining. "Yeah, it's all in there, though it's a bit over my head. I'll have to get Dr. Hastings to look it over before I can give you a final thumbs-up"

"Don't sell yourself short, boy. You surprise me on a regular basis with your insights."

"Boy? Anyways, it should be in your stack. If Mister Master-of-All-You-Survey can find the time, perhaps you can take a look at it too."

"Don't get snippy with me. I've had more than enough provocation today to fire somebody, and I don't want it to be you by accident."

Nathan grinned. "Oh no, when you fire me, I want it to be on purpose. You should plan your day around it. Finally, to be free of that Nathan Kelley!"

"Smartass. What about Jackson Labs?"

"Nothing new. They haven't beaten the differential heating problem with the diode laser stack. They still crack at any output approaching 10 megawatts. We can probably get around it by using a series of 5 megawatt stacks and then using optics to combine them, but that adds space, weight, complexity, and more stuff for Murphy to screw with. It's workable, though, if they can't fix the problem."

"Fine, fine. Keep on them, but I agree we can live with a workaround. Now what about the layered armor for the Whipple shields?"

"I'll be calling Corning's Albuquerque offices tomorrow morning to conference with the armoring team. They're still having problems making unitary plates more than a square meter in size, but they said they were narrowing down the problem. I'll put some money pressure on them, see if some negative reinforcement gets the brain juices flowing better."

Lee sighed over the connection. "No. A phone call's no good. I want you out there in person. You're my bulldog, and your bark isn't nearly as intimidating as your bite."

"Ummmmm, thanks?"

"It *is* a compliment, Nathan. You have a presence with these science types that can't be denied. Maybe it's your time in the military, that automatic assumption that the people you're dealing with have to follow your orders."

Nathan smiled wryly at Lee's naiveté about order and discipline on paper versus reality. "You obviously haven't met many sailors. Sometimes I had to do quite a bit of convincing to get my subordinates to do what they already knew they needed to do. Depended on the sailor—just like it depends on each individual scientist, engineer, or manager."

"Well, whatever it is you do, you do it well. So, you'll be in Albuquerque tomorrow?"

Nathan grimaced. He had a date with a bank assistant manager the next night, back home in California. That no longer looked likely—yet another sacrifice on the altar of Gordon Elliot Lee's insane engineering project. "Yes, Gordon, I'll be there."

"Excellent!" Lee paused for several seconds, during which Nathan tried to compose what he would tell this latest girl. Lee interrupted his train of thought, though, and continued. "We still have time. Not as much as I'd like, but . . . . We have designs and facilities, and now we have building materials, armor, and we're starting to get some no-shit Star Wars weaponry. We almost have ourselves a space navy, Nathan. Maybe we should start thinking about crew selection? There's this Army light colonel by the name of Wright that's about to retire. He'd make a great counterpart for you." He could almost hear the grin in Lee's voice.

Nathan shook his head, unseen. "Sure, Gordon, there are a couple of old shipmates I'd like to bring aboard too, but I think you need to rein yourself in a bit. At the moment, all we have is a really expensive ground-based weapons emplacement. Until we have some way of powering the damn thing and then getting it off the ground, it's not a spaceship, so thinking of a crew is probably somewhat premature."

He called up a new file on his suite and the screen filled with a CAD

drawing of the project's first design. A somewhat pyramidal wedge—bristling with weapons and sensors—surmounted a long open strut, filled in with radiator panels. Just aft of that, things became vague, with two big circles and question marks identifying a reactor section (Fission? Fusion?), and a propulsion section (Magic Space Drive goes here!).

It was almost a real spaceship, mankind's first space-based combat vessel and their bid to save the planet from the approaching alien threat. But it would not be going anywhere until they broke the design deadlock surrounding their power source and propulsion method.

When Lee spoke again, he sounded very circumspect. "Well, I may have a line on some reactor components."

"Really?"

"Yes, really!" Lee responded, defensive. "But you don't need to worry about it. This is my contribution. You just worry about getting everything else together, including our drive section."

Nathan wondered why he was being so evasive about their power source, but it did not really matter. He knew the Department of Energy had turned down their request for an experimenter's license to acquire fissile materials, but Lee had a lot of initiatives going on at once, many about which Nathan had no knowledge. Perhaps one of them had panned out, such as a reversal by the DOE or a partnership with an established research outfit. Still, progress on one front did nothing for the complete failure on the drive front.

"You make it sound so easy, Gordon. Our problem is that every dollar you've sunk into advanced rockets and reactionless drives has bought us exactly nothing. This is our number one showstopper. If we don't have something to match their super-rocket, we'll have to make our stand within the inner solar system, and that's a bit too close to home for me."

"Me too, but don't worry. Something will turn up. After all, the aliens do it, so we know there's an engine out there that can do what we're asking. We just have to figure out how they do it."

"Once again, boss, you make it sound like that's so simple."

"There's a way, I promise you. Faith and courage, boy, faith and courage. It'll come to us."

Nathan wrapped up the call and docked his suite on the dash of the Beemer. Ozone blues, Nathan's current music of choice, surrounded him from the car's ribbon speakers. He started the hybrid turbine up, its engine betraying only a high pitched whistling whine. Four hub-mounted electric motors propelled the metallic blue sports coupe smoothly and silently out

of his space and onto the road.

Two sedans pulled out at the same time and followed.

Nathan rocketed down the access road toward Virginia Beach, foregoing the congestion of the highway for the white-knuckle thrill of speeding along the two-lane road with its nonexistent shoulders. He drove entirely too fast, which was how he first noticed the two sedans—they not only kept up with him, they were closing in.

"Damn it, Gordon. What did you do?" Nathan knew it was nothing he himself had done. He had been dealing in proprietary technology and beyond bleeding edge weapon systems, but nothing shady or illegal. Some of Lee's plans, however, were more esoteric than others.

A third sedan, as dark and nondescript as the other two, suddenly pulled out from a hidden driveway along the access road and stopped in Nathan's lane, blocking him. Two suited heavies scrambled out holding weapons.

Instead of coming to a screeching halt, he floored the accelerator and swerved into oncoming traffic. Alert drivers and collision avoidance logics drove all but one of the few cars there off into the tall grasses abutting the road. As Nathan zoomed by the men and their car, an old minivan appeared in front of him in the oncoming lane. They both swerved into Nathan's right-hand lane, still headed for collision.

Nathan checked his turn at the last instant and the two vehicles scraped by one another in a shower of sparks and flattened fenders. The BMW fishtailed down the centerline while the minivan spun around and came to a stop just in front of the third sedan. Nathan got his car under control and slid back into his lane, flooring the power to the wheels once more.

It was all for naught. Apparently deciding the sedans and armed heavies were not enough, two tactical vehicles merged onto the access road and blocked both lanes. Their occupants exited bearing automatic weapons. Nathan continued to debate his options for escape, but then he saw the letters emblazoned on the sides of the tac trucks: DHS.

Nathan cursed and slammed on the brakes, bringing the coupe to a screeching sideways stop. The three sedans arrived and also came to screaming halts, arrayed behind him to block any escape he might still be considering. There were guns everywhere, all pointed at him, and he still had no idea what this was all about.

A severe looking woman in a dark gray suit emerged from the back seat of one of the first sedans. She held up an ID, though it was impossible for Nathan to read from this distance. "Mr. Kelley, this is the

Department of Homeland Security. Step out of the vehicle and come with us. We have some questions for you."

He carefully opened the door and climbed out of the low-slung car, hands held high. No sooner was he out than there were three agents in black utilities on him, his arms held painfully against his back, his face and chest pressed hard against the hood of the car. They frisked him with brutal efficiency while others began rifling through the car and cracking the encryption on his suite. He heard the rapid clipping of heels on asphalt and the female agent, undoubtedly the leader of this merry band, was behind him, whispering in his ear. "Why were you running from us, Mr. Kelley?"

Nathan fought a losing battle to keep the pain out of his voice. "Why were you chasing me? I didn't know who you people were until your trucks showed up! You didn't exactly go out of your way to introduce yourselves."

"Mr. Kelley, we often find introducing ourselves to someone like you merely an invitation to bullets or the destruction of evidence. My sincerest apologies for any discomfiture you may have experienced, but you'll have to excuse us for learning from our bloody past."

A fresh jab from the man holding his arms elicited a long groan. Nathan gritted his teeth to cut it off and said, "What do you mean, 'Someone like me'?"

"Nuclear terrorists, Mr. Kelley. And one of our modern war heroes as well. How very sad."

"What!?"

Nathan's spluttering denials and protestations went unacknowledged. They dragged him from the hood of his car and walked him into the back of one of the tactical trucks. In a few more minutes, the access road had been cleared, and their convoy moved along the highway with both trucks, the three sedans, and Nathan's BMW. They were gone before the first regular police arrived with an ambulance to check over the frazzled occupants of the old minivan.

In the well-appointed back seat of the truck, Nathan sat with two dour-faced agent/soldiers in black utilities. The female agent sat across from him on a rear-facing bench seat. They drove in silence for several miles until Nathan could stand it no longer, exactly as they had intended. "I'm not a terrorist, nuclear or otherwise."

"That remains to be seen. I am Special Agent Stanton, Homeland Security. We're acting on credible intelligence received concerning you and your employer's recent activities."

"Mr. Lee isn't a terrorist either."

"Which I am sure will be either confirmed or not in the very near future, but everything depends upon your cooperation. Do we have it?"

"You have it! Absolutely. Nothing would make me happier than to help you, especially given your kind and gracious offer to chauffeur our meeting."

"You can lose the sarcasm, Mr. Kelley. Sarcasm ends this interview and gets you safely behind lock and key as an accessory in the illegal trafficking and use of nuclear materials."

Nathan glared. "Belaying sarcasm, aye, ma'am."

She glared back at him for several more miles in silence. Nathan used the opportunity to try to assess his situation. They had not arrested him yet. In fact, they had not even bound him, with the obvious exception of the two hulking guards on either side. That probably meant that though they suspected him of something, they did not have enough certainty or evidence to proceed with impunity. In fact, if they did arrest him, he could probably have it thrown out of court because of the manner of his arrest. Homeland Security might have become overcautious and extreme in their procedures over the years, but they were still ostensibly a law enforcement agency. Nathan tried not to repeat that to himself as a mantra.

This was a fishing expedition. Not only that, but it had all the classic trappings of a shakedown rather than a legitimate interrogation. These people were likely experienced at this sort of thing, and did not appear to be stupid. That meant that their method of snatching him could hardly be an accident. It was intentional, calculated, probably intended to intimidate him or cow him into a cooperative frame of mind. He was unsure of what that meant for him, but it did serve to relax him somewhat.

Special Agent Stanton saw Nathan settle a bit from his earlier position atop pins and needles. It only seemed to infuriate her. No longer content to wait for his frightened, nervous babbling of what they wanted to know, especially since it did not seem to be working, she started in. "Who is Lee working for?"

"As far as I know, Mr. Lee only works for Mr. Lee."

She smiled. "So Lee is taking it upon himself to become a nuclear power? He's trying to acquire weapons grade and reactor grade fissile material for some perfectly legitimate reason?"

Nathan winced inwardly, hoping his poker face betrayed nothing to the Homeland Security agents. "Overseas procurement problems," Lee had said. It had been nothing for Nathan to worry about—that is until he had been snatched up by the most paranoid, overreaching law enforcement/defense agency since Hoover's FBI. Now, it might be considered Nathan's problem.

"Ma'am, if something that outlandish were true, I'm sure that Mr. Lee would have a perfectly legitimate reason. As it's not true, I think this discussion is probably unnecessary."

"Oh, it is indeed true, Mr. Kelley. We're not quite sure how involved you are, but since you're the head of Windward's Special Projects division, we would surmise that you are fully briefed."

"Fully briefed on what exactly? Your wild speculations?"

She folded her hands demurely in her lap. "We have international data and voice intercepts of your employer attempting to procure nuclear material from several nations which are not on the best of terms with the United States. I would advise you to drop the false innocence and start digging your way out of this."

Nathan tried to think of something. Repeated pleas of his virtue would fall on deaf ears here, and staying quiet would do no good, not when this whole operation seemed focused upon turning him into a babbling informant. Unfortunately, there was nothing for him to babble, even if he had been so inclined. He had not done anything, but Stanton and her underlings would never be satisfied with that. He had to give them something, and though Nathan's thoughts turned at a furious rate, they uncovered nothing. Then he smiled.

There was no lie half so good as the truth.

"Okay. Though I knew nothing about the specifics of what he was up to, I do know that he has been looking for some way to power and arm a spaceship in order to defend the planet from a marauding alien force." He paused, but she said nothing in return. "That's probably what he was doing."

Stanton frowned. "You'll enjoy extra-territorial rendition, Mr. Kelley. Sun, tropical beaches, four by eight cells, no ACLU or UN interference ..."

"I'm being serious."

"Spaceships and aliens? That is the polar opposite of serious and definitive proof that you doubt our own willingness to find the truth through whatever means necessary."

"I'm not saying you have to believe it, and I'm not saying I believe it, even after seeing years' worth of his evidence. But you do need to believe that Lee believes it."

"So you're honestly proposing that Lee is trying to acquire nuclear materials in order to hold off an alien invasion?"

Nathan folded his arms and nodded. "Yes, or at least that's what he believes is happening. I know this isn't the first time you've heard this. It's been an internet rumor for years."

"Yes, I've heard it before—the Deltan invasion, but I put it in the same category as Walt Disney's head being frozen. NASA debunked this whole thing almost ten years ago. It's some sort of comet or something, right?"

"A rogue stellar fragment that coincidentally happens to be between us and Delta Pavonis, but yes, that's what they say."

"Very well, but this also raises the very likely possibility you're telling me this in order to shield your real activities behind some innocuous absurdity."

Nathan leaned forward. He felt his two guards tense up in response, but he ignored them. "I'm not lying to you, and I'm not a terrorist. You have nothing on me, because I haven't done anything. All that you have on Mr. Lee is that he's some harmless kook with too much money and not enough sense. No one is ever going to give him nuclear materials, and if he did actually manage to buy some, you'd be there to snatch us both up. We wouldn't be having a pleasant conversation in the back of your über-truck."

She nodded slightly, though to what part of Nathan's comment, he could not tell. "And what is your part in all of this, Kelley?"

"I'm building his spaceship, but we don't have our magic space drive yet."

Stanton sneered. "I'm going to enjoy interrogating you away from prying eyes."

"It's a date, then. I'll try to bring some flowers."

The convoy pulled off the highway and into a bank parking lot just outside Virginia Beach. The truck opened and Nathan was unceremoniously shoved out. Stanton leaned toward him from her seat. "It would be ill advised for Lee to continue with his proscribed activities, ludicrous reasoning or not. As a valued and trusted employee, and someone with a noose around his own neck as well, I would recommend you persuade him to cease and desist. This argument is no doubt being made to Mr. Lee himself by my California counterpart at this very moment, but it would not hurt to have you backing up our injunction. I do so hope that we will not be seeing each other again, Mr. Kelley." The door slammed shut and the five Homeland Security vehicles sped off, leaving him alone in the parking lot with his beat-up BMW.

"Bye." He walked over to his car and climbed in, one side of his mouth turned down in thought. His suite lay on the passenger seat, none the worse for wear. Nathan extended the screen and scrolled through files. Nothing seemed to be missing, but the access log did show a download of all contents, in spite of the heavy encryption he had bought for it. He grinned a bit, thinking of how confused Stanton would be when the files only confirmed everything Nathan had been saying.

Even if she believed he and Lee were not terrorists, they still would not be allowed access to nuclear materials. Windward as a company had already been denied any legitimate business in atomic energy or weapons development circles, so they could not get what they needed through the established channels. And now they were under surveillance, so they would not be able to get any through extra-legal means either. Lee's plans now had two insurmountable obstacles: power and propulsion. And even if they somehow acquired a reactor and were able to remain out of jail, there would still be the impossibility of getting into space and out of the solar system.

Nathan was forced to acknowledge that what he had said to Stanton was indeed true: even after spending three years on this project, he was still unsure who to believe. Believe Gordon, his cronies, and their following of conspiracy bloggers that the approaching light was an invading hoard from Delta Pavonis, the Deltans? Or believe NASA and their explanation for the blue light, that it was a large, long period comet reflecting light along a fortuitous axis due to its shape and composition, and that it was neither as far away or moving as fast as Lee's data seemed to suggest? Nathan thought NASA's explanation involved a lot of coincidences and hand-waving, but every time he tried to put belief in Lee's aliens, he seemed to feel the world dropping out from below him.

Nathan shook his head. It was his job to build a space combatant, not to believe in its purpose. He shut the screen on his suite and called up Lee's home number. He heard it ring, followed by Gordon's weary answer, "Hello?"

"Hey, Boss. It sounds like we need to have a talk."

5: "BLUE LIGHT SPECIAL"

July 26, 2039; University of Texas at Arlington, Physics Department; Arlington, TX

The conical array was innocuous—nothing but a six inch diameter, six inch long, hollow, double layer cone of cerium-strontium-silver-sulfate superconducting nanowire mesh and frost covered cooling lines, surrounding a tightly spaced series of toroidal magnetic coils. The cone was held aloft by stout bracing within the accelerator's target chamber, which lay directly in the path of UTA's moderate energy electron linear accelerator. The LINAC, essentially a modified injector from the old, bitter days of the Superconducting Super Collider, looked equally cobbled together and home built. This was the sort of place where C average students did third-rate science for the biggest, most apathetic commuter school in East Texas. It was physics hell.

But it was Kristene Annalise Muñoz's own slice of heaven.

She finished looking over the cone and all its various connections and then closed the door to the target chamber. The wheeze-pop of the vacuum pump started loud but quickly faded to background, and she smiled at her contraption. There were no telltale wisps of gas from the cooling lines. No leaks, everything had held. The chamber had been evacuated and they were ready. She turned to her fellow post-grad student, Leo Buchanan, with two thumbs up, sending both her iridescent purple pigtails flailing about. "Good to go!"

"What the hell does that mean? This isn't fucking mission control. This is us blowing the last of our damn grant on your screwed up shit. We are anything but good to fucking go."

She sidled up next to him and batted her eyes. "Awwww, doesn't Weo wike me anymore?" She topped it off with a devastatingly cute pouting of her lower lip.

Leo shoved her over with an elbow, but he could not stop the embarrassed grin that cast off his glowering frown. They were, in many ways, antagonists toward one another, but they both knew he carried a small torch for his oddly hued lab-mate, piercings, ink, and all.

Kris straightened up, smiled back, and moved over to her computer.

"Besides, you can't blame me for being the only one to come up with an idea that actually works when our wacko benefactors threaten to pull the plug."

"Works, my ass. You've got dubious science backed up by crappy engineering, Kris. The only things that we're going to get out of running your rig are some smoked magnets. That and a zero balance on the piss-poor pittance Windward let us keep."

"And I suppose we would have been better off running your simulations? Again?" She shook her head and began her program. A loud hum issued from the LINAC as its magnetic fields built slowly.

"Yes, we would. Gravity wave propulsion is about as mature a science you can get in this field, and I've got the simulation data to back my ideas up. I'm doing real fucking physics, not tinkering like some garage inventor. I'm following in the footsteps of established trailblazers, not just throwing ideas at a wall to see if anything sticks. I've got a friggin' heritage to uphold! After all, my father was with NASA's Breakthrough Propulsion Physics Group."

Kris keyed in the parameters for the next phase of her program. The cone shook briefly, silently in her target chamber. "Please! He was a grad student attached to it for like two months before it was disbanded! Just don't bring up your father again. If I have to hear about him at BPPG, or NASA, or JPL one more time, I'm gonna spew."

"Screw you, chica. I'm not the one with daddy issues."

She pointed a finger at him, and the look in her eyes froze Leo. "Do not even *think* about continuing what you were about to say. You will regret it. Your unborn great-grandchildren will regret it." Kristene was a kooky, happy-go-lucky sort of genius, but there were two things that were absolutely off limits in regards to her. The first was any criticism of the way she chose to decorate the canvas of her form, whether that be her ever-changing hair color, her nose or brow ring, or the colorful tattoos crawling up her left arm. The second was the subject of her father, an abusive loser who had done only one good thing her entire life—abandoning Kris and her mother when the young girl was only ten years old. Kris hid the damage he had done to her, but the damage was still there.

Leo closed his gaping mouth. "I'm just saying that Windward would probably be more appreciative of some established, cutting-edge science. If we'd spent the money on my sims, we could have shown Dr. Hastings my gravity shield effect, we could have shown him my grav wave impeller, and the next generations of the Alcubierre warp drive, whatever."

"Yes, Leo. Your sims are very pretty, but they also require these huge, impractical, and impossible to achieve energy densities. Face it, the only easy way to generate useful grav waves is by shaking a neutron star, and we're fresh out of those. Now if you could come up with some sort of big bang in a box, your fancy sims might be workable, but without a suitable power source you just have some elegant theoretical physics. Thing is, Windward doesn't want theories. They want an engine—and three guesses why, if you believe the internet about Gordon Lee. But they gave us a grant to build an engine, and K-Mart is the only shot we have left."

Leo shook his head and turned to check the bank of gauges and oscilloscopes supporting Kristene's experiment. "'K-Mart'. That has to be the worst fucking name for an experiment in the history of science. Why not just call it a photon drive so everybody knows what a dead-end it is?"

She pouted. "It's clever. It's all about the 'blue-light special'."

He tapped a coolant pressure gauge and then turned back to her. "Yeah, yeah. Anyways, you're probably right. I wouldn't expect some soulless corporation like Windward to have anything approaching the sort of vision you need to appreciate my level of science. I mean, Hastings is all right, but with this sort of company it's usually just bottom-line bastards like that Kelley guy."

The cone began to glow with a soft cerulean light, and Kristene nodded. "I don't care if what's-his-name's got a vision, or a soul, or anything else. As long as he's got a checkbook and a job for me after school, I'm good."

Leo grinned. "Mercenary."

"Potty-mouth." She grinned back. Kristene took one last look at the computer and blew a long, apprehensive whistle. "LINAC's charged, K-Mart fields are oscillating at target frequency and sync'd up, and beam lenses are good. I'm ready to make me some history!"

Leo shook his head at her beaming face. "Where did you say you put that fire extinguisher?"

"Oh, ye of little faith." She turned back to the test chamber. The blue glow from the conical array scintillated captivatingly. Her finger hovered over the ENTER key. "3 ... 2 ... 1 ... Go!" Kristene jabbed her finger down, executing the program and triggering a stream of powerfully accelerated electrons from the LINAC.

And the lab promptly exploded.

It was not precisely true to say that the laboratory in the basement of the Physics Building exploded. It would be more correct to say that half the lab was flash irradiated to the point of brittle failure, and the other half of the lab was blown outward in the pressure wave cast by the passage of the rapidly accelerating conical array. Once the transient pressure wave passed, the irradiated half of the lab was then torn apart by the rebounding air. In essence it was closer to a linear eruption than a classical explosion. The line of demarcation between irradiation or pressure wave was defined by the test chamber and the plane perpendicular to the cone.

When the beam of high energy electrons from the LINAC entered K-Mart, the toroidal string of magnets smoothed the stream into a regimented flow of particles, while the last magnet in the string defocused the stream, spreading electrons uniformly over the inner surface and first layer of the superconducting nanowire mesh cone. The high frequency electromagnetic field generated by the mesh absorbed the significant energy of the electrons and stopped them cold, leaving them to drain off the mesh at a very low potential. The energy absorbed by the field passed without loss through a region of spacetime with some rather unique boundary conditions, and into the synchronized field set up by the closely spaced outer surface and second layer of the cone. This field, so intimately linked with the first field, sought some way of coming back to equilibrium and achieving restoration of the specially bounded region between the fields, and so it did.

The blast of photons that emerged from the cone's outer field were more than mere braking radiation from the halted electrons. They were the universe's attempt to maintain the conservation of momentum and energy in the face of an unstoppable force coming up against an impenetrable barrier. Photons of an energy not seen outside quasars and the birth of the universe itself rocketed out from the cone and struck the target chamber, melting and blasting off the door, and then burned down the rest of that half of the lab.

Kristene was lucky enough to be directly in front of the door. The scorched, flying plate of stainless steel struck her in the face and chest, knocking her across the room and breaking her nose, two ribs, and her left collarbone and arm, but it also served as a shield against the worse part of the radiation. As it was, she received some rather nasty second-degree burns and nearly her maximum lifetime safe dose, but she was alive.

While the cone emitted its impossible blast of radiation, it also rocketed forward, propelled by the high specific impulse and thrust of the dense, mass-less, light-speed emission. The melted struts holding the cone in place gave way, and the fragile experiment accelerated forward at a rate of over a thousand gravities. There was no way for the array to survive this incredible burst of motion, but even after it disintegrated its shrapnel continued to carve swaths throughout the front half of the lab, leaving behind torturous shockwaves to bleed the debris' sudden kinetic energy into the surroundings.

Leo received a chunk of copper cooling tube through one of his shoulders and then was blown back against the wall. Glass, metal, and concrete blasted outward, penetrating the walls and ceiling into the surrounding rooms. Fortunately no one else was injured. The jury-rigged, venerable linear accelerator, one of the last working parts of the failed SSC, was demolished, taking with it UTA's last bid to remain relevant in the world of experimental physics in the 21st century.

In the next instant—after the blast wave passed and the dust settled— silence reigned. Minutes later, shouted voices could be heard, and then rubble began to shift as people started to dig through to search for survivors. Leo was found, logy and bleeding, but alive. Soon after, he was able to compose himself well enough to complain, loudly.

Kristene was pulled free of the ruins by paramedics soon thereafter. She was hurt, but alive and lucky to be so. The EMT's saw the aftermath of the explosion and simply shook their heads in amazement. Part of their shock was due to the level of damage in the lab compared to her relatively minor injuries, but most of it was due to the broad, unconscious smile plastered across her face when they freed her.

▰▰▰▰▰▰▰▰▰▰▰

July 29, 2039; Arlington Memorial Hospital; Arlington, TX

Kristene scooped up another spoonful of jiggly red goodness and began debating the merits of doing her dissertation on the recuperative, therapeutic properties of Jell-O. She had gorged herself on enough of the stuff in the last few days to become a subject matter expert, and it had some definite plusses in its favor. For example, it rarely, if ever, exploded and put you in the hospital.

That was one thing it had over physics.

Additionally, she could probably collect a large amount of data from the comfort of her bed, unlike the large amount of data and equipment that was now, no doubt, destroyed in her last and final experiment. Her K-Mart, her Blue Light Special, her bid to join the groundbreaking minds of the age was now irretrievably lost, along with her notes, her data, and her observations.

She smiled, even as the depression began to creep through the cracks in her will. She had spent far too much time since the accident crying over everything she had lost. At least her last try had gone out with a bang—a big, bright, blue bang. It had been an "event", an unexpected, seemingly impossible … something, something which hinted at a deeper effect, some previously unknown facet of physical law.

She thought about it, obsessed over what she had seen, what she thought she had seen, and what it all meant, if anything. Like every other conscious moment since the accident, she bent her will to the mystery, but came up short. This time, though, Kristene was still for several minutes, then her eyes widened as all the puzzle pieces finally clicked into place.

She dropped the empty cup of Jell-O from her mostly immobilized left hand and reached out with the right for her pink, crystal encrusted suite. Opening the extensible screen from the handheld tablet and tapping on it with her stylus, she winced. It was unseemly to do such potentially important work on what amounted to a pink cell phone, but her primary computer had been lost in the explosion, and something was better than nothing. She began to scribble furiously across the screen.

An unknown time later, but long enough for the sun to set from the afternoon sky, there was a knock on the door. She looked up as it opened and saw a man in his late 30's come in. She did not recognize him, but his plain, serious face brightened remarkably as a broad smile appeared, giving life to the laugh lines around his mouth and eyes, making him far more attractive and compelling. She smiled back. It was hard not to, given her usual preference for older men.

He nodded to her, still smiling, and opened his sports coat to put his hands in the pockets of his khakis. "Hi. How are you feeling?"

She gave a little half shrug with her right side. "Pretty good. I get to stay in bed all day and eat prodigious amounts of sweets. How would you be?"

He laughed. "That would kill me, I'm afraid." He stepped forward and held out a hand. "Sorry. I'm Nathan Kelley, from Windward Tech."

Kristene gave it a shake. "Kristene Muñoz, but you probably already knew that. I've heard of you. You're Dr. Hastings' boss, right?"

"Only in so far as you can be the boss of someone that can think circles around you. Let's just say that I give Hastings a direction and then try like hell to keep up with him. He actually wanted to be here to check on you, but since I came in at the last minute, he's checking out the remains of your lab instead. I figured if you went to all the trouble of blowing yourself up for Windward, it's the least I could do to come out and see how you are."

"Well, thanks! Protecting your investment? Or avoiding a law suit?"

Nathan frowned a bit. "You're not going to yell at me like that Leo guy, are you?"

She relented and shook her head with a lopsided grin. "Naahh, just messing with you. Now, I may have to talk to Hastings about his priorities next time I see him, but I really do appreciate it."

"I'm so sorry about your lab. We knew you were close to completion. It has to be frustrating to be so near the finish, and then have it all taken away."

Kristene looked surprised. "Frustrated? That last experiment was spectacular!" She cocked her head to one side, and put on a devilish smile. "It was a blow-out, a smash success."

Despite Nathan's grin, he looked concerned. "How many meds are you on?"

"I am relaxin' on a little tapentadol, but I'm not that doped up. I'm serious. The only problem with that last test was that I didn't understand everything going on, so I miscalculated. It didn't fail to work—it worked all too darned well!"

Nathan turned, grabbed a chair, and took a seat by her bed. "I'm starting to get a little behind here. Why don't you take it back a few steps?"

She sighed and handed over her suite. Nathan accepted it gingerly and saw it was full of curves and equations, only about half of which he even recognized. She saw the confusion and relented. "Okay. I don't understand everything yet either, but when has that ever stopped me? Basically, you guys asked us two questions: what kind of engine would produce a specific blue light of such and such spectrum and such and such energy, and was capable of massive thrust with very little or no reaction mass, and secondly, how do we create an engine capable of interstellar travel?"

"Yes, and you and about a thousand other people have been working on those questions for the past 15 years with absolutely nothing to show for it."

She nodded. "Okay, I'll give you that, but, truth be told, most of those guys just took your money, shunted it to other research, and then fobbed off some old Breakthrough Propulsion Physics ideas on you."

Nathan's face colored slightly. "Yeah, there were some folks with a bit less integrity than others."

"Because you gotta admit, there are some pretty loopy rumors about what you guys are trying to do!"

"I thought you said you were going to explain why your lab blew up," he said, waving her suite around.

"Oh, I am, I am. It's important to know where I'm coming from is all. You see, I don't think you guys are nuts. I believe in the Deltans!"

"You believe we're being invaded by aliens?"

Kristene's grin faltered. "You mean you don't?"

"Honestly? It depends on the day of the week. I'm putting off making up my mind until I can see some less ambiguous evidence, like maybe from the SSBA, if they ever allow us tasking on it."

"It's not ambiguous. That rogue stellar fragment theory that NASA keeps sticking by is a bunch of hooey, and it looks worse every year they refuse to change their minds. The only reason nobody will publicly challenge it is 'cause they don't want to admit to believing in aliens."

He nodded and then looked down at the suite's screen again. "So you're a true believer. How does that apply to this?"

"Well, everybody else has been focused on the usual suspects for your interstellar engine: warps, bias drives, gravity waves, wormholes, reactionless motors, and stuff like that. But all that stuff is either impossible, improbable, or is gonna take some sort of miraculously magical power source to run. And the only realistic alternatives to the pie-in-the-sky dreamers have been your advanced plasma and ion engines. They can do the job, and we're building them now, stuff like VASIMR, and FEEP, and Hall Thrusters, but none of them have the endurance to really go interstellar, not like the Deltans anyways."

"Okay, so what did you do?"

She beamed. "I killed two birds with one stone. I figured if the aliens were doing it one way already, it probably indicated all those other ideas were full of crap. So why waste my time figuring out how to open a wormhole when some advanced extraterrestrials couldn't even do it? I focused my efforts on answering the first question in order to answer the second one!"

Nathan smiled. "We actually hoped most would do that, but we didn't want to shoot down potentially useful tangents, so we phrased it as two different questions. You aren't the first person to link them, but you are the first to claim to have figured it out."

She wagged her right index finger at him. "Figured it out and have the busted-ass lab to show for it."

"Maybe. That's what Hastings is trying to do by piecing your lab back together. He said the wreckage was very interesting."

"Well, I'll tell you what he'll find. It's what I found and what the Deltans are likely using: a photon drive, but better. Inconceivably better."

"Go on."

"Photon drives have been on the drawing boards for years, but the negatives have always outweighed the positives. Basically, it's a cross between an ion drive and a flashlight. Photons are particles, at least for the purposes of this theory anyway. We won't worry about the wave properties of light at the moment, so just think of them as particles. Specifically they're massless particles, but they still have momentum and energy because they move at the speed of light. There's a whole bunch of different examples of photon momentum in nature, and we've even tried to make space propulsion systems using solar photons for free: solar sails for instance.

"Now a flashlight or a laser is already a photon drive, shooting photons out one end and accelerating in the other, but they're so damn weak you never feel the push. The best they can do efficiency-wise is a Newton of thrust for every 150 to 300 megawatts expended. To make a useable engine you need to produce a LOT of photons at some really big energies, which takes gazillions of gigawatts of power.

"Now, you look at the spectrum from the Deltans' ship, and it's this high energy curve, but it's not a blackbody spectrum like photon drives are traditionally figured for either. Nor is it a coherent monochromatic source."

Nathan shook his head. "You're losing me. My basic physics was a long time ago and ... ."

She nodded. "It's okay. It doesn't look like a star's emissions, or any thermal source like a rocket, but it doesn't look like a laser either. It's different, weird, but what it does resemble is an antenna emission, only with the central, main frequency a lot higher than we're used to, somewhere in the high ultraviolet. The blue light we see from the Deltans is just the tail end of their emission spectrum.

"I guessed that maybe there was some sort of benefit to having the photon drive's exhaust in a narrow frequency band rather than a broad blackbody spectrum. So, I tried to duplicate what they had already done. It took a lot of freakin' brilliant work on my part, but eventually I came up with the cone. I call it K-Mart."

He screwed up his face, but then said, "K-Mart? Blue-light special?"

Kristene suddenly felt a lot warmer than the room seemed to be. She gave him a coy half-grin. "Oh, I knew I liked you."

Nathan grinned back, but shook his head. "Anyways ... ."

"Anyways, it's essentially an antenna, keyed around the same central frequency as the Deltans', but no material I know of could handle the power output needed to give this thing any sort of thrust, so I used a pair of coupled field effect antennas. They emit from the fluctuations of an EM field, with one field receiving and the other transmitting. So you put power in one side, and the other side emits your photons for thrust. It's not reactionless, which is impossible, but you don't need reaction mass either. You just need power."

Nathan stood, excited by the possibilities, but still apprehensive. He began to pace. "Okay, for the sake of argument, let's say it worked. Why did your lab explode?"

She shrugged with her right side. "I don't know. It shouldn't have. The cone should have these huge losses from one side of the antenna to the other. It was only supposed to produce a couple of millinewtons of force, about what you'd get out of a standard ion drive. Not the sexiest interstellar engine, but it'd work. Thing is, not only did it not show any loss from the electron beam to the photon emission, that explosion seems to show that it released more energy than was even present in the beam!"

Nathan turned to her. "That's impossible. You can't create energy from nothing."

"I don't think I did. It'll have to be proven out, but I think the cone took *all* the available energy from one side and converted it to photon thrust. That's the energy in the beam, the energy in the LINAC's fields, the radiant heat and light in the target chamber, hell maybe even vacuum energy, but I doubt it. It took everything available and turned it into thrust. The beam started the ball rolling and it just took off from there on its own. If I could do it over again, I bet I could show that whatever type of energy you shove in to the receptor field, it can use it to make thrust. It's the ultimate rocket: the highest possible specific impulse, at a high thrust, high efficiency, and zero need to cart around reaction mass."

Nathan approached the bed and gripped the handrail with both hands. "So, this ... enhanced photon drive—could you do it again? And without blowing yourself up this time?"

She pouted. "Well, maybe, but it turns out that someone cut my funding off."

"Assuming Dr. Hastings can translate what you have here," he said, holding up her suite, "and assuming he buys off on it, you can consider your funding restored, and this time as a direct employee of Windward."

Her pout became an impish grin. "In that case, you bet your ass I can do it again, and a lot better this time. We're going to the stars, Mr. Kelley!"

6: "OF PICTURES, PRAWNS, AND POSSIBILITIES"

December 10, 2039; Calvert's Gumbo Room; Alexandria, VA

Nestled in the corner of one of Alexandria's oldest buildings downtown, the quiet little restaurant existed as neutral territory in the battlegrounds of scandal and ideology, enjoying the coverage of an umbrella of discretion and anonymity that few establishments retained for as long. This sort of unspoken agreement of private civility between the press and the upper echelon patrons of the dark, wood-paneled Gumbo Room meant that Calvert's would never be fabulously successful or famous, but it would allow the little place to become an important footnote in the unwritten history of the nation.

Here, senators could dine with their mistresses in style, without too great a fear of discovery. At this table, the majority and minority leaders could share a drink and a laugh over how divided their public personas had become, while the actual difference between them had never been narrower. At that table, the conservative talk show host, the liberal editor, and their respective publicists and advisors could all gather round heaping piles of steaming blue crab and divide up the political landscape, working out talking points and scathing rebukes of one another, all the time keeping a keen eye toward maximizing their individual market share.

As a direct consequence of Calvert's unacknowledged place in the political universe, an unofficial non-meeting could be held there which might receive undue attention were the principles to meet in an actual government office. Many a nation-altering deal had been brokered secretly and safely above the Gumbo Room's varnished tables and embroidered maroon tablecloths. Thus, at the table in the far corner, isolated from the rest even in this sanctuary of isolation, the Assistant National Science Advisor, the Deputy Secretary of Defense, and their tardy guest could quietly change the course of the world and the human race.

Lydia Russ smiled softly and contemplated her glass of wine in silence while Carl Sykes, Lieutenant General, USAF (retired) seethed over their guest's continued absence. He jabbed a toothpick violently into another olive from his small plate, swished it through his untouched martini, and devoured it with a growl and yet another look toward the entrance.

No one was there. Sykes shook his head and snapped his toothpick, tossing it negligently behind him. "Where the hell is he?"

Lydia took a sip of wine. "He'll be here. Stop worrying."

"I'm not worrying. I'm pissed. It's unprofessional and rude to make us wait. You'd think that someone with his ego would jump at the chance to cackle at us."

Lydia smiled more broadly. "You don't know Gordon like I do. His ego wouldn't allow him to be here on time even if he had nothing to crow about, and now that he does, he probably considers making us wait some form of payback. He'll be here, though. It's the opportunity he's been waiting for, after all."

Sykes grunted and snatched another toothpick from the small open jar among the condiments at the center of the table. He was just about to angrily spear an olive yet again when Gordon Lee's smug voice behind him caused him to snap the pick instead.

"Imagine my surprise! After being persona non grata in this town for the past 16 years, suddenly, people are accepting my calls. Suddenly, the whispers that I've got one foot in the loony bin quiet down a bit. And if that wasn't nice enough, I suddenly get myself a personal invitation to the Beltway Bandits' own secret dinner club. Whatever could be the reason for this startling reversal of fortune?"

Sykes looked back and saw Gordon Lee, shedding an expensively tailored tan trench coat and straightening his jacket and tie, a tie, he noted, that was covered in little Flash Gordon-style rocket ships. Sykes shook his head and said, "Maybe Christmas arrived early this year."

Gordon's smile became tighter, more vicious. "Somehow I doubt that." He approached Lydia's side of the table and bent down to squeeze her hand and gave her a kiss on the cheek. His lips were cold from the chill wind blowing outside, but his eyes were warm with the embers of their past. "Lydia, you are lovelier than ever."

She canted her head to one side and gave him a saucy grin. "And you are a manipulative, gloating liar, but I wouldn't have it any other way. How have you been, Gordon?"

"Lonely ... and angry, but excited, too. I've got a whole bunch of stuff to show you, both of you, stuff that you'll never believe."

Sykes smiled. "Something of a habit for you isn't it, Lee? Showing off things no one in their right mind would ever believe in?"

Lydia held up a hand to forestall the barb Gordon was about to fire back. "We have things to show you as well, Gordon, but first let's get the important stuff out of the way. Drinks?"

Unobtrusive waiters dressed all in black, with long, dark green aprons appeared. Within a minute, Gordon proceeded to banish the last of his chill with a cut crystal tumbler half filled with straight single-malt highland scotch. Lydia had taken the liberty of ordering for each of them already. Gordon's tastes were known and she figured the Gumbo Room would be a special treat for him. Sykes was a bureaucratic insider with a lifetime of government service in war, in peace, and in the special infighting peculiar to the Pentagon and the Washington Beltway. Second in command of the nation's defense or not, all he would care about was getting a free meal.

By the time the servers backed away, they had all had their drinks freshened, and steaming, spicy cups of Cajun gumbo had been placed in front of them. Different from the Creole gumbo Gordon was used to, he used his spoon to break up the ball of white rice in the center of the cup, mixing it with the dark brown soup and the plentiful shrimp, onions, and celery settled below the surface. Savory, piquant heat radiated out from the first spoonful, and Gordon smiled broadly to his hostess and friend, acknowledging her good choice.

Gordon wiped the corner of his mouth with his napkin, and caught their eyes with his own. Sykes stopped endlessly stirring his gumbo and devoured another martini-dipped olive. Lydia wiped her own mouth and looked back at Gordon. The head of Windward Tech and the man she had helped to ostracize years ago grinned tightly. "So, what happened? Why the turnaround?"

She responded by reaching down to her purse and extracting her suite. Lydia laid it on the table between them and extended the screen from the side. Displayed on it was something he'd grown very familiar with over the years: the constellation Pavo. A familiar, chillingly enigmatic blue star shone next to the position of Delta Pavonis. This picture appeared to be recent—the separation between the blue light and the star it came from was the most pronounced he had seen, parallax making the approaching light oscillate wider and wider across its origin.

Gordon looked up at her again. "That's not really any more compelling than the ones I showed NASA originally. I believe they downgraded it to a 'stellar fragment' and me to a nut-job crank."

She nodded. "True, unfortunately, but how about this." She tapped the suite and the image changed. Now, instead of all of Pavo, it zeroed in on Delta Pavonis and the blue light. Another tap and just the blue light filled the screen, fuzzy and indistinct. Another tap and the blue light shrank away, the fuzziness sharpened to distinct threads of light and optical glare, but there was something else there as well. It was a broken halo, something reflecting reddish in spots around the star of pale blue.

Gordon leaned in and she tapped the suite again. The picture became artificially sharp, a false color image designed to bring out the details in the captured blobs of light. At the center was a sharp circle of bluish white, the scintillating edge of the alien photon drive. Around it, an equal distance from the center and arranged in a somehow familiar fashion, there were four reverse shadows, the edges of four immense objects surrounding the drive flare, illuminated with a red brilliance and spots of blue bright enough to obscure anything else from view. Gordon's heart hammered excitedly within his chest. He looked back up to Lydia. "What the hell is it?"

She shook her head. "We don't know, but it is structure, and it's definitely not a rogue fragment ejected from a star."

Gordon grinned. "I'll tell you what it is. It's my damned aliens! This is it! Proof, incontrovertible proof that they're coming here, just like I always said."

Sykes shook his head. "Hold on, Lee. It's 'something'. Whether or not it's proof of your pet aliens is another matter entirely."

Gordon shooed his hands at Sykes, dismissing him and focusing on Lydia. "How did you get these shots? What are they from?"

"Optical interferometry. They're from the Solar System Baseline Array."

"I tried to get my astronomers tasking on the SSBA since it became operational, but we always got the brush off. They told me it was because the 'fragment' was a low order priority, but I always figured it was just another sign of the box I'd been put in."

Lydia frowned. "You're closer to right than wrong, but not everyone who believed was isolated like you were. You had more than a few supporters within the community. Eventually it became more suspicious to reject their requests than it was to let them get their pictures. No one in the administration ever imagined it would reveal something like this, though."

Gordon's eyes narrowed slightly. "And which side were you on, Lydia? Were you one of the believers or one of the ones blocking them?"

She returned his glare steadily. "The administration is my administration, Gordon, for better or worse, but I also have faith in my friends. I'm the one that authorized the re-tasking of the SSBA. Is that good enough for you?"

He nodded, his expression softening. "I'm sorry. It's just been a long time out in the cold is all. I'd become of the opinion that I didn't have any friends left out there anymore." Gordon shook his head and smiled again. "But what are we doing here? We should be planning our press conference! We have to get the word out as soon and as wide as possible."

Neither of the others said anything. A hint of a smile touched the corner of Sykes' mouth. Gordon looked from one to the other and then sat back, dismayed. "You're still not going public, are you? You have pictures of the damn thing and you're going to sit on it?"

Lydia's voice pleaded for his understanding. "We have pictures of something, something that backs up your original assertion, but it's still not proof. The images we have come from a new satellite constellation that most people don't understand, and that brings with it some doubt. We only arrive at a final image by mathematically combining the images from space based telescopes positioned in different orbits all around the solar system. For most people, that brings in even more doubt, some degree of un-believability. And to get the final image of the … object, we had to process it even further."

Sykes cleared his throat, inserting himself in the conversation. "That picture doesn't really exist, and it won't exist. It's a computer-manipulated image from an unproven system that backs up the claim of an industrialist most people regard as nuttier than Howard Hughes in a straightjacket. No one is going to publicly stick their necks out to support you, and they're certainly not going to give you a budget to assist with your little science fiction crusade."

"So we work harder to convince them!" Gordon downed a slug of scotch. His expectations had grown so high in moments, and now they had been sent crashing. His nerves were a mess. "We support some pretty screwy shit in this country with no justification whatsoever, and now that we have something real and verifiable to show people, we're just going to say that it's too risky? That there's not enough there to back it up?

"This could be either the best thing to happen to the human race in its whole history, past or future, or it could be the end of our history, the end of everyone, timid politicians and innocent soccer moms alike. Either way, people have to be prepared. By the time we have the type of evidence that will convince the administration to go public, we won't need it, because everyone will be able to just look up and see the aliens in orbit!"

"Oh, get off your soapbox, Lee. You had the chance to go public years ago as well, right after you got the brush-off from the government, but you didn't do it. Where were your press conferences then?" Gordon said nothing, so Sykes continued. "No, you didn't go forward with telling everyone because you knew that the standard for convincing people about aliens is higher than it is for other things. It's higher than some weird kinematics off a bunch of telescope sightings, and you know that it's higher than some doctored photo of a bunch of red and blue blobs that look nothing like our concept of a spaceship. You stayed underground and let the evidence exist as some internet rumor because that's as far as you could go until you had more to show. We're the same way. We can't go forward on the basis of this photo."

Then Lydia smiled. "But maybe we can stop holding you back."

Gordon looked at them both sharply, but they said nothing. The servers returned with food and fresh drinks, whisking away their half-eaten cups of gumbo and replacing them with steaming, sizzling dinner plates. Sykes was served some sort of squash risotto alongside an immense blackened porterhouse, a dollop of butter melting on top. Both Lydia and Gordon were each served shrimp.

In this case, shrimp was an oxymoron. These were prawns, three grilled, butterflied tails apiece, each one four inches long, spiced with flakes of red pepper and herbs, lying atop a bed of sticky white rice, drizzled and surrounded by a rich crawfish étouffée, and topped off with a sprinkling of lump crab meat. Gordon looked down at it and smiled. He glanced back up at Lydia. "For this, I forgive you of nearly half of the crap you've pulled."

"My, my. That much? And we haven't even gotten to coffee or the desserts yet. I just might be back in your good graces by the end of the night."

"Don't push your luck." Gordon sliced off a forkful, making sure he got a piece of everything. He tasted it cautiously, but as the myriad spices, sauces, and meats inundated his senses, he began to chew with gusto. No one flavor or spice stood out. It was an exercise in exquisite balance, with the resulting mélange of flavors nothing less than arthropodic bliss.

In so far as it is possible to define a person in simple terms, Gordon Lee was a man of great drive but little philosophy. One of the few beliefs he held, aside from an almost religious devotion to preparing for the Deltans, was that there was a definite moral equivalency to being part carnivore. If an animal had to die for his dinner plate, he felt that it should have an honorable death, and that its passing should result in something greater than just the filling of his belly.

Fast food, for the most part, was simply wrong and the vast majority could be replaced surreptitiously with Vegan fare without anyone noticing a thing except for the drastically improved health of the nation. On the other hand, a really good burger could represent a sublime ascendancy, placing a simple cow in the bovine equivalent of Valhalla. For a bacon cheeseburger, the moral cost was correspondingly higher, the dish then involving the lives of two farm animals, including one that was arguably more intelligent than a dog. For Gordon to feel good about it, it had to be *really* good bacon and on a *really* good burger. If one of them failed to measure up, the whole thing was in a moral deficit.

Gordon had had more than one ethical crisis over club sandwiches.

Though crustaceans were pretty far down the sentience/morality ladder, having three different varieties on the same plate was still more than enough to raise the equivalence bar pretty high. That Gordon dug in with relish and without any sort of soul searching or sense of existential guilt was testament to just how good Lydia's choice had been.

They passed more than a few minutes without saying a thing other than to comment upon the food. Sykes, who did not share any of Gordon's philosophies toward meat, merely grunted in seeming agreement, cutting off bite after bite of bloody, seared steak. Eventually, Gordon began to emerge from his culinary fugue and looked down at the remains of his dinner with equal parts satisfaction and embarrassment. He permitted himself another bite and then carefully laid down his knife and fork. He enjoyed another bit of scotch and then bid his hosts' attention with a look from one to the other.

Sykes and Lydia caught his look and paused a moment in their dining as well. Gordon smiled, but there was a hint of menace in it. "So, aside from plying me with good food, how exactly is the administration going to help me? Or was that 'obstruct me less'?"

Lydia smiled back, but it was somewhat cagey in response to the less than friendly nature of his own expression. She wiped the corners of her mouth with a cloth napkin and then demurred, "Oh, I think we could probably swing a little of both. The thing we can't give you is overt support. There's just not enough good evidence to sell the Deltans to the nation … or the world."

Gordon nodded slightly. "Okay, maybe I'll grant you that. Now where exactly have you been holding me back?"

"How about everywhere, Lee," Sykes said around a mouthful of risotto. He took a drink of water and then wiped his mouth as well. "You don't think all those rumors started on their own, did you? It took a lot of effort to make sure you didn't get recognized by anyone respectable. If someone with some actual credentials backed you up, it might have forced the administration to support you without some more concrete evidence.

Could have been an embarrassment, or worse, an actual waste of money."

"Gee, I'd hate for an alien invasion to put anyone out of sorts."

"Don't get petulant now that we're playing fair, Gordon." Lydia leaned forward, seemingly eager, with a hint of the excitement Gordon always remembered her having. "However, you have done some pretty amazing things stuck out on the fringe. Is it true you've come up with a new kind of rocket?"

Gordon tried to play it cool, but failed. The menace was gone from his smile now, caught up by her enthusiasm. "It wasn't me, but yeah. We've decoded the Deltan's method of interstellar travel and we can duplicate it. That's just the icing on the cake, though. We've developed new structural materials, sensors, computer architecture, armor, you name it. The only sticking point I've got is in power. I always figured that propulsion would be the long pole in the tent, but reactor design is where we've been held up the longest. Due to your little passive aggressive crusade to marginalize me, I've been kept from any real research or development in any sort of serviceable fission power plant. Every time I get close to hiring somebody or investing in someone else's project, somebody official shows up to investigate me. Do you have any idea how many times I've been searched by Homeland Security?"

Sykes smiled. "Actually, I know the number exactly, as well as the number of times we've hacked your data without a warrant. We've only been able to decrypt a few of your intercepted files, but it's allowed us to keep tabs on you. That's how we knew about your little photon drive. We weren't sure if we believed it, though, since we couldn't decrypt any of the theory or application to confirm it. I thought it might have been something to lead us off on a tangent, some sort of joke you were having on us."

Gordon arched an eyebrow at Sykes blasé admission of his illegal data mining. "Huh. Well, it's real, and I found a way around the NRC and all your reactor opposition anyway. It's the one thing I had to farm out overseas, but I was able to get a little French company to develop an advanced pebble-bed reactor for me. Now if I could just get your timid administration to let me bring the prototype over to the US, perhaps I could get some real integration done."

Lydia nodded. "In the interests of removing obstacles, I think we can give that one to you. Consider your work with the French outfit officially authorized. You'll have your reactor as soon as they can ship it."

Sykes finished off his steak and wiped his mouth, leaving the napkin on the bloody residue covering his plate. "'Course, that raises the question of why you didn't just farm out everything overseas. We blocked you everywhere you turned. If you're open to French nuclear power, why not German armor or Chinese computers? If you did that, you might have an actual spaceship by now."

"And I also might have given away a capability beyond anything in the whole US arsenal. This tech is designed to fight aliens should that become necessary, but it could just as easily be used against humans, and our fellow man has been a confirmed threat for a lot longer than the Deltans have been doing their thing. The drive alone could be put to pretty devastating use if you pointed it at something other than empty space. Call me a patriot, or call me a provincial nationalist, but I trust my country more than the others, flaws and all, allies of the US or not. Personally I'd rather face the Deltans with a bunch of spit wads than face our potential opposition with this sort of capability."

The Deputy SECDEF grinned. "Will wonders never cease? There's something we agree on after all."

"Don't take that as blanket approval, Sykes. I'm not a hundred percent on giving this stuff over completely to the US either. We don't have the best track record as the arbiters of human decency, and hearing you talk about all the times you've tried to access my research doesn't make feel all warm and patriotic inside."

Sykes had nothing to say to that, either in defense or in confirmation. Lydia frowned and then asked, "We know your goal is to get direct intelligence on the Deltans with a probe mission. If you had everything you needed, how long before you could independently put up a mission?"

"Independently? Never. Windward is stagnant and stockholders are dropping like flies. I've sunk every dollar and every bit of attention I could spare into this project, and the company has suffered as a result. Lockheed and Orbital are killing my market share. I may be okay personally, but I'm no longer one of this country's ten richest industrialists. I'm probably not even in the top 100, and Windward Tech's stock has fallen over 40 percent. If I don't get at least a little assistance, my company is either going to fail or I'm going to have to start releasing some of the project's developments, and that's risky in its own way."

Sykes nodded. "No doubt. You might give away intel to other countries, other companies, or even the Deltans, if they're watching us with any sort of keen eye. You declassify it, you lose control."

Lydia put a hand over Gordon's and squeezed. "I'm sorry, Gordon. Again. I know how much building Windward up has meant to you. It's been your life, and now you're losing it because we wouldn't believe in you."

Gordon favored her with a bittersweet smile. "Honestly, I've been so caught up in the project that I let the company slide. It's not your fault I let it come to this. What you did didn't help, but I'm the one ultimately responsible."

"Well, along with removing obstacles, we probably could free up some indirect funding. I mean, we bail out corn and railroads, why not spaceships?"

Gordon smiled softly. "Okay, give me six months and a little quiet funding, and I can give you a probe that will bring back the intel you need to go public with the Deltans. Support me fully, and I can give you a damned warship that'll give anyone pause, alien or not."

Sykes grunted. "And here we'd been getting along so well. I'm all for peace through superior firepower, but there's still a few too many unknowns to go the warship route yet. We haven't even assessed a threat, and you're ready to fire the first shot anyway."

Gordon's brow sharpened as he looked at the retired Air Force general. "I'm ready to be ready for anything. If the Deltans are benign, no big deal. Whatever we spent on preparations will be eclipsed by everything we gain just by being in their presence. If they're indifferent to us, we've taken at least the first steps at meeting them as equals and forcing them to take notice. And if they're hostile, if they're inimical … well we'll be ready for that too."

"Ready? As if you could ever be ready for anything as unknowable as a hostile alien force. They're coming here from twenty light-years away, Lee. They've expended massive amounts of energy and resources to fly here physically for whatever reason they have. How could we possibly hope to contend with them as any sort of real adversary?"

"Interesting position for the Deputy SECDEF, don't you think?"

Sykes' face darkened. "I've fought for this country in and out of war for 36 years. I've seen even battles and I've seen when one side clearly outclasses the other. I know what to do for each situation, whether it's on the offensive or defending territory. In this case, it's ludicrous to believe that we could hope to really contend with the Deltans in any sort of combat sense. What we've uncovered from your plans is that you and Kelley are planning an offensive defense-in-depth, hitting them far out, heavy, and often, should it prove necessary. But don't you see that's doomed to failure? They've already expended more energy than we've released as a species throughout all time and shown off more than enough capability to prove that they can destroy us without a second thought.

Your tech is impressive, but it's not alien-overlord impressive."

"What would you do then, General?"

"I'd face up to our limitations. I'm all for your probe, and I'd even back up a manned mission if you have the tech to make it happen, but as an ambassadorial effort only. Try to reason with them or divert them, and in the meantime work on defenses here at home. Your tech could be used to build some very effective bunkers and fixed emplacements. We don't know what they want, but it can't be to simply destroy us. If that was it, they wouldn't have even bothered to slow down. They could kill the whole damn globe with kinetic energy alone. And they can't be coming to our system for resources alone. They've had to pass by too many closer solar systems and they've expended too much energy for this to be about simple materials."

"I've said much the same thing before, and I agree that we should be applying ourselves to expanding our planetary defensive capabilities, but how can you believe it's better to begin the fight here rather than off the planet, whether we have any reasonable chance or not?"

"I don't want to begin any fight at all, Lee. Our only option is to try to work out a benign contact, and then prepare for a dug-in defense in case that fails. All an early attack will accomplish is to piss them off, ruining any chance we'd have at a diplomatic solution, and increasing the likelihood that they would just glass the planet when they got here."

Gordon threw his hands up. "You can't possibly know that! We have some pretty effective weapons in our arsenal, and that's before I've even turned my project engineers toward upgrading and adapting them. We might be a hell of a lot more capable than you're making out!"

"That's wishful thinking on your part. What little you might be able to send against them in the next 15 years or so would just be nuisance making, and a distraction from developing our defenses on the ground. Face it, when you saw their turnaround flare it was already too late."

His face turning red, Gordon snarled, "I might have been ready to send more if you people had given me the support I asked for when I first came to you!"

Lydia laid a hand on both of their arms, taking over before more than words were exchanged. "This is not the time or the place for this. Let's just take it as accepted that both of you have … passionate but differing views about the details of our defense. That's not what this meeting is about, though. This is about finding out what you need for now. We can work out the next step, calmly and sanely, later when we all have more than personal arguments to go off of."

She waited for them to nod before moving on. "Six months and funding will get us a probe, right?"

Gordon took a slow breath, pointedly looking away from Sykes. "Yes."

"And I'm assuming one probe won't satisfy anyone with any experience in space operations, so more funding and a little more time will give us more probes, right?"

"Yes. I can't give you a better production time until we make up the prototype, but I'm assuming it will be a lot less than six months for each probe."

"And how long will it take to get data back from those probes?"

A hint of a smile touched the corner of Gordon's mouth. "Well that depends on a lot of things: how far away the Deltans are, how fast the probe is going, and what sort of flight profile you send it on. Do I send it straight at their ship for a fast flyby, or do I send it in for a meeting situation? And do I maneuver it overtly or covertly?"

"It's your probe, Gordon. The administration officially has no involvement, so you tell us."

"Okay. If they continue tracking as they have, the Deltans are now 1.7 light-years away and moving at 20% the speed of light. If we shoot out a probe and accelerate it at one g continuous for a fast flyby, I can have some intel back in about two and a half or three years. That includes the time to travel out there, and then the time for the report to come back here. Now that's somewhat misleading since that assumes we can maintain that acceleration for that long, or that a probe could even survive approaching 90% the speed of light, and even if it could, you're going to get some piss-poor photos at those passing speeds due to Doppler shift.

"A better bet would be to arrange some sort of covert meeting situation, where we accelerate off-axis and then reverse our acceleration halfway out, while still keeping our drive corona pointed away from the Deltans. That lets us match speeds and approach them from the side without totally giving away our presence. That's the same profile a manned mission would take as well."

"Better plan, Lee," Sykes grumped. "If there's only going to be a couple of these probes, we don't want to waste one of them on a recon that only nets us a blurred picture or two. I'd rather wait than waste a shot."

Lydia nodded. "How long a wait?"

"That's a little tougher. I can't exactly back-of-the-napkin that sort of maneuver, but call it six to eight years to get data back, or maybe a little less."

Sykes frowned. "It's the better plan, but that's still a long time to wait for intel."

Gordon shrugged and said, "It is what it is. Voyager has been traveling for over 70 years, and it's only in the Kuiper Belt. We're talking about something *light-years* away and getting back information in a matter of a few years. You're just stuck thinking in terms of a single planet. For these sorts of speeds and distances, under a decade is practically real-time data."

Servers appeared around them, clearing away plates and dropping off yet another fresh round of drinks, as well as a pot of coffee and three cups, cream, and sugar. Lydia smiled and began pouring coffee for each of them. "So we can help you out with a couple of probes, and then in six to eight years we get to find out if it was money wasted on a comet, or if the whole world is about to change. What do you plan on doing in the interim? Or, rather, what would you like to do with all your secretive government funding while you don't have to worry about pesky things like justifying its use?"

Gordon grinned. "I'll be working on the ship, the prototype for, I hope, all those warships that we're going to build as the last line of defense we have against the Deltans. The probe is just a starting point. An actual ship with people and weapons aboard is hundreds of times more complex, and it's going to take years just to figure out what the best design is. And then that first ship will be *the ship*. The prototype is going to be our ambassador to the stars."

"How poetic." Sykes drank his coffee black, swallowing the whole cup in a single gulp. "And what sort of things are you looking to develop for this ship still?"

Gordon began counting off on his fingers. "Environmental support, oxygen replenishment, living arrangements, waste management, radiation shielding, sensors, weapons—"

Sykes pounced without leaving his chair. "What sorts of weapons?"

"Well, I've already sunk money into electromagnetic guns, launchers, and laser systems. Those are all bearing differing amounts of fruit, but I recognize that those sorts of systems won't be enough to stop the Deltans alone, should they need stopping. What I really need to work on is missiles, and specifically warheads. Along with freeing me up to work with reactor components, how about releasing me to work on weapons-grade materials?"

Sykes pushed away from the table and gestured for his coat. "Nope.

Forget it. You get the authorization to work on nukes when the Deltans prove they're a threat. Figure out something else, include space for missiles from our existing arsenal, or, better yet, forget the offensive systems and go with an ambassador ship."

"Our ballistic missiles are developed for hitting stationary land targets, not an enemy warship in space. They're totally inadequate for this purpose."

"Then leave them off."

"What about ensuring peace by preparing for war?"

Sykes coat arrived. He stood and slipped it on. "Did you forget? I don't think any ship you send out there is going to have a snowball's chance in hell. If you send an offensive capability out there, at worst you'll piss them off, ruining any sort of diplomatic defense we might be able to make, and at best you'll give away what little capability we do have. So no nukes. No plutonium, no lithium deuteride, nobody from Los Alamos, nothing." He turned to Lydia and gave a short bow. "Thank you for a fine meal and a very weird conversation, Ms. Russ. I hope this all turns out to be this nut's fantasy, because if it isn't, we're screwed. Good night to you both." Sykes downed his martini and headed for the door. He disappeared into the cold, black night.

"I don't think we're going to be friends." Gordon shook his head and turned to Lydia. "I'm hamstrung if I don't have the access to build some sort of ship-to-ship nuclear weapons."

"I'm sorry, dear. We're just the heralds of a much higher-ranked decision group, and even then only two representatives of a much bigger organization. I'm the science side, he's the defense and never the twain shall meet. I can make decisions on funding for development, but not for weapons development."

"Is there anyone I can appeal to? The SECDEF himself?" Gordon looked desperate.

Lydia tried to show as much compassion in response as she could. "Who do you think they're going to side with? You've only freshly shucked the mantle of shame." She reached out and held both his hands. "Don't worry about it for now. You've got years yet to change their minds. Focus on everything you've achieved tonight and forget about the rest, if only for a little while."

He squeezed her hands and looked back at her, his frustration slowly giving way to gratitude and the pleasant shades of memory. "It is so good to see you again, Lydia. It's been too long, with too much left unsaid."

She smiled. "I've missed you too, Gordon."

Gordon arched a brow. "I believe you mentioned something about dessert?"

Her smile took on a decidedly different character and she gestured to the wait staff for the check and their coats. "I just might wind up back in your good graces tonight after all."

7: "THE PROMISE"

Kristene Muñoz found her quarry in the wood, granite, and stainless steel kitchen of Gordon Lee's sprawling house. Nathan Kelley sat on a stool with his back to the swinging door, leaning over the center island with his attention split between the steaming mug of coffee in his hand and the suite expanded before him. Kris had no idea what he was reading so intently, but she was in no hurry to stop him.

She carefully stopped the swing of the kitchen door and just leaned back against the wall, a sly smile turning up a corner of her mouth. If he was content to catch up with his reading on their big day, she was content to admire the view. Lee maintained a gorgeous estate, a slice of central coast California heaven, but this had to be her favorite new vista.

It was too bad Nathan was completely clueless, she thought, because he could wear a pair of jeans really, really well.

The last year had been a whirlwind dream for her. She first hobbled into the world of Gordon Lee and his secret project at Windward Tech, still recovering from the injuries she had sustained in her discovery of the enhanced photon drive. As her body healed, she had been read into the mysteries of the Deltans, along with all that Lee had developed and hidden away, and all that he still hoped to achieve. It was a heady time for her— just out of college and the undisputed star of the interstellar program, but she had been far too busy to let her ego swell too much. The drive required refinement and definition, with all the tedious hours and tests – and failures, so many failures – that it took to change scientific serendipity into engineering surety. And now, with the removal of governmental obstruction, her drive became the centerpiece of the next great step in their march to the stars.

Throughout it all, Nathan Kelley had been a constant presence at her side, guiding her, correcting her, mentoring her. It was Nathan that tied all the designs together, and he loomed large in her relationship with Windward. She was also fully aware that her initial attraction to him had deepened as she had gotten to know the man. Kris knew she was now lost somewhere between an unacknowledged crush and unrequited love. It was a rather uncomfortable and lonely place to be, but it thrilled her enough for the moment that she was content to wait things out, to see how long it would take him to catch on, and whether or not he would reciprocate. She self-consciously rubbed her hand over the tattoos on her left arm, something the straight-laced Mr. Kelley would never have.

Nathan took a sip of coffee before turning his head and catching sight of Kris watching him in his peripheral vision. He started, but just managed to avoid spilling the mug on himself. Pushing the suite away, he turned his stool to face the colorful, slender girl. She looked not only like the cat who had eaten the canary, but who greedily regarded the next canary in line.

He answered her smile with a cautious grin of his own and said, "Hey, Kris. What's up?"

She shook her head and failed completely to adopt an innocent face. "Nothin'. What are you reading?"

Nathan reached back and picked up his suite, stowing its screen and returning it to his pocket. "It's your proposal. There's some pretty freaky stuff in there."

Kris shrugged and pushed off from the wall. "Don't blame me. It was yours and Gordon's idea." She walked over to the coffee pot and poured herself a mug, liberally dumping in the cream and sugar.

"No, it was Gordon bitching about not making any progress on the weapons, and me bitching that it was too bad we couldn't do something with the high energy density of your drive. But this," he said, patting his pocket, "this is ... how do I put it? The perfect mix of my greatest hopes and my worst nightmares?"

She held her mug with both hands and slurped it loudly. "No big deal. We've blown up so many early iterations of the drive that I was already thinking in terms of explosives applications. I just changed the emitter geometry from a cone to the interior of a sphere to produce a compressive shockwave instead of linear thrust. Throw some lithium deuteride in there, flash the field, and boom: mini Bikini Atoll, and no mucking around with the government's precious radioactives."

Nathan shook his head. "A pure fusion weapon ... the mythical 'red mercury' finally achieved. They're going to shit bricks when they find out we just did an end run around the whole arms control process."

"Screw 'em. They don't want to let us play with nukes in order to defend the planet, we'll do 'em one better."

"Sure, but what I'm saying is that your tech and the relative ease of acquiring heavy hydrogen means we just made it that much simpler for the little guys to become nuclear powers."

"Hey, I tinker. Others can worry about security, and all the ethics and politics."

"Nice. How very un-Oppenheimer of you."

Kris shrugged again and took another slurp of coffee. "I yam what I yam. Besides, it's not all doom and gloom. If my setup works, we can make some friendlier nukes."

"Friendly nukes?"

"Friendly-ER. Since this eliminates the radioactive cladding, the tampers, the neutron sources, and the fission primary, we can use any fusible mixture we want in the core. We can even eliminate the residual radiation that you get from a D-D or D-T bomb entirely by using some aneutronic reaction like hydrogen-boron or helium-3. It's a slightly lower yield, sure, but you can plant flowers right after the blast wave passes and the flames die down."

Nathan shook his head again, this time in dismay. "You can be one scary chick."

Kris dimpled cutely. "I try."

He stood and stretched, once more missing the lingering appraisal she gave him over the rim of her mug. Relaxing, he smoothed out his shirt and walked over to refill his mug. Looking sideways at her, he squinted. "Green?"

She reached up and twirled a curl of her brightly colored hair around her finger. "No! That would just be weird. This is teal."

"Right. Teal is so much more conservative. What are you trying to be? An anime character?"

"I looked into getting surgery to have my eyes blown up to the size of saucers, but Windward's HMO wouldn't cover it. I do have a miniskirt schoolgirl outfit though. Wanna see it?"

Nathan spluttered on his coffee and pulled it away from his burned lips. "Maybe some other time. Did you come by for coffee or to torture me?"

"Both and neither. There's a storm front moving into the launch area, so they're advancing the timetable."

Nathan looked worried and glanced at his watch. "To when?"

"I believe Gordon's words were, 'We're lighting off as soon as Nathan Kelley gets his lazy ass in here!'"

"Jesus, Kris! Let's go." Nathan dumped his coffee in the sink and left his mug to be washed later. He turned and trotted from the kitchen, sending the door swinging wide.

Softly to herself, Kris said, "Run, Navy-boy, run." She took another loud slurp and then strolled out, chuckling.

Nathan slowed when he reached Lee's personal office. It was a cozy place, stacked high with walls of books, but unlike the gentleman's study it was meant to emulate, the shelves were filled with technical manuals, science texts, and pulp sci-fi rather than the staples of Western literature. Newly installed banks of HD flatscreens and communications gear cluttered up the space, further spoiling the old-fashioned aesthetic, but it was far more appropriate for Gordon.

Gordon Lee spoke by video teleconference (VTC) to a number of talking heads arrayed as windows on one of the flatscreens. Another flatscreen was filled with weather forecasts, shipping and aviation data, as well as radar sweeps for a location far out in the Pacific, a spot approximately 200 nautical miles north of Guam. The third flatscreen was a video feed, focusing on a stable sea launch platform lost amid the low waves surrounding it out to the distant horizon. To one side of the platform, the skies darkened with the first signs of rain.

Despite going from preliminary design to majestic reality in only six months, the probe was much more than spit and bailing wire. Upon finally gaining access to their French reactor, Lee and Nathan had brought together all the speculative technologies they had built up over the last several years in order to build humanity's first interstellar probe. Allocarbium frame, lead laminate radiation shields, crystalline alloy skin, pebble bed reactor, and physics-defying enhanced photon drive, the probe brought together so many unproven technologies in one package they were either assured of spectacular success ... or else the whole damn thing would blow to bits upon launch. Conducting the launch away from prying eyes only seemed prudent.

One of the talking heads on the VTC screen was speaking, this one wearing USN blue and gray digi-cammies and a warship's ball cap, complete with a line of gold fretting on the brim, a commander's single serving of "scrambled eggs". "Control, we have verified the range clear of air and surface tracks. The VT-UAV is RTB and will be outside of the danger zone in five mikes."

Gordon nodded. "Thank you, Captain. I have no idea what you just said, but I'm assuming that means we're free to launch?"

The Navy commanding officer scowled. "Yes, sir, you may launch in five minutes. *McInnerney* out." He turned away from the camera and the destroyer's crest replaced his image on the flatscreen.

Nathan shook his head. "You knew exactly what he said. It's not necessary to punch the buttons of every single person you meet."

Gordon turned to regard him and then returned to the checklist he carried in his hand. "Ah, Nathan. Glad you could attend. And I know that, but humorless superior bastards like our good Captain Geary just remind me of the sort of officers that forced you out of the Navy. He punches my buttons just by being."

Nathan shook his head. It was unavoidable, especially these days. He had left the service behind years ago, but in an ambiguous, unfinished way. Nathan's own feelings about it were a confusing mess. He could not reasonably expect someone on the outside to understand his departure any better. "No one forced me out, Gordon. I resigned. And I never even met Geary when I was in."

"All the same, he bugs me. He shouldn't even be involved in the launch. I could have hired my own range safety observers. I didn't need Sykes assigning a naval escort. The government insists on keeping me at arm's length like some shamed mistress, and then they pull this!"

Nathan smiled. "You should look at this as a gift. Now you don't have to pay for it, you're assured of having a professional job, and no one keeps a secret worse than a sailor. Instead of having only a few tracking stations aware of this, now you'll have 200 blue-shirts bragging about it in the next port they hit." He motioned a rocket blasting off with his hands. "'There I wuz, watchin dis rocket shoot up inta space. Lemme tell youse all abouts it!'"

Gordon grinned. "The ranks of my faithful grow: first it was just a few UFO freaks, and conspiracy bloggers, but now I have the junior enlisted of the USS McInnerney. I have truly arrived."

Nathan walked over to the flatscreen with the radar of the encroaching storm. "This probe is supposed to travel at a significant fraction of the speed of light. Are we really worried about a little wind and rain?"

"Space is an empty vacuum, while the atmosphere is decidedly not, but it's not those that bother me." Gordon walked over to the flatscreen with the video of the probe and sea-launch platform itself. He jabbed a finger at the dark shape of the probe. "This carries an experimental nuclear reactor and the most powerful motor ever designed. Do you really want to see what happens when it's struck by lightning?"

Nathan opened his mouth to answer, but was cut off by Kristene sweeping into the room. "That would be a 'No', boys. Not after seeing what was *not* left of the test pad after our first full-scale drive went out of control. I think we might get in trouble if we nuked a hole in the ocean." She smiled at them and then rushed over to the VTC screen, reaching out to touch one of the pictures. "Dr. Hastings, how are we doing?"

Hastings, a bald man with a weathered, pockmarked face, looked up from whatever he had been doing and into the camera. An identifier below his image listed him as being aboard the Launch Direction Ship, a recently acquired container vessel by the name of *Morningstar*, which operated in company with the *McInnerney*, a mere fifty nautical miles from the probe's launch platform. "Hi, Kristene. We're a bit frantic over here, but we're coping. As far as the probe is concerned, it could launch now or when it was supposed to, five hours from now. I've updated the timeline and initial launch vector on the computer and it's conducting the pre-flight. No problems thus far."

Kris smiled. "Computer" was such an understatement that the word almost no longer applied. Situated somewhere in the technological stratosphere between the fuzzy logic expert systems that managed the nation's air and ground traffic and the dream of true artificial intelligence, the system aboard their probe was the current pinnacle of computing capability. Comprised of eight different massively paralleled processors, each of which utilized both linear digital and nonlinear quantum elements, as well as 100 terabytes of flash memory with optical storage backup, the system was expected to accomplish the nigh impossible task of operating and piloting the probe across light-years of space, locating and rendezvousing with an alien vessel for first contact, and then reporting back to Earth.

"Computer" was practically an insult.

"Sounds good, Doc," Kris said. "Go ahead and begin the power ramp once the pre-flight finishes running. We'll launch from here when you give us the go-ahead."

"All right, we'll contact you then. *Morningstar*, over and out!" Hastings grinned with a mischievous gleam in his eye.

Nathan winced. Hastings knew that sloppy comms procedures were his pet peeve. Anyone with any time among radio circuits knew it was either "over" or "out", but never both together. Kris looked back at him and grinned. They all loved tweaking his somewhat rigid professional sensibilities.

Out in the vast Pacific, practically lost among the rising waves surrounding it, the launch platform was a lonely island of stability amid the chaos of the seas. Nestled at the bottom of a gantry rising a hundred feet from the surface of the ocean, the probe squatted with burgeoning power. It had a purposeful, enigmatic appearance, singular in design, unlike any other rocket ever launched.

The top of the probe was covered with a white aeroshell covering the instrumentation and antennae underneath, which would be jettisoned immediately after leaving the atmosphere. It was also the sole linking factor to any previous design. After that, the probe's shape was designed solely around the needs of its mission.

Beneath the aeroshell, the probe was a slender, flat black spire, the top half bristling with sensors, cameras, and dishes. The middle length of the elongated body was given over to reactor cooling, a nest of radiator fins sticking out perpendicular to the fuselage like the petals of some midnight black bloom. The bottom half was a tapering, stepped pyramid shape, the inverse of the usual flared venturi common to all previous rockets. It was different but reminiscent of Kristene's disastrous first design of the photon drive, improved by a greater understanding of the force she had unwittingly unleashed.

Hidden at the center of the probe, surrounded by the radiator fins, the pebble bed reactor came to life. Neutron baffles withdrew, allowing thousands of tennis-ball sized "pebbles" to mix for the first time. The spherical pebbles were each tiny fission reactors in their own right. Tens of thousands of encapsulated pellets of enriched uranium were sandwiched within a silicon carbide matrix and then wrapped up in a thick graphite shell. The shell moderated the fast neutrons from spontaneous fissions and allowed them to drift back among the pellets, increasing the probability of absorption in the uranium and the chance of an induced fission reaction. Group enough of the pebbles together, and the whole assembly became supercritical, raising the rate of fission and the reactor temperature until the graphite expanded and the process became self-limiting. It had a high operating temperature and efficiency, but a meltdown was virtually impossible, making the pebble bed perfect for their use: safe, simple, and powerful enough to reach the stars.

High pressure helium was forced into the reactor, flowing between the channels naturally formed by the bed of spherical pebbles. The helium carried away the heat of fission to the thermogenerators surrounding the core. Electricity began to flow and the radiator fins grew white hot.

Hastings spoke from the VTC screen. "Control, this is *Morningstar*. The probe is on internal power with pre-flight complete and satisfactory, no discrepancies. Ummm. That's it, I guess. We're ready to launch. Who's pushing the button?"

Kris turned to look at Nathan, and then she and he both turned to stare with intent at Lee. Gordon looked from one to the other and back until he shrugged. "Okay, if you insist. I'll push it."

Nathan grunted. "Right, as if one of us trying to push it wouldn't be the quickest way to the unemployment line."

Gordon grinned and approached the completely unnecessary Big Red Button he had installed just for this moment. He lifted the button's cover and cleared his throat. "This is our greatest moment. With this simple act, we answer the promise of generations that have come before us, and we make a promise to the generations that follow. Mankind has always reached for the outermost fringes, the distant horizon, and the furthest frontiers. With the launch of this probe, we expand the sphere of our influence upon the universe and reach out to neighbors unknown. We hereby swear an oath to the future that we shall continue our intrepid journey, no matter the obstacles we face, and we shall reach out to embrace whatever fate holds with courage, honor, and ever increasing wonder."

Kris stifled a laugh. "My, my, that sounded completely spontaneous."

Nathan nodded. "Very humble, boss."

"Posterity is lost on you jerks." Gordon stabbed down on the button. "Fare well, *Promise*."

The button sent a signal to the distant *Morningstar*, which in turn sent a complex activation code to the probe. Valves shifted within the reactor and superheated helium was forced into the inlet of the photon drive. The primed fields stopped the gas cold, instantly converting its internal energy into linear kinetic energy. High-energy photon thrust streamed out of the terraced steps of the drive pyramid, blasting down into the surface of the Pacific.

Clouds of steam and superheated air exploded out from the launch platform, expanding outward in a supersonic wavefront. The sea within the ring was flattened to a glassy surface, and a hollowed out cone of steam and light formed beneath the rig. The *Promise* hesitated for the briefest of moments and then crawled higher and higher up the gantry, building speed, power, and acceleration. As it reached the top of the launch platform, it finally began moving at a respectable rate as it clawed its way free of the Earth. The cone of steam collapsed in upon itself, no longer able to deny the pressure of the surrounding ocean, sending a solid plug of water up toward the rig. And as the probe cleared the gantry, its thrust inundated the platform, burning it away even as the sea hammered it from below.

The probe rocketed up, its star ascending toward the dome of the heavens, cast out from the planet of its birth, never to return. Waves of white noise followed in its wake, the air screaming in tortured frustration as the *Promise* escaped the pervasive clutch of gravity. The star climbed higher and higher, but unlike most rockets, it never tipped over to apply its awesome thrust to achieving orbit. Its destination was far beyond anything so mundane as circling the planet. The endpoint of its journey lay at the near edge of infinity.

Three minutes after Lee pushed the button, the probe left behind the nominal outer reaches of the atmosphere. The aeroshell blasted away from the main body, discarded by the *Promise's* still accelerating form. Reveling in the vacuum and darkness of space, the probe performed a slow loop about its outbound vector, testing its maneuverability. Satisfied by its performance, it deployed its main dish and sent a brief message back to Earth.

Hastings and Captain Geary each yelled excitedly from the launch-tossed decks of their respective ships. Hastings turned to the VTC camera to engage the beaming, awestruck faces of Kris, Nathan, and Gordon Lee back in California. Continuous thunder rolled in the background. "It's gone! It was here and now it's gone! The whole launch platform is sinking and the probe is already out of the atmosphere. You should have felt the blast! It made the shuttle feel like a Roman candle!"

Geary cut in. "Congratulations, Mr. Lee. It was quite a thing to see. We're collecting tracking data now, but it's almost outside even our expanded radar range."

Kristene's smiled so widely, it must have hurt her face. "Gordon, we're getting a transmission from the *Promise*. Comms, sensor telemetry, power, and maneuvering all test perfect. A flawless launch and a perfect probe—we couldn't have made it go better if we had planned it that way!"

Nathan laughed. "What are you talking about? That's exactly how we planned it!"

Gordon shook his head, his own grin faltering slightly. "Yeah, but we also had backups for the backups on our backups, and not one of them was tripped. It's stupid NASA superstition, but you always expect *something* to go wrong. And we've had our fair share of failures before this. But, a perfect launch might just mean something is destined to go wrong later when the mission is beyond your reach." He paused, doubt changing the character of his subdued smile. "And that begs all sorts of uncomfortable questions. Like, what if this is the wrong move after all, and the aliens would have been friendly had we just left them alone and not investigated them? We're committed now, we've played our first hand in the big game, but what if our glitch is the mission itself?"

"Dun, dun, duuunnnn!" Kris intoned. "Cue the ominous music. Bring on the grim sense of foreboding. Come on, Gordon! Forget the doom and gloom and let's celebrate! We just launched an interstellar probe, for God's sake. We've made the first step in solving the mystery of the Deltans and we did it when the whole damn world figured we were a bunch of freakin' crazies. It's champagne time!" She reached out and hugged both Gordon and Nathan together, then turned and trotted off back to the kitchen.

Nathan patted Lee on the back. "Good work, boss."

"No, no, good work to you, Nathan. None of this would have been possible without the two of you and all you've done." Gordon walked past Nathan, looking back at the screens. The one showing the storm front now showed a cataract of disrupted air impinging on the smooth curl of the cloud mass. The other screen, upon which had been the aerial view of the launch platform, now showed a graphic of the projected course of the probe out of the Solar System and on through the emptiness of space, all the way to their rendezvous with the unknown, years and light-years distant. "So much that we've done, so much that we still have to do, and no telling if any of it's going to do any good."

"What next?" Nathan said, at his side.

"We finish the second probe. Then we lay the keel of our ship, yesterday, and we answer all those questions that we've been putting off."

Nathan smiled. "Like how the hell to build a manned space combatant *slash* ambassador ship?"

Gordon laughed. "Yeah, like that."

Kris reentered with the ringing of champagne flutes, a magnum clutched under one arm. "Well, all that crap can wait until tomorrow. Right now y'all are having a drink with me." She handed each of the men a glass, and then passed hers to Nathan as well. With a twist, she popped the mushroomed cork from the bottle without launching it or spilling a drop. She poured a respectable amount in two of them, while carefully filling one to the top. After setting aside the magnum, she claimed one of the regular glasses, leaving Nathan with the brimming one. She dimpled. "Cheers!"

Both Nathan and Gordon looked askance at the full flute, but Nathan just shrugged and drank deep.

Lee shook his head. "This looks to be a memorable evening in a variety of ways."

Kris nurtured a soft, contemplative smile. "Surely does. More bubbly, Nate?"

Up in nearby space, the *Promise* kept accelerating continuously out from Earth. Within a few hours, the dark, unreflecting probe would become the fastest manmade object in history, but it would not pause even then. The probe adjusted its thrust vector, backing down to a third of a gee of continuous acceleration and changing its course to achieve a hyperbolic escape orbit from the Solar System. It settled with its blunt, lead laminate shielded nose pointed several degrees to one side of the distant blue star of its destination, eschewing the direct meeting for an oblique, non-threatening approach.

Destiny, for good or ill, lay in its path.

8: "AN UNEXPECTED GUEST"

April 5, 2043; Windward Tech Development Facility, Ingmar Rammstahl Ltd. Shipbuilding; Santa Clara, California

The ship's hull rang like a bell as the supercavitating torpedo narrowly roared by, detonating 100 yards off the destroyer's beam. Everything strapped down moved along with the hull as the underwater explosion battered the ship, shocked but survivable. Anything not strapped down kept its position within three dimensions, in harmony with the laws of the universe, but suddenly at odds with the realities of war.

Captain Anthony "Tony" Jones flew through the air, over the tightly packed consoles in Combat, and crumpled to a heap next to the padded steel bulkhead, his head at an odd, telling angle. Sparks fountained outward from power panels and consoles, lighting the dark, somber contours of the captain's suddenly lifeless face. From his seat in front of the TAO console, LT Nathan Kelley had an unobstructed view of his commanding officer's resting place, and he could not help but think about how serenely artful the terrible scene was.

Then the regular lights went out, the brighter lights of the emergency fluorescents came up, and the artistry was gone, snuffed out as quickly as Captain Jones' existence. Nathan turned back to his console, barking orders he no longer remembered, feeling the shudder as another torpedo detonated, this one further away. Despite the deaths and destruction, they were still in the game. They had gotten their shots off and they were surviving the attack. Nathan felt as one with the surface warriors of the last century, akin to the fighting sailors off Samar in WWII.

He turned to Senior Chief Edwards, a question upon his lips. What had he been about to ask? What had he been about to say that could not wait until they were out of danger? What could Nathan have done differently to avoid what happened next?

Edwards smiled, but not as preface for one of the bad jokes he always had at the ready. A ferocious, teeth-baring grin overwhelmed the bottom half of his face, counterpoint to the angry glare from his eyes as he punched buttons and watched the tracks move on his flickering display. Then the last torpedo struck, detonating below their after keel.

There was a moment of discontinuity.

The world ceased to be, and then came back to Nathan in bleary flashes of sight, sound, and sensation: the screams over the sound-powered phones; the spider web pattern

79

formed by his forehead on his blank tactical display; the chairs and consoles broken free of their mounts, crushing their occupants against the forward and aft bulkheads; the insane rolling of what remained of the Rivero …

And Edwards lying on his back atop his broken chair, his console snapped free and slicing into both of his broken legs . . . .

▰▰▰▰▰▰▰▰▰▰▰▰▰▰

Nathan opened his eyes into darkness, now so familiar with the dream-memory-nightmare that it no longer made him jump. He had also passed the stage of crying out into the night, but that did not mean his heart no longer experienced the terrifying trip-hammer flutter it always had upon waking.

The vision did not come for him every night, but more often than not, and it was always the same, never clouded by fantasy or revisionism. He sometimes prayed for a little dramatic license, for something to blunt the continuing horror of the attack, but after 12 years dealing with it, the memory was burned into unchanging stone.

Waking up was slightly different this time, however.

Nathan lay back on the couch in his shipyard office, having fallen asleep working, yet again. The hours he had devoted to figuring out the kinks in their ship design took a heavy toll. He found himself spending more nights here on his hated couch than he did in his Santa Cruz apartment. He usually woke up in the pre-dawn hours with a horrible crick in his neck and a desperate need for a shower and a direct infusion of caffeine. This time, though, he did not find himself clambering desperately off of the couch.

A warm, fragrant presence lay against him, inviting him to stay for a while, and Nathan found himself heeding the call. Kris had taken to working late with him as well, but she usually left before it became *too late*. This week, though, there had been a lot of integration issues with the environmental systems, the reactor, and the drive, so she had been staying later and later. Tonight, she had apparently stayed too late.

Her loss of sleep was evidently his gain.

Nathan leaned forward and inhaled deeply from her wavy, bright maroon hair, partaking guiltily of the fruit and spice essences the strands hinted at. He laid his head back and closed his eyes, enjoying the sensation of her warmth against him, his arm conveniently draped across her as she breathed in and out, ever so softly. However had she wound up on the couch with him?

His eyes snapped open, narrowing. Nathan was no idiot. He knew exactly how she wound up there, and why. A blind man would have noticed the way she looked at him, the way she acted around him. She actively sought opportunities to work closely with him and had changed her manner of dress, losing her nose and brow rings, and wearing conservative, long-sleeve blouses and shirts in order to cover the tattoos upon her arm, features that he had honestly never minded. He might have assumed she was just maturing, trying to be more professional, but there were also the looks she gave him, all the sly double entendres, the flirting. She had done everything but throw herself at him, and anyone else would have done something about it by this point, whether that meant bowing to the seeming inevitable or putting an end to her coy advances.

Only Nathan would have kept himself utterly oblivious on purpose.

He carefully slid out from her side, laying her down with hardly a stir from Kris. He stood and stretched, wincing as his vertebrae and joints snapped and popped. Nathan stifled a groan and turned back to look back at her peaceful face, feeling an unwanted, but undeniable longing.

Things were safe and simple between them. She had the ideas they needed to make the mission a reality, he had the design and organizational skills to see it to fruition. It was coming together. They would be ready to intercept the Deltans. They would. All they needed was the data from the *Promise*—that, and no complications.

He and she, either together or as a dead issue, were a complication.

Nathan forced himself to look away and walked to the clear glass wall that separated his darkened office from the building's fourth-floor circumferential walkway along with the open construction bay it surrounded. Down on the bare concrete first floor, pieces of their future had started to become reality. A radiator panel here, an allocarbium structural member there, with photon drive components, radar sets, hull-plates, environmental scrubbers mixed among them in a jumbled, disordered mess that nonetheless made complete sense to Nathan and the rest of the Windward Special Projects team. The only system obviously by itself was a laser diode emplacement, undergoing power drain testing and well cordoned off from the rest of the mess.

Nathan could look at all the various components in their various states of completion and imagine the realized whole: a spaceship in the truest sense of the word—not the fragile, spindly constructs of NASA and the ESA, but a real workhorse, capable of rocketing them out of the solar system and into destiny, ready to face whatever fate handed down to them, be it for good or ill, war or peace.

He sighed in frustration. He could see a future of science fantasy made fact, but he could not see the way ahead for himself and Kristene, not one in which they both got what they clearly wanted and deserved, and also allowed them to complete the ship with little to no derailing personal drama.

Kris murmured softly in her sleep and rolled over. Nathan turned and let his eyes linger over her, so close, yet firmly isolated by his own mores and idiosyncrasies. They had orbited around each other for four years now, engaging in brief and not-so-brief opposing relationships, relationships that the other always remained discreetly apprised of. And when each of these dalliances with the outside world invariably failed, they always found themselves circling closer and closer about one another, whether the other was completely available or not. And it was always Nathan who kept them frustratingly and unreasonably from coming together.

Nathan found himself wishing she would just take the hint and move along—even as he dreaded her ever giving up on him, not when their future after the ship was finished was so wide open.

He turned back to his view of the construction bay and approached the window, shaking his head at his own screwed-up train of thought. Waking up with her like this had made him excessively maudlin. All-in-all, it would have been easier to keep a firm resolve if she would just stick to taking naps in her own damn office across the way.

He looked into her third floor office as he thought this and noticed that it alone of all the glass-fronted rooms had light spilling from it. Her computer monitor, dormant for hours, inexplicably lit the otherwise darkened level. A mild buzz of alarm crawled across the nape of neck, but the monitor could have been left on for any number of reasons.

Then the light shifted as someone walked in front of her screen.

Nathan jumped back into the uncertain security of deeper shadows. The telltale monitor glow shifted in color and brightness as whatever it displayed changed. No one came to her window, though. Nathan remained undiscovered, apparently.

He turned and picked up his phone. Relief flooded through him as the dial tone called out strong and clear.

Four digits later, the phone in the complex's security office rang. And rang, and rang, and rang with no answer. Nathan stifled a nervous curse, his mind conjuring all manner of dire images, foremost among them the vision of his night guard's lifeless body, lying only inches from the incessantly ringing phone.

Nathan hit the hook and dialed again, this time calling the shipyard's security office. There was no ring though—only the insistent, staccato buzz of a busy signal. But their office was never busy, especially not this late at night. Dismissing further visions of a trashed office filled with bullet-riddled bodies, Nathan dialed the number again. This time, instead of a busy signal, he received three strident, piercing tones. "We're sorry. Your call cannot be completed as dialed. Please—"

He slammed down the phone, wincing at the sharp crack it made. He looked down at the phone that had somehow become his enemy and shook his head. He was loathe to do what necessarily came next, but he had little choice.

Nathan picked up the phone gingerly and dialed 9-1-1. Whatever technical secrets their potential intruder failed to uncover would undoubtedly be compromised by the police and their eventual investigation. There went all their remaining operational security.

The phone did not ring or answer, though. Instead, he heard, "We're sorry. You have reached a number that has been disconnected or is no longer in service. Please check—"

Nathan set down the handset in its cradle with a mixture of relief and anxiety. Something had obviously screwed with the landlines, no doubt as a preface to the break-in itself. He briefly considered the cellular suite in his pocket, but knew that was a bust. Security for the project had been as tight as they could make it. They were dealing with world-changing ideas and technologies, and Gordon had been adamant that none of it get out until he was ready to release it. As a result, none of their sensitive computers had a connection to the outside world, and the entire place was wrapped in the electromagnetic cocoon of a Faraday cage. Wireless signals would never make it outside their complex.

There was no help coming.

Crouching down, Nathan shuffled back to the couch and leaned in toward Kris. He shook her lightly, and then harder as she stayed asleep. Eventually, her eyes fluttered open, confusion and annoyance at being woken up drifting smoothly into an expression of coy innocence as she saw how close he was to her.

She smiled at him, the corners of her mouth amused by the potential of their relative positions. "Oh, I'm sorry. Did I fall asleep?"

Nathan placed his hand over her mouth and received a flash of renewed annoyance from her eyes. He whispered, "Kris, there's someone messing around in your office and the phones have been fucked with. I think someone's trying to steal the secure files."

"Who?" she demanded, her loud whisper muffled by his hand.

Nathan pulled his hand away and put a finger to his lips, glaring at her to stay quiet. "I don't have any idea, but there's definitely someone down in your office, working in the dark. I tried to call security, but no joy."

Kris jumped up and approached the office's glass front, only to be jerked down to her knees by Nathan, still crouching. She pulled her arm free of his grasp, her annoyance now the beginnings of anger, but he only shifted around to grasp both of her shoulders firmly.

"Stop!" he said, firmly but quietly. "Wait a second and listen to me! We don't know who it is and we don't know what they're prepared to do, but they seem to be trying to stay covert. Otherwise, they'd just pull the drives and steal whatever wasn't nailed down, but that's going to change if whoever it is realizes someone's still up here. You go off half-cocked, you're going to make things worse and you might even get us killed."

Kris turned toward him, hissing her words in the barest semblance of a whisper. "Nathan, we can't let them have our designs! Another company would be bad enough, but what if this is some other country? Can you imagine the Chinese mass-producing these systems? The world would change overnight, and not for the better if my opinion is worth anything!"

"Don't you think I know that!? I'm not proposing we cower up here."

"Oh. Then what do you propose?" she asked, an edge to her voice.

"We're going to stop him—or rather I'm going to stop him while you get outside and call for help on your suite."

She looked at him, saying nothing, and he could read nothing from her expression. Soon, the corner of her mouth turned up slightly. "Really, Rambo? You're going to stop the professional industrial super-spy all by your lonesome? Correct me if I'm wrong, but wasn't your military specialty surface warfare rather than special warfare?"

His eyes narrowed in exasperation. "I'm not going to jump him or anything, but I can't let him just break our encryption and download anything he likes."

"So what are you going to do, and why couldn't I do it too? What happened to not dividing your forces before the enemy, oh great tactical wizard?"

Nathan shook his head and held his own suite out to her. "Don't mangle aphorisms at me. And I don't know what I'm going to do, yet, but I do know what you're going to do. You're going to take our phones and you're going to get to the open and you're going to call in the damn cavalry. You've got the critical job here. I'm just going to try to keep him on the premises until security shows up. Do you understand or do you just want to keep arguing?"

She responded by snatching the cell suite from his hand and pulling out her own phone. Both phones worked, and both showed zero signal strength. "Reception sucks out here, even beyond the building. It may take a few minutes to get the word out."

"Whatever. Just call them in before I get my ass shot or garroted or whatever it is super-spies do these days."

"Who do you want me to call?"

Nathan smiled, but failed to keep the nervousness from his eyes. "Everybody."

Kristene smiled back, then darted in before he could turn away, kissing him.

Surprise and his own rationalized objections aside, he found himself kissing her back, a hand on the back of her head, his fingers tangled in her brightly colored hair. Eventually, his misgivings and the mission at hand reasserted themselves, and he pulled away with a flash of guilt.

Before he could say anything, she turned away and crawled to the door, favoring him with a suddenly more enticing view. Kristene slowly swung the glass door inward, then crawled out and to the right, headed for the distant stairwell exit.

Nathan followed along behind, but turned to the left instead, heading toward the mid-platform stairwell, the shortest route to Kristene's office and whatever fate awaited him.

He rose from a crawl as soon as his knees hit the diamond grating of the industrial walkway, his joints crying in protest. Crouching low and keeping close to the shadowy wall, Nathan made his way to the stairs, cursing the sound of his footsteps, but utterly unable to make them any quieter. He tiptoed down the stairwell, splitting his attention between Kristene's partly lit office and the darkened stairwell he was trying to negotiate. To his credit, he made it all the way down with barely a misstep, except for when he misjudged the distance down from the last step and slammed his foot on the grating with too loud of a footfall.

To Nathan's ears, the sound of his shoe on the metal walkway reverberated through the building, ringing and clanging on and on like church bells at noon, but he convinced himself a moment later that most of the sound was only in his worried head. Whether it was or not, no one emerged from Kristene's office, ready to deliver the same unknown fate to Nathan as he had to all the facility's guards.

Now moving even slower, he crept up to her office, approaching low and close to that level's wall. He stopped immediately before the glass-fronted face of her office, close enough to hear the clicking of keys and a mouse, but unable to see the intruder directly without giving himself away.

Nathan crouched, slowly beginning to fume with doubt and self-recrimination. Here he was, mere feet from the possibly murderous thief who threatened to steal all the research they had devoted themselves to, who would undoubtedly release it to a known enemy, giving them a capability even the US did not enjoy, and he could not see a damned thing. He now knew less about what was actually going on than he had from cowering in his own office across the way. The impotency built and built until he gave a silent curse and allowed himself to peek around to peer into the glass front of the office.

Seated in front of Kris's desktop, a man in a Windward security uniform typed a few letters, grimaced, clicked upon a mouse and shook his own head with frustration. The thief looked disconcertingly bland: Caucasian, slightly out of shape, brown hair and eyes, with soft features and a not-too-intelligent look about him. Nathan winced. He could describe this man exactly and still have trouble distinguishing him from a host of others. In fact, from a distance, he would look like their own usual night security guard.

Arrayed in front of the fake guard, alongside the keyboard and mouse were a number of things that were forbidden from the building because their very nature was counter to ensuring security. There was a high volume flash deck, probably upwards of a 100 terabytes of storage, but only the size of a pack of cigarettes. Beside it was something that appeared to be a standard cell suite, but was undoubtedly not, judging from the wisps of vapor streaming off it and the tiny steel gas vial plugged into its side. Only one kind of computer would need active cooling, one that was infinitely more powerful than a suite, or even the desktop the device was plugged in to.

Nathan panicked, but also felt a rush of geeky envy. The thief had his own "quacker." A quantum code-breaker, it could make short work of any encryption system or security algorithm, pitting its super-cooled qubits against a normal computer's registers of logical ones and zeroes. It essentially performed in seconds the same code-breaking feats that would tie up a near-AI level supercomputer for months or years. It was only due to Gordon Lee's infuriating insistence on multiple layers of encryption (despite the way they slowed going from one file to the next) that the thief had not already absconded with everything on the entire server. It was just a matter of time, though.

Only one thing kept Nathan from charging the false guard immediately. Next to the linked flash deck, quacker, and desktop was a slender, lethal, semiautomatic pistol. Before he could even make it through the door, Nathan was sure he would find out just how destructible he was. The fate he had narrowly avoided twelve years before would be all too ready to catch up with him, at least with this guy's able assistance.

He could hardly allow the man to continue using the quacker with impunity, nor could he stop him directly. And there was no way to tell how long it would take Kris to alert the authorities, or how long it would take them to get here. By that time, the thief might well have enough time to decrypt all of their research and designs and get away clean. Once again, no help would arrive in time. It was up to Nathan.

There was no reason for the grin that began to spread across his face, but it appeared nonetheless, unbidden.

Abandoning any semblance of cover, Nathan jumped to his feet and pounded loudly on the glass partition, over and over again, yelling as loud as he could. The doughy man in the security outfit almost fell from his chair, his arms flailing in shock. He succeeded in knocking the keyboard, quacker, and pistol from the desk, leaving only the mouse and the flash deck hanging from their cables.

For the briefest instant, Nathan considered trying for the door and entering the office, to search for the gun before the thief could recover it. Before he could complete the thought, however, the man reached down and pulled the pistol up from the floor. Nathan grimaced. Doughy and surprised though he might be, the man was no amateur. Seeing the gun come up, Nathan dove to the left, landing hard on his back upon the diamond steel grating. He looked up to see spider-web cracks blossom from two points of impact in the glass office front, along with a blue flash and a shower of sparks.

Sparks. Nathan groaned and rolled over, coming to his feet. He now felt the grin fully upon his face. Their thief had all the latest gadgets: high capacity flash decks, quackers, and even capacitor stun rounds for his weapons. Whoever the man worked for, murder had not been high on their agenda. The capacitor rounds, plastic bullets which carried enough piezoelectric-induced charge to knock a man unconscious, were the ultimate fusion of gun and stun-gun. Nathan's prospects were not much improved, but it did mean he would probably survive the night – which opened up all sorts of new possibilities.

The door opened and Nathan ran, weaving from side to side unevenly along the walkway. Two capacitors exploded on the railing and stanchion next to him as Nathan darted down the path, leaving his left side tingling from a brushing of the charge they carried. He cried out and dodged again as a capacitor round hit the opposite wall, even closer this time.

But that was enough. Nathan's brief stint as an action hero was over. He stumbled and rolled, passing right beneath the lower railing on the open side of the walkway, and fell. His hand lashed out and grabbed, clutching for a moment on the diamond grating, but his fingers slipped. They held him just long enough to check his headlong dive into open space, and he swung back toward the catwalk below.

Nathan fell atop the railing on the next lower walkway, the second floor. The topmost safety rail slammed into his side and he felt the crunch as his ribs cracked, something of which he had a passing familiarity given his earlier experience. He fell further, but this time on the proper side of the walkway, safe on the floor below his attacker.

Not that the thief had any further intention of going after him. Nathan heard frantic steps upstairs, unknown movement and unknown labors, and then the thief was out of the office and pounding down the walkway in the opposite direction Nathan had run, in the same direction Kristene had gone, toward freedom and the loss of all their secrets.

Nathan had already paid too much to keep those secrets safe only to let him get away now. He struggled to his feet and limped toward the mid catwalk stairway that the first and second levels alone shared. "Screw this. You wanna play with capacitors, I'll show you some goddamn capacitors."

He reached the production floor just as the thief reached the far stairwell, only three flights and a short jog away from the exit. Nathan looked around frantically among the jumbled pieces of the ship, nowhere near being put together, and some of them still in the midst of testing. One system test stood out in particular.

Beyond a number of high-voltage danger signs and two perimeters of caution tape, one of the intended weapons of the ship stood at full power and readiness. Part of a capacitor bleed test, the CMEDLA (Collimated Multiple Element Diode Laser Array) had all of its components installed, from the many farads worth of ultracapacitors, to the pulse stretching power inductors, and even the diodes and optics assemblies. Any component that could potentially bleed off a trickle of power from the fully charged ultracap bank was present, in order to see how long an effective charge could be maintained in the array, a very important tactical consideration. Everything was there except for the complicated operating system, but Nathan had no need for complexity with what he planned to do.

Passing by the lens trunk, Nathan shoved the rolling concrete safety target out of the way and then eyeballed the base of the stairs. He bumped the trunk with his hip for a gross aim adjustment and shrugged as the thief jumped down onto the last flight of steps. Nathan limped back to the trigger assembly that separated the power section from the beam-forming section and frowned at the delicate tangle of diodes and relays, all useless without their operating systems and the computer programs on the eventual bridge.

"I always said this was an unsafe design," he mumbled. With that, Nathan picked up a long wrench and tossed it across the trigger assembly, shorting the ultracapacitor bank to the 100 megawatt elements of the diode laser stacks.

There was a purple flash and a crack of lightning, followed closely by a blast of heat and ozone-soaked air that knocked Nathan on his back again. He cried out as his cracked ribs ground against one another, paralyzing him with pain for several breaths.

Looking up from his back, his eyes saw only a green afterimage of the shorted capacitor bank and heard a continuous series of sizzle pops from the wrecked bulk of the laser array.

Soon, though, the pain in Nathan's side faded just enough for him to notice the dull pain over all his exposed skin, especially along the front half of his body. He struggled to his feet, disregarding his fresh flash burns, and found that he could see, after a fashion. He began to limp forward, heading toward the hazy, far end of the building. He could make out very little detail, given the smoke and his temporary flash-blindness, but something was definitely different.

He approached and saw that his aim had been a little off – not bad considering the haphazard way he had fired the system. The laser beam, only partly collimated by the inactive lens trunk had not confined the beam to a tight, parallel stream or a devastating pinpoint, but rather more of an irregular oval. He knew that because that was the shape of the hole.

The hole through everything.

The bottom half of the last flight of stairs was gone, either melted, or blasted, or vaporized to nothing. Also gone was the base of the steel girder supporting the weight of the stairwell, the lower portion of the outer wall bounding the stairwell, and the right foot of the person who had been climbing down the stairwell.

The malformed beam had caught the thief just as he had been stepping onto the last run of stairs, destroying his foot and cauterizing the stump. Then the accompanying heat bloom of the beam in atmosphere had blasted him off the stairwell to crash into the opposite wall, where he now lay unconscious.

Nathan checked the burned and blasted man's pulse, found it satisfactory to his layman's touch, and then rooted around for the flash deck. He found it just as the tactical team from Windward security burst through the doors at both ends of the building. Standing above his victim, and holding the deck high in the air for the benefit of all the automatic weapons pointed at him, Nathan gave them a lopsided grin. "S'all right. I got it."

Whereupon, he immediately passed out.

<hr />

"Hey there, Tex. You just waking up from your little siesta?"

Nathan opened his eyes to half-slits, and even that hurt. Kristene looked down at him, a smile playing along her mouth, but a nervous cast to both her eyes. He closed his eyes and reopened them a moment later, disliking the way his eyelids felt papery and stiff, as if he had received a massive sunburn. He licked his parched lips and coughed, causing a flash of pain all over, but especially from his side where he had fallen.

He glanced around, taking in the hospital room in which he lay, and then looked back toward Kris. She still appeared concerned beneath the mask of her smile. "How long have I been out?"

"Not too long – just a few hours I'd guess. They've got fluids and a bitchin' cocktail running into your arm. They said you'd wake up when you felt like it, but nothing was hurt too badly."

Nathan moved a tentative hand toward his side, feeling his skin crinkle slightly. She saw the movement and gently pushed his hand back down by his side. "You broke three ribs, but nothing got punctured. Aside from that and a hell of an impromptu tanning session, you're okay. You look a damn sight better than the other guy, believe me."

She smiled for real this time, her nerves relieved. "Listen, just lay there and let me tell the nurse you're awake. Okay?" Kris turned and left, with Nathan watching her as she walked away, his mind a tumult.

A minute later, Gordon walked in, with Lydia Russ following close behind. She was slowly becoming a more common feature around the offices, but whether that was for government oversight or because of the bond she obviously shared with Gordon, he did not know. Nathan nodded to her and turned to focus upon his boss.

Nathan thought the man looked worse than he himself felt. Lee's skin was deathly white with a grayish-yellow pallor, and he looked panicked, worried beyond all hope of recovery. He looked like a man who had very nearly lost everything.

Upon seeing Nathan, the corner of his mouth turned up in a grin and he sighed audibly, relieved. Gordon reached up and fished around in his jacket pocket, producing a small bottle of pills. He popped a couple into his mouth, dry, and winced as he swallowed them down.

Gordon sat down beside Nathan's bed, color already returning to his pained face. He placed a hand over Nathan's and gave it a light squeeze that Nathan tried not to cry out from. "You had us worried, boy."

Lydia nodded sagely from across the room. "That's right."

Nathan smiled as far as he could without involving the muscles in his cheeks. In a raspy, dry voice he said, "I just wanted a little R & R, Boss. I figured this was safer than asking you for time off."

"Well, next time just route a request like everyone else. Damn, it's good to see you awake – even if you do look like hell."

Nathan thought that was a bit hypocritical. It was not often that Lee showed his age, but today he seemed far older than his actual mid 60's. "I'll bet, Gordon, but I've at least got a reason. Have you looked in a mirror lately? Is there something wrong?"

Lee let go of Nathan's hand and stood, pride making him suddenly closed and distant, though he was only inches away. "I'm fine, so don't you join the nagging crowd of my doctors. It's like they worry the smallest little emotional roller coaster will send me into palpitations. I've got pills. It's nothing you need to worry about. It's nothing at all."

Lydia frowned. "So you say, Gordon."

Nathan tried to make light of it. "As long as you don't keel over on me, I won't nag. My skin is very sensitive right now and your dead weight might make me un-comfy."

Gordon's eyes narrowed. "Your compassion and concern are noted."

At that point, Kris reentered, ahead of a wave of nurses and doctors. She and Gordon stood off to the side with Lydia as Nathan was poked, prodded, queried, and quizzed. Soon enough, his IV bag was changed, a fresh round of pain killers and antibiotics administered, and his guests were cautioned not to keep him up for too long.

Kris saw the last of the medical staff out and then closed the door, leaving the four of them alone. Gordon had grown far fresher during Nathan's examination, so his medication was apparently effective. The man's health and his own discomfort no longer his primary concerns, Nathan could hold back his questions no longer. "So what the hell happened at the shipyard? Who was that guy? Have we questioned him, found out who he was working for?"

Gordon's slight smile dropped. "Before I tell you, I want you to keep in mind that as soon as you're better, I'm going to beat you unconscious again. You blew up an entire laser emplacement and burned a hole through three buildings. You're supremely lucky no one was killed, including yourself! What were you thinking?"

Kris appeared to have no concern over Nathan's chosen method of stopping the thief, her approval obvious from her expression. "Yeah, good shootin', Tex, but talk about overkill. You gave us a new north exit, and made our unexpected guest footloose and fancy-free. What were you planning on doing if the laser didn't work? Nuke him with a ship-to-ship missile?"

Nathan grimaced. "I really hoped I'd misremembered that. Did I really burn his foot off?"

She shrugged. "Let's just say Hopalong's going to be stepping very carefully around you from now on."

"Enough of that," Gordon interjected. "This was a serious security breach. We're hoping that we were lucky and this was the first such incident, but just because you caught him last night doesn't mean he hasn't been stealing from us on every previous night."

"How did he even get in?"

"Well, you may not have even noticed, but he bears a striking resemblance to Bill Blake, our night security chief – rather, our former night security chief who had a bad habit of drinking himself into a stupor when he was supposedly on watch. Last night, your thief made sure Bill was drugged enough that he wouldn't wake until morning, dropped a virus in the telecom server so no one could call in or out, and made the rounds himself. We don't know who this man is yet, or who he worked for, or even whether he's a spy or just an industrial agent."

Lydia spoke up. "He's been taken into DOD custody. So far, Under-Secretary Sykes has clamped down on even my access to info. We don't know anything about the thief yet, but when we find out, you'll be among the first to know."

"One thing is for certain, though," Gordon said, "and that's that not everyone believes our pots are cracked. Someone out there, besides our late-arriving government sponsors, believes in what we are doing and they want that tech for themselves. This is the first attempt we've stumbled across, but it might not be the first attempt and it certainly won't be the last. Between the launch of the *Promise* and your somewhat open use of an offensive laser, we are building up some actual stories to go along with our crazy theories. People are going to continue to try to get access."

Nathan winced. "Let me guess: tighter security?"

Gordon nodded. "At the very least. More encryption, more electronic and manned security, more government oversight, whatever it takes."

"That means slower work and more frustration, and that's not even counting the time lost due to the laser 'malfunction'. Can we afford that?"

"It's a little late to be asking that question, Nathan! It will take whatever time it takes, time we have less and less of every day. Soon, we should get our first close-up pictures from the probe. What we've received thus far hasn't been much better than what we've already gotten from the SSBA, but I guarantee the new data will impact our timeline. The closer we get, the more we define the threat, if there is one, the more pressure we're going to start getting from above. We either adapt to it and continue to show progress, or we risk them 'nationalizing' us and removing us from the process entirely. Understand?"

Nathan wished he was not lying down. He wanted to reassure Gordon, and he could not do that very well from such a position of weakness. "Yes, sir. We'll tighten things up and we'll get back on schedule. We'll get our ship operational before the probe makes contact. I guarantee it."

Lee's stern expression softened a bit. He gripped Nathan on the shoulder, one of the few places he was not really burned. "I know you will. Rest now, work later."

With that, he nodded to Kristene and then turned and left. Lydia came up and gave him a gentle, motherly kiss on his flash-burned brow, then followed Gordon out, closing the door behind them. Kris watched him leave and then sat next to the bed, carefully holding Nathan's hand. She looked down at him, a smile rising on her cheeks. They were alone.

She was about to say something, to do something. Nathan could see it, and now with all the new pressures being put onto their construction, his reasons for putting things between them on hold made even more sense—damnable, terrible, hatefully cold sense, but sense just the same.

He hated it, hated himself, but he still rushed to speak before she could say anything. "Kris, about last night . . . ."

She smiled. "I was just about to mention that. I know it might seem a bit sudden, but when you look at it another way, it's been a long time coming."

"Nothing happened."

Her smile faltered. "Well, something obviously happened. I seem to remember us kissing in your office."

"*Nothing happened.* We're coworkers and friends, and we both work closely together. Sometimes that ... closeness is easy to misinterpret. And with everything going on last night, we got confused."

Her mouth was now set in a firm line. "I wasn't confused."

"Kris, we can't afford to mix work with … whatever else. I just don't have time for a relationship right now."

"Correct me if I'm wrong, but didn't you just break it off with your latest? Or was it the other way around?"

"I'm sorry. I mean that *we* don't have time for a relationship, not a relationship like that."

She fumed now. "I'm perfectly capable of keeping my job and my personal life separate."

"Good. Then this won't be awkward when I get back to work." Nathan closed his mouth and stared back into her glaring eyes, refusing to look away first.

She broke contact, stalked to her purse, and went straight to the door. "You can be such an ignorant ass, Nathaniel Kelley. I know what you want and what you can and can't afford to do better than you do. Hopefully, you can get a fucking clue before I'm done with you and this project." She slammed the door behind her as she left.

Nathan was alone. He laid his head back carefully, his skin no longer painful, but still noticing the stretching and tingling of his epidermis. He closed his eyes and tried not to think. He tried to banish all thoughts of the new pressures the project was under, the thief he had injured, the way Gordon had looked, and Kris, Kris, Kris.

His will failed. All his thoughts wrapped around those central ideas and spun faster and faster, sucked down a dark drain. An hour later, still awake, he felt numb with self-loathing, and he wished for anything else to dwell upon, even the nightmare-memory of the *Rivero*'s death.

9: "CATHEDRALS IN AIR"

The *Promise* fulfilled its name with unemotional efficiency. From the moment of its launch, the probe continually modified and refined the approach, attempting to arrange a meeting with an unknown alien presence traveling toward Earth at nearly one fifth the speed of light. To a person, this might be a daunting task, dogged by doubt, uncertainty, and trepidation. To the expert systems of the probe, it was merely a matter of numbers.

The Deltans, at the time of launch, were 1.69 light-years away, traveling at 0.18 c toward Earth, and decelerating at a hundredth of a standard Earth gravity, or approximately 0.01 c per year. The *Promise*, presumably far smaller and less refined than the approaching alien, was nonetheless capable of greater accelerations.

The probe set out from Earth at a third of a gravity of acceleration, more than thirty times the rate of the Deltans. Angled down out of the ecliptic, that rough plane in which the planets revolved around the sun, and to one side of the blue spark which defined the approaching alien, *Promise*'s course allowed it to direct its drive corona away from Earth and all the inquisitive amateur astronomers who might ask too many hard questions about the secretive probe. It also allowed the probe to make an oblique approach upon the alien—covert, ostensibly non-threatening, and as stealthy as one could get while radiating at a high temperature.

Promise stacked up a list of accomplishments, all unacknowledged. Only hours from its launch, it surpassed Voyager 1 as the fastest man-made object, despite never going through the complicated rigmarole of planetary gravity assists. The probe's enhanced photonic drive allowed it to brute-force itself past the record, to speeds which boggled the imagination. It rocketed across the orbits of each of the outer planets in turn, skirted by the wide expanse of the Kuiper belt and punched through the heliopause, where the pervasive solar wind was ground to a halt by the all-encompassing gasses of the interstellar medium. More than a hundred times the distance of Earth from the Sun, *Promise* entered true interstellar space, surpassing all previous probes.

But Gordon, Nathan, and Kris's modest creation paid little attention.

Its journey had only just begun.

The drive kept up a continuous massless thrust, using unimaginable photon pressure to muscle the probe to nearly relativistic velocities. At the speeds it traveled, a single grain of dust impacting the probe would be disastrous, so it protected itself by, once more, brute force methods. A laser continuously scanned the space immediately preceding the probe, lighting up and ionizing any particle massive enough to do *Promise* harm. The burning, ionized particle was then pushed out of the way by the strong electromagnetic field set up in the bow like a battering ram. Even with this defense, though, the probe could do nothing to stop the resulting radiation and cosmic rays that inundated it. For that, *Promise* relied upon thick layers of shielding and redundant, self-repairing electronics.

For twenty months, *Promise* kept up its uninterrupted course. Then, when it had built up a staggering velocity of nearly half the speed of light, the drive shut down, more than 10,000 astronomical units from Earth, halfway to the inner edge of the Oort Cloud. It turned, centering the Deltans in its sensors, and re-evaluated its approach. It made some minor adjustments, turned to point its drive at a nearly right angle to the target, and lit off again.

By starting out its journey driving at an angle to the Deltans, the probe had built up a significant velocity away from both the aliens and the Solar System. Now, after turnaround, it had to negate both that lateral velocity and the relativistic approach speed it had built up. The practical upshot was that the drive corona was now pointed away from the Deltans versus directly at them, allowing the probe to close relatively unannounced. It was wasteful in terms of energy expended, but the chosen route was as much of a defensive measure as the sandwiches of shield material blanketing the probe.

The days continued to add up. *Promise* reached the Oort Cloud, that diffuse spherical grouping of icy rocks from which Halley's comet was born, and burned its way through the Cloud's nearly 30,000 AU expanse. Two and a half years after its launch, the probe exited the last structure of the Solar System, over three quarters of a light-year from home. Months later, the probe flew past the arbitrary but significant milestone of one light-year from its origin, but it paid no attention.

At 1.08 light-years distant, the probe was nearly at rest to the Solar System and still accelerating. *Promise*'s motion reversed and it began to close then, building up speed in the approaching direction in order to match speeds with the Deltans. The Deltans themselves were no longer just a blur of blue light, but began to take on definition to the diminutive sensor package mounted on the probe.

The processors aboard the *Promise* woke up, commencing the endgame of its journey. At 1.05 light-years from Earth, at a speed of 0.14 c, the probe turned again and reduced its drive to only a fraction of its earlier intensity, matching the nearby Deltans. The shielded side panels of the probe came free and the *Promise* blossomed, extending sensors, auxiliary probes, and twin communication dishes—one pointed at the objective, and the larger one pointed back toward Earth.

Promise scanned and photographed the mysterious alien presence, so long unknown and now revealed. The probe launched smaller measuring devices in order to increase the scope of its investigation and retransmitted the reams of data it produced back to Earth, though the information would take just over a year to be received. The Deltans endured this scrutiny without reacting, seemingly inert.

Then *Promise* said hello.

February 18, 2045; Lee Estate; Santa Cruz, California

Gordon sprawled lazily in his chair, leaning as far back as the soft leather seat would go, his feet propped up on the desk in his home office. The door stood closed, with Melinda Graciola, his personal assistant, holding all distractions at bay from her place just outside the office. Gordon was free to lay back and just *think*, something which he rarely had time to do these days despite the dividends such uninterrupted concentration usually paid.

In each hand, Gordon held a glossy print, slowly bringing them together again and again, not really noticing the soft crashing noise he made every time the pictures touched. In his right hand, he held a picture of all they had worked to achieve—the ship, lying on its side in its floating hangar. It was a nameless, gunmetal gray monstrosity, a plated hexagonal pyramid covered in hatches, domes, sensors, and cables as workers crawled over it with last-minute labors, readying it for its rapidly approaching launch date. Nathan would be there now, overseeing the final outfitting, worrying over it like a mother hen. But that was good. It was his job to worry over such things.

Gordon Lee had other things to worry about.

In his left hand, he held the mystery—the clearest, most recent processed photo of the Deltans from the SSBA. For all of the array's vaunted resolution and capability, though, this picture was little improvement over the one Lydia and Sykes had shown him years before. The glare from the Deltans' photon drive simply blocked out all but the grossest of detail, and what was left behind looked like no ship Gordon could imagine. It was a false-color image of the central drive corona in brilliant blue-white, surrounded by four reddish shadows on the periphery of the drive's circle.

The spacing of the shadows always seemed to suggest something to Gordon, but he had never put his finger on it. The three largest shadows formed the vertices of an equilateral triangle around the drive, with the smaller shadow nestled on the perimeter halfway between two of the vertices. And, as subsequent exposures showed, the four shadows rotated about the drive, always keeping their relative positions to one another, but rotating rigidly around nonetheless.

He softly crashed the pictures into one another again and then arched an eyebrow as a thought occurred to him. "Lagrange?" he asked to the empty room.

Before he could pursue that line of thought any further, there was a rapid knock upon the door and Melinda opened it without prompting. She had been a knockout when he hired her thirty years ago, primarily as eye-candy for jaded bureaucrats he tried to sell to, but she had proven to be capable beyond just her looks, a true asset to the company. In the intervening decades, she had traded gorgeous and voluptuous for glamorous and regal. Gordon was usually pleased to see her, but not when she interrupted him on the verge of something so big. "Damn it, Melinda—"

"Gordon, Castelworth's duty monitor is on the line. She says she has an encrypted stream for your authorization."

Gordon scowled. Castelworth was his Australian telemetry station, tracking and monitoring all the constellations of satellites Windward Tech maintained for both government and corporate clients. Why the hell would they need him to personally decrypt a transmission? "Can you ask—"

"Sir, it's the *Promise*."

Gordon shut his open mouth and nodded. He carefully laid his two photos down on his desk, one atop the other. He squared them precisely and then moved them off to the side, and tried to appear calm. Calm was not a good descriptor, though. Now, without anything to occupy his hands, his fingers drummed a rapid, complicated rhythm on the desk, a counterpoint to the numerous disparate trains of thought that tried to traverse his mind at the same time.

He looked up at Melinda and cleared his throat. Softly, he said. "Oh. Well, could you do me a favor and get in touch with Nathan for me. He should be here when we decrypt it. And Lydia Russ. Yeah, Lydia will never let me forget it if I leave her out. And Kris Muñoz and the Contact Evaluation Team, and the Physics Group, and the Astronomy Group, and, oh, and the *Promise* team, and—"

She smiled at his nervous fumbling. "How about I just follow your preplanned response? All those and more are already listed in the contact section. Remember? You wrote it before going senile a couple of minutes ago."

"That would probably be for the best." He tried to return her smile, but only got half of a crooked grin out.

Melinda shook her head and came up to the desk, reaching out to put one hand over his in reassurance. "You did it, Gordon. That's what this means. The *Promise* is a success." She squeezed his hand and then left, off to inform the company and the world that first contact had been made.

Shocked, Gordon continued to just sit there. He looked at his desk as if it might explode. Accessible within its active electronic surface was everything he had hoped for, prayed for, and feared for the last 22 years. He was a few keystrokes away from answers to questions that had consumed his life, but now at the critical moment, he was frozen in trepidation.

Besides, he reasoned, he really should wait for the others. It would mean more, experiencing it all with that highly elite crowd. That was the right thing to do.

He would not allow himself to be turned into some petulant child the night before Christmas. There would be no shaking of presents on his watch.

Gordon refused to spoil this.

No way.

Then his half grin broadened and lifted into an uncomfortably feral smile. "Yeah, right. Screw 'em if they can't handle being second."

He tapped a capacitive control flush with surface of his desk and an integral keyboard and touchpad swelled out of the desktop, while a large expanse of the black lacquered surface became a wide monitor. Gordon logged on to Windward's secure global network and clicked around until he was into Castelworth station's server. There he performed a second login, scrolled over to the active and waiting telemetry streams and found a single icon that caused his heart to beat noticeably within his chest: the *Promise*.

Gordon held a breath for a moment and selected the icon. Streams of memorized pseudorandom digits tumbled forth from his fingertips and the decryption algorithm began to un-spool the compressed, jumbled data into several channels, all transmitted more than a year before.

One was a telemetry stream, which would help evaluate the health of the probe and the details of its encounter, but which would be completely unintelligible until processed by systems mirroring the probe itself. Then there was a communications log and a recording of all transmissions sent and received, the robotic equivalent of a cockpit voice recorder. Gordon hovered his cursor above this stream, anxious to hear what exchange there might have been with the aliens, but he did not select it. One of the other streams held an even greater allure.

The video log was an overview of all visual data and telemetry. He could see the encounter with the Deltans from the very moment *Promise* turned on its cameras. Though not as detailed as what would be found in the telemetry stream, it was immediately accessible.

Gordon selected it and saw that 43 minutes of video had been received, with more streaming in. He laughed. Due to the limits of relativity, from his perspective, *Promise*'s encounter was still "live". Even though it had been transmitted a year before, to Earth it was as fresh as breaking news. To him, first contact was still going on. No one on the planet was as close to the Deltans as he was now.

Gordon started the video stream and leaned in, getting as close to the log and its various inset cameras as his in-desk monitor would allow. His eyes grew wide and he gasped in awe when the object of all his speculation swung into view. "It's not a ship at all. Good god . . . ."

The probe grew closer to its quarry and he sighed, the only sound he made for minutes as history unfolded before him. Ten minutes later, he said to the empty room, "So that's it. I was right—Lagrange points. Huh."

Nothing happened after that, and Gordon grew impatient. He fast-forwarded the stream a bit, watching the encounter happen at four times the normal speed. Then, in minutes, he slowed again. "Here we go. Enough of this timid crap. Transmitting. Our first official words to the galaxy."

After that, he froze, unable and unwilling to speed it up anymore as events unfurled faster and faster. His heart began to beat harder, growing from a noticeable thumping in his chest to a pounding pulsation in his ears, and then a burning agony that failed to subside. Sweat rolled from his face and Gordon clutched his chest as if to contain a heart that threatened to burst from him, but he refused to look away.

On the screen, the video stream ended with the abruptness of a filmstrip ripped from the projector. Gordon saw nothing but static, but the last images would be burned into his mind for the rest of his days, not that he really had any of those left.

Nathan pulled up to the house with a spray of displaced gravel flying out from his truck's tires. He noted with a wince that Kris's motorcycle was already there, but then smiled when he saw her rushing up the front steps. He jumped out the door and ran across the driveway, pushed by the twin drives of future history and the need to not let Kristene beat him inside.

He was up the steps and standing next to her before she had even finished knocking. He gave her his most dazzling smile, and she responded with a shake of her head and a half-smile of her own. "I still won," she said.

Nathan shook his head. "Noooooo. I believe the taunt was, last one inside's a rotten egg. No inside-eee, no win-eee."

"You cheated. You started out twice as close as me. I had to get over here from the shipyard, through worse traffic."

"While no doubt doing about Mach seven. It all evens out. I drive a truck bound to the laws of physics, while your little turbine-cycle follows rules no one's ever thought about defining. Tell me, do you outrun the police or just teleport out of their jurisdiction?"

Kris smiled. "Neither. I'm invisible to radar when I'm up to speed."

"Ah, that explains it." She reached forward and knocked again. "Besides, it's not as if one of us will actually see the video before the other. Gordon's probably going to wait until we all get here so he can make a grand event out of it—the Great Unveiling of my Mad Endeavour."

Nathan laughed. "Of course, he's probably watched the whole first transmission himself by now."

"And marked all the good parts," Kris added.

They both nodded and said together, "That's Gordon for you." That made them both laugh, and Nathan took a half-step closer to her, to which she responded with a half-step of her own to keep the space between them. It was a subtle little dance they shared but never acknowledged, the legacy of Nathan's rejection.

For a month after their confrontation in his hospital room, Kristene had avoided any and all contact with him, and he despaired that not only was their friendship doomed, but the project was as well. She could not stay mad forever, though. It was anathema to her nature.

What had begun then was a gentle return to the status quo. They were friendly, but it was work-friendly, not the exciting and playful friendship of a pair of acquaintances on the verge of becoming something more. She resumed her bright, joking effervescence, but now without any hint of flirtation.

And Nathan missed it terribly.

The project was on track, their interaction was pleasant, and there was little to no awkwardness, but where before the future had lain significantly before them, now there was only the present and the memory of a discarded past. He knew he had perhaps made his life's biggest error.

Nathan opened his mouth to say something, anything to her, but the door finally opened and Melinda waved them inside, a cell suite tucked between her shoulder and her ear. She said into the phone, "Thank you. Yes, we're all assembling at the estate, and we'll review the files when everyone arrives. No, you don't all have to be here—just a representative, though Mr. Lee is quite anxious for everyone to view it and give their opinion. Yes. Thank you, Dr. Chen. We'll see you soon." She took down the suite from its perch atop her shoulder and smiled at Kris and Nathan. "It's so good to see you two. What I just said only applies to the riffraff. You can both go in and take a look now, if he hasn't seen it all a couple of times by this point."

Nathan smiled. "Thanks, Melinda. I think we'd both like to get a look at the telemetry before the huddled masses begin arriving. Is he in his office?"

She nodded. "Just knock and go in. I've got a few dozen more calls and e-mails to make, and I haven't even gotten to the official government contacts yet."

They nodded to her and both began walking through the house. As they made their way through the rooms and corridors, they shared a glance and a nervous smile. Kristene began walking faster, edging ahead of him. "Big day, don't wanna be late."

"You're going to be the late Ms. Muñoz if you make me run through Gordon's pretty house." Nathan took longer strides and kept pace, causing Kris to jog forward a few steps as preface to a run, but then she bumped a table and rebounded limping and cursing. Nathan shook his head and slowed his walk to match her now much slower gait.

They reached the estate's home office together. Nathan knocked and held the door open for Kristene. He opened his mouth to say something, but it died away unsaid when he heard Kristene's cry and saw for himself the scene in Gordon's office.

Gordon lay on the floor in a pile of papers, face up and gasping, trying to raise himself up by pulling on the desk. His cheeks were sunken and a gray pallor covered his face. Static played on the surface of his pill-strewn desktop, and his chair was knocked over on its side.

Nathan rushed in, knelt at his side, and immediately felt the old man's neck. The pulse was so rapid and light it was nigh indiscernible. He turned to capture Kristene in his gaze and commanded, "Call 911! Then get Melinda in here with the defibrillator. Go!"

She rushed out the doorway without a word, and Nathan laid Gordon flat on the floor, grasping his hand firmly, and catching the suffering man's panicked gaze with his own eyes. "Gordon, lay still, we're getting help." He glanced at the top of the desk and saw all the little white pills scattered over its surface. "Your medication? Did you take your pills, Gordon?"

It took a moment for Lee to get control of his pained, gasping breath, but eventually he said in a harsh, broken whisper, "—es ... took 'em ... no good."

"Okay. Just lay back and rest. Melinda's getting your AED and Kris is calling for an ambulance. You just stay still and concentrate on not dying, all right? The last thing you want is me giving you CPR, you know?"

Gordon grinned behind a mask of pain. "Ugliest ... damn nurse ... ever had." He winced, arched his back and clutched his chest and left arm as another attack hit him.

Nathan looked desperately to the doorway as he held Gordon still, but no one appeared there. "Melinda! Hurry up!"

Lee reached up, grabbed Nathan's arm and dragged him down close. He seethed through his clenched teeth, hissing, "Listen ... saw it ... bad. All bad ... worse than I feared."

"Gordon, lay still and calm down. Don't worry about that now."

"Not a ship ... worse ... cathedrals ... burning stars for engines ... Nathan ... you have to go ... soonest ... have to test them ... must start now."

"We will, boss. The ship's ready, and the crew's ready, but don't worry about that now! You'll be there to see us launch and you'll be there when we get back."

"Don't understand ... government ... wasn't real before ... is now ... they'll take it ... from us ... can't let them ... our ship ... not theirs."

Nathan felt Gordon's grip slacking off. His eyes took on a faraway look as he lay back down. Nathan followed him to the floor, straining to catch every increasingly softer word.

Melinda and Kris ran into the room, frantic, eyes lined in red, but working together in quiet confidence. Melinda broke open the large orange case of a portable Automatic External Defibrillator and began to lay out the unit next to Nathan and Gordon, ripping off plastic wrapping and peeling the paper off a pair of sticky panel electrodes while the unit charged up. She pushed Nathan to one side and ripped open Gordon's oxford shirt, exposing a smooth chest with unnaturally yellow and grayish skin. Melinda attached the electrodes as Nathan moved out of her way, still keeping his ear close to Gordon's mouth.

The old man's words were little more than breathy whispers. "Take up my sword ... you must ... take up my sword ... save us ... how's it go ... liberty ... or death."

With that, his pupils dilated and the last hint of rosy vitality faded from his skin. He seemed to deflate slightly and the AED, which had been giving Melinda verbal instructions unnoticed by Nathan, spoke out again in a calm, female contralto, "No cardiac rhythm detected. Unable to regulate rhythm. Perform CPR until rhythm re-established."

Melinda and Kris cried openly. Nathan moved the secretary over and then settled his hands over a point an inch or so above the base of Gordon's sternum. He locked his elbows and then pushed down and released, pushed down and released. He kept it up for a count of thirty and then sat back, looking to Melinda, who was still fiddling with the AED, trying to get it to magically bring their employer and friend back to life, instead of just repeating the same unhelpful statement over and over again.

"Melinda!" Nathan said sharply. "Breath for him. Two breaths."

She nodded and wiped pendulous tears away from her eyes with the back of her hand. She tilted Gordon's head back, lowered her lips to his, and breathed for him, twice. Nathan rose up to begin chest progressions again, and paid no attention to the tears that coursed down his own cheeks. He and Melinda alternated back and forth, listening to the AED repeat itself and watching Gordon's unchanging body without hope.

Kristene looked from one to the other, shaking her head and moving gently in to relieve either Nathan or Melinda if their will began to flag. The three of them kept it up for ten minutes, silent for the most part, until the ambulance and EMT's arrived, ready to do all that was possible to hold Gordon to the corporeal realm.

But Gordon Elliot Lee, who had cast such a large shadow for such a slight man over the course of his 68 years, had already left this world for the next, surpassing even the *Promise* in the scope of his final journey.

Hours later, Nathan re-entered the house and shut the door numbly behind him. He stood still and *listened*. No one was there. Melinda had gone home from the hospital with Kris in tow, both of them discussing funeral arrangements in somber, quiet tones. The paramedics, police, and a baker's dozen of reporters were gone, their questions asked and answered with quiet respect and understanding, for the most part. The house staff, who always tried to be pretty much invisible, were indeed gone, the object of their labors no longer having the need for such care.

Nathan was alone.

He listened deeply, trying to block out the sound of his own breathing and the movement of his clothes. All was silent. There was nothing left. Gordon Lee could fill a room with his presence, and his spirit could keep it brimming with excitement even after he left, but none of that lingered now. Gordon was gone and not even a ghost remained to shepherd them through what lay ahead.

He shook his head, returned Gordon's keys to his pockets and walked over to the immense terracotta warrior that dominated the foyer. Nathan looked up at it, bowed his head slightly in respect, and then proceeded on through the darkened, quiet interior of Gordon's former home. He moved with a purpose, for he had one, but nostalgia and grief gave him a halting gait as he passed objects which had been merely part of the background, but now took on the significance of a thousand memories.

After the pain of losing his place in the Navy, this place had become his life and his home. It was not where he lived, but it was where his life had regained meaning. Gordon had given him something beyond any mere job or project. Gordon had given him purpose, had made Nathan matter again to the world, and made the world matter to Nathan. It was a debt he had not even realized he owed before, and now it was too late to ever repay it.

Nathan reached the home office, lit only by the frozen static on the desk screen. The stream was still logged in. He knew that the telemetry stream had already been viewed by almost everyone on the short list with access to the server, but he himself had not had a chance to review it yet. Nathan stepped carefully around the desk, self consciously avoiding the spot where Gordon had died, and sat down. He shook his head and scrolled the cursor around, clicking to begin the video log again.

The static cleared and a video divided into four images began. First was a visible spectrum, light-enhanced view out of the main camera. Next to it was the same scene, but in a false color, multi-spectrum view. Below the first images was the video from the sub-probes *Promise* had launched, switching from one unit to another every few seconds. The last image was a view of the *Promise* itself, taken from a spar extended from the main hull.

The probe looked to be in decent shape—discolored slightly, with multicolored burns and pockmarks around the shielded nosecone, but nothing appeared to be broken or missing. The other images showed nothing but stars and space. Then the main views rotated and the Deltans were revealed for the first time.

They filled the images. Either the probe was *extremely* close, the magnification was all the way up, or the approaching aliens were really, really big. Nathan's jaw fell slack and he forgot to breathe for a moment. The "ship" was unlike anything he had expected. And it was not really a ship at all.

The most immediate feature was the Deltan drive. It was not a photonic drive or rocket as they had surmised, though it might ultimately produce a similar effect. This was, for all intents and purposes, a sun.

It appeared as if someone had lassoed a star and forced it to radiate in only a single direction. Blue white light blasted forth from one pole of a distended ball of plasma. The tortured sphere of the drive had its own roiling purple white and golden red radiance, but it was far outshone by the thrust of the drive. Where the "star" was constrained, brilliant ropes of silvery light bound it, forcing it out of its natural form and putting it to work for the ornate bodies orbiting it.

Surrounding the drive, but unconnected to it by any visible means, were four shapes. The configuration of those shapes had perplexed Gordon for years. He had never figured out what significance they had, but it all seemed obvious to Nathan upon seeing it now. The bodies orbiting the Deltan drive were positioned directly upon the classic Lagrange points—three of the shapes in an equilateral triangle around the drive, with the fourth shape stuck in the middle of one of the sides.

For any two bodies in a gravitationally bound system, where one body is much more massive than another, there were points of gravitational minima and maxima, where another body so placed would be in equilibrium with the first two bodies and the whole system could exist in stable harmony. These were known as the Lagrange points, designated L1 through L5, and these were the points that the four constructs surrounding the drive were configured around.

The drive obviously filled the role of the central, massive body. The other body of the "two body problem" was the smallest of the constructs. Illuminated by a brilliant violet-red glow from the equator of the drive, this vessel was the most starship-like of the four. It appeared as a dully metallic, plated ovoid, with various projections and hatches of unknown purpose adorning its hull. The vessel had none of the comforting normalities of a human construct—no recognizable docking points, solar panels, thrusters, or view ports. Nathan could hardly even tell the front from the back. The overlapping rings of plates which formed the hull gave it a vaguely arthropod-like appearance, but Nathan was probably more closely related to a lobster than these things were. Below this vessel, all of the silver-white bands of energy around the drive sphere came together, though for what purpose, Nathan was not ready to guess.

At the L3 point, directly opposite the first vessel across the drive, was an irregular sphere of plated metal. It looked … incomplete. The coloring was not uniform, and there appeared to be nothing purposeful or special about it. There was no reason to believe he could tell anything from first appearances, but to him it looked like nothing so much as a junk heap. It was easily twice the size of the first vessel, but if this really was a Lagrangian configuration, it would have to be much less massive.

At the L4 and L5 points, 60 degrees ahead and 60 degrees behind the first vessel in its orbit about the drive, were the last two constructs. Similar in size and basic shape to the junk pile at the L3 point, these appeared in no way incomplete. These were nothing less than the cathedrals Gordon had spoken of in his last words.

The one orbiting at L5 was somewhat spherical or polyhedral, and was covered with long, curving chambers defined by angular ribs, adorned with almost gothic arches. The structure appeared to be made of dark gray, polished stone blocks, accentuated by copper and silver edgework and statuary. There were no lights to reveal its darkly shadowed alcoves, but half of the structure was illuminated by the deep carmine glow from the drive. Nothing about it seemed practical or spaceship-like. Instead, it appeared to be the illegitimate offspring of Notre Dame and Westminster Abbey as interpreted by Salvador Dali or M. C. Escher.

L4 sported a construct similar in purpose to the gothic structure at L5 (in so far as it bore no relation to either of the two main bodies or the junk heap at L3), but completely different in style and appearance. It was also somewhat spherical, but appeared lumpy and organic. Domes, spires, and hollows adorned the structure, configured in a pleasant, orderly fashion, but which seemed to have been extruded naturally rather than built. It looked to be made of an off-white plastic or polyp, lit on one side by the drive's reddish-purple glow, while complex geometric designs of intersecting whorls of color and dark, looping lines broke up the uniform surface coloring. By the way the light played over the designs, they appeared to be cut into the surface of the construct vice merely drawn upon it.

The four structures of the Deltan "system" revolved slowly around the equator of the drive, rotating about their common polar axes so that no one side was tidally locked toward the star-like sphere of plasma. Whether this system was indeed gravitationally bound like a planetary or solar system, or whether there were other forces at play, Nathan would have to wait for the telemetry analysis, but he felt himself making his own assumptions about the system regardless.

The drive seemed to be an enormously powerful and skilled manipulation of several forces, well beyond Earth's own capability, but it did not feel magical or beyond all understanding. The drive was apparently controlled by the lobster-like ship, and produced a massive thrust in order to slowly accelerate its immense bulk from star system to star system. The other constructs were then dragged along behind, bound to it by gravity, electromagnetism, or some other force unknown to humanity. The constructs themselves inspired a number of different interpretations, none of which had any validity other than the feeling in Nathan's gut.

For the junk heap at L3, Nathan felt nothing. It was a non-entity, neither alluring nor threatening. For the ornate structures, gothic and organic at L5 and L4, Nathan felt a sense of wonder and enticement. They practically invited exploration as works of art and design—design along two completely different aesthetic frameworks. The whole system was alien, and every part of it seemed alien to every other part.

Only the lobster-like control ship carried with it any negative connotation. It looked menacing, though not one element of it could be pointed out as threatening, and it did nothing but revolve about the drive, same as the others. Staring at it, though, he could not help but feel a sense of dread. Perhaps he attributed too much to it because of what happened to Gordon, but the plated vessel appeared to be vaguely threatening.

The view devoted to the sub-probes came to life as one or another made a close flyby of each structure. More detail was seen of the individual vessels, but nothing indicated any life aboard. The vessels cruised on, dragged by the forces of the drive to an eventual rendezvous with the solar system, but they did so without change or response. They appeared to be either dead or asleep. Nathan wondered what the telemetry would show.

Getting nowhere with the sub-probes, *Promise* would move to the next step. Lights came on around the probe—with flashing indicators above the auxiliary communication disk and the lidar transceiver, declaring its presence for all to see in case any potential viewers had missed it. He could not tell from the video, but he knew the probe would now begin transmitting to the four vessels, attempting to make contact.

Nathan began to tap a rhythm on the desk—one, two … one, two, three … one through five … one through seven, and so on. It was the classic "first contact" transmission, the first thirty-three prime numbers, from 2 to 137, the inverse of physic's fine structure constant. It was a decidedly nonrandom set that would communicate a variety of things to any potential extraterrestrial visitors. Namely, that humanity knew what a prime number was, and its significance, that we were a mathematical, reasoning species, and could thus be seen as potential peers to the advanced race dropping by for a visit. Whether or not this implied message would get across to these particular aliens, Nathan had no idea, but it always seemed to work in the movies.

Promise would broadcast the prime transmission at a number of different frequencies and rates, from long wavelength radio, to microwaves, visible light, and ultraviolet, hoping to come across something the Deltans would notice. It would keep this up for 24 hours, repeating the sequence over and over again until some response was received. If a response came in, it would reply in kind and then broadcast the greeting message on the appropriate frequency, thus beginning the long process of forming a primer for common communication. If no response was received during that first 24 hours, *Promise* would release additional adjunct probes, this time attempting a physical touchdown and contact with one of the alien structures.

Nathan tapped out the twelfth prime (37) when the Deltan system stopped revolving.

He sat up straight in Gordon's chair. There had been no other change in radiance or activity, but the four structures suddenly ceased their ponderous orbits about the drive. They stood still, frozen in their positions, belying the necessities of orbital mechanics. Obviously, there were other forces involved than mere gravity and inertia. He wondered how it worked, how much sheer energy it must have taken to stop the motion of those enormous masses.

Then, even more rapidly than they had come to a stop, the system spun in the reverse direction until the main, arthropod-like vessel was aligned closest to *Promise*, whereupon it stopped again. Nathan shook his head, in awe of this moment. He could hear his own heartbeat in his ear. Was this sudden activity what had led to Gordon's attack?

Promise would have noticed this change in motion and likely taken it as a response. The prime transmission would have ended and the welcome message would go out, a robotic probe acting as mankind's first ambassador to the stars. In his head, Nathan heard the words in Gordon's own voice, "Greetings to you, our unknown visitors from a nearby star. We welcome you to our solar system in the name of all the free inhabitants of Earth. Please allow this probe to exchange data with you in our stead, such that we might form some bridge for open and enlightening communication between our two species." Whereupon, the probe would begin a math lesson, graduating from there to sounds, letters, and pictures, and from there to concepts and actual negotiations.

Mankind had come far from the days of a golden record slapped onto a beeping probe. Not that it mattered in the least.

Before Gordon's message would even have had a chance to finish, the Deltan system responded. Threads of silvery light lanced out from each of the structures to the adjunct probes *Promise* had fired near them. Telemetry on the third screen turned to static. The silvery light flared about each mini-probe until they were all supplanted by spherical clouds of sparkling dust. The dust clouds then began to break up and stream toward the articulated plate hull of the be-shelled vessel.

Each stream of dust was drawn up into the main ship through unseen vents, soon vanishing completely. Nathan let loose a ragged breath, unaware he had been holding it. Some of its capability and intent now revealed, the ship appeared even more menacing than it had before.

A silvery beam, either larger and brighter than the others or merely closer, shot out from the primary vessel and struck the *Promise* mid-frame. Where the beam made contact, the surface of the probe wavered and became indistinct. The effect slowly spread out from the point of impact, and static began to show up in the remaining camera views.

Promise had been programmed for hostility, though.

The photon drive fired at full thrust, forcing the probe out of the beam's path at several g's of acceleration. The spar holding the probe's self-camera bent down under the thrust, pulling the probe out of the central view. Despite that and the vibration from the engine, *Promise* was still visible and still transmitting.

The beam moved to re-engage the probe, causing *Promise* to shift and redirect or reverse thrust each few seconds. Every time the beam skated by with another glancing blow, the new hit began to waver and become indistinct like the first. The effect was not reliant upon the beam either. Damage from the first strike and every subsequent one still spread further, albeit at a slower pace than when the beam had been feeding it. Sparkling dust streamed away from the probe, crumbs left behind by whatever invisible forces were eating the hull.

Promise made a valiant effort, but it was doomed from the start. Whoever it was that controlled the silver beam soon grew tired of the probe's attempt at being elusive. An invisible beam, its presence revealed only by its devastating effect, stabbed out from the ship. A brightly shining cut opened up the reactor and the drive chamber, appearing almost at once. Chunks of molten debris exploded from the photon drive and the thrust cut out, leaving the probe adrift and twisting.

Static filled the screen and faded away, cycling in and out as the transmission dish was pulled past the limits of its gimbals and it lost the lock on Earth. The laser did not bother making a second pass, its operator content with only crippling the agile probe.

Maneuvers at an end, the silver beam returned, locking on to a single spot on the probe's hull. The disintegrating effect continued on, hull plates, framework and components swiftly transmuting into so much scintillating dust, all of which streamed away to be collected by the ship.

There was a flicker, a flare, and then static. Nathan watched the static until it froze at the end of the video stream, and then continued to sit there. His heart pounded at the confirmation of everything they had worried about, and a vision of Gordon gasping upon the floor returned to him, unbidden.

If he was absolutely honest with himself, he had to admit that he had never really, truly believed in the Deltans. Seeing them disintegrate something you had built with your own hands had a way of convincing even the harshest skeptics, though.

It all came crashing in upon him: the invasion, Gordon, the ship, Kris, the government, his failure aboard the *Rivero*. Nathan was one man, caught up in events that had already battered him about, but this was huge, bigger than himself, bigger than anything he had ever been prepared for.

What the hell am I going to do?

He stood and rubbed his face vigorously, trying to banish the chills he felt through sheer manual effort. He wandered about the office, thoughts wild and unfocused, veering between reasonable worries and irrational, unreasonable terror.

Eventually he stopped, unsure whether his misery would be better dispelled by crying for his lot or laughing at the utter futility of all they had done. He settled for shaking his head and just looked down. He found himself standing in the spot where Gordon died.

Nathan resisted the urge to sidestep. He stood his ground and looked down at the carpet that had been Gordon Lee's deathbed. Slowly, but with a noticeable salutary effect, some of the wild emotion dropped away, supplanted by clear, orderly purpose.

Gordon had faith in him. Gordon had chosen him to do this, and Gordon had invested everything in Nathan, sure that he could indeed handle whatever might happen. Nathan felt that he himself was a lesser man than his mentor had been, so how could he possibly have the audacity to doubt him?

The fear fell away. The worries fell into a hierarchy of concerns, none of which was insoluble. The misery faded. In their place rose a new emotion, an emotion that could be just as debilitating, but which also was key to striving and succeeding.

Anger.

Nathan knelt, placing one hand on the carpet where Gordon's head had lain and one hand on the frozen static of the desk screen. The Deltans had claimed their first victim, the one man who had risen up to defend humanity against an unknown threat, and if Nathan had anything to say about it, he would be the last victim they would ever claim.

10: "FATEFUL MEETINGS"

February 24, 2045; Joint House/Senate Secure Briefing Center - TS/SCI Level; US Capitol; Washington DC

The image on the large display screen dissolved into a wash of static, and the assembled lords of government responded with complete silence. Nathan hit a button on his remote and the static froze, to be replaced by a diagram of the trajectories defining the rendezvous between the Deltans and the *Promise*. He turned back to his audience in the somber, austere top-secret briefing chamber.

His table and the screen behind him were the focal point to stepped tiers of stadium style seats taking up the majority of space in the wood-paneled, brushed-steel room. Seated there along the four rising levels, favoring him with unknowable expressions in the darkness, were senators and representatives of the House and Senate Armed Services committees, DOD officials, NASA representatives, and key Cabinet members, including the President's Science Advisor, the Secretary of Defense, and the National Security Advisor. Little, unlit placards with thin lettering identified each person, but he could only make out a few. He recognized even fewer by sight alone, such as the Security Advisor and the SECDEF.

Nathan smiled grimly. His nerves at confronting such a high-powered audience had mostly settled down, but the video and the stark memory it brought up had set them jangling once more. Still, there was no alternative, no choice. The project needed him here, on their turf, in the basement of the Capitol itself. He needed to do this and do it well, both for Gordon's memory and for their own potential survival.

"Ladies and gentlemen, all telemetry ends soon after the conclusion of the video-stream. We must assume that the *Promise* was either destroyed or was captured for study. The radar and lidar telemetry, as well as the passive sensor data support what the video shows for the most part." Nathan clicked his remote again, changing the diagram to one of the Deltan ship-system. "The aliens travel in a convoy of sorts, with their ships in orbit around their main drive. It looks a bit like a miniature solar system, with the vessels laid out almost perfectly on the classic Lagrange

113

points, but the drive is not a star, and the vessels are not planets.

"The drive is the largest component, a constrained sphere of plasma approximately 1000 kilometers in diameter, emitting a photon reaction thrust along one polar axis. The vessels all maintain a circular orbit around the equator of the drive, at a radius of approximately 800 kilometers, held there by some mix of electromagnetic fields, gravity, and possibly some undetectable forces.

"The vessels are as follows," he said, highlighting each in turn with a click of the control. "The control ship. The junkyard. The cathedral. And the polyp. The control ship is the smallest at twenty kilometers in diameter, and the others are all about the same size at 45 kilometers each. We don't know the purpose behind any of them, or why their designs all vary so greatly. All we know is that the control ship seems to take an active role in controlling the drive and the rotation of the convoy, and that it collected all the debris from the *Promise*'s sub-probes. Presumably, it gathered up the probe itself after it stopped transmitting."

Nathan set down the control and looked over the darkened assembly. "That's pretty much all we can say about the rendezvous. You each have full briefing packets before you which cover the video and telemetry analysis in greater detail. If you have any questions, please ask, but remember that all we know is there in the briefing. Anything else is nothing more than pure speculation, at least until *Promise II* makes its rendezvous. That includes conjecture over whether or not this was an overtly hostile act, whether it was some form of defense, or even if this was just a common, innocent reaction that we're simply misinterpreting. We won't know the answers to those questions until we are in direct contact. Now, given that, are there any questions before I continue with current ops plans and any future initiatives?"

The lights in the room came up somewhat, and he now faced a room peppered with expressions ranging from shock, to incredulity, to fear, and to amusement. He scanned over the room of darkly polished wood and brushed steel, hoping there would be no redirect, that he could continue before his confidence had a chance to falter, but in a room filled with people who were paid to pontificate, there was little chance of that.

One senator stood in the third tier, behind the cabinet members, but Nathan did not recognize him. He nodded to the man, wishing again for a set of congressional flash cards or at least some brighter placards, and then sat. The tall, stately, white-haired gentleman from Nebraska looked somewhat adrift, but he flashed his most challenging glare and addressed Nathan directly, though his comments were meant for the crowd. "Aliens.

You gathered us together, interrupted our very tight schedules, shoved a bunch of spurious charts and analyses in front of us for … what? For aliens?"

Nathan responded from his seat at the table heading up the assembly. "Yes, Senator. I know it's asking a lot. I, myself, didn't really believe for years, but none of us now have the luxury of time to indulge our doubts. Unfortunately, you need to get on board almost immediately. There are decisions that have to be made, and you folks are the only ones that can make them."

The senator just shook his head. "The Deltan invasion has long been the province of charlatans, madmen, and the ignorantly paranoid. But now that you have your little movie and your charts, you expect us to join up with the conspiracy theorists and just open the coffers to you? I really don't think so. How do we even know this telemetry is real—that your probe is real?"

Nathan started to speak, but a hand closed over his own to stop him. Lydia Russ sat beside him, holding him still with a look. Instead, she rose gracefully to her feet, standing as the newly appointed head of Windward Inc., as decreed within Gordon's updated will. "Senator James, do we really need to start grandstanding in here? This brief is above Top Secret. None of your constituents will ever see it. C-SPAN Six won't be covering any part of it. There will be no sound bites, and no lobbying. Today is about planning and policy, not politicking.

"Now, how exactly do you think we even got you all in this room today? Was it because of my winning personality? Because I'm a veteran Beltway Bandit? Perhaps out of belated respect for my predecessor and friend, a man who gave so much to this nation? Not likely in this crowd. No, we did it by proving the data, to the satisfaction of the DOD, NASA, and top minds in the fields of science and industry. If you would have bothered to open your briefing, you'd have noted that every bit of it has been vetted and verified already.

"The probe was real—we have video of its launch, as well as eyewitness testimony from our own naval ships. The telemetry is real—it was received by numerous tracking stations who will each confirm that it was transmitted from deep space. And though it's possible that we could have performed some sort of Hollywood magic to show the rendezvous, the briefing package will clearly show that is not the case. It's all real: the probe, the data, and the aliens, certified by your own top government experts.

"So denying the situation at this point is the equivalent of screaming to us that the Earth is flat or that Washington is a bastion of virtue—not only is it crazy, it's naive, short-sighted, and a waste of time. Given the evidence we've presented, no one should have to stretch their credulity any more than we do for any other piece of actionable intel. Face it, this is our new reality, and we're already late in confronting it. We simply don't have the time for business-as-usual. I recommend you start accepting that and stop obstructing the business of this committee."

Senator James opened and closed his mouth like a gasping fish a few times, but he soon noticed something important among his paperwork and he sat down quietly to examine it further. Nathan suppressed a grin and stood as Lydia sat. He looked at her. He could tell why Gordon had liked her so, why his will had appointed her as his successor. They were kindred spirits.

He turned back to the room. "Any *other* questions?"

The conference chamber was quiet for a moment, but eventually a congresswoman stood in the fourth tier of seats, smoothing her dress and capturing the room with her gaze. When all eyes were on her, she spoke. "Mr. Kelley, I just want to express what most of us here are probably feeling. This whole situation has taken us aback. I don't want to be obstructionist, Ms. Russ, but briefing package or no, this is something that's going to take some getting used to. There are questions that need to be asked, and we can't even formulate them until we can get our minds around the basic situation.

"Aliens? Where are they from? Why are they coming here? How can we prepare for them without making some critical misstep? Should your fears prove justified, how can we possibly defend against a capability so firmly beyond our own? And most importantly, how do we couch this new reality to the people of America and the rest of the planet?"

Nathan nodded. "Ma'am, I cannot answer all of those for you. I'm just an engineer now. The man whose later years had been devoted to coming up with those answers is no longer with us, unfortunately. We can only carry on with his vision and try to do our best. You ladies and gentlemen have to determine what that best is." He favored her with a slight smile. "But we do have a few answers for you.

"If you will open your briefing package to section three, you'll see summaries of the technical initiatives Windward and the DOD have been involved with for nearly twenty years. Realizing our best chance began with making first contact away from Earth itself, we've been developing a number of groundbreaking technologies in the areas of propulsion, power, structural materials, and computing. These have culminated in our first true spaceship, a vessel capable of interstellar flight within a reasonable mission-time, capable of greeting the Deltans outside of our solar system and establishing diplomatic relations, or, if necessary, of dissuading their further approach should they prove hostile."

Nathan turned to the screen and clicked his remote. For a moment, the room faded away from his senses, and all he could see was the display. On it, a schematic and an artist's rendering of their ship stood side by side, the long, stark lines of its hexagonal wedge and its chevron-like radiator panels unlike anything the world had ever seen, but familiar and nostalgic just the same, an image from fevered sci-fi dreams. He could almost feel Gordon standing next to him.

"This is the *Sword of Liberty*, the first in a new class of spacecraft. Numbered DA-1, for Destroyer-Astrodynamic, she is 800 feet long, with a beam of 100 feet by 130 feet, divided into three sections: mission hull, radiator, and reactor/drive. The ship masses about 6500 tons and is powered by a 10 GW plutonium pebble bed reactor, cooled by radiative emission and drive effect. Propulsion is via a breakthrough technology known as an enhanced photon reaction drive, enabling us to produce a continuous g-level thrust without need of any bulky reaction mass, and is similar, if not identical, to the Deltan's drive."

"Excuse me, Mr. Kelley!" Nathan stopped and turned around. The congresswoman, whose name he still did not know, but who had spoken up before, raised her hand up from her seat. "Do you mean that this is what you are planning on building or what you have built?"

"I mean that the *Sword of Liberty* is built, fitted out, and ready for launch into orbit. As we will discuss in greater detail in a moment, our intention is to launch with our full crew aboard, conduct a brief series of trials and tests in orbit, and to proceed on our own rendezvous mission soon thereafter."

He turned back to the screen, clicking the remote to reveal the *Sword* in her floating launch hangar outside Santa Clara, laying down on her side, with cables and workers arrayed over the dark gray surface. "We have installed a wide variety of communication devices, each linked to linguistic databases, intelligent translation software, and first-contact primers developed by experts in the, until now, theoretical field of exo-linguistics. It is intended that a US ambassador and staff employ these systems to open negotiations. Room has been reserved for this diplomatic element, and we only await your guidance in order to finalize our crew.

"And in case communication should prove futile, the *Sword of Liberty* is a destroyer in fact, not only in designation." Nathan clicked the remote to reveal another schematic, this one highlighting the weapons and sensors arrayed over her hull. "We have no way of knowing what weapons would be effective, so we've included a variety, stretching the limits of our own technology." A green laser point appeared over each system as he briefed them.

"You can't build an honest-to-God spaceship without lasers, so we installed them. The *Sword* is serviced by six independently powered and controlled diode laser stacks, each capable of producing a multi-megawatt beam of high-UV light, coherent out to a focal limit of 1500 kilometers. Though that seems a significant range for a direct-fire weapon, it's fairly short for encounters in space, especially with something the size of the Delta system. Therefore, while the lasers are capable of aimed fire out to their extreme range, they are optimized for autonomous defensive fire, and thus constitute the primary active defense of the ship.

"The ship also mounts a spinal railgun running down the centerline, firing forward. The railgun fires a number of different projectiles ranging from electronics rounds, to explosive rounds, to tungsten kinetic rounds, all of which can be fired at a selectable velocity—up to 60,000 meters per second, at a cyclical rate of 30 rounds a minute. Given our targeting capabilities, the railgun has a longer effective range than the lasers, but it's ammunition limited, unlike the laser stacks."

Nathan paused to survey the audience. They were rapt for the most part, with a few flipping back and forth through the briefing packet. Nathan reached down and poured himself a drink of water from the ubiquitous crystal pitcher and glass on his table. Those who had been reading looked up at the interruption while he drank. The cool water did little to slake his desperate, nervous thirst, though. His mouth seemed even dryer than it had been a moment before. This next part would be tough.

Damn Kris and her bright ideas.

He favored the audience with a half-smile and then turned slightly back to the screen. "Excuse me." His green laser ran over a set of small, individual hatches arranged in six groupings of eight on each flank of the ship. "These hatches cover the main armament of the ship. Each of these 96 hatches tops a missile cell, much like our ships' current Vertical Launch Systems. Within each one is a ship-to-ship offensive missile of our own design."

Nathan clicked to the next slide, showing a schematic of the missile in profile. "This is the Excalibur Mark 1. It's pretty much a small spacecraft in and of itself, consisting of a guidance and sensor package, a limited AI, and a photonic reaction drive powered by a sacrificial ultracapacitor bank. Each missile carries six variable-effect munitions capable of either deep penetration, contact, or proximity detonation. Each munition also has a fourth, untested detonation mode: lasing. One of the primary tasks for our orbital trials will be to validate the performance of the Excalibur in all four modes."

Nathan heard a scraping of a chair and he looked over to see who had moved. Upon seeing the culprit, he stifled a groan. Not only had he inherited Gordon's responsibilities on the project, it seemed he had inherited his headaches as well.

Secretary of Defense Carl Sykes, formerly Deputy SECDEF, stood with an unreadable expression on his face. "Excuse me, Mr. Kelley, but might I ask what type of explosive your missile is using? 'Munitions' is rather vague and you seem to have left it out of your otherwise fine briefing."

Nathan squared his shoulders and faced off with Sykes across the room. "Not an oversight, Mr. Secretary—an intentional omission. We've relied heavily upon the largesse of the US government in order to get this ship built, but certain conditions and restrictions placed upon our preps could have derailed the whole effort. We knew what needed to be done, so we did it, even if it meant circumventing a few of the limits placed over us."

Sykes' eyes narrowed. "What are those missiles armed with, Kelley?"

"Thermonuclear warheads, Secretary Sykes."

A few representatives and senators popped to their feet, with genuine outrage in some cases and carefully crafted platform stances in others. The incensed legislators frothed so automatically that they all started speaking over one another. "Nuclear warheads!" "This was never authorized—" "What about our treaties—" "—the damn Non-Proliferation Treaty—" "I bet it was that idiot in the White House—" "Where were those missiles built? My constituents—" "Whose securing these—"

"Quiet!" commanded Sykes, briefly returning to his former role as a senior general in the Air Force. And though the assembled indignant congresspersons were not the types to defer authority easily, his tone and their genuine level of discomfort with the situation allowed him to assert his control. "Ladies and gentlemen, I assure you that the office of the President and the agreement under which this ship was constructed did not include the outfitting or development of controlled weapons. In fact, they specifically barred the acquisition of weapons-grade nuclear materials."

The SECDEF glared each of the reps back to their seats and then turned back to Nathan and Lydia. "Since that was indeed our agreement, would you mind telling us how you got highly-enriched fissile material through our screening process? All you were approved for was reactor-grade fuels, and I personally vetted the nuclear-security procedures set up."

Nathan smiled tightly. "Yes, your procedures were very effective—effective at slowing down every aspect of reactor construction, but don't worry. No one violated your materials control process."

"So how the hell did you build nuclear warheads?"

"We did it by not using any nuclear materials at all—yours or anyone else's. Our fusion warheads are triggered through a completely different process, developed in-house as an offshoot of our drive technology. There are no plutonium or uranium primaries. Instead we use a pure fusion process more closely related to laser ignition—the photonic compression sphere." Nathan turned away from Sykes and addressed the audience as a whole. "I know this may be a special shock, in a day filled with shocks, but believe me when I say that this was a necessary step. Without a weapon of this energy level, we'd have no hope of competing with a tech-base capable of interstellar travel."

One of the senators who had stood before, the man who had cried foul about the Non-Proliferation Treaty, stood up in the second tier again to address Sykes and Nathan. "Mr. Kelley, Ms. Russ, I'm Paul Yardley, senator from Nevada. I'm sure you felt this was a necessary weapon. It's obvious that you've had to make tough decisions about issues that most of us have never even imagined before, but this decision, this choice, has repercussions beyond merely your project.

"You've looked at this like an engineer, finding a solution that neatly avoids the obstacles placed before you, but you've also just invalidated decades of armed diplomacy and enforced compromise. All our arms control safeguards are built around monitoring and controlling the use of processed radioactives. If you can get the same effect through what are essentially ballotechnics rather than controlled materials, then you've just made it possible for small groups or even individuals to make their own WMD's. You built over 500 of them in Santa Clara, and no one even noticed."

Nathan nodded grimly. "I realize that, Senator, which was why we took so much care with security—security so effective that the fact that our warheads were actually thermonuclear devices went completely unnoticed by our DOD overseers. They thought the missiles were armed with kinetic-kill submunitions only. The warhead components were all built by different sub-contractors under oppressive non-disclosure agreements. Not one of them knew what the components were meant to do, or what they connected to, or how they connected together. They were each assembled, mounted, and installed in the ship at our Santa Clara facility. Aside from the intended crew and the people in this room, there are only ten other people who know what the devices actually do, and I trust them all implicitly."

Sykes grunted. "I'm sure your personal assurances are more than enough to soothe our nerves, you know, with uncontrolled nuclear arms proliferation on the table, and all that. By the way, wasn't there a break-in at your facility?"

"Which we stopped—"

"And you still have no idea as to the identity of this thief, no knowledge of who he was working for, or how many other secrets might have leaked out before this?"

"He's in your custody, Mr. Secretary! You should be able to answer that better than anyone! But you're correct—our mystery man is still a mystery. However, no related tech has been seen in the outside world and we are sure that no other break-ins have occurred before or since."

Lydia stood, placing a hand on Nathan's rigid shoulder. He resisted for a moment, but soon responded to her gentle insistence and sat. She looked over the room, catching Senator Yardley and Sykes with her final gaze. "You're right to be worried, Senator. This tech changes everything, and it makes your jobs both harder and more dangerous. But this device is, if anything, more complicated and difficult to build than even a 'normal' hydrogen bomb. It is not something your average Timothy McVeigh or Abdul Massharaf will be able to develop on their own. Rest assured, it was a necessary and vital development for the project. Don't forget the stakes we're dealing with here. Our failure to go through with this possibly ill-advised step could lead to our extinction or enslavement by an alien race. Remember that.

"Besides, when you think about it, this warhead tech is only the tip of the iceberg. Everything about this ship and its mission is going to change the planet."

Senator Yardley cocked his head to one side, a signature gesture he used when he thought someone was lying or exaggerating. "I would be hard pressed to believe that anything could be more potentially upsetting than an uncontrolled, off-the-shelf nuclear weapons technology."

Lydia smiled. "Then you obviously don't understand what we've been sitting on for the past twenty years. While I myself wouldn't characterize the weapons tech as 'off-the-shelf', it's not my chief worry. At this point it's covered in a blanket of secrecy. As long as we don't blab about it, there's no reason for anyone to suspect it differs from other nukes. It's relatively 'safe.' But when we launch for trials and the mission itself, other aspects of this tech won't be nearly as safe.

"If you launch something this big, with this much energy, people will notice. The probe was tiny, yet it still caused significant interest, which we were able to successfully deflect. When the *Sword of Liberty* goes up, it's going to be the story of the millennium and there's no way we'll be able to hide it or its destination. All of a sudden, the US government will have to come clean about its cover-up, and about the truth behind the Deltans. Suddenly, we won't be alone in the universe. I expect that the societal and religious disruptions that'll cause will more than dwarf the unreleased fact that we have a fancy new warhead.

"The international community will be angry we didn't involve them or the UN. Every preacher of every faith on the planet will wonder what this means in terms of our place with the Almighty, what it means about our souls, or about the aliens' souls. The stock markets will experience an upheaval that no one can predict. Other emerging superpowers will try to beat us to the punch with their own first contact efforts, which means they'll either go up with existing tech, try to develop their own, or try to steal ours—and there's a lot to be stolen besides just the warheads. The structural materials like chromatic plate and allocarbium will spawn new industries and wreck the existing steel and composites economies. The laser and railgun tech will revolutionize the defense and power industries. Our computing tech is a good five to ten years ahead of what's commercially available.

"But the big upset is the drive tech. Orbit is no longer difficult to achieve. The solar system is now days or weeks away, not months or years. There are mountains of ore just waiting to be smelted and processed out there in the asteroid belt. And don't discount the tourist industry! Everybody is going to want to see Saturn's rings for themselves.

"No, this ship could have deployed armed with nothing but sticks and stones, and it still would have turned the world upside down. Worry about the warheads if you like, but this august assembly had better worry about the other aspects of this situation a hell of a lot more. The good thing is that our beloved US of A is starting out at the top of the heap. You gentlemen and ladies have to figure out how this country's going to capitalize on the opportunity before it blows up in your faces."

Lydia sat to renewed murmurs and excited, concerned discussion. She turned to Nathan and whispered to him, "That's got 'em buzzing. Good god, Gordon would've gotten a kick out of this."

Nathan nodded. "He'd eat it up, but he's not as smooth as you are. He probably would've had a tantrum and attacked a senator by this point. Of course, we haven't dropped the big question yet. You could still pull a Gordon."

She feigned an expression of exaggerated shock. "Me? I thought you were the one who would make the Grand Request." She smiled, looked over the room and then locked in on Sykes again. "He's been too quiet. After sticking him in the eye on the whole warhead thing, I figured he would have to be dragged out of here."

"Maybe it wasn't as much of a shock as you thought it was. Gordon warned me about him. He's supposed to be pretty shrewd."

"Mmm hmmm. Shrewd and not the biggest supporter of what we're trying to do here." Her eyes narrowed. "He's up to something. There's a reason he hasn't protested much yet."

Before Nathan could respond, Senator James took advantage of a lull in the room's chatter and stood. From his position on the third tier of elevated seats, his tall frame towered over the chamber, causing all eyes to go toward him. "Excuse me! Excuse me. My dear Ms. Russ, your little presentation has us all atwitter, which I'm sure must be exciting for you, however what do you really need from us? You've got your ship, your crew, and your smug sense of duty. Why bother informing such an insignificant body as the United States Congress? Why not just go on your mission and write yourselves into the history books without us?"

Lydia stood, smoothing her outfit. "Members of Congress, Secretaries, the *Sword of Liberty* is only the start, but it's all that Windward Tech could hope to accomplish with its own budget and the black funding from the DOD. As of this last quarter, the company I now head is in the toilet. Windward has to turn away from exterior concerns and focus on the business of business, or else we'll be gobbled up and cast to oblivion.

"The reason we're briefing you, aside from your simple need to know, is that DA-1 is not enough. The *Sword* will make first contact, and hopefully that contact will prove the aliens benign. Should it prove otherwise, it will then attempt to find out what, if any, of our tactical preparations are actually effective. Should it become necessary, DA-1 will engage the enemy, determine its tactical capabilities, transmit that data to Earth, and, God willing, withdraw. But it is not the final defense of Earth, only the first sally.

"You all have to make sure that's not in vain. While DA-1 is in transit, you must begin construction on DA-2, and then DA-3, and 4, and 5, and more and more until we have a fleet of *Sword*-class destroyers. You must build them, outfit them, and crew them. You must start thinking about the defense of our planet. You have to start thinking about orbital mine fields, asteroid laser and missile emplacements, sensor nets, electronic warfare stations, supply depots. Frankly, you have to authorize and shepherd our way to a space-based defense right out of Star Wars or Star Trek within the next 13 years, because that's the world we're in now, and we're starting this game already behind."

Senator James sneered at all the reps who nodded their heads at her request. "You're talking about putting us on a war footing! We don't know that such a thing is even necessary, or how it might color our first negotiations with these aliens! And how do we know that your destroyer will be effective in the least?"

"We don't know, but that question is almost useless. If we prepare and they prove friendly, what we gain in terms of technological distribution and new tech will make the expense and effort almost minor. If our preps make them uncomfortable, well, we're human, and such a step is only supported by our history as a species. If they know anything about us, they should know it's the sort of thing we're apt to do. Hell, it's a moderately friendly action compared to some of the things we've done right here on Earth when faced with the unknown. Of course, if we prepare and the *Sword* is totally outclassed, there's always a chance we can adjust our defense in time, but more likely they'll just wipe us off the face of the planet. Then no one will be left to complain about how much we've spent.

"And certainly, there's the distinct possibility our preps will be completely justified. If the *Sword* is moderately successful, then building a defense at home might very well save all our lives. Of course, then there's the worst case scenario: you don't allow us to prepare as we're urging, the aliens prove to be the nasty sort, and we all end up dead. Then you can try to balance the cost of these defenses against the price of everyone's lives, all the way to your grave."

Senator Yardley stood as James carefully returned to his seat, his face troubled. Yardley appeared thoughtful though. "Ms. Russ, that all sounds quite a bit like Pascal's challenge concerning the existence of God. But, let's move away from the philosophical and narrow down on the practical. How much would the defensive measures you're advocating end up costing us? Can we even afford what you're asking of us? Are you asking us to start issuing war bonds? Are you asking us to do this in collaboration with other nations?"

Nathan took over from Lydia. "Those questions are the meat of the matter, Senator, and that's what you folks have to determine. We've done what little we could to aid your deliberations, though. If you'll all turn to section four of your briefs, you'll see a Defensive Cost Analysis—"

"Wait one moment, Mr. Kelley!" Sykes stood with the briefing package open in his hands. He smiled in an unpleasant way. "I'm not quite done with section three yet, on your ship and mission."

"Here it comes," Lydia said softly from her seat, where only Nathan could hear her.

Nathan nodded. "Very well, Mr. Secretary. Go ahead."

"I just have a few questions regarding your crew selection."

"Ask away."

"A few of your choices seem … unusual. With a crew totaling just 35 people on a potentially tactical mission, only fifteen of them have any military experience at all."

Nathan smiled. Something was building here. "Well, of those 35, thirty are identified, with the remainder to be decided upon by the DOD and the State Department. Half of my portion of the crew have extensive military experience, primarily in the Navy and the Air Force. We also have one Marine thrown in for good measure. That's not too bad a ratio, in my opinion. Of the remaining fifteen, seven have private pilot's licenses, two are former Merchant Marines, one's a trauma surgeon, another's a general practitioner, and the others are the primary designers for several of our most complex systems.

"All of our identified crew has trained for over a year on operating and developing the combat and engineering systems aboard the *Sword*, and each crewmember has undergone extensive cross-training so they each know the others' jobs. The whole crew has been through a private version of NASA's astronaut training program, and they've gone through the full space station psychological battery. When it comes to having an expert crew able to handle any eventuality or casualty, I'd go with this one over any other."

"One of your veterans is a double amputee, Mr. Kelley."

Nathan's eyes narrowed. "That particular gentleman has gotten by quite ably for the last thirteen years on prosthetics, and in microgravity that handicap should be a moot issue. In addition, he's a tactical and technical wizard, a decorated former Senior Chief in the US Navy, and I'd trust him with my life anytime, anywhere."

Sykes shook his head. "Would you trust him with every life on this planet?"

"Yes."

Sykes grunted and looked back down at his briefing. "And who is the commanding officer of this 'expert' crew?"

Nathan said nothing and looked down. He sighed and scanned the crowd. A few followed along in their briefs, but most simply stared at him and Sykes.

He turned back to the antagonistic Secretary of Defense. "I'm the captain of this mission. I had a major hand in designing the ship, in determining the tactical mission parameters, and in assembling the crew. My past naval experience and my skill-set in particular were sought out by Mr. Lee. I was his first and last choice to lead this mission. There may be someone out there with more battle experience than I, or more sea time in command, but no one has more experience aboard this type of ship on this sort of mission. Gordon Lee wanted me to be the CO, and I plan to carry out his wish."

Sykes nodded and looked around at the audience. Now all eyes were on them. "Correct me if I'm wrong, but wasn't your last seagoing assignment as a mere lieutenant department head, an assignment that ended with your ship sunk and half your crew killed?"

Lydia shot to her feet. "That's a damned low blow, Carl!"

Sykes raised placating hands. "I'm not disputing the valor with which you served, nor the medals you justly received for your actions off the coast of North Korea. I merely want everyone here to realize to whom they're entrusting the wellbeing of our nation and the entire human race."

He turned completely around, looking up from his seat in the first tier to address the joint House and Senate committees. "I would be the last person to disparage a seasoned, bloodied hero of our Navy, but I also won't allow them to capitalize on my honor and respect in order to steer this body onto a dangerous course. What LT Kelley did in 2031 is far removed from what he's proposing to do now. Years can change a man.

"See it this way, if you will. Do you feel safe entrusting first contact to a man who has already lied to our government? Who lied for the purpose of building his own nuclear arsenal for use against an alien presence that has not definitively proven itself hostile? Who will be far beyond the systems of checks and balances and controls that our own trained, vetted ballistic missile sub captains operate under? Who may, possibly, be suffering from the effects of Post Traumatic Stress Disorder, or who may have something to prove for past blood and lost glory?"

Lydia began to step out from the table, held back only by Nathan's firm grip on her wrist. "God damn you, Carl! There's not one bit of truth to anything you just said! You're twisting things!"

Nathan surveyed the room, purposely avoiding Sykes' eyes. To their credit, several senators and representatives looked appropriately shamed, unable to lock gazes with him. Eventually, Nathan forced himself to focus upon Sykes. "I suppose you have an alternative plan, Mr. Secretary?

Sykes smiled slightly. "As a matter of fact, I do."

February 24, 2045; Kelley residence, Vista Del Mar Condominium Village; Santa Cruz, California

Nathan slammed the door on his car and looked toward his front door with a mix of dread and relief. At this, the tail end of the longest, toughest day he had ever endured, all he wanted was to lay down, shut his eyes, and sleep. But surrendering to sleep also meant giving up the fight, even though he had already lost before he even knew he should be fighting.

Gordon predicted this, he thought. He saw this coming, he warned me with his dying words, and I still failed him.

Nathan shouldered his overnight luggage and trudged up the path to his first-floor condo. Looking at the cement walk, fumbling for the key on his key-ring, he failed to notice Kristene sitting on his porch until he almost fell over her.

"Hey! Kris!" He smiled down at her, momentarily glad despite how the day had gone. "What are you doing here?"

She looked up at him and slowly rose to her feet, her wildly disarrayed phosphorescent red hair offset by the dark expression she wore. She stepped forward to block his access to the front door. "Anything you want to tell me about your trip, Nathan?"

He sighed. "There's a lot I want to tell you, that I need to tell you, but not right now, okay? I was up at five AM East Coast time and it's been a hell of a long day. All I want to do now is get some sleep."

Anger flashed in her eyes. "Yeah? Well I want some freakin' answers! Why is all my access cut off?! Why are there Army types crawling all over the shipyard and the dock? What the hell did you do in DC today?!"

"Army types? Damn, he works fast."

"What is that supposed to mean? I called Lydia and she said she couldn't tell me over the phone. She told me to go and ask you. So here I am. I'm asking! Why have you two cut me off from my work? Am I not on the team anymore, now that you're in the big leagues with Washington?"

Nathan shook his head, confused for a moment, and then he looked at her and grinned slightly. He laughed, but choked it off when he saw her expression turn fiery. "Okay, all right. Let's go inside so I can put this shit down. I'll tell you everything, but it's not what you think."

She stood her ground for a few seconds and then stepped to one side. "It's not?"

"No," he said, "it's much worse."

Nathan unlocked and fumbled through the door, dropping his gear on the other side with relief. The place was pristine, ordered, but not because he himself was. He was virtually a stranger in his own apartment. All his time, his devotion, his passion was spent at the shipyard. This place was furnished out of Swedish catalogs, updated with all the latest electronics, cleaned and maintained by a service, and enjoyed by virtually no one.

Kris entered behind him and shut the door. She looked uncomfortable, the heat of her anger cooling slowly. Nathan favored her with as welcoming a smile as he could muster, given how tired he was, but he could not help it coming off more melancholy than friendly.

Realizing he could not make her feel any more at ease, he dropped the smile, and meandered through his place. He felt unaccountably nervous. It had been a long time since a woman had been in his apartment, but this was Kris. That was a non-starter. It could not be that.

He wandered over to the one area of his apartment that he truly thought of as "his". A wall entirely devoted to bookshelves was filled to overflowing with paperbacks, hardcovers, UV-ROM movies—science fiction, thrillers, and military all, with a few engineering and speculative science texts thrown in for good measure. Interspersed among the books-stacked-upon-books were bits and pieces of his former life. Ball caps, signed pictures of the three ships he had been on, photo albums, cruise books, memorabilia—snapshots of a time when he had served something greater and nobler than his own interests. Nathan had hoped to add another ship's icons to those shelves.

But that would not happen, not now.

He shook his head and turned back to Kris. Her anger had ebbed enough that she could see how deeply he hurt. He could see the compassion rising in her eyes. Nathan took a step closer. His voice dropped to a near whisper. "We lost it, Kris. It happened just like Gordon warned it would, and there wasn't a damn thing we could do to stop it."

"What—"

"They nationalized us," he said in a louder, grimmer tone. "Sykes must have been planning for this from the very moment the government began bankrolling the program. Now that the ship is done and the mission is no longer political suicide, he made his move. It's not just you who's lost your access. It's all of us. As of this afternoon, the *Sword of Liberty* and the entire Special Projects division of Windward Technologies Inc. are wholly-owned properties of the United States government, managed by the Department of Defense."

Anger colored her face again, almost making it match the glowing crimson of her hair, but this time her ire was not aimed at him. "They can't do that! You said Gordon had agreements, contracts that clearly laid out the boundaries of who owned what!"

He nodded sadly. "That's right, but you'll find that contracts are hard to enforce when the things they concern are classified at a higher level than any court that's authorized to work out disputes. We relied on the magnanimity of the Beltway, which goes completely by the wayside when you start edging up on national security issues. And when Congress found out we had our own unregulated nuclear arsenal, and that a bunch of non-military eggheads were going to be negotiating with an advanced alien race for the fate of the planet ... well, they were only too happy to back up the SECDEF in his power grab."

Kris looked like she was about to scream, but then her face just fell, her fury shorted out. He could see all the emotions she had built up through hours of wild speculation and worry over betrayal simply vanish, leaving behind a numb, empty shell, another soul hollowed out by the bureaucracy. To Nathan, it was a recognizable moment, that realization of defeat.

She turned and sat down on the couch, moving slowly as her mind tried to sort things out. Nathan was grateful. His fatigue and his own drained emotions conspired to sap him of whatever energy still kept him standing. He walked over and flopped down on the plump tan couch next to her. The cushions were bliss. He laid his head back.

Kris leaned over, her elbows on her knees, her hands massaging her temples. "What happens now? Are we out-out? Or are we just out for the moment?"

He looked over at her. He was so tired, but he had worked through all of this hours ago and he did not want her to rack her mind through all the permutations he himself had turned to and discarded, one by dismal one. "Yes, we're out-out. Apparently, we're national assets, you more than me. We're needed down here, to oversee and guide the construction of the fleet, assuming of course that they even decide to build one."

"A monkey could do that now," she snarled, some anger still alive within her. "The ship is designed! Anyone could take our specs and build another. I'm not needed for that. I'm needed where the damn first contact team might run into something we never planned on!"

Nathan shook his head. "Be that as it may, your new place is here. A combined Navy-Air Force crew will take up *Liberty*, and they'll make first contact. They're dependable. They're expendable. They're not us."

"So I build their damn starship, and I don't even get a ride? That's complete BS!"

He shrugged. "I know, but Lydia and I were able to get a couple of concessions, at least. We will get to go up. We'll launch the ship, carry out the test trials with the military crew, and then we'll return to Earth. One ticket, one joyride, but no mission."

She slumped back on the couch, to slouch as he was. She looked over at him. "And what about the mission? What about the whole reason we built the ship in the first place?"

Nathan smiled tightly. "The ship will stay in orbit while they re-evaluate the mission plan, and train on the operational systems. When the DOD decides they're ready, they'll go. I'm sure we'll get a nice mission patch or something, but as of this afternoon, the fate of the world no longer rests on our shoulders."

Kris turned her head and stared at the ceiling. "Good god, this sucks."

"Yeah." He looked at her in profile, smiling softly to himself despite how horribly the day had turned out. Kristene was here, and for some reason that seemed to make everything all right. He watched her stare ahead, working furiously and hopelessly through all the angles of their new reality for as long as he could. But after a few moments, his eyelids drooped, the world fell away, and he slept, admitting defeat at last.

▰▰▰▰▰▰▰▰▰▰▰▰

After some unknown time, as quick as an eye blink, or as long as hours, the world came back. He awoke refreshed, renewed, and unreasonably content. The worries of his long day did not seem to matter as much. Something was different, with either himself or the world, but the difference was a welcome one.

As he rose further from the comforting depths of sleep, he realized that something indeed was changed about the world, a world defined at the moment by just his senses of touch and smell. Now, before he dared to open his eyes, the limits of his existence were bounded by the pleasant warmth and the reassuring pressure of someone by his side, by the fresh, indescribable scent of a woman's hair.

Nathan opened his eyes and looked over to see Kris' head lying against his shoulder. She looked back at him with red-rimmed eyes, unspent tears gathered at their corners.

She said nothing, gave him no explanation for why she was there, for why she might have been crying. There was nothing that needed to be said, however. For her, things between them had never really changed, only delayed. For him, the only thing that had changed was the realization that his stoicism and his denials had been for nothing. His rejections had not saved the project. They had only put off what they both wanted, what they both knew was the right and necessary thing.

His reasons for doing what he had done had been valid and objectively wise, but they also no longer applied. They did not need to hold him back anymore.

Nathan circled his arms around Kris and leaned toward her. She reached up and drew him into a kiss, gentle and slow, the fulfillment of an unspoken promise that had been made in his office one night nearly two years before. Over time, time that passed unnoticed and unheeded, their kiss grew more heated, more insistent.

The pleasant warmth that lay between them became an unbearable heat. Lying on the couch together, they each quickly shed their encumbering clothing and yielded to the pull of unrealized needs, to the weight of years spent orbiting about one another, waiting for this moment.

Later still, so late that it was early, Nathan lay back in his bed, holding her close to him, reveling in the sensation of her skin in contact with his own. His hands roamed aimlessly across her back, tracing the colorful tattoos that extended up from her left arm and across half her back, massaging or idly stroking with no rhythm or regularity. It was just something to do, something he had always wanted to do, but which he had never admitted to himself before. He enjoyed the slight shivers that went through her when his touch was lightest.

They looked at each other and, seemingly on cue, they both started giggling, laughing over nothing but new-found joy. It was as if they were two children who had discovered the hidden wonder and magic in the everyday world, like suddenly finding the rainbow spun off a crystal in sunlight.

Kris rolled over and lay next to him on her back, in contact, but not so close now that he could feel every heartbeat. She pulled the sheet down, carrying nothing for modesty and happy for a chance to cool off. She looked at him. "You know, I've been thinking … ."

"You can still think?" he asked, smiling. "Wow. That's one up on me."

Kris smiled back. "Stop it. I've been thinking, is the SECDEF a bad guy, someone who just wants the tech for himself, under his control? Or is he right, that we shouldn't be trusted with something this big, that just because we thought it up and we built it, we aren't necessarily the right choice to actually go?"

Nathan frowned and reached for her hand, entwining her fingers with his own and kissing them gently. He brought their arms down between their prone forms, still holding her hand lightly. "I don't know. I don't know him well enough to say. Just because someone didn't get along with Gordon or Lydia, doesn't automatically mean they're evil or wrong."

"But it's not exactly a vote in his favor, either."

"No, definitely not. Still, Gordon had his quirks, and not everybody appreciated them. I guess I'd have to hope that Carl Sykes did what he did out of a genuine sense of duty and concern for the nation. But I was there. I saw him and the way he operates. He may have nothing but altruistic motives, but how he gets his way is nothing short of criminal."

Kris rose up on one elbow and turned toward him, making it difficult for him to concentrate suddenly. "Eyes up here, fearless leader." He locked gazes with her and they both smiled. She nodded. "Tell me, is what Sykes doing the right thing or not? Is this mission delay and crew swap a better plan in the end, objectively? Or do you stand by the crew you picked out, the mission you've been planning?"

There was no hesitation on his part. "Getting out to the Deltans sooner rather than later is a better plan. Going out there with the people we trust and who we've worked with for so long is the right plan." Nathan sighed. "But it's out of our hands now. Why ask?"

She leaned in to him, her lips brushing his earlobe, whispering, "Because if we only get one chance to be on that ship, we'd better make it count for something."

11: "TRIALS AND TRIBULATIONS"

March 6, 2045; USS Sword of Liberty (DA-1), aboard RLV Cauldron; Pacific Ocean, 400 nautical miles off the California coast

Miles and miles from any shipping lane, and barren of any unauthorized traffic, a very unusual naval exercise was underway. The carriers, cruisers, and destroyers of the US Pacific Fleet had scoured the waves for days, working in concert with satellites, aircraft, towed-array sonar surveillance ships, and submarines to ensure not one person was within weapons or sensory range of that particular spot in the ocean.

Having cleared the seas, the naval assets withdrew to a safe distance of 100 nautical miles and formed a defensive ring, allowing no man, boat, sub, plane, or leviathan to cross their barrier.

At the center of this ring, a very unusual ship sat alone, doing a very unusual thing.

The Reconfigurable Launch Vessel *Cauldron* had served as the womb of mankind's first true spaceship. Within this strange, boxy vessel, the ship that would change the world had been assembled, in pieces, under the shadowy oversight of the US government at the innocuous Ingmar Rammstahl Shipbuilding Company in Santa Clara, California.

For the last two and a half years, the *Cauldron* had floated high in the water, with her vast, enclosed bay's floor well above the ocean's surface. But as the child of the future grew in her belly, her draft had slowly grown deeper. This mothership was more of floating drydock than a ship in her own right, but she could do things that no respectable drydock would ever be caught doing.

Now, alone at the center of the US Navy's costly ring of solitude, the *Cauldron* appeared to be sinking. Over the span of hours, her bow lifted into the air while her stern dipped below the waves. Yet, she was not the victim of some random, tragic casualty. This was by design, through the careful pumping of ballast from one tank to another.

The angle of her hull increased steadily as her bow lifted up and up into the salt-laden sea air. Eventually, the drydock vessel became less of a ship and more of a tower—a tall, stable, enclosed gantry, floating isolated in the middle of the Pacific Ocean. And once the tower was finally erected, the bow blossomed open to reveal another, very different bow hidden inside.

For a brief moment, the wind and the sea gave pause, becoming calm and glassy, as if the sight of this strange ship/tower about to give birth to another ship were enough to shock nature itself into stillness. Then, silence and calm vanished as the *Cauldron* exploded in light and sound. Here, a new force of nature was unleashed upon the planet.

Blue-white energy stabbed down into the ocean, instantly boiling tons of seawater, producing superheated clouds of steam that pushed outward with the force and the speed of a nuclear detonation. The hollow bulkheads and frame of the *Cauldron* came apart like kindling and the *Sword of Liberty* was revealed for the first time, balanced upon her hexagonal stern, riding atop a lance of pure energy in the center of an expanding crater in the ocean.

The enormous, wedge-topped tower of the spacecraft fell slightly as her thrust built—but then the fall reversed itself and she began to rise, faster and faster, driven by a force equivalent to firecracker strings of nuke, after nuke, after nuke. The ship rocketed upwards at ever climbing Mach values, wind tearing at the thin aeroshells that protected her bow, antennas, and radiator panels.

The drive effect pulled away from the surface of the ocean and floods of seawater rushed in to fill the steamy, conical depression carved out in the ocean by the launch. Water geysered up hundreds of feet into the air, a final, petulant slap at the ship from Mother Earth, for having stricken her so deeply.

The attending ships, their crews gawking in awe at the spectacular launch, were unfortunately forced to turn away from the show by the simple need to survive. Atmospheric shockwaves from the continuous torch of energy were bad enough, throwing out hurricane-level gust fronts to set the ships heeling over, but the tidal wave was worse.

The transition of that much water to steam, and the accompanying inrushing flood and geyser were enough to set the whole ocean ringing like a bell. Solid bands of physical force expanded out from the launch point at the speed of sound through water, many times that of sound through air. The height of the ring fell steadily, but the energy remained, undissipated. The surface shockwave crossed the safety buffer of 100 kilometers in a few short moments and struck the warships with the abruptness of a hammer-fall.

Smaller ships were nearly tossed out of the water, lifted up high by the front of the wave and then left hanging as its sharp tail receded in a flash.

Steel frames warped and cracked to such a degree that it would be years before all the ships would have a chance to go to drydock for repairs. Then the tidal wave vanished over the horizon to spread its influence around the globe, leaving the dazed sailors behind.

It would strike the California coast with the greatest ferocity, crunching a few seaside homes which had long staved off the creep of the Pacific, "safe" upon stilts. Wrecked too were several ocean-view roads, and an older pier or two, but no one died, having been mysteriously pre-warned by NOAA and the USGS who had uncannily predicted the likelihood of a small tidal wave in the immediate future. Elsewhere, the wave would strike limply, causing no real damage. It simply spread out, distributing its energy uniformly, bouncing and rebounding off of coastlines and seamounts, passing back through the ocean over and over, becoming less and less pronounced, until its presence was indistinguishable from the normal ebb and flow of the seas.

High above, and becoming higher still, the *Sword of Liberty* pierced the atmosphere and left the confines of the Earth. The blue skies of the western hemisphere faded to black, and the roar of air molecules rushing by the hull faded away, leaving the ship to pass on in silence. The drive effect made no real sound when it was not burning air or water to plasma. However, if it could have been possible, an observer pressed against the hull might still have heard one thing—a singular voice crying out into the darkness.

"*Yeeeeeeee Haaaaaaaaaaa!!!*"

Lying on his acceleration couch in the bridge/control room of the *Sword of Liberty*, Colonel Calvin Henson, USAF, NASA, winced and keyed his microphone. "Ms. Muñoz, can you please refrain from doing that?"

Her emphatic cry cut off in mid-*Haaaa* and she cleared her throat. Kris smiled despite the two gravities of acceleration pushing her down in her own couch in Engineering and answered in her most demure and respectful tone. "I'm sorry, Colonel, I really don't think I can. If I only get one ride on this tub, I plan to make the most of it. Now then, *Wooooooooo Hooo—*"

Her voice vanished as the new Commanding Officer of the United States' first space destroyer cut off the intercom circuit to Engineering. He muttered to himself and tried to keep up with the massive streams of data inundating him from his displays and automated status boards. Nathan risked turning his head to look at the frustrated veteran astronaut seated next to him and tried not to smile too broadly.

Henson made some adjustments to the data he frantically monitored on his personal screen, and mirrored on the main screen. He keyed into the now silent command circuit again. "Pilot—I mean XO, standby to cut thrust.

Stable orbit in five, four, three, two, one, and shutdown."

Before the Executive Officer, Commander Daniel Torrance, USN, could touch the control to cut off the drive, the computer did it for him, having completed its programmed launch flawlessly. All sense of weight disappeared and the XO jumped slightly as he began to feel like he was falling. The former submariner stayed his hand from the superfluous shutoff command and keyed into the command circuit instead. "Captain," he said, feeling unnatural addressing a non-Navy officer as such, "shutdown completed on schedule, stable orbit ... achieved." As he finished, another unnatural feeling began to overwhelm him.

Henson recognized the XO's hesitation for what it was and keyed into the general announcing circuit, overriding all of the other comms circuits. "All personnel, this is your CO. We have reached orbit and are en route to rendezvous with the International Space Station. We're finished with the scary, exciting part, so all we have to look forward to at the moment is the hard part, the actual work of space. There's a lot to be tested and verified before we move on to the tactical phase, so I urge you to focus on your task list and try not to spend all your time doing somersaults and bouncing off the bulkheads.

"Now, for many of you, this is your first time in microgravity, so this sensation of weightlessness might be new to you. I caution you: don't try to tough it out! If you feel the need, use the osmotic meds you're carrying. It happens to a lot of us and it's no reflection upon you if you need them. You can't do your job if you're getting sick everywhere. All right, all stations report in and commence space-worthiness checks per your checklists."

Nathan released his harness and gave himself a short push, floating off the couch and into thin air. Despite the changes that had occurred, the setbacks they had all endured, and despite Gordon not being there, they had made it.

He looked around at the semicircle of acceleration couches and maneuvering coffins mounted to the deck, one for each bridge watchstander. The couches were each coupled with a set of flat touch screens and a communications panel, from which most operations of the ship could be controlled. Larger displays covered the padded, cable-strewn bulkheads, lighting up the bright white and navy blue bridge with information, while speakers and ducting crowded the overhead, setting up a background buzz of voices and noise that defined a ship underway.

Nathan grinned wide and foolishly as he tried to take it all in at once, unable and unwilling to put up a stoic front. He was here, in space, weightless, aboard his own ship. It almost made up for not being in command any longer. His was a jumble of emotions: excitement, anger, joy, nervousness, and even a touch of guilt.

The new commanding officer looked at him, bemused. "And how do you find it, Mr. Kelley?"

He turned to Henson. "Captain, Superfluous Civilian Consultant reporting in with nothing to do, sir!"

Colonel Henson frowned for a moment, considering, then pushed off of his own couch, directly at Nathan. He touched, grabbed hold of Nathan, and carried them over to a corner of the bridge, stopping them both much more adroitly than Nathan would have ever managed alone. Nathan briefly envied his experience, but Henson cut off his thoughts with a sharp whisper.

"Mr. Kelley, I need to know now if the two of you are going to continue to be willfully difficult for the rest of these space trials. If you are, I may be forced to have you confined to quarters until we can use the SSTOS to take you back down. Is that what you want?"

Nathan stared at the officer's eyes, trying to gauge whether he was serious or not. What he saw failed to comfort him. "No, it's not what I want."

"Good. I don't want that either, but I will do whatever is necessary to make these trials a success. Our launch is going to cause enough problems down on Earth, that I don't need another set up here. Understand?"

"Yes, sir."

Henson smiled tightly, forcing himself to be somewhat more pleasant. "I really thought we had gotten past our ... circumstances, Nathan. You and Kris have been nothing but helpful this past week, giving us a crash course on the *Sword of Liberty*."

Nathan nodded. "We both want you guys to be successful. It's in everyone's best interests. I guess it's just a little different being up here and knowing we're not going all the way. But, that's not your fault and we shouldn't be taking it out on you."

He blew out a long, slow breath. "All right, we'll be good. I'll have a word with Kris and we'll stop pushing your buttons."

"Thank you. Because while your instruction on the ground was excellent, I'll admit that most of us are still too new to not be nervous pushing this bird's buttons. We're glad to have you along."

The military skeleton crew and their two civilian consultants went to work, verifying the *Sword of Liberty* was safe and ready to continue with her trials. Coverall adorned crew flitted about the ship through bright white passageways festooned with handholds, cables, ducts and padding. The decks of the ship were all aligned perpendicular to the centerline running from bow to stern, set up for either weightless operations or for the pseudogravity that existed when the ship was under a standard one g of thrust, turning "forward" to "up" and aft to "down".

Kris darted around the corridors and access trunks like a fairy on too much caffeine, excitedly checking every internal seam and pressure boundary, each accessible valve and indicator, ensuring her ship was safe and ready for the stars. A trail of Navy and Air Force engineers, both astronauts and non, struggled to keep up, taking notes on everything she touched. After verifying no air was leaking out and that everything had survived the launch intact, they proceeded to reconfigure the ship for actual operation.

The aeroshells were jettisoned, revealing nests of antennas, cameras, and sensors which would connect the destroyer with the universe around her. Larger shells came free from the amidships third of the 800 foot long spacecraft, exposing her immense, fragile, chevron radiators and their support struts, lying between the mission hull and the reactor/drive section.

The *Sword of Liberty* shortly matched orbits with the International Space Station, coming to rest 100 meters from the nearly forty year old, cobbled-together monstrosity. They were a study in contrasts.

Where the ISS was a spindly, boxy structure of scaffolding and connectors, mismatched tubes and capsules, discarded experiments and obsolete solar panels, the destroyer was defined by its solidity and functional lethality. Her forward third was a stealthy collection of oblique angles, clean lines, and sharp boundaries: a plated, irregular, hexagonal wedge bristling with antennas and laser emplacements. Lines of missile hatches covered the wide faces of the long wedge, while a pair of active phased array radar domes stood out from the two narrow faces.

On one narrow side, designated the "dorsal" side even though such things were completely arbitrary in absence of a consistent gravity, an armored, retractable panel covered the ship's Single Stage To Orbit Shuttle, or SSTOS. Essentially a miniature version of the ship itself, it could carry the entire crew complement to and from the surface without worrying about stages, boosters, or refueling. Opposite it on the ventral side, a similar set of roll away panels covered a pair of pods for use in space, as either lifeboats, repair vessels, or inter-orbit transports.

Amidships was dominated by the radiating panels, large, reddish, reflective squares arranged in a series of chevrons along the long axis of the ship, each set of panels perpendicular to the next set. These panels all glowed dully, giving away to space whatever waste heat the pebble bed reactor, environmental systems, and weapons produced.

Since there was potentially a lot of heat to dump, heat that could and would give away the vessel's presence, the panels had been vastly overbuilt. A pair of the sets was sufficient to handle most normal heat loads while the others could be shut down. Was the crew to only use the ones facing away from the threat axis, they would be able to approach much closer before their residual infrared signature gave them away. In cold, empty space, thermal stealth was nearly impossible to achieve, but this design would make the best of a bad situation, reducing their detection range from interplanetary scales to merely planetary ones.

The aft section consisted of the pebble bed reactor and the photonic reaction drive—a gigantic reflective "nozzle" capable of emitting and focusing the thrust of their enhanced photon drive, as well as a number of smaller nozzles for station-keeping and maneuvering. Though more refined and many times the size of the experimental setup Kristene had developed at the University of Texas at Arlington, it was nonetheless almost identical in operation. Of course, this one, they all hoped, would not explode like her original had.

Aiding in the maneuvering of the destroyer, the main drive was duplicated in miniature upon four triangular pylons on the forward hull, aft of the banks of missile cells. These pylons each supported a trio of photonic emitter nozzles facing in opposing directions, a reaction control thruster system with each emitter more powerful than a shuttle's main engine. Used in concert with the main drive emitter and the similarly-sized aft nozzles, these photonic thrusters could maneuver the ship at high g-levels more nimbly than an air-bound fighter jet. They could, in fact, maneuver the destroyer at rates far in excess of what its soft tissue crew could physically withstand.

The crew of the ISS took all this in over the next couple of hours, gawking unceasingly through the habitat windows while the destroyer crew completed their readiness checks. The *Sword of Liberty* had made this stop-off in case the destroyer should prove unsafe to continue on with its tests. In that case, the ISS would have acted as a last ditch refuge of sorts. However, with his new ship performing flawlessly, Colonel Henson had another duty to perform.

With the bridge cameras rolling and transmitting, Henson and the others floated back to their seats around the ship, strapping in for maneuvers. The colonel sat up and addressed the camera directly, "Crew of the ISS, peoples of Earth, this is the United States Ship *Sword of Liberty*, designated DA-1, the first step in our journey to the stars, ready to face whatever may come with honor and courage, in defense and support of our planet, but against no man or terrestrial power.

"This ship represents a promise to all nations that we will go forward together, in unity and fellowship, to a new age, a golden age where we are no longer fighting over the limited bounty of Earth, but are instead working in harmony to discover the universe for the benefit of all mankind. We stand atop the achievements of those who have come before us: the trailblazers, the pioneers, the voyagers, those who have given their lives for the advancement of all. And in the spirit of their past accomplishments, we go … forward."

At his last word, the destroyer's main drive fired and the ship accelerated effortlessly away from the ISS at a single gravity of continuous thrust. The new guard had saluted the old. The torch had been passed.

Commander Torrance, the XO, jumped up again and fell solidly back down to the deck. He smiled at Henson and Nathan. "This beats the shit out of that freefall stuff, sir. You astro-nuts might like it, but I'll take the pull of terra firma any day, thank you very much."

The destroyer had been underway for hours now, toward its planned tactical operating area, and the trials had gone flawlessly. They had gone so well, in fact, that they were all waiting for some setback, for Murphy to make his presence known. But the other shoe had thus far refused to drop. Both in orbit and underway, they had tested every system, cycled each valve and every switch, with nothing but a few minor faults that had no real effect.

Henson shrugged at his XO's teasing, but said nothing. Nathan smiled and clapped the XO on the shoulder, saying, "I'm with you, but don't forget, there's no terra firma here to pull you down. We have pseudo-gravity only while the drive is firing at a continuous one g. It cuts out or we maneuver, and you may find yourself in an uncomfortable position."

Henson clicked off his display and stood, stretching loudly. He enjoyed the comfort of gravity himself, not that he would ever admit it to his non-astronaut Exec. "That's right, Dan. Stow for space, just like you stowed for battle. Move around and secure things as if gravity could turn upside down or at right angles without notice. It's a pain in the ass … but you lonely squids should be used to pains back there."

"Ha-ha. Homophobia, the last bastion of insults for the intellectually disarmed. Don't make me pull out my bag of Air Farce-isms, sir. Between me and my former Navy compatriot here, we could reduce your mother-service to shreds within seconds."

Henson held up his hands. "Ach! Truce, truce. Besides, we're part of a whole new service now—the Aerospace Force. The terrestrial forces will have to come up with all new insults for us, and I expect you to have my back, XO."

Torrance looked as if he was considering it. "Call it the Aerospace Navy and you've got yourself a deal."

Nathan figured that was a good trade-off, but he said nothing. There was so much different about their new ship, it would take a lot of getting used to. Neither the astronauts nor the regular officers had any particular advantage, either. And of all things, simply getting around took perhaps the most getting used to.

With the thrust on standard, forward and aft were tricky concepts. On a wet-Navy ship, those terms meant "toward the bow" and "toward the stern" respectively, but here the planet-side definitions were at odds with common sense. Instead, toward the bow was "up" and the stern was "down", essentially turning the angular wedge of the destroyer into a tall, regal tower, thrusting upwards through the heavens.

For ease of reference in varying thrust conditions, forward and aft kept their naval designations, even though they also meant up and down with the main drive running. Continuing with that convention then, the other ship coordinates worked themselves out: ventral was to the narrow side with the work pods, which had faced down when the ship was constructed laying over on Earth. Dorsal lay opposite this, along the narrow side with the STOSS hangar, which had faced up during construction. Port was to the left when facing ventral or forward, and starboard was to the right. These designations were firm as well, no matter if they were in microgravity or accelerating along some non-standard vector. Re-orienting their coordinate system to apparent gravity would not only have been maddening, it would have made meaningful communication impossible.

Nathan sat and checked their progress on his screens. Earth had been left behind, becoming just a small circle no larger than a dime held at arm's length. But they were not alone in all that vast emptiness. Grown into visible range before them was another body—a small, seemingly insignificant mountain of iron compounds and silicates, which had the unfortunate distinction of being their target.

To prevent a sudden, limited pass-by past their rocky objective, the *Sword of Liberty* had flipped around to thrust into the opposite direction once they were halfway to the Near Earth Asteroid, 2006 UA22. And aside from a slight wobble in their apparent gravity at turnaround, thrust and acceleration as well as the direction of up and down remained constant. They quickly matched orbits with the target, the pair of them pretty much alone in space.

Nathan split his attention between the bright marble of Earth and the gray-brown pitted ovoid of the asteroid. He shook his head to no one in particular, and wondered which of the two bodies were going to be hit harder by what they were about to do.

Kristene popped through the doorway, excitement and anticipation evident on her face. "Are we there yet? I'm anxious to blow something up."

The CO and XO both laughed and Nathan grinned and stood. She sidled up to him and he kissed her, with only a twinge of self-consciousness at the critical looks Henson and Torrance gave him. Nathan responded, "Patience, patience. We're farther out than anyone has ever been, in just a couple of hours no less, and it's still not fast enough for you."

Torrance checked his display and nodded. "The young'uns these days. As a matter of fact, we are approaching range of the target, and have reached the planned crossing velocity. Recommend cutting thrust and proceeding with the tactical trial."

"Very well. Cut thrust and line us up on the asteroid. All personnel to Battle Stations Alpha," Henson commanded.

Nathan sat and made the necessary selections. From speakers all around the ship, a cool feminine voice announced, "General Quarters, General Quarters. Now set General Quarters, Alpha Stations. The ship may engage in high g maneuvers without warning. All personnel will move in an orderly fashion to their General Quarters stations. All personnel will secure for maneuvers and minimize all internal transit unless specifically authorized by the Commanding Officer."

Suddenly, all trace of weight vanished as the drive cut off and they were again in microgravity. Most of the skeleton crew of fifteen officers aboard were in position, but more than a couple overcompensated for the return to freefall and launched themselves into the overhead with painful results. Those few winced and proceeded to their designated acceleration couches, to monitor and control the weapons tests from there.

Alpha Stations allowed them to work from their usual consoles and seats without suiting up, while Bravo Stations forced them to work from within protective vacuum suits, just in case the ship took damage and lost air integrity. The final condition, Charlie Stations, required them to don vacuum gear as well as relocate to the "pods" or "coffins", special one-person chambers capable of being pressurized with a force-dampening gel which would enable them to withstand higher g-loads than they normally could endure.

Nathan glanced over to Kris, where she had strapped into a spare couch between the XO and the Weapons Officer. He locked gazes with her and gave her a significant look. "We all ready, Kris?"

She smiled. "Born ready, Mr. Kelley, sir! Let's launch us some nukes and shoot us some guns."

Henson glanced from one of them to the other. "Ms. Muñoz, if you would, please monitor the Weapons Officer and assist LCDR Gutierrez with the launch. This will be the first time any of us have fired these missiles and we would prefer not to have a set of six fusion warheads go astray. XO, please monitor Mr. Kelley in the use of the railgun and the laser emplacements. Computer, main screen, enhanced targeting view, go."

The large flat screen that took up half of the ventral portion of the bridge switched from an overview of environmental, ship, crew, and sensor data to a false-color display showing the highlighted asteroid on a field of black. Vectors and outlines shifted continuously over the rock's surface as radar and lidar picked out surface features and the computers made automated threat evaluations.

This particular nameless asteroid had been chosen for one reason only, and a cynical, informed observer could not help but notice that the planetoid's shape and size bore a striking similarity to that of the Deltan control ship. Nathan had suggested the target and Henson and Torrance had been happy to agree with it. None of them would admit to having pre-conceived notions of the aliens' intentions, but neither would they object to being prudent.

LCDR Rudy Gutierrez made some selections on his screen to which Kris nodded. Elsewhere on the ship, in CIC just dorsal of them and in the missile deck monitoring station several levels above, his selections were taken as commands to the officers working there, who carried them out and acknowledged them almost automatically. Gutierrez turned to the CO. "Captain, all weapons stations report ready. Track 0017 targeted at range 674.3 km, bearing 340 by 075 relative off the port dorsal bow, bearing and closure rates negligible. Asteroid target and ownship at zero thrust. One missile, portside dorsal cell 12, selected for launch. Weapon, drive, and tube capacitors are charged, and ripple warhead pattern selected. Ready for nuclear weapons release on your authority, sir."

Colonel Henson looked over at Nathan. "Mr. Kelley, assure me there's no chance I'm going to end up raining meteors down on Earth should this test be successful."

Nathan frowned and double-checked the missile vector and their relative positions of the Earth and 2006 UA22. Eventually he shrugged. "There's no way I can give you a hundred percent certainty, but the missile is detonating on a line between the asteroid and the planet. Any debris we get should be aimed away from that vector. I can't say nothing will ever change orbits and fall to Earth, but the chances against it are … astronomical, I guess you could say."

Henson narrowed his eyes and turned to the Weapons Officer. "Batteries released. Shoot one."

Gutierrez stabbed down harder than necessary on his touchscreen and was rewarded with a quick thump-THUMP and a slight shake of the whole ship. Outside, on the forward port dorsal face of the hull's wedge, one of the square missile hatches flipped open. Powerful coils surrounding the missile tube then flexed with magnetic force, expelling the missile from the tube with sudden, violent efficiency. It shot out from the ship at a constant speed and the hatch closed behind it softly.

Fifty meters from the ship, the missile's sacrificial capacitor bank began to break down, converting its blend of electrolytes, activated carbon cells, and dielectrics into a froth of free electrons. This explosive cascade of electric charge funneled down through platinum waveguides into Kris' photonic drive and the small missile erupted into brilliant life.

Gutierrez nodded as a new track appeared on their screens. "Missile ignition. Accelerating to target at 300 meters per second squared. Fifty seconds to warhead separation, 67 seconds to contact."

The missile flew out, quickly closing with its quarry. For twenty seconds, it flew straight as an arrow, but then it began to jerk erratically about, tracing an uneven corkscrew through space. Strobes of light and flares of invisible radiance exploded from it for seemingly no reason.

"Electronic countermeasures and terminal defensive maneuvering engaged—no faults."

Henson nodded at Gutierrez, his eyes remaining riveted upon the screen. "Good. Of course, there's no proof they'll be effective in the least."

Nathan shrugged, but kept looking at the main screen as well. "Can't hurt to be prepared. It's impossible to hide the drive effect on something that small, so we had to give it some sort of defense or it might never reach the target. Besides, *Promise*'s telemetry showed its maneuvers were somewhat effective at avoiding that alien disintegration beam, and it was both bigger and slower than our missiles. Have faith."

At fifty seconds, several large lobes of the missile broke free, their own smaller drives igniting in turn. The corkscrew blossomed second after second into a small squadron of six arcing points of light.

Gutierrez's voice was almost a whisper in anticipation. "Warhead separation. Ripple fire in three, two, one . . . ." They all held their breaths.

With the warheads now widely spaced from one another, the first detonated, 100 kilometers from the asteroid. A secondary bank of sacrificial capacitors dissolved into plasma, driving a spherical, inward-looking photonic mesh and an outer coil of superconducting wire. The resulting implosion compressed a solid core of lithium deuteride into a plasma as dense as the core of a star, forcing it to fuse. This plasma rebounded and exploded outward with nearly a megaton's worth of pure energy, but was largely wasted, detonating much too far out from the target.

Yet it was not a complete waste. Even as the components of the missile were vaporized, they were put to work. A small pinch of electromagnetic energy from the secondary coil forced the protons and electrons of the newly generated helium plasma into a brief, rigid order. Photons clumped and streamed down these channels of subatomic particles and the fusion blast became something more. Nearly ten percent of its explosive energy was suddenly converted to coherent x-ray laser light, orders of magnitude stronger than the ship's primary lasers.

The beam speared invisibly past the other five warheads and stabbed into the asteroid, blasting and vaporizing a chasm into its surface. Seconds later, at fifty kilometers out, a second warhead exploded in laser mode, sending another lance of heat and light piercing into the same spot. Then a third warhead lased, burning their target shaft still deeper.

On the bridge, the crew sat in slack-jawed awe, staring at the strobes of light puncturing the enormous mountain of nickel, iron, and silicates.

The fourth warhead detonated in proximity mode, eschewing the lasing coil for the brute heat of a close-by thermonuclear explosion. Though there was little concussive force to the blast outside of an atmosphere, its radiance a mere kilometer out was powerful enough to vaporize and melt away a significant portion of the narrow laser wound's entrance. This wider shaft allowed the next two warheads to fly deep into the rock itself.

The fifth and sixth warheads crashed through the softened minerals of the twenty kilometer diameter asteroid's interior and detonated in rapid succession, the first on contact with the inner surface of the wound, the second moments after burying itself into a few tens of meters of lava. These blasts were largely hidden from the crew, blocked and absorbed by the bulk of the rock itself, but their effect was immediately apparent.

2006 UA22 shattered, exploding outward in an oblate shockwave of fire and pulverized, glowing debris. Five pairs of hands shot up in the air on the *Sword of Liberty*'s bridge, the two civilians and the military crew all shouting in triumph together. They laughed and yelled, matched over the intercom by the twelve other officers and enlisted crew, all of whom had been watching the weapon test.

Torrance gripped Nathan's arm, shaking him and grinning. "Good lord, Kelley! You all certainly can kill some rocks!"

Henson shook his head in dismay. "We just vaporized Mt. Everest."

Gutierrez turned away from the main screen and looked at Kristene, his sense of astonishment shifting from the vanished asteroid to the designer of the Hell-weapon he had just fired. "Ma'am, may I tell you something? I'm sorry if I offend, but you are one *scary* person."

Kris did not look offended. If anything, she preened. "Why thank you, Rudy. That's very sweet."

Henson and Nathan both shook their heads at that, then Nathan zoomed the display out from former site of the asteroid. Chunks of debris, from the size of office blocks and houses down to pebbles and sand crowded the screen with individual tracks and vectors, each streaming away from the annihilation. Nathan pointed and motioned for the CO's attention. "Sir, please note there are no debris tracks on a direct course for Earth."

"Thank you, Nathan. Now, how about debris on a direct course for us?"

Nathan smiled and made several selections on his touch screen. "Of those we have an abundance. Standing by for phase two of our tactical trial."

Henson nodded. "Very well. Batteries release. The helm is yours."

"Aye aye, sir." Nathan made a few final selections on his screen under the watchful eye of CDR Torrance. Graphics crowded in on his tactical display, showing power and temperature states for all six laser emplacements, as well as power, temp, and ammunition magazine states for the forward railgun. Everything showed up in the green.

Nathan gestured to the main screen before them all, drawing the attention of the CO, XO, and Weps. Kris stayed focused on her own panel, working at a furious pace, sweat glistening upon her upper lip and brow. Nathan highlighted several hurtling meteors. "We'll focus on the largest rocks on a direct collision course first, then we'll work our way out. I'll be firing a number of different munitions from the railgun, from explosive, to unitary kinetic, to flechette, and we'll just see which ones work best where. Now, since the gun is too big for a stable turret, it only has an aim swing from its cradle of 10 degrees to centerline. Anything outside of that arc will require maneuvering of the ship, but we can slave the helm to the gun target line with just the push of a button. Like this."

Nathan reached out and made another selection. The ship's bland feminine voice then sounded from every speaker. "All hands, brace for maneuvers. Acceleration may change without further warning while engaged in gunfire evolutions."

"From this point, aiming and fire is automatic," Nathan said. "There's no way an operator could ever effectively aim these shots over the ranges we're talking, so whoever you assign to gunnery will only have to manually select targets and monitor performance, or else he can program in his own target selection doctrine and let the computer do everything."

Torrance grunted. "If it works anything like Navy weapons doctrine, we'll be shooting at every Gemini urine bag and discarded Russian satellite the radar can track."

Nathan grinned and nodded. "Well, I never said it was perfect. I'm still a big believer in man-in-the-loop, myself. So, now that I've manually designated all my targets, I back it up with auto laser handoff. Any chunks or secondary debris that makes it past the gunfire will then get targeted by the lasers to be burned away."

Kris looked up from her preps. "And that's it. Easy, squeezee: your basic cone of impenetrable destruction. These rocks won't know what hit 'em, and neither will the Deltans. We're ready on my end, babe."

"Thanks, Kris. Firing … now." Nathan caught Colonel Henson's gaze and firmly pressed the blinking icon on his own panel. The screen chimed and the ship immediately shook. Then again, and again, and again, once every two seconds, as the railgun fired its way through the target list. A distant thumping ring sounded with every bump, transmitted through the hull by the violent electromagnetic pressures building and releasing up in the bow.

Outside the ship, white light flashed with every round, a soundless bolt of lightning and plasma jetting forth on the heels of each shot. Over time, the plasma boiling away from the twin rails of the railgun would begin to degrade their surface treatments, preventing the shell armatures from firing effectively, but that moment was thousands of shots away. For now, the system worked flawlessly, sending blinding shot after blinding shot straight out into the void, directly down the gun line.

Having serviced the targets inside its firing cutouts already, the railgun began to guide the ship to new targets. The *Sword of Liberty* started to jerk erratically, dodging from vector to vector to bring its massive gun to bear, her pylon thrusters firing at seemingly random intervals.

Kris started to feel queasy.

Downrange, the massive tons of meteors met the irresistible forces of the railgun rounds. Unitary rounds—slender sabots of hardened tungsten alloy—struck the largest boulders, converting their enormous kinetic energy into heat, light, and shattering force. The meteors cracked up into hundreds of smaller pieces, and each one was tracked in turn and added to the firing queue.

Flechette rounds deposited their momentum and kinetic energy in a different way, breaking up into a cloud of diamond hard slivers before striking their medium size targets. The dozens of smaller sabots worked in concert to pulverize these rocks into dust and pebbles, sizes which could be more reasonably handled by the ship's point defense and armor.

The smallest targets—man-sized chunks of rock and tight formations of rock and debris—received the attention of the explosive rounds. These larger railgun shots were directional blast fragmentary rounds, cylinders of scored steel plate sandwiched with sheets of octaazacubane (N8) explosive. Striking and detonating with the combined kinetic energy and explosive force of thousand pound bombs, their targets were obliterated and dispersed into relatively harmless detritus.

Aboard the ship, the crew watched as the darkened storm of incoming meteors blossomed into clouds of light and gas, coloring the infinite black with violently hued destruction. Henson shook his head. It was impressive, even graceful, but he shuddered to think about what would happen if such a weapon was turned upon something more significant than asteroidal debris. From its high perch in orbit, the *Sword of Liberty* could potentially devastate any city with impunity.

In its own way, it was even more terrifying than the sudden apocalypse of the nuclear warheads. That mind-boggling terror had been over in a literal flash. This was enduring, relentless, chewing away at chunks of solar history like some voracious colony of insects.

He looked over at Nathan. The former sailor was a decorated veteran, a hero and a patriot, but Secretary Sykes had warned him that he was also driven by an almost religious need for the ship to be a success. Such an intimately profound sense of motivation could easily turn and twist into something darker. Nathan Kelley had been nothing but helpful to the new crew, but he was also bitterly disappointed in the current state of affairs.

Henson suddenly realized how glad he was that this would be the first and last time Nathan would be handling the ship.

He cleared his throat and said to Nathan, "Well it certainly looks impressive. How is it working?"

Nathan shrugged. "It's working pretty much as planned, breaking up and dispersing all the incoming, but the debris front is still moving toward us. We'll have to see how we weather the storm."

Kelley spoke up. "Targets reaching point defense boundary at 150 km. Lasers are cycling to auto."

Henson nodded. "Very well."

While the ship continued to jerk and swing, and the railgun continued to thump and fire away, the diode laser banks on each of the six emplacements began to track and fire. There was little sound from these weapons, only the repeated snap and hum of continuously charging and discharging capacitors. The railgun power supply made similar sounds, but that was lost next to the awesome crack of a shot ablating down the rails.

Invisible beams sought out chunks of rock, starting with the nearest and the largest inbound threats and working out from there. Though the beams were not apparent, their effect was unmistakable, as hurtling meteors flared bright, turned to vapor and slag by the energy of the beams. Where a meteor was too large to be burned away completely, the section of it that was burning would outgas, pushing the chunk onto a new vector away from the ship.

It was a success. All the weapons worked. What had begun as a mountain floating in space, an ancient leftover from the birth of the solar system billions of years before, was now a continuously expanding sphere of rocks and meteors—and one side of that expansion had been further reduced, pummeled and vaporized into harmless pebbles and dust. Nathan sat back and smiled, letting the system wrap things up for him.

Flawless, he thought.

Kris's voice cried out suddenly, strident and fearful. "Leaker! I've got a track on a collision course, no weapons pairing!"

They all looked at her and then at the main screen. Highlighted on it was a single track: a two meter wide, irregular mass of iron streaked through the gunnery sector without an engagement and broached the self-defense line without a laser reacting to it. It stayed on a constant bearing, its range ticking quickly down on a collision course with the ship.

The system failed to react and there was no time to engage it manually. Nathan's eyes widened and he shot out a hand, striking a control on the emergency panel between his and the XO's seats.

The strident beep of a collision alarm sounded. At the same time, the ship's voice cried out, "Brace for shock!"

The destroyer lurched to one side, jerking them badly in their seats. The lights flickered, then died, returning a moment later on half-lit battery backups. Static washed over their control screens and the gun and laser emplacements were silent.

They all set dazed for a moment, until Colonel Henson shook his head and looked at the four others. "What the hell was that? All right, SITREP. Find out what's up, what's down, and where we are in terms of that blast front. XO, get comms re-established and get us a head count."

Nathan, Torrance, and Gutierrez each responded simultaneously with, "Aye aye, sir." Kris answered numbly with a slow nod of her head.

The static cleared from their screens as the system reset itself. A few moments and keystrokes later, they had Henson's answers. Weps spoke up first. "Sir, the railgun shows 136 rounds expended, bore clear, no apparent casualties. All lasers have green boards. I have charged capacitor banks on all weapons, but the detection and tracking systems are down due to loss of power. Radar and lidar are down for the same reason. The system is dead reckoning all tracks in from their last good radar sweep and we should be okay. All major, potentially damaging rocks were destroyed, and the blast front is approximately two minutes out. We may get peppered, but unless there's another pop-up leaker, we should be all right."

Henson nodded. "Very well. Engineering?"

Nathan answered. "Power is down, obviously. Engines are down and the reactor is scrammed. Helium coolant pressure is zero. Reactor room air pressure is zero. I've got hull damage alarms and radiation hazard alarms for the whole of Engineering, and all the safety airlocks for that section are in lockdown. My guess is the leaker penetrated us right over the portside radiator, and breached the reactor vessel. I'll have to suit up to confirm it, but it's probably a hard vacuum back there, with clad plutonium pebbles spilled out all over the place."

Henson nodded and looked at the XO. Torrance responded, "We got lucky. If we had a full complement, we would have lost at least two or three people, but no one was in the locked down area. I've got reports of some bruises and a whiplash or two, but everyone's still alive and functional, Colonel."

The CO relaxed slightly and rubbed his own aching neck. "Lucky. And astronomically unlucky as well. Mr. Kelley, this is an inauspicious beginning for your space fleet, don't you think?"

"It's disconcerting, sir, but I don't think it invalidates what we're trying to do."

Henson's lip turned up on the threshold of a grim smile. "It doesn't? We were just taken out of the game by an inanimate hunk of iron. Our hull is open to space and we're practically in the dark here. We could have lost men's lives. How do you think we'll fare against your technologically advanced aliens?"

Nathan held up his hands in protest. He was about to speak, but a sudden patter of dinks and bangs sounding from the hull gave him pause. They all listened to the meteor storm front sweep by them, worried and almost convinced that there would be another collision and another breach.

Their earlier weapons fire had been effective, however. All that struck them was sand and pebbles, moving at a slow enough relative speed that the destroyer's chromatic armor plate could successfully shrug it off.

The noise faded after a few moments. Nathan lowered his hands and sighed in relief. "Colonel, this is a glitch, a bug, Murphy's Law. Nothing more. I don't know why that meteor was able to sneak through our defenses, but it does not invalidate what the rest of the trial showed. We investigate this, we make repairs, and we try it again. And then you fine gentlemen go make the Deltans wish they had never heard of Earth."

Henson and Torrance exchanged a look and a nod. Henson turned back to Nathan. "Fine. Now, what about repairs? Can we get the power and engines back online?"

Nathan and Kris looked at one another, and she shook her head. He motioned for her to go ahead. She flushed and stammered slightly. "C— Commander, Colonel, we, uh, we can't fix this here. Assuming the only thing that was damaged was the reactor itself, and that's a big, bad assumption, we can go EVA and slap a patch on the hull and the reactor vessel. We can clear away the rad hazard and maybe re-pressurize with helium, but there's no way to tell if the reactor safeties will even allow us to bring it back online, and we're going to soak up a lot of REMs while we're making the attempt. Also, if we can't get it done in six hours, which we can't, the air is gonna get awfully stale."

Nathan nodded. "Our only real option is to abandon the ship in the SSTOS and come back with a proper engineering team. It'll take about three cramped, uncomfortable days to make the trip home. Then a few days to gather personnel and materials, another three to return, a week or two for repairs, and then ... ? Figure on the better part of a month before we can get the *Sword* underway again and back to Earth orbit."

Henson punched his seat's armrest in frustration. "Shit. There's no other way?"

Nathan shook his head. "Not with the resources we have out with us at the moment. I'm sorry, sir. This trial is over. You have to focus on getting your crew home now."

"I know that." His tone was sharp, but he relented a second later. "It's just ... I had a lot riding on this mission as well, you know? Fine. Mr. Kelley, you're sure the shuttle has the range to get us all home safely?"

"Absolutely, sir. That was one of the safety constraints for the mission. It won't be that pleasant, but the SSTOS has the delta-v and the resources to get us all back to Earth safely."

"Very well." Henson slumped slightly in his seat, in so much as one could slump in microgravity. "Issue the order, XO. Abandon ship."

Torrance nodded and reached down to the comm panel. As he began to speak to the rest of the ship, relaying what has happened and what they had to do now, Nathan and Gutierrez worked in concert to shut down and safely power off all the charged weapons systems, using what computer control they still had while the various battery backups were still active.

Kris unstrapped from her seat and floated up, her face stricken. "I'll go pre-flight the SSTOS," she said softly. The CO simply nodded, staring at the bulkhead. As she passed by Nathan, she reached out a hand and squeezed his shoulder.

He reached up to catch her fingers and drew them to his lips. He kissed the back of her hand without any of his earlier self-consciousness. "It'll be all right, babe. This is just a setback, but we'll work our way past it. Okay?"

She attempted a smile, but failed to pull it off. Kris nodded, her eyes limned with tears that could not fall, and then turned in mid-air and dove out of the room. Nathan went back to his work, refusing to notice the other three men watching him.

Around the darkened, quiet ship, personnel began to make their way from their stations toward the dorsal interior of the destroyer and the large shuttle hangar there. They pushed their luggage before them or dragged it haltingly behind, struggling with their massive packs now that inertia had been divorced from the aid of either gravity or pseudogravity.

Inside the hangar, the line of Navy and Air Force officers and crewmen drifted into the sleek, gray, single-stage-to-orbit-shuttle. A slender, lifting-body design, it had been adapted from NASA's somewhat successful sub-orbital spaceplane. All that differed was the power plant, replacing the turbo scramjet/chemical rocket hybrids with a small thermoelectric fission reactor and a photonic reaction drive.

While the skeleton crew stowed their gear and went back for several days' worth of rations, the adapted shuttle came to life, its ventilation fans, pumps, and motors providing welcome white noise to the crew. It was not acknowledged among the uninitiated, but sailors of all stripes secretly feared the silence.

At sea, at sail, silence meant a dead calm, awaiting a slow death while lingering in the doldrums. In later generations, silence meant the end of engines and power, forcing the tin cans and iron men of 20th and 21st century navies to negotiate with the capricious elements, at the mercy of forces they had long since conquered.

Aboard the *Sword of Liberty*, the silencing of technology's pervasive noise meant they were stranded on the furthest, most isolated, most inhospitable reef man had ever ventured toward. Out here, there was nothing that would not kill them, from the implacable vacuum to the impenetrable cold of space. Seeing the SSTOS come to life let many of them release bated breaths they had not even realized they had held.

The last to go aboard, Colonel Henson allowed Commander Torrance to precede him into the shuttle. Nathan placed himself just inside the shuttle's hatch, ready to close it and conduct his door check. Henson stood at the threshold, halfway in the destroyer, halfway aboard their forlorn lifeboat. He looked wistfully at the ship. "One month. I'll see you in a month … I promise," he said, his voice a whisper.

He turned and pulled himself into the SSTOS. "XO, is everyone aboard?"

"Yes, sir. LCDR Oneida and Major Keller are in the cockpit, and Ms. Muñoz is back aft, completing the reactor and engine checks." Torrance began putting on his five-point harness, settling in.

Henson pulled himself forward, drifting to his own seat next to the XO. "Very well. Mr. Kelley, if you would get the hatch, plea—"

The hatch, firmly shutting on his request, gave him pause. He turned around, just as everyone else began to crane around in their seats to get a look. Nathan Kelley had indeed shut the hatch to the shuttle.

Except that he was on the outside of it.

A horrible possibility suddenly dawned on the colonel, and he jumped off and flew to the hatch. He tried the auto release, but it would not work. Fumbling with the manual release cover, he opened it to find that the operating mechanism had been removed. The colonel growled in betrayal.

Henson spun around to glare at Torrance. "You said Muñoz was aboard? She's back aft?"

"Yes, sir! I saw her go back there myself."

"Is there another hatch back aft?"

He had his answer when the XO went pale and began fumbling to release his harness. Henson cursed and jetted himself into the cabin and then flew up onto the flight deck. He jerked open the door and stared at the pilot and co-pilot in the cockpit, going over their checklists. "Oneida! Do you have controls? Is your board up?"

The pilot looked confused and turned to his panel. He flipped a few switches, and tapped a few keys, but nothing seemed to happen. "That's funny. It was working a minute ago . . . ."

"Damn it! Get it back online! Do whatever you have to." Henson turned and flew back into the main cabin, just as the XO emerged from his trip into the shuttle's small engineering space.

Torrance looked as if he did not know whether to be sick or to throw a fit. "She's gone and the aft emergency hatch has been disabled."

Henson growled and sought out his Chief Engineer among the assembled, strapped-down crew. "Commander Marcus, did you actually see any of the meteor damage? Any at all?"

The Navy astronaut looked around at his men and then shrugged, embarrassed. "Well, no, sir. The cameras were offline and the doors to that section were sealed for a vacuum and rad hazard. I thought we would at least do an EVA and survey, but the Muñoz woman said there wasn't enough time. We had orders to spend the time shutting down and evacuating."

"Good god, I'm an idiot." Henson ran a hand over his face. Everyone else in the cabin stared at him, unsure of what to do, of what to say.

Pilot Oneida's voice called out from the cockpit. "Colonel! You're going to want to get up here."

Henson re-entered the cockpit and saw Keller manipulating his controls to absolutely no effect. It was easy to see his fruitless efforts because the lighting in the hangar was fully on, no longer on battery backup. A red flashing light strobed over their heads. The two immense, armored hatches that separated them from the vacuum had each begun pulling away, revealing the stark black of empty space. Ship's power was restored and the hangar had already been fully evacuated. In a few moments, he felt sure they would be left stranded in space.

Oneida held out a communications headset to his CO. Henson grabbed it and put it over his head, positioning the microphone in front of his mouth.

He keyed the mike. "Kelley, this ship was never hit, was it?"

Nathan's voice came back instantly. "I'm truly sorry, Colonel. Did I neglect to tell you about the rather robust damage control training simulation program the ship has? I really should put that in the next familiarization course."

"I saw that meteor. I felt it strike the ship."

"No, you saw a meteor test track overlaid on the actual tactical feed. You felt the engines pulse to provide the tactile simulation of a hit. And then the system closed off the appropriate locks and gave the expected alarms for this type of casualty. If we had gotten partial power restored, I could have even shown you video of the damage. But, no, we were never hit."

The SSTOS lurched slightly, and Henson saw them float slowly up, out of the hangar and into the infinite void. "Kelley! What the hell do you think you're doing?"

"I'm doing what I have to do. I'm fulfilling a promise I made to a man who endured the doubts of an entire planet to prepare mankind to defend itself." The SSTOS cleared the hangar doors, revealing the trapezoidal armor plates of the destroyer's forward dorsal hull. It looked stark and unreal out there, all alone, without the enveloping protection of the hangar in which it had been born, without the comforting proximity of the Earth's broad horizon below it.

Nathan's voice came over the headphones again. "Oh, look, Colonel. You seem to have abandoned your perfectly good ship for no reason at all. I'm afraid I'll have to claim her as salvage before some ne'er-do-well absconds with her."

Henson growled in frustration. "You can't steal back your ship, Kelley. It's not only petty, it's treason!"

"I suppose I'll have to rely on the vindication of history."

"You have no crew, no shuttle. And what about the ammo and reactor power you expended thus far? I can guarantee you that you won't be visiting any filling stations between here and the Deltans."

Nathan's voice was vaguely disappointed in response. "Let's try to proceed on the assumption that I'm not a complete idiot, okay? This ship is fully stocked and has enough reactor power and delta-v for four years of continuous operation. As for the ammo and crew, trust me. I won't be going off half-cocked or ill-prepared."

Colonel Calvin Henson screamed with rage. Oneida and Keller stared at him, joined by Commander Torrance who appeared behind the CO to stare agog at the blackness of space surrounding them. Henson gripped the mike, as if to force his words into the instrument and through the ether. "What gives you the right, Nathan? What makes you think you're entitled to first contact? What makes you believe you can do it better than we can?"

There was a long pause. Then, "I suppose it's faith, faith in someone who had faith in me, faith that I've been tried in the crucible once already, and I'm tempered for whatever comes next."

Below them, the *Sword of Liberty* began to pull away, acceleration building quickly to a full g. The wedge of the forward hull moved forward, followed by the dully glowing radiator panels laid out in front of the reactor vessel, and then the brilliant blue thrust of the photonic drive, boiling away with corpuscles of light so intense they seemed to be physical objects in and of themselves.

Nathan's voice called back over the increasingly widening gulf. "Your controls should unfreeze in the next thirty minutes. Then, just follow the recorded flight plan to Earth and reentry. You should be there in about three days. Farewell, Colonel. Don't take this personally, please. I hope to see you in command of the next *Sword* when we get back from our mission. You deserve one of these.

"But this one is mine."

BOOK TWO: "TEMPERED"

12: "ECCENTRIC ORBITS"

"And we're back!"

"Hey, all of you out there on the drive to work, welcome back to Pat—"

"And Terry—"

"In the Morning!!"

"If you missed the first hour—"

"Ya lazy bums."

"Terry! Anyway, if you missed the first hour, we're talking about what everyone seems to be talking about—namely, the unprecedented surprise launch of the *Sword of Liberty* off the coast of California yesterday. Now, I don't care if you're an old-timer and you remember the hey-day of the space shuttle, or maybe Apollo and the moon landing, or hell, perhaps you're ancient and you remember Sputnik, Gagarin, and Shepard, but this is seriously the coolest thing to happen to space in maybe *ever*. I'm totally geekin' out."

"Yes, you are a total geek."

"Terry! Well, *I* think our devoted listener-ship is with me on this one. This thing is *big*. This thing is fast, powerful, and *sexy*. It's the answering call to all the dashed dreams of generations of enthusiasts and starry-eyed hopefuls. This is sci-fi made real! Forget multi-month missions to Mars to pick up rocks. Forget robot probes and halting, tentative steps into space. This is Space with a capital 'S'."

"Yeah, yeah. It's cool, Pat. It makes those fragile little NASA rockets look like bush-league amateurs. But while you're having a geekgasm, think about what this really is: they didn't call it a space-explorer. They don't call it a solar system surveyor. They called it a destroyer. Think about that!"

"What are you trying to say, Terry? Who cares what they call it?"

"I care! And you can bet your sweet wife's fanny that the Chinese and the EU care. Our government, who only has our best interests at heart of course, has just weaponized space to a degree unheard of before now. Hell, I couldn't even count the number of international treaties violated if I used both my fingers *and* toes. Why? C'mon, there's gotta be a reason for all those missiles and lasers. And what's with that little speech Colonel Henson gave? '—ready to face whatever may come … in defense and support of our planet, but against no man or terrestrial power.' If it ain't against no man or earthly power, who the hell is it against?! Is there some non-earthly enemy they haven't let out of the bag yet?"

"Ha! Terry, I'm the Trekkie, but you're the first one to jump on the 'aliens from space' land mine? Listen, there are no little green men on Mars. The balloon people of Jupiter aren't coming to steal your cable or drink your beer. And the grays are just a bunch of society-influenced collective hallucinations by some sad little lonely-heart crazies. The *Sword of Liberty* is up there for the same reason we put up any new combat system—to defend the red, white, and blue against all enemies, foreign and domestic. We put up the first one, and I'm sure we'll find out within the year that it was in response to something the Chinese or the Algerians intended to put up."

"Yeah, Mister The-Flag's-Never-Dirty? What about the Deltans?"

"Conspiracy theories, Terry? Please! That's worse than a simple garden-variety belief in UFOs."

"Hear me out, Pat! Who's the major contractor on the *Sword?* Windward Technologies Inc. And who was the founder and former CEO? Gordon Elliot Lee. And who was the guy that first claimed the Pavonis comet wasn't a comet at all? Gordon F-ing Lee. You're trying to tell me there's no connection between the company that built the first interplanetary star destroyer and the conspiracy whack-job that's been warning us about an alien invasion for the last twenty years? Come on!!"

"You folks out there in radio-land can't see it, but Terry just put on a tinfoil beanie, propeller and all."

"That's it, Pat, laugh at the crazy man wearing his underwear on the outside, but mark my words—there's aspects to this whole space-based destroyer thing that the administration hasn't told us about yet. The other shoe? It has yet to drop, my friend!"

"I am happy to concede the point that our beloved military-industrial complex has not been completely forthcoming—not that I would truly want them to be, but that's the difference between us. Now, are you willing to put away the conspiracies for a minute and just agree with me that this is cool and that if anybody has to have such a thing, at least it's our own dedicated, honorable military?"

"Okay, I'll grant you that, Pat. It is indeed cool and I'm really damn glad that it's USA-cool rather than Somebody-Else-cool. I'd shudder to think what this thing would be like in the hands of another nation or some private group, rather than our boys in the Navy and Air Force."

"You and me both, brother. You and me both."

March 7, 2045; Windward Technologies, Inc. Test and Evaluation Airfield; Vallejo, CA

"I don't know, sir. I think I need to call the watch commander."

Dave Edwards, retired Senior Chief, fellow *USS Rivero* survivor, and current co-conspirator, looked up from the wheelchair he hardly ever used and gave the young Air Force guard his most withering glare. The look from his thick, leathery face included a mixture of contempt for the Air Force Technical Sergeant's youth, rank, and service, as well as a special disdain for the non-com's temerity to delay one such as he.

Edwards rolled forward until the pants-covered stumps of his legs touched the soldier's camo trousers. "Boy, do you have any goddamn clue about who the hell I am, or about the clusterfuck you're attempting to insert yourself in?"

The Tech SGT took a quick, wide-eyed look at the crowd of civilians facing him and then looked down at Edwards' challenging glare. "Um, yes, sir—I mean no, sir—I mean yes, sir, I know who you are. I know who all of you are, but that doesn't make this any less irregular. More, truth be told."

Edwards gave him a feral smile, causing the SGT to back up a step. "Well, Airman, let me make it more clear for you. There's this big fuckin' spaceship up there and everybody's all abuzz about it."

The SGT bristled at the purposeful misstatement of his rank by the retired Navy non-com. He growled out, "I'm aware of that, sir. This facility is at a heightened security posture for that very reason. Which is why—"

"No, no, screw that," Edwards interrupted. "You're talking about security postures and I'm talking about pissing off the President of these United States. Here's the way it is—that big ass ship up there is too damn large to ever land again, and now that it's on its way back to Earth, the President has pretty much got jack and shit to show off to the people of the world during her big welcome home for the asteroid-conquering heroes.

"Now, when the crew returns and lands at Andrews Air Force Base, she sure as hell would like to show the world more than one dinky spaceplane. And since she can't present the big, impressive destroyer, it sure would be nice if she could at least show off a light squadron of spaceplanes!" Edwards pointed behind the SGT to the two Single Stage To Orbit Shuttles sitting side by side within the Windward Tech hangar. The two SSTOS were identical to the one the *Sword of Liberty* carried in her dorsal hangar.

The SGT glanced back at the two sleek, lifting body aerospace craft in the cavernous hangar behind him and shook his head. "I don't know, sir. Nothing was mentioned about this at watch turnover."

Edwards threw his hands up, exasperated. "Hence the definition of a clusterfuck! Listen here, Sergeant. I'm an old enlisted man myself, and I don't have to tell you how screwed up and anxious officer types can get when someone changes plans at the eleventh hour, but that's just what's happening now. Some PR flunkies decided the Commander-in-Chief needed to present something tangible to the press corps in order to justify all the damn money they've spent on a destroyer no one's ever going to see. And they decided who better to show it off than the original crew and the ones who designed the damn thing. So now I've got 26 civilians and two spaceplanes to fly to Washington DC and get in place before the *Sword of Liberty* regains orbit.

"If you go contacting the watch commander, he's gonna think something funny is up—just like you were, don't deny it—and he's going to call his boss. And his boss is going to wonder why a watch commander is calling him for an authorized and fully legitimate flight, and he's going to call his boss. And so on and so on until the White House and the freakin' SECDEF are wondering where their damn planes are! Now I'm just a civilian nowadays, but I don't ever recall anything good coming from the brass wondering why some mid-grade enlisted man was obstructing their grand, FUBAR planning. Do you?"

The SGT looked worried but determined to stand his ground. "Sir?"

Edwards relented. "Okay, Sergeant, you're making this more complicated than it needs to be. Despite the fact that this whole joint's been nationalized, and you got stuck over here to guard these here planes, do they or do they not still belong to Windward?"

The SGT opened and closed his mouth, uncomfortably trying to decide on an answer. "I really don't know, sir, only that we're supposed to guard this facility and everything on it."

Edwards nodded, commiserating. "Yep. I spent plenty of years as a mushroom too. The answer is yes, they do, and these are still our planes. The government only owns the one on the ship. Now, do we or do we not have a properly filed flight plan?"

The soldier glanced down at the paperwork in his hand that Edwards had given him earlier. "It would appear so."

"And are we on restriction? Are you under any guidance to interfere with our work here? Are we perhaps Chinese spies in disguise? Terrorists?"

The SGT smiled for the first time and looked at the assembled Windward employees and their stacks of luggage and equipment, sparing a lingering glance at Edwards' own wheelchair. "No, sir, no restrictions. We, in fact, have orders to restrict you as little as possible."

Edwards sighed and slumped in his seat. "Well, if I'm not a secret legless hijacker spy, and you've got no orders stating otherwise, how about you give us a break and let us just do our damn jobs?"

The SGT cinched his assault rifle up closer to his shoulder. He looked at the group, then back at the SSTOS in the hangar, and eventually just shook his head. "You win, sir. I've got rounds to do."

The crew all smiled in relief and grabbed up their luggage. As they filed into the hangar, Edwards popped a quick wheelie and turned to face the sergeant as he began to walk away. "Many thanks to you, Sarge. I promise to take back at least half the bad things I ever said about the Air Force!"

The receding guard waved a hand and continued on, soon passing the hangar door and disappearing around a corner. The genial smile immediately dropped from Edwards' lips and he spun about, just as Christopher Wright, the crew-training lead from the original team and another member of the conspiracy, came up behind him to push him at a run toward the shuttle. The former Army colonel asked, "Are we good, Edwards?"

Edwards shook his head. "I'd like to begin our little adventure with a prayer. Here's mine: Please, Lord, let us get outta here before my web of bullshit flies apart and they shoot us all for treason. Amen."

March 7, 2045; White House Situation Room; Washington DC

Secretary of Defense Carl Sykes stood straight under the baleful glare of his President and revealed nothing of the mixed anger, embarrassment, and inexplicable sense of vindication that he actually felt. He was silent, allowing the Commander-in-Chief to process what he had just said.

President Annabel Tomlinson sat primly at the center of the room's long conference table, surrounded by the anxious expressions of her staffers and military advisors, chewing the inside of her cheek and regarding Sykes as if he were a bug. "What do you mean, 'It's been hijacked'?"

Sykes smiled tightly. He could feel Gordon Lee laughing at him from beyond the grave. "Precisely that, Madame President. The timeline we've established thus far would indicate no other possibility."

"Perhaps you should let me decide whether or not we have another possibility, Carl. Your experience, while valuable, sometimes has a tendency to limit rather than expand your outlook." Her features were stone still, betraying not a whit of emotion.

While he could detect no malice or disdain in her voice or the cast of her eyes, he knew it was there, an undercurrent that pulled along all of their interactions. It was an unfortunate confluence. Sykes was the best possible person for his job, the rare, wise Beltway Bandit who had worked his way up to his position through patience, politicking, and unarguable professional competence. President Tomlinson was the outsider who had swept to a landslide victory, in part, on a platform of dismantling the usual Washington machine—more or less a "throw the bums out" policy.

In Sykes' case, he was the only competent bum she had to choose from, so he alone of all his compatriots in the previous administration had remained. Many days, she regretted her decision to advance him from Under-Secretary to SECDEF. They were fire and ice, matter and antimatter, and the day was not far off when the two would finally clash with cataclysmic results.

The last fifteen months had been more than a little strained.

Sykes sighed. "Very well, Ma'am. Here's what we know for certain—I'll let you be the judge. Approximately two and a half hours ago, immediately after the successful strike on asteroid 2006 UA22, all telemetry from the *Sword of Liberty* ceased. We queried the ship without success and telemetry did not return. Imaging radar and direct telescopic visuals showed the ship was intact, though resolution at that range prevents us from assessing directly any hull or radiator damage. One hour and twenty minutes after going offline, we witnessed a track split."

"Track split?" she asked.

"Her radar return split into two distinct returns. Imaging showed that the destroyer had launched its single-stage-to-orbit-shuttle, or SSTOS. There are any number of reasons for this—they could have been sending the shuttle out as a staging platform for repair work, they could have been investigating some of the asteroid debris, or they could have been abandoning ship in response to damage incurred during the asteroid strike.

Without comms or further visuals, we could not determine the actual reason. However, when the *Sword* itself got underway, heading back to Earth at a higher acceleration and a half hour before the shuttle started moving, effectively abandoning the smaller vessel, it left few other reasonable possibilities other than hijacking."

President Tomlinson reached out and took a sip of her coffee. "You say 'few other possibilities' but you only give me one. Is that laziness on your part, or is there something else which supports your hijacking scenario?"

Sykes stood at ease for a moment, simply staring at her, but he eventually responded. "Yes, ma'am. While there could conceivably be some other reason for the ship to abandon its shuttle and head home immediately, there is no reason for the unauthorized launch of two additional SSTOS from the Windward Tech air field in Vallejo. That occurred an hour and a half ago, after the *Sword* broke off telemetry, but before it abandoned its own SSTOS and we ramped up our security posture. The reason given for these SSTOS flights was so that they could appear at Andrews for an impromptu media blitz involving you ma'am. By the time that filtered up to us and we sounded the alarm, both shuttles were off the designated air lanes and were making for high orbit. They are currently orbiting the Earth at an altitude of 3500 kilometers and have refused all attempts to communicate.

"Now, while there might be a slim possibility that these two events are unrelated, that potential becomes vanishingly small when you figure in who was aboard those shuttles and what went missing from Vallejo at the same time." Sykes held up a finger. "That is the original *Sword of Liberty* crew, and," he held up another finger, "the reserve resupply kit stored at Vallejo."

Tomlinson stood up, shaking her head. "All right, all right, Carl! I yield. It's a hijacking and Kelley's taking back his ship. But why? And how the hell did a bunch of civilians make off with two shuttles and a mission resupply kit? Aren't there weapons in there—secure, nuclear, WMD-type weapons?"

Sykes shrugged. "Answering your second question first, it's a matter of hastily implemented procedures and narrow expectations. The Vallejo field was a civilian site with a brand new military security detachment devoted to thwarting an outside aggressor or spy, not a bunch of workers going about their own 'routine'. And as for the weapons, they're all inert. The railgun rounds contain no controlled explosives and the missile has no fuel and no radioactives. Unless you have a *Sword* class destroyer handy, they simply won't do you any good. So, unfortunately, the security team had not been required to implement nuclear safeguards. It's the sort of thing that would have been fixed on review of security procedures, but no one's been in place long enough to call for a review.

"Honestly, Madame President, this sort of thing is a lot more common than anyone in the business likes to admit. We can handle almost any known threat with ease, but present us with something unique or unexpected and we either overreact or get rocked back onto our heels. If another group tried to repeat what Kelley and his crew have accomplished here, there's not a chance in hell they'd get away with it."

Tomlinson frowned. "But that doesn't change where we are at the moment." She turned and approached the large flatscreen dominating one side of the Situation Room, her wall-of-knowledge. On it was real-time telemetry of the approaching destroyer and the two orbiting shuttles. "You know Nathan Kelley, Carl. Why are they doing this? Why didn't they throw in with us and Colonel Henson's crew? Why would they purposefully commit treason for this mission of theirs?"

Sykes walked over to stand beside her. "For the answer to that, you'd have to have known Gordon Lee. Did you ever have the pleasure of his acquaintance?"

She smirked. "I'm an elected official and he was a wealthy industrialist. Of course, I met him. He was a major contributor to my runs in '36 and '40, but it was strictly political insurance on his part. I can't say we ever had a conversation more than five minutes in length."

"Well, I had the displeasure of knowing him for years—both as a Beltway operator and in relation to this project specifically. Gordon Lee was brilliant, arrogant, and of the firm conviction that he was always right. Unfortunately for anyone arrayed against him, though, that belief was too often correct. And even though the miserable old bastard is dead, he rubbed off on Kelley and the rest of them in a big way.

"They come assured by the closest thing to God on Earth that there is only one way to do this, and they mean to do it that way. This mission is theirs to accomplish, and not you, me, or the collective will of the nation is going to keep them from doing it. They couldn't care less about treason when the alternative is violating Lee's vision."

The President nodded and turned away from the screen and began walking the length of the room, acknowledging one by one the other people filling it out in silence. The Chairman of the Joint Chiefs of Staff, General Volescu, nodded to her in support, support echoed on the faces of her staff and advisors. They were all behind her, but she was the one who had to make the difficult choice in this unprecedented case, and no one else wanted to be the one to take the blame in the event it turned out badly.

Suddenly, she appreciated Sykes' unwavering frankness, even when it put them at odds with one another.

"Options? Recommendations?" she asked the room at large.

No one said anything. Whether they deferred to Sykes in his role as SECDEF, or were merely afraid to say anything, she could not tell. Perhaps "throwing all the bums out" had been rash.

Sykes stepped forward and gestured to Volescu. "Ma'am, there are three main courses of action available." The general brought up a series of text slides on the wall-of-knowledge and Sykes continued talking. "First option is the most difficult, with the highest potential for disaster, but it gives us the most clear-cut win. We have approximately six hours until the *Sword of Liberty* can make orbit and rendezvous with the two stolen shuttles. Undoubtedly, she will onload the resupply package and transfer the old crew aboard, then take one of the SSTOS with her, abandoning the other for later retrieval. The shuttles themselves are not armed, and none of the civilian crew is special forces trained.

"We have a Joint spec-warfare team in Pensacola that's been trained for zero-g, vacuum combat. We've never had a need for them before, but it always seemed like a good idea to have the capability. We can use our one remaining SSTOS to rendezvous with the two stolen shuttles, deploy the team, and retake those ships. We put a military crew onboard both, then when Kelley brings them aboard, we retake the destroyer."

Tomlinson looked askance at him. "That seems very much like a 'best case' outcome."

Sykes looked at Volescu, saying nothing until the Army General groaned. Volescu stood and turned to his Commander-in-Chief. "Madame President, it could go wrong at any one of a dozen points. The team may not be able to prep in time. We will be using untested pilots to do a first-time-ever rendezvous in orbit with *two* other shuttles who will undoubtedly be maneuvering to avoid us. Assuming we can link up, the hatches are not designed for a commanded entry from the exterior while in orbit, so we would have to blow them, which will kill the renegade crew and make it obvious to Kelley and Munoz that something is up. Then we have to get aboard the destroyer without it lighting us up, which is pretty much an impossibility. Best case, we purposely destroy the shuttle carrying most of the crew, kill all the civilians, convince the resupply shuttle to give up or die, and use the two remaining shuttles to somehow sneak aboard the *Sword of Liberty* and then take the big ship. Probable loss of 25% to 100% of the team, two shuttles, and maybe even the destroyer. More likely, none of it works at all and Kelley smokes our team from orbit because they're still trying to take one or both of the stolen shuttles."

Tomlinson grunted. "It seems like the two of you have already discounted that option. Very well, what's next?"

Sykes turned to the next slide as it came to the fore. "Option two has a chance of succeeding, but the cost may be … prohibitive."

She did not bother reading the slide, reading the two men's eyes instead. "And that cost is?"

Volescu answered. "We use our anti-satellite and BMD inventory and take out the shuttles and the destroyer. A deadly weapon system, arguably the most advanced, destructive weapon system ever developed has been stolen, and we have no guarantees that Kelley and his crew only want to take it out into deep space to greet a bunch of aliens. He could intend to extort the whole world. Were this situation duplicated in a more familiar, terrestrial sphere, there would be no question. We would take the hijackers out."

"Granted, General, but this is no simple stolen plane or tank. It's not even a stolen submarine. This is currently our one and only existing defense against these Deltans."

"I am aware of that, Madame President, but it is our most conventional recommended response, and it is the one I prefer. We have a decade or more before the Deltans arrive. We can build another."

Sykes grimaced. "I agree with the General that we can build another, but not for some time. However, his option assumes we *can* shoot the damn thing down. I'm sure our arsenal would be effective against the stolen shuttles, but I am a great deal less sure about attacking the destroyer. It's a good two or three tech generations beyond our missile defense network. And assuming Kelley is inclined to go off mission and is considering an attack on a terrestrial location, we would be ill-advised to make an ineffective first strike upon him. 'Ms. Nuclear Retribution' isn't a real winner as far as re-election campaign slogans go."

Tomlinson quietly considered the two men, looking from one to another. She shook her head and focused on Sykes. "Noted. Option three?"

Sykes turned to bring the last slide forward on the screen, but hesitated. "I can't believe I'm saying this, but our third option is the one I'm going to be recommending. You, however, are not going to like it."

"Get on with it, Carl."

"Yes, ma'am."

March 7, 2045; USS Sword of Liberty (DA-1); En route Earth Orbit; Mission Day 2

Nathan Kelley lay back in the Commanding Officer's acceleration couch and looked at the Control Room's central display. It revealed a beautiful, annotated, illuminated image of Earth with thousands of false color satellite tracks encircling it like rings, a chaotic, iridescent Saturn in miniature. It was an awe-inspiring view, but Nathan was left oddly hollow by it. He seemed to not know how to feel. At that moment, his emotions were a wild mixture of anticipation, exhilaration, contentment, and guilt— especially guilt, and for a couple of different reasons.

There was, of course, the matter of his theft of the *Sword of Liberty* and the risky abandoning of her innocent joint military crew. But that was largely offset by his conviction that this was the right way to go about things, that such a move was essential to the success of the mission. No, the main source of his guilt—as well as a not insignificant degree of gleeful satisfaction—was because of something he had done which was almost completely unrelated to the *Sword's* intended purpose.

Kris popped up off of him with a mischievous smile. She grabbed up her shipsuit, slipping it and her underwear back on with a leisurely grace that he found much more enthralling than the fantastic image of the Earth from space.

She slapped his leg as she finished, interrupting him mid-stretch. "C'mon, spaceman. Get your skivvies on and shake a leg. We're almost to yon orbit and'll be strikin' the mainsail and dumpin' the scuppers. Ye don't want to be caught in ye olde freefall with your ass hangin' out all nekkid-like, do ye? Arrrrr."

Nathan grinned and sat up, reaching for his own coveralls and paraphernalia. "It doesn't matter how long you talk like that, you still aren't a space pirate."

"Space privateer, maybe?"

"Definitely not. That would involve government sanction—more or less the opposite of where we find ourselves."

She shrugged. "Oh well, at least I'm a charter member of the 10,000 Mile High Club. And the 50,000 Mile High Club. And the 100,000—"

"And I can't believe we did that. I've always been firmly against hanky-panky aboard ship. Contrary to good order and discipline and all that."

Kris grinned, stepping in close as he finished dressing. "Well if it's discipline you want … ." She leaned in and kissed him. "I'll have no guilt out of you, slave. What else did you think would end up happening? A brand spankin' new couple, alone on a damn spaceship, with nobody around for hundreds of thousands of miles, on the run from the law as it were? Face it—they'd have kicked you out of the Dude Union if you hadn't gone for it. You're practically a pioneering hero now!"

He smiled and kissed her back, his expression easy now, free of tension. "You're right, Pirate Mate. Consider your leader properly abashed. Now let's get ready to cut acceleration and maneuver for orbit."

"Aye, aye, Cap'n! Arrrrrrr!"

They tidied up the Control Room to military precision again, then checked the instruments, verifying their position and velocity. Nathan began to search through the thousands of potential tracks as they approached, but the two SSTOS carrying their compatriots were right at the top of the track priority list. He selected the two shuttles, checked their orbital parameters, and let the computer automatically come up with a rendezvous course. With a few keystrokes, the new course was laid in and executed.

The main drive cut off and they were immediately in freefall. The ship bumped briefly as it turned to a new vector and then "gravity" returned—much reduced—as they maneuvered to join up with Edwards and the rest of the crew.

Nathan scrolled through a number of different displays, checking the status of each of the ship's many, many mutually supporting systems. He paused at the defensive systems summary, relieved that the threat track list was blank for the moment. He had worried that as the *Sword of Liberty* closed with Earth and their treachery became apparent, Sykes or another trigger-happy type might try something. For the moment though, they were un-shot-at, and Nathan was glad that the fully ready laser emplacements and railgun had not been employed against missiles or other weapons from his own country.

Kris checked her own displays at her engineering console, verifying the status and health of the reactor, drive, auxiliary, and environmental systems. She really wanted to go check them out herself, but without a crew onboard, there was simply too much that remained to be done for her to have times to place hands on. Satisfied for the moment, she nodded and drifted to each of the other dedicated consoles on the perimeter of the brightly lit bridge/Control Room, squeezing Nathan's shoulder in passing.

They continued in comfortable, busy silence for a few minutes, until

Kris broke the calm with a low, "Oh, shit . . . ."

Nathan jerked his head up from his console and looked over to her. Kris floated, bent down over the Comms station, not bothering to sit in the miniscule gravity. "What's up, babe?"

She turned to him, a half-smile frozen on her face. "You want the cool news or the 'Holy Christ' news first?"

He cocked an eyebrow, perplexed. "Well, if we're not being shot at, give me the cool stuff and lead me up to the other. You do it the other way and it'll suck all the coolness out by comparison."

Kris grinned in full. "I'm tapped into the web, telecom network, and cable news via satellite uplink, and we're pretty much the talk of the planet. The 24-hour news stations and sites are All-*Sword-of-Liberty*, all-the-time. Our website and e-mail queues are busting at the seams with traffic, and there are practically an infinite number of cell and radio-telephone calls in the hopper."

"Are we answering any of them?"

"Nope. Just like you said, the auto-hailer and voicemail are shut down and we're running silent, but they're waiting anyways."

"Any of those broadcasts or webcasts covering the hijacking?"

She shook her head. "Not a one. As far as the hoi polloi know, Colonel Henson, his military crew, and their two civilian riders are one big, happy space-family."

"There's no way they can't know by now. Even if Henson's STOSS is still too far away to make a direct call home, they have to have flagged our behavior as soon as we broke comms and left the shuttle behind. So they're keeping things quiet. Okay. What about Dave Edwards and the others?"

Kris nodded. "I've got a burst data receipt from both STOSS's. Everything's quiet on their end and they're standing by for rendezvous. Encryption is good and Edwards and Rainier both used the 'Valkyrie' code word. They're not under duress."

Nathan nodded back and grinned as well. "Well, everything seems to be coming together better than I hoped. That is cool. Now what's the big news?"

Her smile grew more, flashing teeth. "The President's on hold for you."

Nathan's grin dropped and he looked appalled. "Damn it, Kris. Voice or visual?"

"Visual. I'm putting it on the main screen, Star Trek style. Hope you're zipped up, lover-boy."

He shook his head in dismay and sat up straighter in his seat, facing the Bridge's primary viewscreen. The view of Earth and her myriad orbits vanished, replaced by a close-in view of Annabel Tomlinson, looking perturbed. Behind her could be seen a conference room and several silent figures, generals, admirals, and civilians alike. Nathan set his jaw firmly and nodded. "Madame President, it's an honor."

There was the briefest, too-long pause as his signal crossed the minute gulf between them and her response flew back at the speed of light. Tomlinson's expression remained hard, her voice icy. "How nice. Well, I would be honored if you would explain just what the hell you think you're doing, Mr. Kelley."

"I would've thought that would be completely obvious by now. We are proceeding on our mission as originally proposed and approved, before Sykes, and you, I suppose, changed things."

"So you're just going to take the ship that the US government built, that the taxpayers unknowingly paid for, and go haring about the galaxy to satisfy your own personal whims? You have a lot of gall."

Nathan shook his head. "No, Ma'am. We have an essential mission for which we have trained and qualified, as well as a sense of dedication to our country and our leaders which won't permit us to let this asset go with a lesser crew. I'm not trying to insult Colonel Henson or his team, but they are rank amateurs compared to the original Windward complement. If we wait for them to become our equals, our timeline for intercepting the Deltans at a relatively safe distance will fall by the wayside. We can't permit that, and you should just accept it. To tell the truth, you should embrace it."

The pause was a bit longer this time, despite the fact that every second brought them closer to Earth. Finally she spoke, her eyes seeming to lock with his even through the intermediaries of the screens and cameras. "I appreciate your position, Mr. Kelley, and I respect it in a way, but the fact remains that you are all civilians. You are not bound to the wishes of my administration, the will of the nation, or the strictures of the US Constitution. It would be criminal for me to allow you to go about your mission and enter negotiations with an alien race for this nation or for this planet. You simply haven't the authority."

"Well, Ma'am, then we find ourselves in a quandary, because while I might not have the authority, I'm the only one with the means. And I'm not going to give that up."

Another pause, longer than the tiny light-speed lag. She appeared to be thinking, calculating. "Perhaps I should proceed as has been recommended, and simply shoot you down."

Nathan's eyes narrowed and a corner of his mouth turned up. "I don't think 'simply' would be how I'd describe it. I'm not so arrogant as to believe that you couldn't shoot this ship down—I have no idea what sort of directed energy or missile technology the DOD might have hidden away, perhaps even some tech used in the *Sword*'s own design. I think it would be a nasty fight, though, and not one you are guaranteed to win. In addition, I would fear for the collateral damage—both the physical kind from a statistically probable miss and the political kind when everyone sees the US shooting down her own destroyer. Madame President, I would think very carefully before listening to anyone advising you to do that."

She nodded, more quickly this time. "I had come to much the same decision, though you might be surprised to note that I couldn't really care less about the political firestorm such an action would unleash. Believe that or not. No, we aren't going to shoot you down and we aren't going to have you forcibly boarded. Instead, we are going to employ a much more subtle weapon against you.

"You are a man of honor and duty, willing to even break the law, to endanger your future as a free man if you see that as the course honor dictates. You sacrificed much in the wake of the *USS Rivero*'s sinking, but the biggest casualty was your tie to the traditions of military service. Both you and the Navy lost something when you resigned. I'm happy that you have found another cause to believe in, another worthy task in which to invest yourself, but your desires and your goodwill are not enough. If this mission is to be undertaken by you, the interests of the United States must be served first and foremost. Secretary Sykes, if you please."

Nathan looked at Kris, confusion evident on both their faces. He looked back to the main screen to see the President move aside and Carl Sykes take center-stage. Sykes glared at him. "Nathan Kelley, please stand and raise your right hand."

Nathan did so, numbly, hardly even thinking.

Sykes cleared his throat and stood at attention, his Air Force training coming to the fore. He did not bother with a note card. This was a passage each of the men knew by heart. "Repeat after me. I, state your name—"

"I, Nathaniel Robert Kelley—"

"—do solemnly swear that I will support and defend the Constitution of the United States against all enemies, foreign and domestic; that I will bear true faith and allegiance to the same; that I take this obligation freely, without any mental reservation or purpose of evasion; and that I will well and faithfully discharge the duties of the office on which I am about to enter. So help me God."

Nathan repeated the oath of office, oblivious to the open-mouthed stare Kris gave him from off-camera.

Sykes relaxed and grinned with more than a hint of malice. "Checkmate. I know you, Commander Kelley. I know how you think, and no matter how you may have been intending to do business, you'll do it the Navy way now. You're my boy, and don't you forget it. Now, Ms. Muñoz?"

Kris, fear making her eyes huge, peeked over into the edge of the camera's field of view. Sykes smiled wide when he saw her. "Raise your right hand, Missy."

13: "THE LIBERTY LETTERS"

SAT TRANSCRIPTION QUEUE: XXX SUPPRESSED XXX
DTG RECEIPT: 09 2219Z MAR 2045
DTG TRANSMITTAL: 09 2217Z MAR 2045
TIME-DISTANCE LAG: 000:00:02:1.3 D:H:M:S

FROM: Nathan Kelley, CDR, USAN
[KELLEY.NATHANIEL@SOL.WINDWARD.NET$
USAN.MIL;
CO@SOL.WINDWARD.NET$USAN.MIL]

TO: Paul Kelley
[CLANKELLEY0819@WEBRUNNER.COM$PHILA.PA.GOV]

SUBJ: Guess where I am?

MSG: Hey, Pop.

As you've no doubt discovered from the 24-hour news coverage and such, I've gone on a little trip. It's been a whirlwind couple of days (as you might imagine), but now that we're all aboard, settled, and on our way, I managed to find a little free time, so I wanted to write and let you know the whole truth on everything—the truth that I wish I could have shared with you and Mom before this.

First, let me apologize for that. I know you've had to put up with my secrets in the past, like during the investigation following what happened on the RIVERO, but until recently, there was nothing officially classified about what our project. Yeah, there was a lot of it that was fairly UN-believable, but there wasn't really anything I had to exclude you on. I guess, at first, it was simple embarrassment. I mean, I had this great job, working for one of the most fascinating innovators in the world, and what was I doing? Oh nothing insane … like building spaceships to go visit aliens, perhaps.

Sure, some of it was technical or industrially sensitive, so I really wasn't inclined to say anything (nor would you have been that interested), but as for the Big Idea, as for what I was really doing and why, I never should have kept that from you two. And now, with the crazy way things have finally come together, you had to hear about what your son's been doing from the TV and the web rather than from your own flesh and blood.

Well, no more. Now that we're underway, further out and faster than anyone has ever gone before, and with so much longer a journey still ahead of us, there's no reason to hold anything back. Here it is, the whole truth, some of which is already out there, some of which is covered by misinformation, and some of it yet to come out (sorry about the NDAs the Feds are making you sign, by the way):

The Deltans are real. We've visited them with one probe, and have another on the way, and they are just as real as Christmas. We don't know why they're coming here, but they'll arrive in about 11 years. We're going out to say, "Hi, whatcha doin'?" and, if we need to, swat them on the nose.

To do that, Gordon Lee and I (and a few others, I suppose) built this ship, the USS SWORD OF LIBERTY (DA 1), the flagship (OK, the ONLY ship) of the United States Aerospace Navy. I guess I didn't learn my lesson from RIVERO. So, I'm back in the service, though, technically, it's a brand new service.

You might hear a couple of different versions of how that came to be, or about crew swaps, about being press-ganged into re-taking the oath, or some crap about us hijacking the SWORD, but allow me play rumor control.

None of that happened.

The DOD, the administration, and Windward have all been in lockstep agreement throughout this process, and while we did take up a different shakedown crew at launch, they were just there for the trials and not the mission.

In fact, that crew was aboard only because they needed to see how things will be run on their ships, which will be laid down any day now. In the meantime, the SWORD OF LIBERTY, and our main crew, mine and Gordon's crew, will be taking the long ride out to our future visitors, proudly flying the flag and representing the interests of Earth. Don't let what passes for reporters these days tell you any different.

This ship, and the journey we're all on are marvels in the truest sense of the word. The things it can do and the punishment it can withstand would simply boggle your mind. Case in point: rendezvous. Ever since this morning, we've been accelerating at a steady one-g, and we're going to keep that up for the next 16 months, non-stop. Already, after just a day of acceleration, we're so far out that it takes two minutes for my e-mail to reach you at the speed of light. We're moving at over three million kilometers per hour—over 12 times faster than the fastest man-made object ever before—and only getting faster and faster as we continue along.

The intention is to approach just over 3/4 the speed of light for the first half of the journey, then flip around and match speeds with the Deltans on the second half. As we get further and further out, you're going to see the lags between messages get longer as well. Don't worry about it—it's just the way things are because of the distance the messages have to travel. There shouldn't be any really bad Einstein-ish relativity effects at that speed.

At rendezvous, and pretty much our furthest distance from Earth, we'll be almost half a light-year from Earth. We could do it a bit faster than 16 months, but we're approaching from an oblique angle like the probes, so we don't accidentally threaten the Deltans with our exhaust radiance or overly highlight our approach.

Of course, that's just getting out there. Coming back will take longer, even though it's a shorter trip. This ship is pretty swift, but it's not magical. When we rendezvous, we'll have expended over half of our reactor power and available delta-v, so we'll have to come back on a slower, but more direct route. Can't have it all, I guess.

Well, it's late, ship-time here, I've probably overloaded your heads, and I need some rest. Still lots to do tomorrow. Now that we're officially military, I've got to take a look at the crew to streamline and formalize the chain of command a bit, and divide people up into department heads, division officers, and enlisted. Some of these folks were never military before, so it's going to be quite an adjustment for them. Then we have to plan the rendezvous and drill, drill, drill. The ship may be different, but shipboard routine stays pretty much the same.

I'll write again soon, Pop. Give Mom a hug for me and, please, don't worry! This whole thing may beyond your wildest dreams, but it's not beyond my biggest plans. We're ready for this. First contact is in the bag.

I love you both.

— Nathan

PS: Almost forgot! I've met someone. You'd like her. More later!! (Ha! Mom is soooo going to throttle me.)

XXX EOM XXX

SAT TRANSCRIPTION QUEUE: XXX SUPPRESSED XXX
DTG RECEIPT: 17 1156Z MAR 2045
DTG TRANSMITTAL: 17 1016Z MAR 2045
TIME-DISTANCE LAG: 000:01:40:22.2 D:H:M:S

FROM: David Edwards, MCPO, USAN

[EDWARDS.DAVID@SOL.WINDWARD.NET$USAN.MIL;
COB@SOL.WINDWARD.NET$USAN.MIL]

TO: Collette Markey
[BUNNIETOES4CM@ALLITEK.COM$SDGO.CA.GOV]

SUBJ: Same Shit, Different Service

MSG: I miss you, Bunny-girl.

Sorry I didn't write yesterday, but our first full-fledged General Quarters battle drill turned into a complete clusterfuck. It took hours to get the computer to release us from a training environment, and then even longer to reset the simulated damage and get the engines and other systems back online. I'm definitely impressed with the simulation fidelity the Windward engineers managed to coax out of the ship's network in the short time they had, but there's something to be said for a longer test and evaluation period. If it wasn't for them damned aliens and their not-to-be-delayed schedule, I'd have opted for at least a few months in orbit before we got underway.

Our beloved Skipper Nathan took it all in stride (after a little ribbing from me, anyway), but the XO was some kind of pissed. It seems that when good LCDR Christopher Wright was in this man's Army, they didn't put up with any wonky computer B.S. Yeah, right. You ain't in the Army now, buddy, but even when you were, you still got saddled with some buggy shit. I'll guarantee it, especially in the Armored Cav Army. Hell, I remember the Centurion II. This isn't any different—just a new uniform and a new setting.

That setting can be a little disconcerting, though, when the air shuts down and the engines go off and they both refuse to turn back on. We are a long, long way away from home, and there ain't no way back but on this ship. I mean, right now I'm a hundred light-minutes from you, babe. That's 1,790,000,000 kilometers—beyond the orbit of Saturn—and we're moving further away at nearly two percent the speed of light.

If Kris Muñoz's little contraption ever realizes exactly how many laws of physics it's breaking, we are completely screwed.

Some of the crew, particularly the ones who didn't have any time in the service before coming under Gordon Lee's wing, didn't take the brief "unplanned interruption of systems" that well. A few of them pretty much lost their shit when it dawned on them that this stuff was real and not just theoretical any more (it's amazingly easy to forget that, when we're all walking around in a continuous one g, even though we're in deep space).

Nathan proved himself. He has this steady, companionable style, like he knew this was coming all along, and that calmed most of them. I joked a few others out of their death spiral (Note to Self: reminding folks that our ship's initials could also stand for *Shit Outta Luck* may not soothe as much as intended). But a couple of our newly "enlisted" spacers just could not get it together. I was thinking about some alternative counseling techniques, old-school Chief-style, Nathan was wondering about sedating them, but neither method turned out to be necessary.

The XO waded in and yelled them into submission. Started going on and on about how they weren't civilians anymore, that they were technicians in the US Aerospace Navy and that they had a tradition of duty to uphold. Tradition? Our service is just over one week old and it has a manpower of only thirty people. Still, he sold it. Said they might well be at war and if they didn't shape up, he'd shove them out an airlock, friends or not. That was a bit much, but I'll be damned if the guy didn't almost have me scared to attention as well.

I guess there's something to be said for strait-laced, humorless Army-types after all. I may give him a ration of shit (it's my oath-given right), but he'll make a good XO, certainly better than me or Kris Muñoz, Nathan's other two candidates. Kris is too egghead flaky, and I'm a Master Chief, damn it—don't go screwing with my self-image at this point. As XO, I wouldn't have a leg to stand on!

Ba-dum, chiii!!! Thank you, thank you, I'm here all week, folks!

Well, enough of this Navy crap. Let me wax philosophic about those lovely feet of yours. Oh—

XXX SUPPRESSED FOR OFFICIAL RECORD - NO MISSION CONTENT XXX

XXX EOM XXX

SAT TRANSCRIPTION QUEUE: XXX SUPPRESSED XXX
DTG RECEIPT: 11 2217Z APR 2045
DTG TRANSMITTAL: 10 1341Z APR 2045
TIME-DISTANCE LAG: 001:08:36:18.8 D:H:M:S

FROM: Kristene Muñoz, LT, USAN
[MUNOZ.KRISTENE@SOL.WINDWARD.NET$USAN.MIL;
CHENG@SOL.WINDWARD.NET$USAN.MIL]

TO: Maria Muñoz-Turner
[MMTURNER2037@Q-MAIL.COM$HSTN.TX.GOV]

SUBJ: Pass this to that son-of-a-bitch
MSG: Mamma,

I'm so, so sorry that you have to go through this by yourself. I know, Ron is there for you, and I'm thankful you have him, but I also know he doesn't like crossing the orbit of you, me, and Dad, so he's probably going hands off. But I'm too far away to send the bastard packing, so your husband really needs to get over his "respect for family boundaries" and punch that father of mine in the dang nose.

I can't believe the sheer temerity (I'd prefer to say balls or gall, but I know how you are about strong language) he has to start claiming credit on the news for me being up here. He doesn't give a damn about me and he hasn't since he walked out on us when I was in GRADE SCHOOL! Ugh!! He makes me so mad! I'm just a paycheck to him, his chance at 15 minutes. You should call those same shows and let him know just how involved he was in my upbringing. I'm here in SPITE of him, NOT because of him.

Sorry. I don't want to waste my ration of bandwidth on that jerk. How are you otherwise? Did your showing go all right? Things here are ... boring. I never would have believed that a voyage through outer space would become tedious, but, yep, that's what it is. The first day blew our minds. The first week was really, really cool and different and exciting, the second week was the same thing over again, the third week—same. Fourth—ditto.

I mean, all we do is cruise, and drill, and study up on culture and fine art and literature (that's the XO's doing—who knew such a dour hard-ass would have a bachelor's in Art History) and watch gauges that don't move. I guess I'm happy that my stuff works so well, but the last bit of excitement we had was that power and propulsion failure a few weeks ago, and that was only a software glitch.

It would have been a nice change of pace to do a flyby on a planet and see one for the first time up-close, but our course took us down out of the ecliptic, and no worlds were on our line of bearing anyway. Anyways, we're too far out now regardless: 35 BILLION km out at .088c—pretty much past the Kuiper Belt and the scattered disk, right at the heliopause, where the interstellar "wind" stops the solar "wind" (not that we felt anything different. Particle densities got way higher, but nothing our shielding couldn't stop.). Ah, astronomical gobbledygook. Ask Ron to go over it with you.

Point is, while interesting from a numbers standpoint, in a social sense it's duller than dirt. All we do is sit around and watch the same movies and have the same conversations and wonder about the same things, over and over again (Deltan stuff mostly). Oh, my Captain, my Captain is still an entertaining toy (can you see me blushing down to my bright chartreuse roots all the way from Earth?), but Nathan is being affected by the boredom same as everyone else.

Problem is, he's the responsible, serious type, and he and the XO use their massive spare time to one-up each other on contact scenarios and engagement options—which only underscores how utterly alone we are on this mission. Chief of the Boat Edwards and I try to keep them from getting too lost in all the infinite dire possibilities, but it's tough.

So, bored is me. And now I'm worried about you and what that ass is up to. You know what I think you and Ron should do. I'll leave it at that, but for one last thing, which you should absolutely pass on to my dear father:

Dad, your little girl, the one who has nothing but antipathy for you, is the inventor of both the most powerful engine in the world, and the most awesomely destructive weapon known to mankind. I did this in response to a POTENTIAL threat to those I love. Should you become an ACTUAL threat, or should you ruin mine or my mother's names, what do you think I'll come up with in retribution for that? I may be a universe away, but I'm still close enough to squash you like the bug you are.

There, I'm off to mess with one of my division officers' heads (can you believe Nathan actually put ME in charge of PEOPLE?) down in Engineering.

Your loving, ever faithful daughter,

Krissy.

XXX EOM XXX

SAT TRANSCRIPTION QUEUE: XXX SUPPRESSED XXX
DTG RECEIPT: 23 0818Z JAN 2046
DTG TRANSMITTAL: 11 1434Z NOV 2045
TIME-DISTANCE LAG: 072:17:44:28.7 D:H:M:S

FROM: Nathan Kelley, CDR, USAN
[KELLEY.NATHANIEL@SOL.WINDWARD.NET$
USAN.MIL;
CO@SOL.WINDWARD.NET$USAN.MIL]

TO: Lydia Russ, CEO, Windward Technologies Inc.
[RUSS.LYDIA@CORP.WINDWARD.NET$NWYK.NY.GOV;
CEO@CORP.WINDWARD.NET$NWYK.NY.GOV]

SUBJ: Broken Promises
MSG: Lydia,

I'm more than a little concerned by the fact that you've yet to receive contact telemetry from PROMISE II. I can only hope that sometime during the next two plus months it takes this message to reach you, you'll get it and send it winging our way, but I'm not holding out a whole lot of hope. By our figures, even accounting for the growing time lag between our positions, we should have gotten the probe data over three weeks ago.

I appreciate your assurances and I know all about the myriad normal things that could have gone wrong with the probe, but, frankly, that's a NASA holdover and not something we anticipated at Windward—especially when the first probe was such a success. What I have to worry about out here, what we have to plan for, is the worst case scenario—that the Deltans were on the lookout this time and destroyed PROMISE II before it got into transmission range. And while the destruction of the first probe could have been deemed an accidental or curious act, destroying the second probe before it could make a close approach seems unambiguously hostile.

As mission commander, I have to allow for the fact that I could be wrong, that despite the evidence, the Deltans are indeed friendly. So, while I'm certain that I know how this is going to go, I can't just go in guns blazing. We have to try to make first contact work. We have to convince the Deltans that we are thinking, rational beings—that we are deserving of joining whatever galactic civilization they come from. But I already have it in my mind that things are going to go south.

We're prepped for either eventuality, though. One good thing: Chris Knight has really stepped up to the plate. Originally, he was going to be our liaison with the diplomatic element, but now, with the "reorganization," not only has he proved himself as our XO, cracking the whip as necessary, he's also been a very able teacher. It may go against standard thinking, but with his background in languages, diplomacy, and cultural history, I'm going to have him take the lead in contacting the aliens, vice doing it myself as captain.

Of course, if Chris can't make the Deltans understand, if they attack or make their intentions to do so clear beyond a shadow of a doubt, well, we'll be ready for that too. Drills and simulations have allowed us to develop some fairly strong tactical options, but I was really counting on that additional probe data. I don't like going in without seeing how they act a second time.

Of course, this may point to exactly how they're intending to act.

It all leads back to the original, central question. Why, Lydia? Why are they coming here like this? It doesn't make any sense at all unless they want something physical from us, something they can only get from a populated planet. If it was just information they wanted, they could just call and ask us for it, with a lot less danger and energy expenditure. If it was resources, they could presumably mine them from a much closer system or belt. And we doubt it's food. Doc Smith figures that it's highly unlikely they could ever efficiently metabolize our proteins, given the lack of a common ancestor and environment, so "space carnivores" are probably right out.

That means they want something from US, mankind, for good or ill. If it's for good, they sure have a funny way of allaying our fears. And if it's not, if they're coming all the way here to kill us up close and personal (or enslave us, or convert us, or absorb us, etc.) it still seems like a horrible waste of resources.

What could possibly be of that much value to an alien race? What do we have that they cannot get from anywhere closer than twenty damned light-years? What makes us special? What about our transmissions and broadcasts attracted them to us in the first place?

And why come here so slowly? Kris poised that question the other day, and it doesn't seem like a logical query at first, but she does have a point. Think about it.

They're only accelerating at a hundredth of a gravity, well below what we primitives can do with technology we developed from watching them. It has to be because of all those different ships they're bringing and that overly massive drive "star" of theirs. Why bother bringing so much mass with them that it takes eighty freaking years to make the journey? Does the size of their convoy have anything to do with why they're coming here? Why are all the vessels of their convoy so different from one another?

I just can't wrap my monkey brain around our lizard overlords' intentions and it's pissing me off.

I'm sorry, Lydia. I didn't mean to lay so many angst-driven questions on you. It's just that we're nearing turnaround, and we're so far from home, that the loss of PROMISE II makes me worried all over again. Forget it. We'll figure it all out when we get there.

Switching tracks, I saw that they laid down our next three destroyer hulls. Outstanding! But what about the allied technology transfers? We're going to need a lot more than three other destroyers to stop these guys should it come to a battle. When are the other NATO countries going to be starting their own hulls? What about the other defense systems?

That's my bandwidth limit for today. Hope this finds you and yours well. Take care, Boss.

V/R,

NATHANIEL KELLEY
CDR   USAN

XXX EOM XXX

SAT TRANSCRIPTION QUEUE: XXX SUPPRESSED XXX
DTG RECEIPT: 20 2307Z FEB 2046
DTG TRANSMITTAL: 03 0746Z DEC 2045
TIME-DISTANCE LAG: 079:15:21:18.6 D:H:M:S

FROM: Kristene Muñoz, LT, USAN
[MUNOZ.KRISTENE@SOL.WINDWARD.NET$USAN.MIL;
CHENG@SOL.WINDWARD.NET$USAN.MIL]

TO: Leo Buchanan, Associate Researcher, Sandia National
Laboratory
[LEO.BUCHANAN@SANDIA.GOV$ALBQ.NM.GOV]

SUBJ: Suck eggs, Gravity-Boy!

MSG: Oh, hey there, Leo.

Yeah, I just wanted to drop you a line, let you know where my stupid little experiment's taken me. Well, we just did a turnaround on our least-time transit, constant acceleration brachistocrone trajectory. Seems we got all the way up to 70.6% the speed of light on our little journey, and we gotta slow down to say hi to the space aliens that surely don't exist.

Yep, I'm about a quarter of a light-year away from you, so you won't get this message for quite some time, but I hope that when you get it, I'll still be able to hear you cussing a blue-streak all the way out here. Ooooooo, feel the burn, lab-mate! Work yourself up into a good, righteously indignant lather.

Hey, how's your gravity wave propulsion experiment going, by the way? That badly? Really? Awwww. And you looked so very promising and full of yourself back in our university days.

Have fun scratching on chalkboards, Leo, I gots me a date with destiny!

Toodles,

Kris Muñoz

XXX EOM XXX

SAT TRANSCRIPTION QUEUE: XXX SUPPRESSED XXX
DTG RECEIPT: 28 0616Z JAN 2047

DTG TRANSMITTAL: 14 1822Z JUL 2046
TIME-DISTANCE LAG: 197:11:54:10.4 D:H:M:S

FROM: David Edwards, MCPO, USAN
[EDWARDS.DAVID@SOL.WINDWARD.NET$USAN.MIL;
COB@SOL.WINDWARD.NET$USAN.MIL]

TO: Collette Markey
[BUNNIETOES4CM@ALLITEK.COM$SDGO.CA.GOV]

SUBJ: A Final, Dismal First for the LIBERTY Crew

MSG: Hey, Darlin'.

Today is not a good day. Things have been tough for a while now. This trip has been long, too long. People are getting on each other's last nerves.

The food, most of which has been "processed" on board, tastes pretty much like the recycled shit it is. All the movies have been watched, all the variations of relationships have been tried (and don't worry, I've been a good boy, as have most of the other married folks, with a few notable exceptions), and the fact that we are both at our furthest point from Earth and about one month out from rendezvous … well, the pressure is pretty intense.

Too intense for one.

I don't know if you remember Diane Rutherford or not. You probably know her better from her official crew biography than you do from personal experience, but I know you met her at least once—maybe at that last Windward Christmas party.

She was pretty but plain. Diane had hair that couldn't decide if it wanted to be blonde or brown, but she didn't care. She was smart as a whip—an electrical engineer with a Master's from Stanford, and she knew reactor control systems like nobody's business. Of course, with a crew as high-powered as this one, that only translated to her being one of our support personnel: an enlisted Electronics Technician First Class. Diane didn't mind being designated enlisted like some of our crew did. She didn't want to be an officer, and she thought being forced into the military before we left was funny as hell. She was from somewhere in the mid-west, Kansas City I think, and she was divorced with no kids, but she was really close to her dad.

I'm talking about her in past tense because she's dead. When we reached our furthest point from Earth, at rest relative to the solar system, more than half a light-year away from home, she purposefully stuck her hands into a reactor power main bus box and electrocuted herself. We know it was on purpose because she left a note.

Diane had been depressed for months. She'd gotten more and more pessimistic about the mission's chances, especially when we missed the second probe's telemetry. She worried about dying out here, with her dad never knowing for certain what happened to her. She was just so damn homesick.

And she wondered if her soul would be able to find its way to heaven so far away from Earth.

We all talked to her, tried to cheer her up, but the problem is, when you've been around the same thirty people for so long, your patience for everybody's annoying little quirks wears pretty thin. Folks just began rolling their eyes when she would start to lose it. I even snapped at her, told her to stop freaking out and get refocused on the mission.

I know, babe. I don't really blame myself for her committing suicide, but damn it all, I could've been more supportive. I'm the COB. It's my job to know the crew's minds so I can keep everything running smooth. I'm supposed to listen to 'em, especially when they're having problems. Of course, I'm supposed to kick 'em in the ass when they need it too. Shit.

So, we've had our first death. In accordance to her wishes, as specified in her suicide note, we committed her body to space. Yeah, I can guess what you're thinking—it doesn't seem too damn consistent with the particular worries she was having over her soul and all, but I don't think rationality was her strong suit in those last few days. It may not make sense to any of us, but it's apparently what she'd been waiting for weeks for.

Nathan said a few words, we said a prayer, and we all jumped back into work. Things are quieter now, more polite, more introspective, I guess. I'm not sure that's a good thing, though.

Diane's death is like a slap in the face. It woke us up, but it also put us on the defensive. Folks aren't talking to each other like they should be. This is when we need to be finalizing things, polishing off our diplomatic and tactical plans. It's almost game-time and we should be looking for ways to come together, not drift further apart. On top of everything, her death was the last thing we needed.

Everybody is taking it hard. Nathan is beating himself up. Kris too. The XO isn't beating himself up—he's pissed at her instead, but I'm not sure that's in any way a better thing.

I'll give 'em all another day to play the self-blame game (myself included) and then I'll commence to kicking everybody's ass. We have got to get our heads straight—Nathan most of all. These Deltans aren't going to give a shit if we're tired of each other, or depressed, or worried, or whatever. They know what they're about, they have their own agenda, and they're going to follow it, whether we're ready or not. We have to be ready.

That's it, babe. I realize that by the time you get this note, we'll have already made first contact, so it'll all be over, one way or another, but pray for me anyway. We're going to need all the help you and the man upstairs can provide, belated or not.

I love you.

— Dave

XXX EOM XXX

14: "FIRST CONTACT"

August 16, 2046; USS Sword of Liberty (DA-1), 0.48 light-years from Earth, 2.0 light-seconds (600,000 km) from alien formation; Mission Day 529

Alone in the vast darkness, a sword of light slashed across the void. So far from the life-giving radiance and warmth of Sol, the only star mankind had ever known as more than an abstract point on the matte black canvas of the sky, there was no real illumination other than what the brilliantly lit vessel produced on its own. The blade of this rapier-like ship was crafted of light itself, a long contrail of focused energy, so strong and so fiery that its very emission was enough to drive the ship through the night. The sword's hilt, the source of that shining blade, was a tiny thing lost in the vastness, a warm, dully glowing construct of metal, carbon, and unflinching will.

Abruptly, the blade of light vanished, shutting off its driving radiance after seventeen months of near-continuous operation. The *USS Sword of Liberty* coasted through space, lit only by the dull reddish glow of the radiator panels running down the middle third of her length. Her forward third—a maul-like hexagonal wedge of dark gray crystalline armor, antennas, radar panels, weapon emplacements, and missile hatches— flashed with lances of blue-white light, smaller, but no less brilliant than the illumination produced by her main engine.

These pulses of radiant thrust slewed the ship around and then arrested her traverse, such that she was now pointed bow-on toward the only other artifact in their small bubble of space—a bright spark of violet with a forward leading contrail of blue brilliance all its own. This, the quarry that had driven the crew to build their amazing little ship, was a constrained sphere of plasma, a star-in-miniature that the visitors somehow used as their drive. And circling about this angry, roiling ball of gas were four constructs, invisible to the naked eye from this distance—the enigmatic alien ships of the Deltans themselves.

The *Sword of Liberty* was not limited to the naked eye, though. Telescopic cameras dotted her hull and combined their data in phase, effectively giving the destroyer a virtual lens as large as the ship herself.

The ship channeled the resulting image to the very interested parties in her Bridge Control Room, buried at the center of the forward mission hull.

And within that Bridge, Commander Nathan Kelley, Captain and Commanding Officer of their far flung expedition, looked at the magnified image with an intensity that had built itself steadily over mile upon impossible mile of their journey, until it seemed strong enough to blast through the screen and through the hull, strong enough to reach out to the Deltans and reveal their mysteries all by itself.

Alas, no matter how hard he looked, he was only human, and no such capability existed. Nathan shook his head, and frowned. *So close and yet …*

.

He looked around the starkly silent bridge at his officers and crew. All of them were suited up in slender, form-fitting vacuum suits, and each one watched the steadily growing image of the Deltan formation as intently as he had been. All of them, that is, but Kris, who appeared less concerned over their journey's resolution than she was over the state of the man leading it. She looked back at him with compassion, worry, and love shining from her eyes as brightly as the thrust from her engines.

He reached out to her and grasped her vacuum-suited hand with his own, drawing her floating figure close. As her face came up to his, he ran his other gloved hand through her short, silver-white hair and locked her into a long, emphatic kiss. It was a simple thing, a familiar intimacy, but this time, with all that lay behind them and all that still remained, this time it was special.

As he kissed her, and as she returned it with equal fervor and insistence, all the months of impatience, dread, petty annoyances, and fatigue began to fall away. Now, on the doorstep to discovery, the voyage's slow-building weariness—a weariness which had even begun to strain the two of them—seemed to fade. It had dragged all of them down for week after endless week, but now it passed, leaving them both with a renewed sense of wonder and purpose.

Kris pulled back slowly, languidly, and favored him with a smile that suffused her whole face, her whole being. "Better, mon Capitan?"

"Oh yes, CHENG," he answered, with a grin all his own, the first he had genuinely felt in some time. He let her go reluctantly. As she drifted off, he found that the rest of the bridge crew had also turned away from the frustratingly close enigma of the Deltans and were looking directly at the two of them, most with half smiles on their lips.

Dave Edwards, strapped into the Chief of the Boat's seat to his left, patted Nathan's arm and said, gently, "You know, Skipper, if you two are having a moment, we can put this whole first contact bullshit on hold. After a year and a half of waiting, I'm sure the crew won't begrudge you a quickie with your main squeeze."

Nathan turned to him with an expression gone from serene to baleful. "COB ... ." he said menacingly.

To his right, Christopher Wright spoke up, his tone as professional and serious as ever. "Captain, we're at two light-seconds from the objective, zero thrust, and bow on. Estimate a 015 by minus 20 relative target angle to the formation and opening. No reaction by the aliens, sir. Ready for your orders, Captain."

"Thank you, XO." Nathan turned back to the main panoramic screen forward of them. He touched the trackball control mounted to his armrest and scrolled around the image, highlighting and magnifying target tracks as he continued to speak. "All right, this is it. We are currently about ten times further out than the *Promise*s were when they were programmed to initiate comms. We know that the first probe was safe up to this point, because she wasn't taken out until she was almost on top of them. As for *Promise II*, it's a wash. We don't know if she either never made it this close, or if she made it closer but got smashed before she could reconfigure herself for communication. Either way, we haven't been schwacked yet, so this is probably a safe range for the moment. This is our last chance to alter plans if we need to. After this, we're committed."

Nathan had highlighted and set off into inset windows of their own each of the visible ships that made up the Deltan convoy: the Control Ship, the Polyp, and the Cathedral. The Junkyard, in its quasi-Lagrange position on the far side of the Control Ship, was occluded by the drive-star, but the slow orbit of each of the vessels around the axis of thrust would soon bring it into view and obscure the Polyp in turn.

Nathan looked at the crew seated and floating around him. Along with Dave Edwards and Christopher Wright representing his command staff, and Kris here for Engineering, he also had Mike Simmons from Operations Department and Ivy Cho from Weapons Department, his other department heads. Also seated were four "enlisted" watchstanders at their Bridge stations for Helm/Maneuvering, Ops/Communications, Weps/Sensors, and Aux Engineering, but they kept their eyes on their duties and did not interject themselves into his powwow with the senior officers.

The Executive Officer held up a hand. "I don't see any gains made in changing things at this point. I just want to reiterate that we have only one chance at doing this peacefully. Once we shoot or shoot back, we'll have set the course for the whole planet, so I want to again urge caution and patience. What happened to the probes might have been either hostile or inexplicably benign. We cannot be sure how an alien intelligence would view our physical visitations to them or their reactions to that visitation until we understand their culture. Even if the Deltans take action that could be construed as hostile, I'd prefer to hold off counterfire until it becomes our last possible option. Maneuver defensively, continue attempts at communication, and hope that we can get through to them before they leave us with no other choice."

Edwards shook his head. "I will never be able to get you straight in my head, sir. Gruff Army guy one moment, and pacifist diplomat the next."

Wright smiled tightly. "Your experience in the Navy ranks might be different, but I've found that many of the best soldiers and the bloodiest warriors I ever worked with were, at heart, the truest of make-peace pacifists … something about preferring to argue over a conference table rather than over the sights of a gun, at least while the conference table is still an option."

The Master Chief considered it and nodded finally. "I suppose so, and it's not a bad attitude to have, especially for the guy leading our negotiations." Edwards turned to look at Nathan. "Still, my druthers would be to set off a warhead or six in their path and let them start the talking. We've tried to observe the niceties twice already, and all it's gotten us is two dead chunks of hardware."

Nathan shook his head. "We've been over that, COB. All our simulations indicate that showing off our weapons tech before we use it decisively gave us zero advantage, and like the XO said, it pretty much closes off the diplomatic option. I'm hoping we can still chalk up the probes to a big misunderstanding."

Edwards shrugged. "Hey, you asked. And, besides, you have to allow for the fact that those sims were all made in a vacuum—literally and figuratively. Just like we don't know their motivations in torching our probes, we don't know for sure that a show of force would give them an undue tactical advantage."

Wright leaned back to look at the Master Chief past Nathan's head. "That's true, COB, but it's also an unnecessary violation of operational security. Right now, they don't know that we're even armed. Why release that info and let them see the exact nature of that armament unless we're positive it will give us an advantage? Those simulations may have been done in a 'vacuum', but they weren't done with a lack of common sense."

Edwards held up his hands. "I'm not arguing with either of you gents' logic, I'm just a little more sure about our visitors' disposition than you or the CO are willing to be. It's part of my job description: keep the sailors—spacers, whatever—under control and advocate the hell out of the devil, so you at least have one voice of dissent when the pair of you get to agreeing too much."

Wright grunted. "I appreciate your fervor in that role, Master Chief, but sometimes you enjoy being the contrarian a bit too much."

"Hey, just because I'm contrary, doesn't mean I'm not also right. Provable hypothesis or not, I'd be approaching this official first contact a bit more aggressively, and I think that position's more than justified."

"Which is why I'm in the lead for this, and not you!"

"All right!" Nathan snapped. "Enough. Points are made, and while I have a depressing certainty that we'll be unloading our ammo out the barrels versus the magazine trunks, we're going to stick with the diplomatic plan. No changes." He broke out a crooked smile and looked around at his department heads. "Unless you three have anything else to add to the XO's or Chief's deliberations, that is?"

Ivy Cho, Mike Simmons, and Kris all looked at one another, panicked, and only too quick to shake their heads. Kris, who was constitutionally incapable of remaining quiet, said, "Screw that! It'd be like putting our feet into a bear trap on purpose. I don't know, but you guys seem a little touchy for some reason today. I wonder why ... ."

They each tried to hide their relieved smirks, except for Nathan, who smiled at her warmly. "Okay, that's it. No sense putting this off any more. XO, set General Quarters, Bravo Stations for contact. Let's do this."

Wright turned to his chair's panel and made the necessary selections. The stern, unidentified feminine voice of the ship sounded from every speaker aboard. "General Quarters, General Quarters. Now set General Quarters, Bravo Stations. The ship may engage in high g maneuvers or lose pressure without warning. All personnel will don vacuum protection and move in an orderly fashion to their General Quarters stations. All personnel will secure for maneuvers and minimize internal transit unless specifically authorized by the Commanding Officer."

The already suited crew on the bridge looked around at one another and put their helmets on. Sealing rings clicked in rapid succession, and then the three department heads, whose GQ stations were off the bridge, went around to each of the seated, strapped in crew, performing seal checks, verifying internal air reserves, and ensuring they were all hooked properly into ship's air.

Kris checked Nathan last. When she finished, she squeezed his shoulder and touched her faceplate to his, so her voice would conduct through the helmets. "I love you, babe."

He smiled and reached up to squeeze her arm in return. "I love you too, Kris, but you probably should have turned off your helmet's amp if you wanted that to be private."

She turned red inside her helmet and whirled around when Edwards gave her a familiar slap on the side. He grinned and said, "Honestly, you two kids are just the sweetest things."

Nathan shook his head, and he and Kris released one another. She left the bridge, headed down and aft through the long radiator shaft to the reactor and Engineering Central Control. Ivy and Mike followed suit—she headed forward and up to the Weapons Coordination Center, and he left for the relatively close Combat Information Center, where they would individually oversee the orders commanded from the bridge.

"XO, report when all stations are manned and ready," Nathan ordered gently.

"Aye, aye, sir." Though originally from the Army, the Navy lingo was second-nature to him at this point.

Edwards made some selections on his panel. "XO, Bridge is manned and ready!"

"Very well."

Around the ship, each of the various stations reported in. Including Nathan, Edwards, Wright, and their four watchstanders on the bridge covering the Helm, Ops/Comms, Weps/Sensors, and Aux Engineering, there were twenty-two more crew aboard the USS *Sword of Liberty* in a number of different individual monitoring, control, and coordination posts. From the forward most portion of the ship, there was Navigation Path Clearance and the ship's Railgun Control. Then came the Port and Starboard Missile Module Monitoring stations, Laser Monitoring and Control, and the Dorsal and Ventral Radar Rooms, all of which reported to LT Cho in the Weapons Coordination Center.

In the after half of the mission hull, Operations Department held sway, led by LT Simmons in the Combat Information Center. Reporting to him were the individual combat controllers in CIC who would make use of the weapon systems Ivy Cho's people readied and maintained, should that prove necessary. Outside of CIC, there was the Communication Systems and Signal Exploitation Space—known as Radio to one and all in a nod to the traditional Navy—as well as the Hangar, Flight Ops, and Network Server Control.

Kris, stuck way back in Engineering Central Control between the Reactor Room and Main Propulsion, owned five spaces up forward—the four Aux Propulsion Rooms beneath each RCS pylon, and Damage Control Central which was the aft-most space in the mission hull. She also owned the entire radiator spine amidships, arguably the most critical and vulnerable system aboard, as well as the aforementioned Reactor and Main Prop Room. In terms of real estate, Kris was in charge of just over two thirds of the ship, while Cho and Simmons split the remaining forward third, but her role, and Ivy's for the most part, was simply to support Mike in actually fighting the ship. And all three departments were there in unquestioning support of Nathan and his command team on the bridge.

The *Sword of Liberty* was a complex machine, many times more complicated than her schematics alone showed. Bulkheads, cableways, and equipment enclosures were only part of the destroyer, and the lesser part by any reasonable standard of measure. The people involved, the people who had built her, who had trained and sweat and bled for the last seventeen months in space, who had fought against all the odds to see their vision realized—even to the extent of stealing her outright—they were the soul of the ship, the driving force behind her presence here.

They were the vital cogs in the machine, finely engineered and lovingly intermeshed. As reports of readiness rolled smoothly in, Nathan closed his eyes, savoring this penultimate moment, sensing much as any ship's captain had down through history the bright spirit of his crew that gave their ship life, that had come together to achieve the impossible.

Now he just had to see their sacrifice and hard work justified.

"Captain, all stations report manned and ready, vacuum gear verified. GQ-Bravo Station is set."

Nathan opened his eyes, serene and satisfied. "Very well, XO. Shut all internal pressure barriers and button us up."

"Aye, aye, sir." Wright touched a few icons on his screen and then keyed his intercom. "DC Central, Bridge, verify all GQ pressure fittings and hatches closed and sealed. Verify all atmo sections independent of one another."

Ensign Al-Salaam answered over the speaker from Damage Control Central immediately. "DC Central, aye, sir. Wait one." Silence filled the circuit for a moment and then, "Bridge, DC Central, pressure board is green, all atmo boundaries shut and on independent recirc."

The XO nodded. "Bridge, aye." He turned to Nathan as far as his helmet and seat straps would allow. "Captain, we're as ready as we'll ever be."

Nathan nodded back and blew air out into his helmet in a long low whistle. His momentary serenity vanished, putting him back on edge. "Roger that. Helm, take us in at one g, and close to 100,000 kilometers, parallel course." At that acceleration, it would take almost four hours to close, hopefully enough time for them to assure the Deltans they were friendly and ready to meet, and hopefully to ascertain the same thing about the aliens.

"Helm, aye, sir. Thrusting at one g for a zero relative velocity rendezvous at 0.33 light-seconds. Estimate four hours till in position." Andrew Weston, an enlisted Ops Tech and a former Air Force fighter pilot, went to work on his helm console. Weight quickly returned to them all, pressing them down into their seats once more.

The return of a normal sense of up and down was a welcome comfort to Nathan, and he marveled at how spoiled he had become from Kris' engine. No longer did space and weightlessness go naturally hand-in-hand. He smiled wryly and keyed his intercom. "CIC, Captain, launch the retransmission pod."

LT Simmons responded. "CIC, aye, sir. Deploying pod now." The *Sword of Liberty* had a total of 96 missile cells, but did not actually carry 96 missiles. They had replaced the one missile they had tested at the beginning of the journey, but that still only brought them up to 86 Excaliburs. The remaining ten missile cells were taken up with more diplomatic and scientific cargo.

Eight of the non-missile cells contained subprobes for close inspection of the Deltan vessels, while the other two cells carried retransmission pods, essentially an Excalibur missile frame with the warheads changed out for communications gear. This automated comms probe would monitor the rendezvous and transmit its feed to Earth, as well as re-transmit the telemetry and monitoring data that the *Sword* herself sent back. It was an insurance plan, to make certain that what happened here, however it might turn out, Earth would know.

There was a clack of a missile hatch opening, and then a gentle bump as the re-trans pod was expelled from its tube. Nathan watched video from the hull on a secondary screen, as the hatch swung shut and the pod fell away, left behind by their acceleration. Moments later, the pod's own engine lit off and it moved toward its own holding position and unfolded an immense dish antenna.

"Bridge, CIC, re-trans pod deployed. We have a good link. We'll begin transmitting on your order."

"Bridge, aye," Wright answered. "Captain?"

Nathan nodded, then realized the XO could not see that with his helmet on. "Very well. It's your show now, Christopher. You can begin any time."

"Yes, sir. Weps/Sensors, commence long-pulse radar and lidar surveys of the alien formation."

"Aye, aye, sir!" Yvonne Clark, a former telecom engineer long in Windward's employ, powered up the dorsal and ventral sensor blisters and began sending ranging pulses out toward the Deltas.

Wright turned to Nathan and Edwards. "We won't get much more than range data at this distance, but it ought to be a friendly enough wakeup call in case they're sleeping. And we're still far enough out that we should be fairly safe from any direct fire weapons like they used on *Promise*."

Edwards smiled. "So, there is a cynical old warrior in there after all. I was worried you'd gone all touchy-feely on us, sir."

Wright laughed. "Just because I won't let myself assume they're hostile, doesn't mean I'm not open to the possibility. I'm cautious, not stupid, Master Chief." He turned back to the main screen, watching the imperceptibly approaching alien formation. Range data and some surface features began to augment the picture and information displayed for each contact. "Radar and lidar are good … but no reaction from the convoy."

Nathan shrugged. "That's fine. Considering the success of the last two visits, I'll take no response over a bad one, for the moment at least. Let's go ahead and start sending telemetry back home. We'll let them be frustrated right alongside us."

"Aye, aye, sir. Ops/Comm, lock the main dish on Earth and begin continuous transmission of the tactical log."

"Begin continuous stream to Earth, aye, sir. Transmitting now." Pauline Rivera, a Windward satellite data-systems tech right out of college, hit the appropriate icons on her panel and the largest antennas on the sensor blisters each slewed around to aim at the distant pinprick of Sol and the invisibly distant Earth. What happened now would be picked up in slightly less than six months back home.

"Very well. CIC, Bridge, enable your link to the re-trans pod and start backing up our broadcast home."

Simmons voice sounded promptly. "CIC, aye." Auxiliary antennas on those same blisters slewed around to lock onto the ever more quickly receding shape of the retransmission pod. It, in turn, pointed its own dish to Earth as well and began transmitting its own stream back.

Wright checked on the status of everything set into motion upon his screen and nodded in satisfaction. "All right. Both data streams are going out. Everything after this is on the official record."

Nathan grinned. "Smile nice and pretty, boys. We're on primetime now." He nodded toward the main screen, his smile dropping for an expectant, demanding gaze. "That goes for you too, friends. What do you have to say to the good peoples of Earth, Mr. Deltan? Come on, come on. Talk to us. Why are you here?"

Silence met his questions. For a moment, however ludicrous it might be, everyone on the bridge almost anticipated an answer. Nathan grinned and shook his head. "Seems we need to knock a bit louder, XO."

"Yes, sir. We'll be starting with primes on a number of frequencies, just like the probes were programmed to do. Between each sequence, though, we'll be transmitting the plain language greeting in English, Spanish, Chinese, and Arabic. Hopefully, they'll pick up on one or the other."

"Go ahead. Once again, this is your show."

Wright ordered Pauline Rivera to do as he briefed. Seconds later, a pair of pure tones was transmitted in a number of frequency bands. Then, three pulses were sent, followed by five after a brief pause. Then seven, eleven, thirteen, seventeen, counting up and up through all of the base-10 primes from two to 137, a decidedly nonrandom sequence that it was hoped would prove their intelligence and hopefully lead to a mathematical standard which could then be used for translating between two wildly disparate species.

After a hundred and thirty-seven pulses and a correspondingly longer pause, Gordon Lee's original message went out, slightly altered by computer, his voice haunting the void long after his death. Hearing it again, Nathan sighed, knowing that Gordon should have been there.

"Greetings to you, our unknown visitors from a nearby star. We welcome you to our solar system in the name of all the free inhabitants of Earth. Please allow this ship and crew to make peaceful contact with you, such that we might form some bridge for open and enlightening communication between our two species."

Again, a brief pause, and then the same message went out in the other, most-prevalent broadcast languages of Earth. Nathan held his breath. With the *Promise*, the Deltan convoy had reacted immediately to the transmission of primes. This time … .

"Nothing. No response." Nathan slapped the armrest of his acceleration chair, disappointed beyond measure.

Wright tried to assuage him. "We're still really far out, Nathan. And

Promise only began transmitting after doing an extended flyby and survey of the formation. They may still be dormant. It's possible that they're in some form of suspended animation and takes them a while to come fully out of it."

Edwards grunted. "Yeah. And it's also possible that they want us to get in effective range of their weapons before they light us up."

"Master Chief—" the XO said, a warning tone coloring his voice.

"No," Nathan broke in. "You could both be right. And there's no need to tiptoe around my dashed expectations. It's been a year and a half. Hell, it's been years longer than that, and I really expected them to say something or do something after we came all this way. But ... they'll do whatever they're going to do, regardless of what I want. Let's just stick to the plan. Continue transmitting, continue closing, and keep both eyes on them."

He pointed at the images of the orbiting formation on screen. "And you, whoever the hell you are, wake up. We've come calling, and you have some shit to answer for."

◢◤◢◤◢◤◢◤◢◤◢◤◢◤

Four hours later, and still answerless, Nathan fumed. They reached their hold point at 100,000 km, calling out to the Deltans and dutifully reporting back to Earth, but they had nothing to report other than the continued indifference of the aliens.

Overriding Wright, who wanted to hold at that distance for another 24 hours, Nathan ordered him to carry on with the second phase of the contact. The *Sword of Liberty* moved in again, this time angling ten times closer still.

At 25,000 km, they flushed four more of their non-offensive missile tubes, these carrying recon drones—sub-probes similar to those launched by the *Promise*s. Each one would make a close approach to a different one of the Deltan ships, and make detailed radar, lidar, thermal, and visual surveys of each, transmitting that data back to the *Sword*.

Finally, at 10,000 km and holding, Nathan popped his helmet and set it in his lap. He breathed deep of the cool air filling the bridge. After five and a half hours strapped into his chair, confined to the gradually more pungent environment of his sealed suit, Nathan was hungry, sore, and frustrated beyond belief. He glared at what he now thought of as his adversaries.

The constrained drive-star blazed huge upon the main screen, casting the bridge in shifting hues of lurid purple, red, and blue. At each corner of the screen, bracketing the angry sphere of plasma, detailed windows of data described the four alien ships. They knew everything they could about the outsides of those vessels, short of landing upon them and ripping up hull-plates for analysis, but they knew nothing more of the Deltans themselves than they did before leaving Earth.

The XO unsealed and removed his own helmet, casting a concerned look at Nathan. He had tried every ploy he could think of to make contact with the Deltans. They had been through countless iterations of the prime number sequence, and the multilingual greeting as well. He had tried transmitting short, pulse-driven arithmetic lessons, photos of famous works of art, and video streams in a number of different encoding formats, hoping to pick up on something, anything that the aliens would find compelling. He had even launched off a visual display—fireworks especially designed for shooting out of the railgun. Despite their best attempt at a 4th of July celebration, though, the aliens had continued on unperturbed.

Wright laid a hand on Nathan's rigid shoulder. "Captain, we didn't hold at the 100-k point. Everyone's been at their stations going on six hours now, and I don't know about you, but I'm starting to stink inside this thing. It might be a good idea to break for chow and a change. If you like, we can move back out to 100,000 km, or we can do it from here."

Nathan glanced back at him and shook his head. "No, Christopher. I know we should have held back, and I agree we should probably break off for now, but, damn it, we shouldn't have to. They should have responded in some way by now! We've been hailing them for hours longer than the probes ever managed. We're closer now than *Promise II* ever got, and we're inside the perimeter where *Promise* started broadcasting her prime sequence."

Edwards took off his helmet as well. "Yeah, but we're still outside where the convoy reacted to the probe and began its attack on her. They could be seeing how close we'll get before we get skittish and back off. At this range, the lightspeed time lag is only 3 hundredths of a second, and the tactical reaction delay is under a tenth of a second. Depending on fast we jink and weave, and how fast they can shift their aim, we're potentially vulnerable to the beam weapons they demonstrated before. If we move out now, they could take it as their best chance to fire on us."

Wright's eyebrow peaked. "So, does that mean you're recommending we move back or that we stay here?"

The Master Chief grinned and shrugged. "Neither. I tend to just flap my jaws continuously. I often surprise myself with what comes out."

The XO grunted and tried desperately to hide his slight smile beneath a scowl.

Nathan's gaze had stayed glued to the main screen. "No. This isn't working. It's all canned, automated. We haven't done one unpredictable thing yet. For all they know, we could be just another, bigger probe. *We* haven't made contact yet, so why should *they* bother with responding to us."

"Well, Captain," Wright began, "all other things being equal, predictability often equates to being safe and friendly. If we attempt to surprise them or shock them into making a response, it could be seen as overtly aggressive."

Edwards nodded. "Which is what we really are, XO. Skipper, we're monkeys, animals barely come down out of the trees. We fight with ourselves and when the unknown encroaches on our territory, we lash out at it. If these guys haven't figured that out yet from monitoring our TV shows and news, it's high time we made them aware of it. Permission to launch one across their bow, sir?"

Nathan smirked and laid a restraining hand on Edwards' forearm. "Not quite yet, COB. Ops/Comm, shut down whatever you're currently broadcasting to the aliens and give me an open mike."

"Captain," Wright began warningly, "these first contact comms were diagrammed out a long time ago by men a lot smarter than you or me—and vetted by Gordon Lee himself. Are you sure you want to upset that plan?"

Nathan looked exasperated. "Damn it, Christopher, the Deltans weren't at those meetings and they aren't cooperating with our freaking plans. I respect Gordon more than you can possibly know, but he—and you—both know the maxim that no plan survives contact with the enemy. Now, I'm not prepared to fully classify the Deltans as my enemy, but they for certain aren't trying to be our friends. Now, I'm going to call them up and ask them, essentially, 'What the fuck are you doing here?' Are you behind me on this plan or not?"

No one said a word. Finally, his eyes cast downward, Wright answered. "I'm with you, Nathan, every step of the way."

Nathan turned back to the main screen and pulled a flexible mike mounted to his chair's intercom panel closer to his mouth. He looked at the Deltan formation. Currently, all four vessels were in view, the Junkyard at the bottom of the drive-star, closest to them and preparing to go behind the drive in its orbit. The Control Ship was at the top and swinging down, preceded by the organic form of the Polyp. The Cathedral had just emerged from the limn of the drive. The *Sword's* recon probes beside each vessel were invisible at this distance and magnification, but they were there nonetheless.

Nathan pressed a button for the radio circuit and spoke. "This is Commander Nathaniel Robert Kelley, of the *USS Sword of Liberty*. To the beings in charge of the alien ships now approaching our solar system and world, I greet you in peace. To us, your arrival has been anticipated and dreaded for over twenty years. So much so, that we have done what was deemed physically impossible. We built this ship and climbed within her, and we made the long journey to meet you. We are here, and we only wish to speak with you, to make whatever contact we can.

"You are an enigma to us. You show off a vast technological advantage. You have traveled for twenty light-years over seven decades to reach us, to come to our world physically, yet you have made no attempt to contact us, to let us know why. We are not a people for whom peace comes naturally. It is something we must all work at, and when it fails, through either a lack of trying by one side or another, or in response to a deliberate aggressive act, it is a sad, terrible thing to behold.

"Right now, you, the people we refer to as the Deltans, are a worrisome reality ... either a potential threat which must be dealt with, or a potential friend that we do not want to strike unjustly. I don't know if you understand me, or even if you can hear me, but we are here to resolve that question, and we aren't going to leave until you make contact with us."

Nathan and the bridge crew stared at the main screen. All over the ship, the other crew looked at their own screens as well, following the long attempts at contact with nervous, worried anticipation. Back in Engineering Central Control, Kris held her breath.

Nathan let the silence stretch out. The Deltan formation continued to revolve sedately about. Shaking his head, he pressed down the radio key again. "Please. Please give us some sign that you're alive, that you understand us, that you acknowledge our presence here. Please give us some sign of how things are going to proceed between your people and my own."

The formation suddenly stopped revolving, held in place by unknown, unimaginable forces. Aboard each alien vessel, heat surged to the surface. Before Yvonne Clark at Weps/Sensors or Mike Simmons back in CIC could tell the bridge and Nathan what was happening, beams lashed out from the vessels.

Three of the recon probes were struck down, reduced to slag and vapor by lasers from the Polyp, the Cathedral, and the Junkyard. The

Control Ship also fired, but with the silvery beam it had previously used on *Promise*. As before, the recon probe wavered, becoming indistinct, collapsing into fine, brilliant dust. This cloud of dust then maneuvered of its own accord, streaming into unseen vents between the lobster-like overlapping plates of the Control Ship, rendered and captured as some scintillating prize.

Nathan's gaze turned hard and he released the radio key. Without a word, he put on his helmet and began to check the tightness of his straps. Following his lead, the COB and the XO did the same.

Now speaking over the suit-to-suit circuit, Edwards observed wryly, "As signs go, that one's pretty damn unambiguous. You in agreement there, XO?"

Wright said nothing. He simply turned to lock eyes with Edwards and gave a single curt nod.

Nathan saw it and nodded back. "XO, prep for battle. Ready all weapons for release, evacuate the hull, and shift to Charlie Stations. Let's send them a message of our own."

15: "DEATH FROM ABOVE

August 16, 2046; USS Sword of Liberty (DA-1), 0.48 light-years from Earth, 0.033 light-seconds (10,000 km) from alien formation; Mission Day 529

"Attention all hands! The ship is at General Quarters, Bravo Stations. Now shift to General Quarters, Charlie Stations. Now shift to General Quarters, Charlie Stations for battle. The ship anticipates imminent combat maneuvering and damage. All personnel will move to Charlie Station pods immediately. All personnel unable to do so will report to the Commanding Officer on the bridge. Now shift to General Quarters, Charlie Stations."

The ship's voice—that of a stern, but caring matron who had only the crew's best interests at heart, whether they wanted to do as she said or not—issued her commands all over the ship and then repeated herself. The *Sword of Liberty*'s second pronouncement of the call to Charlie Stations was spoiled, however, by the roar of moving air as each section's atmosphere was pumped out, leaving behind a near vacuum to minimize the progressive damage a hull breach or blowout might cause.

The crew had no need of the air, suited as they were, but it was missed nonetheless. Its removal made reality of a situation that had been only a simulated potential outcome before this. And not only did the dwindling rush of atmosphere isolate each crewmember from one another, it also isolated a future of limitless possibilities from a present along a single, dreaded course.

Nathan felt the confining skin of his suit swell and stiffen slightly in reaction to the drop in pressure, but he had little time to savor the sensation. There was simply too much to do, and after months of preparations and idle time spent wondering how things would go, suddenly there just did not seem to be enough time to do what must be done.

Under his watchful eye, the bridge crew shifted to Charlie Stations. Their consoles and screens went dark and hatches slid open beneath each of their acceleration couches. The couches fell back and the hatches slid shut over their occupants, entombing them within the armored allocarbium structure of the ship itself. The four watches went first, then

Edwards and the XO.

Nathan checked a series of telltales on his one remaining active screen. When it showed twenty-eight green lights and only seven amber, his crew safely ensconced within their pods with only himself, the absent diplomatic team, and poor Diane Rutherford missing, he initiated his own descent.

His couch stretched out and fell backward into its recessed alcove in the deck and then confined him to darkness as the hatch closed over him. As soon as the hatch clicked shut, the interior of the pod closed in, its inner membrane swelling to squeeze him tightly. The space between the walls of the pod and himself and his couch were now filled with a force-dampening gel, an all-encompassing cushion which, it was hoped, would allow himself and the rest of the crew to withstand a greater g-load and the violent shocks of combat.

A specially shaped screen settled over his helmet's faceplate and Nathan was suddenly awash in information, visual data similar to what he could see on his regular screens, but now presented in a three dimensional, comprehensive format. The Deltan drive-star was an immense, false color sphere, almost filling the area in front of them. Along one polar axis, arbitrarily designated "south", a lance of pure energy flowed outward—their thrust corona, instant death if approached too closely. And orbiting blithely around the drive's equator was the constellation of four ships, the Deltans themselves.

Nathan goggled at the imposing whole, of the cosmic forces they were about to challenge and his resolve shrank for a moment. Feeling himself begin to shirk from the task at hand, he gritted his teeth and forced his doubts to the back of his mind. Nathan blinked, re-orienting himself to the combat virtual reality, seeing it not as an implacable whole, but as a series of tasks. Take on one, complete it, then move on to the next. Then repeat. And so on.

His nerves calmed and he flexed his hands, finding his chair's familiar armrest controls even through the confining sluggishness of the force gel. They were comforting in their assured lethality, a system he could have faith in, even when his faith in himself began to falter.

He keyed his mike. "XO, comm check and sitrep."

Wright's voice came through his helmet speakers loud and clear. "Lima Charlie, Captain. I have sat comms with all intermediate control stations as well. Railgun power is at 85% and rising, combat rounds to the autoloader. Laser power supplies are at 60% and tuned. Missile launch coils are charged and holding, and missiles 01-86 are warmed, spun up, and internal warhead and drive capacitor banks are fully charged. Radiator loading is at 38% and reactor power is at 45%. Ready to answer all bells."

Nathan smiled. "Bells" on an engine order telegraph were how steamships ordered up speed changes. It warmed him to hear Wright invoke such an archaic way of describing their readiness. Hopefully some of the spirit of those old steam-powered cruisers and their "Tin-Can Sailors" would be with them today as they initiated the first space battle in man's history.

"Very well," Nathan answered back. "TAO, Captain, I hold us in visual of all four alien vessels. I'm feeling a little exposed. Launch pattern Oscar Four and then get ready to hit the deck. We'll be maneuvering closer to the drive star and heading for the Junkyard to head off any direct fire from the other three ships."

LT Simmons, in CIC as the Tactical Action Officer, responded promptly. "Aye aye, sir. Oscar Four initiated. Be advised: tactical reaction time is estimated at a tenth of a second now. If we close the Junkyard, we'll be increasing our exposure to their direct fire."

Tactical reaction time was a term they had created to account for the peculiarities of long range space combat. In space, there was no horizon. Every target was within visual range of every other target, thus as long as they could see the enemy, the enemy could see—and fire—at them. The only defense they had was distance and maneuverability.

They saw the enemy and the enemy saw them by either the light and radiation they emitted or the light and radiation reflected off their respective hulls. To strike with a direct fire weapon like a laser or a railgun, you just had to point the weapon at the target and fire. If the objective moved enough in the time between emitting its targeting radiation, aiming your weapon, and the weapon beam or shot crossing the intervening distance, the weapon would miss.

At short ranges, lasers could see, point, fire, and hit virtually instantly. At longer ranges though, lightspeed lag and bearing resolution began to play a part. At their range to the Deltan ships, light took 33 thousandths of a second to cross the distance. Double that time and add in any processing time or physical aiming time and one arrived at a tactical reaction time of at least a tenth of a second. Thus they had a tenth of a second to accelerate the ship out of the way if they were going to avoid being hit. And since either they or the Deltans could easily account for continuous accelerations by leading their targets, that meant the *Sword of Liberty* would have to continuously change its instantaneous acceleration every tenth of a second.

This basically amounted to a very bumpy ride, and as a defensive strategy, it would only work if they remained well outside their current range. Closing the Junkyard or any of the Deltan ships would render that lag even less effective.

Nathan considered all of that in an instant and answered Simmons. "Roger that, Mike, but we haven't got much choice. If we stay where we are, we're going to get targeted by all four. Once the star blocks the other three, we can pull out away from the Junkyard and increase the time lag, but we're going to have to get our hull dirty at some point. At least they're a lot bigger than we are and can't maneuver as fast."

"That we know of," Simmons said, with a dubious tone.

"Understood. Execute launch."

In answer, twenty status symbols went from green to red. Between the evacuated hull and the dampening of the pod's force gel, Nathan could not hear or feel the opening of the missile hatches, or the launch of them on their inaugural and terminal journeys, but he focused on them just the same.

Twenty friendly missile tracks appeared around the *Sword*'s own track symbol. Simmons called back. "Initial salvo away. Five missiles designated for each target, ripple warhead pattern. Missile AIs are in autonomous mode."

"Very well, TAO. Break, Helm, dive for the star's horizon and make for a 1,000 km high-v CPA to the Junkyard. Flank acceleration."

"Helm, aye, sir." Nathan could hear the glee in Andrew Weston's voice. Their destroyer was many times more massive than any fighter Weston had ever flown, but it also was stronger and more powerful as well.

Immense maneuvering thrusters flared out in cerulean brilliance, kicking the nose of the destroyer down toward the roiling, angry surface of the Deltan drive-star. Then—checking that swing—the main drive erupted in light, thrusting the magnificent ship just to one side of their enemy, for a closest-point-of-approach of a mere 1000 km.

Nathan grunted and tried to breathe as the air was forced from his lungs. He felt the gel pump to a higher pressure around him, focused on his extremities, much as a fighter pilot's g-suit would do. Unfelt in the discomfort of the sudden fifteen-g acceleration, a cocktail of osmotic stimulants and anti-nausea drugs were injected into him. His vision cleared as his heart and diaphragm pumped harder, forcing the blood and oxygen back into his brain.

Trained pilots and astronauts could withstand up to nine gravities of acceleration in a sitting position, and almost twice that lying down and augmented by modern bio-engineered support systems. Nathan and his crew were not trained to as great a degree, but they would make do. They had no other choice.

Of course, though 15 g's was quite high, it was nowhere near what the ship's composite frame could handle. The hull groaned and popped as its structure was put to the test, but it was only the cracking of prize-fighter's knuckles as he entered the fray. The *Sword of Liberty* welcomed the torturous thrust and begged for more, though more would surely render her crew unconscious or dead.

The twenty missiles, left far behind her, were under no such restrictions. They had no crew to black out, only a mission to complete. After a moment's dormancy to allow the ship to clear, each missile's sacrificial capacitor bank broke down into a storm of free electrons, channeled into their enhanced photon drives. The missiles streaked away from one another at 450 meters per second squared, five heading for the Junkyard in front of them at five wildly divergent angles of attack, and the other fifteen headed in the opposite direction for the three ships clustered on the opposite side of the drive.

The missiles directed at the Junkyard passed the destroyer which had borne them and closed rapidly with their quarry. The jumbled, misshapen alien vessel—reacting to this new activity—fired a pair of beams: one, the silvery beam used by the Control ship to "dust" the Promise and their sub-probes; the other, the laser utilized before with such devastating effect.

It would not be enough.

The laser struck missile simply vanished, shredded into plasma and glowing, high velocity shrapnel. The silvery beam, slowly eating away at the targeted missile's body, forced the weapon's AI to react. It transmitted a warning to its fellow missiles and the *Sword of Liberty*, then deployed its warheads early while it was still intact.

The other three missiles boosted their forward acceleration to a hundred gravities, and began maneuvering wildly across the firmament even as they closed more rapidly. Their motion was lost a fraction of a second later, though, as the six warheads from the harried missile exploded, silhouetting its brethren for a brief instant before dazzling its attacker with multiple beams of coherent x-rays.

The lasing warheads were much too far away to do any real damage, but they did succeed in momentarily blinding the alien ship to what approached. Or, at least, that was the effect as the other three missiles finished closing, unperturbed.

The three unseen shapes suddenly blossomed into eighteen smaller objects, each twisting down in rapidly shifting corkscrews. In a coordinated dance of fire, light, and motion, the individual warheads exploded in sequence. Beams of invisible radiance stabbed into the Junkyard, vaporizing sections of hull and structure. Geysers of plasma erupted from the ship, blowing out chasms of destruction, deep into the vessel. For all its immensity, the alien vessel seemed relatively weak in construction.

The laser warheads fired like the steps of spiral staircase, each one closer than the last. After twelve such successively closer and harsher beams, the remaining six warheads were near enough to switch modes. Two warheads exploded in maximal fusion fire immediately above the mangled surface of the Junkyard, eating deeper in and joining the canyons of carnage together into a glowing, bowl-like depression. The remaining four warheads, driving in at hypervelocity and max acceleration, pierced this softened, half-melted surface, each attempting to drive further and further into the 45 km bulk of the alien ship.

Straining under the oppressive weight of flank acceleration, Nathan could not cheer as the Junkyard flashed into fire and light, but he desperately wanted to. The last four warheads of the salvo exploded almost simultaneously, and every bit of their energy was expended into the structure of the alien vessel. The ship ballooned up with light and broke apart into kilometers long chunks and smaller, skyscraper-sized pieces of burning, out-gassing debris. If it had appeared unformed and purposeless before to their human eyes, its form had been highly functional art compared to what it was now.

Nathan, unable to really move or speak under this level of acceleration, twitched his fingers in the appropriate brevity pattern, sending a text command to Weston on the Helm. Responding to the order, Weston cut the acceleration and slewed the ship bow-on toward the Junkyard's expanding debris field.

Nathan surged upward in response to the sudden freefall, restrained by his seat's straps and the confining gel. His heart raced wildly and his eyes felt as if they were about to pop from his head. It took a conscious effort to slow and shallow out his rapid, gulping breaths. Counter-meds pumped into his bloodstream, slowing his heart to a calmer rate and bringing his blood pressure back to a normal range. He tried moving tentatively, fighting the confinement of the gel.

His movements were sluggish, and every muscle and joint ached in protest, but nothing more adverse seemed to have occurred. He keyed his mike. "XO, Captain, SITREP."

There was a pause, and then Wright responded, his voice hoarse.

"Captain, XO, the Junkyard appears to be demolished, sir. The energy sources we registered with our recon probe before are either gone or they're lost in the haze from the warhead explosions. We aren't picking up any purposeful signals or activity among the major pieces of debris, and we are un-attacked at the moment."

"That's always nice," Edwards said, breaking into the net.

"I'm rather fond of that myself, COB," Nathan answered back, smiling. "How's the crew, XO?"

"Strong vitals on all, sir, but it looks like Sarmiento up in Railgun control and Blake back in Main Propulsion may have been rendered unconscious. WEPS and CHENG are both trying to wake them verbally. The general net is a litany of groans and complaints, if you want to listen in."

Nathan frowned. "No thanks. I'm sure they're just expressing what I feel. On Blake and Sarmiento, let me know if they can't be woken and I'll authorize you to shock them or give them an extra dose of 'happy-wakey'. I don't want anybody out of their pod, though, unless it's a last resort."

"Roger that, Captain."

Nathan shifted his attention back to the debris field. The globe of demolished ruins began to flatten out into an irregular, concave ellipsoid, giving some measure of shape and definition to the unknown fields holding the Deltan ships in position around the drive's equator. Some pieces of the Junkyard had achieved escape velocity and now sailed out into the infinite night. Others had been thrown down below the ship's orbit and burned away in the upper reaches of the drive-star's roiling plasma.

"TAO, Captain," Nathan said into his mike, "How are we for collision avoidance? Do we need to haul out to the north or south of the orbital band, or can we stay in this plane? We're going to need to be close in to the drive at the equator if we're going to only engage one ship at a time."

"Looking, sir. Wait one," Simmons said. It was a quiet minute until Simmons responded. "Sir, if we close to within 300 km of the drive and stay in this plane, we'll avoid most of the debris. The helm may need to dodge a few big chunks, and I may need to shoot some away, but we can get through from this orbit. In approximately 10 minutes, I can have us in position to engage the Cathedral."

Nathan nodded to himself. "Very well, pass your recommended course to the helm and execute."

The ship accelerated again, this time at a more reasonable two g's. After experiencing seven and a half times as much, it felt almost pleasurable—just a subtle sensation of weight on their chests.

Edwards keyed in on a private chat channel, his voice only slightly strained. "Hey, Skipper. What are the odds we're going to find three expanding debris clouds like this one when we cross that fake horizon?"

Nathan shook his head. "I'm not laying any. The Junkyard was the first target reached. The salvoes for the other three ships wouldn't have hit until after this strike was complete, so chances are if they have any sort of command and control channel to the other side of the drive-star, they weren't that surprised by what our missiles could do. And I'll be amazed if the Control Ship proves as easy to take down as the Junkyard was."

"Well, I'm going to do a little positive thinking along those lines. Maybe I can skew fate our way if I wish for it hard enough."

Nathan smiled. "That ever work for you?"

"Not since I was eight years old." Edwards chuckled roughly.

The private channel closed, and Nathan turned his attention back to his three-dimensional battlespace VR. The Junkyard's debris tracks all had false color velocity and acceleration leaders overlaid upon them, with ghostly traces showing where the pieces would be at their closest point of approach. It was a mess, but the layout of the display clearly pointed out the hard spots. The helm's path input showed the course Weston threaded through the swarm of debris, and it appeared as if his maneuvers would neatly avoid any damaging collisions. Nathan grunted his approval and moved on from that immediate problem to the tactical one that still lay before him.

Three ships to go, and to take them one at a time, the *Sword of Liberty* would have to stay as close to the "deck" as possible, that deck in this case being the fiery surface of the drive. That would create a horizon they could peek around, and which they could interpose should they need to beat a hasty retreat. However, it would also further expose them to the heat and radiation pouring out from the miniature sun, cripple their radiator efficiency, not to mention cutting the tactical reaction time even more, and, unfortunately, closing off an entire direction to free maneuver.

In this case, the goods slightly edged out the bads, but too narrowly for Nathan's liking. If he could distract the Cathedral when they made their emergence, though, the odds might improve a great deal.

He keyed his mike. "TAO, Captain, I want to flush another 10 missiles. We know the general location of the Cathedral, right?"

Simmons sounded uncertain. "Yes sir, assuming they haven't shifted their orbit."

"We'll have to chance it. I don't want them watching for us at the equator. Send two flights of five Excaliburs each to the north. Have them cut in along two different longitudinal paths to intercept the Cathedral, and along a higher arc than the one we're making."

"Captain, there's a hell of a strong magnetic field at the north pole, opposite the thrust axis. I can't get the birds too close to it without frying their electronics."

"Understood. Do the best you can. I just don't want them looking to the east when we pop up. Time the intercept so the warheads are lasing when we come into visual range."

"Aye aye, sir. And what if we've lucked out and the Cathedral's already gone?"

Nathan smiled to himself. "Then, by all means, program our bloodthirsty little birds to go for the Control Ship. It's the next one on my target list anyway."

"Yes, sir!" Simmons dropped out of the connection to pass Nathan's orders on to his watchstanders in CIC.

Nathan, in turn, looked at his overall status. Blake and Sarmiento appeared to be awake, and the railgun and lasers fired intermittently, clearing the way in front of them from pieces too small for Weston to maneuver around. It seemed to be working. Their small, impossible endeavor might actually have a chance.

Nathan allowed hope to rise in his heart. Scrolling through the crew status icons, he lingered over Kris's, burning brightly green. For a moment, he nearly keyed her icon to open a private channel, to exchange a small measure of the optimism and pride he felt with the woman he loved, but he pulled back at the last. There was still too much to be done for now. Besides she knew how he felt.

And there would always be time to tell her afterward.

"Launching polar salvoes, Captain," Simmons said, breaking into his reverie.

"Very well," Nathan responded. Again, unheard and unfelt, ten missiles launched from out of the port and starboard cells. In a pair of phalanxes, the missiles streaked away to disappear past the arcing, flaring horizon, each group going at diverging angles to the north.

A private comm channel blinked in the corner of his vision. Nathan keyed it and Wright spoke in his ear. "Captain, radiator loading is at 87% and climbing, but we're operating at a lower capacity than before. We just aren't shedding the heat."

Nathan took a look at the radiator's status bar, confirming the XO's warning. "Roger that, Christopher. This was to be expected for this phase of the attack. Once we get a visual on the Cathedral, we can break for a higher orbit and get away from the drive's heat."

"Yes, sir, but when that happens, we'll be producing a lot more of our own heat as well. We won't be back to a balanced discharge rate until we get out in the black and shut down some of the hotter systems. We have to cool."

Nathan grimaced. "We can't, not yet. Listen, your warning is duly noted, but we do have additional radiator capacity, and if worse comes to worse, we can use the internal heat sinks."

"That's going to cut things pretty tight, Nathan."

"Hey, we're out here beyond the ass end of the solar system, by ourselves, in a still-technically-stolen ship, fighting implacable, mysterious aliens nobody even really believed in till a month or so before we left. Things have been cut tight for a long damn time."

Wright paused, then answered, "Yes, sir. Roger that. I'll keep an eye on it."

"Thanks, Christopher." The private channel icon closed and Wright was gone. Nathan focused again upon the slowly rolling sphere of plasma that filled the lower half of his view. It would be any moment now ... .

There.

Explosions began to ripple across the horizon to the north of the equator. Whatever the beams they spawned were aimed at was still hidden by the fiery limn of the drive. Nathan keyed his mike back into the tactical net. "Heads up, people. Our distractions are underway. The Cathedral should be rolling into view any moment. Let's go ahead and launch a few more while we're still hidden. TAO, designate four more salvoes, two north, two south, five missiles each, targeting the Control Ship and the Polyp. Let's keep them involved in their own affairs while we're finishing off the Cathedral."

"Aye aye, Captain," Simmons said.

"All right. Helm, as soon as we come into view, I want to start evasive maneuvers. They aren't going to be as effective this close in, but every little bit will help. And be prepared to roll the hull if we get targeted by lasers. We'll do better if we don't allow them to concentrate energy in any one spot."

"Aye aye, sir," Weston answered. As he did so, 20 missile icons sprang forth from their ship and disappeared around the drive to the north and the south.

Explosions continued to light up the horizon, each one higher up and closer in, as the warheads maneuvered closer to their objective. Now that the detonations were well above the blazing horizon, though, Nathan could see that not all of them were the brilliant white eruptions of lasing fusion. Some of them exploded more dimly and haphazardly, ignited by counterfire from the alien ships.

He frowned. "Shit."

Magnified by the *Sword of Liberty's* sensors, the Cathedral rose into view. Her gothic arches and ornately carved, stone-like halls were gouged and broken, venting fluids and bright gasses into the vacuum. It was not demolished as they had hoped, but it had not escaped unscathed either. As he watched, another set of warheads flashed into fusion brilliance, and their unseen x-ray lasers lanced deeply into the distant alien vessel.

The Cathedral responded in kind, casting out beams of red light made visible from the gasses and vapors pouring from her hull. Nathan glanced over to see if they intended to take out any warheads, but he lost them as Weston began the maneuvers he had ordered.

Fifteen gravities of acceleration again squeezed him down, but this time they were accompanied by violent jerks from side to side, back and forth. Anti-nausea meds and stimulants flooded his system, allowing Nathan to push the sheer physical torture to the back of his mind, and to still concentrate on the battle.

His fingers jerked as much as they were able under the crushing thrust, sending coded texts to his crew. Four more missiles blasted out from the sides of the destroyer. Nathan did the count in his head. He only had 32 more, but it had been a worthwhile expense, both to cause the damage they had thus far achieved and to test their effectiveness against the Deltan ships' defenses. Should they fail here, that data would be of paramount importance to the ships being built back home.

Determined to give the missiles the best chance he could, but reluctant to expend any more of his dwindling supply, Nathan's fingers twitched again, sending new commands out. Simmons and Weston received the order and took action. The violent jerks the hull underwent smoothed out somewhat and the Cathedral steadied up, directly ahead of them. The railgun locked on and went into continuous fire, sending shot after shot screaming through the narrowing void. The damage imparted by their kinetic and chemical energy might be no more than a nuisance to be endured by the immense ship, but he hoped it would be enough of a distraction that the missiles would have a greater effect.

Now aware of the new threat just risen over the drive's horizon, the Cathedral turned its wounded attention toward the *Sword of Liberty*. Twin beams of laser light flashed out from the ornate arches of the spherical alien ship. Slag erupted from the destroyer's bow, her first wounds in the battle.

High energy photons flayed at the crystalline armor covering the *Sword*. The armor performed as designed, channeling the heat and energy outward from the point of incidence, spreading it over a wider area in an attempt to let it dissipate harmlessly into space, but the power poured in much too fast. Plates swelled and buckled, and finally melted through as the beams continued to fire on the same section of armor.

Alarms sprang up on Nathan's screen as the hull was breached. A wisp of gas erupted from the mostly evacuated space below the breach. Then a crew icon went red—Emil Harmon, the weapons tech monitoring the dorsal radar array, fell off the grid. Nathan winced. He keyed an urgent command to the Helm, but before he could pass along the order, Weston responded.

The *Sword of Liberty* began to spin along her long axis, denying the enemy weapons a single point on which to concentrate their fury. The still-firing beams went from burning holes through the armor to tracing glowing circles and arcs of semi-melted armor all around the mission hull. Hull plates swelled, but now stayed intact, dissipating the energy through the surrounding plates as originally intended. And all the while, the railgun continued to fire.

The spin—coupled with the high acceleration, and a renewed, if lesser, jerking from evasive maneuvers—threatened to overcome even Nathan's anti-nausea doping. He spared a glance at the crew status, and saw that several people showed amber, unconscious or otherwise unresponsive as they all tried to endure Weston's efforts to keep them alive. Nathan's lips were peeled back in an acceleration induced rictus, but he felt his attempt to smile as he saw that Kris's icon was still a strong, vibrant green.

Back on the tactical view, the four missiles launched at the Cathedral reached terminal and separated into 24 maneuvering warheads. The lasers inundating the *Sword* were joined by additional beams seeking out these smaller targets, but before they could take any of them out, small explosions peppered the hull of the alien ship. Railgun rounds rained down upon the Cathedral, unseen and unopposed as they lacked the brilliance of the destroyer's or the missiles' active drives, and since the Deltans did not seem to use any form of radar.

It would take more rounds than the *Sword of Liberty* could carry to destroy the Cathedral with the small projectiles, but the ploy worked. The much-deadlier warheads closed a great deal further than previous salvoes had, and they began to lase at their optimal range.

Flaring out in white light, the fusion blasts cast tightly collimated beams of energy into the Cathedral. Slag and incandescent gas boiled away from the ship's hull. It was a more rugged construction than the Junkyard, but it was by no means rugged enough. Lasers abandoned the destroyer and again shifted their focus onto the encroaching warheads, but they were now too close and too numerous to take out completely.

A pair of warheads came near enough to switch modes. Fusion fire blossomed close aboard and engulfed whole sections of the Cathedral, blasting arches flat and setting its stones ablaze. More importantly, its lasers abruptly stopped as something critical within broke. The ship appeared defenseless, and Nathan cheered inside his head.

Before the last few warheads could administer the coup de gras, though, the Cathedral suddenly swung out of position. The warheads flew harmlessly through the space she had just occupied, their explosions wasted upon an empty void. Nathan jerked in shock and expanded his tactical view.

The Control Ship swept up over the drive's horizon, pulling the Cathedral and the Polyp around it until they were arrayed to its north and south rather than along the equatorial plane. The Cathedral was burned and pummeled, and the Polyp was little better, its organic curves and intricate, tattooed designs marred by x-ray laser gouges and blackened sections of hull. The Control Ship's overlapping, lobster-like metallic plates were also gouged and burned, but to a lesser degree. She looked battle hardened rather than battle bled.

Nathan tapped in an order and the *Sword* broke northward and made for a higher orbit, seeking salvation through distance and greater maneuvering room. The Control Ship would have none of that, however. A dozen lasers blazed from its hull, each striking the destroyer and burning glowing paths along her hull. Now, not only the forward mission hull was at risk, but the radiators and the propulsion module were attacked as well.

The propulsion module, built of the same materials as the mission hull, fared as well as it had under the onslaught from the Cathedral. The radiator spine, however, was unarmored and relatively fragile by necessity. Radiator plates shattered and slagged, spinning away from the rapidly maneuvering ship. Torrents of coolant evaporated from broken lines and heat loads rose threateningly on all the ship's systems.

The radiator had always been their Achilles Heel. Vital to the thermodynamic heat engines throughout the ship, it was their chief vulnerability, and they could not fight or survive without it.

Nathan winced at the options available to him. They were much closer to the Control Ship than he ever intended. He could either turn the *Sword* completely away from the their enemy, and hope they could gain sufficient maneuvering distance before the drive was irreparably damaged—or he could point directly at their enemy and close to knife-fighting range. Either way, he had to interpose the armored portions of the hull between the incoming fire and the radiator, or they were doomed.

Nathan tapped his order in and groaned as the ship swung around. The nose of the destroyer pointed straight at the incoming fire. All four thrust pylons lit up with nearly random jets of light as the ship leapt back and forth along a suicidal closing vector, dodging away from the enemy lasers as much as possible, even as their range fell away to make the beams steadily more effective.

At his order, missiles shot outward from the port and starboard cells, one after another. The railgun fired continuously, targeting each individual laser battery aboard the Control Ship. The *Sword of Liberty*'s laser batteries fired as well, still too far out to cause any damage, but hopefully enough to blind any targeting sensors coming after them.

Damaged beyond capacity, the radiators were no longer able to discard the ever rising heat produced by all the systems running on the ship. Coolant diverted instead to internal heat sinks, blocks of ice nearby every major system on the ship. The blocks absorbed the waste heat, melting, and then boiling away to relieve the crippling temps each system produced. Steam erupted from vents all around the *Sword of Liberty*.

Seen from the distant re-trans pod, the destroyer was a valkyrie afire, a shooting star pouring the most devastating forces the Earth could muster at an enemy that still remained unexplained, mysterious. It was awesome to behold.

And ultimately futile.

Responding to the 32 missiles and then 192 warheads released from the *Sword*, the Control Ship shifted its depressingly effective laser fire away from the destroyer to the individually targeted weapons. Too many flared out into the flames of failure, rather than the brilliant flashes of lasing fusion. Too few closed enough to do real damage with their beams. And the destroyer was still not spared. Now the Control Ship's silvery beam reached out.

The beam of particles struck the spinning, maneuvering destroyer on the dorsal surface first, and then inscribed a tight spiral around the mission hull. Unlike the lasers, though, the damage here was not lessened by the spin. Wherever the strange beam struck, the hull wavered, becoming indistinct and collapsing into dust. If anything, their defensive spin spread the damage around more than if they had remained steady.

Nathan cursed to himself, even as he praised the increasingly accurate fire from the railgun and the lasers. The warheads were mostly expended now, and though the damage they had dealt was impressive, it did not seem to be having nearly enough effect on the Control Ship. The better aimed railgun and laser fire, on the other hand, at least made a few "mission kills"—several laser emplacements aboard the alien ship had gone dark. But soon, those that remained would again turn on the *Sword*.

That assumed they would still be a viable target, though. Whatever the silvery beam did, it appeared frightening in its effectiveness. Silvery dust streamed away from the hull as plates were eaten away. And the damage lingered, growing outward from the stricken areas of the hull even after the beam had passed by. If the rate his hull was eaten continued, it would be through the armor plates and into the pressure hull within a couple of minutes.

A text popped up in his vision. It was from Kris. "NANOTECH. PARTICLE BEAM IS ASSEMBLOR CARRIER. HAVE IDEA. DROP TO LOW ACCEL. MUST EXIT POD TO TRY." Nathan was confused, barely registering what she was trying to say, but he did as she asked, texting the order to Weston at the Helm.

The ship went into near freefall, still aimed at the Control Ship and still firing away. Recognizing the threat, as well as their greater vulnerability while no longer maneuvering, Simmons had his watchstanders concentrate on the source of the silvery beam. While waiting for the shots to reach their target, Nathan focused on Kris's icon. It and that of her Electrical Officer had gone red as soon as they left their pods, and he felt helpless and adrift as he waited for her to come back online.

Explosions flared upon the Control Ship, blanketing the area where the "assemblor" beam fired from. The beam cut out intermittently and then faded away to nothing, shut off at the source. Nathan almost cheered, but the nano-scale eating machines that Kris believed them to be had already been deposited on the hull and continued their destructive work. Whether the beam kept re-depositing them or not, they would eventually turn the ship into dust if Kris was unable to stop them.

Her voice cut in to the tactical net, causing an intense surge of relief in Nathan. "Okay! Since we're fresh outta missiles, I decoupled their power cables from the main bus and grounded it to the outer hull. I'm gonna close the breaker and charge the exterior of the ship. Hopefully those suckers are small and fragile enough to kill with a little excessive voltage."

Nathan shook his head, exasperated. "Stop talking about it and just do it, CHENG!"

"Fine! Just don't be mad if I pop every other breaker on the ship in the process. Here goes."

The speakers in his helmet squealed and popped, and his VR display flickered and went black for a moment, but it came back almost immediately. Red status icons blinked for all of the crew and for a number of systems. Railgun and laser fire had stopped. Panicked, Nathan called out, "Kris! XO! COB! Report."

"Captain, XO, I think we're okay. It's just the monitoring systems and weapons that have gone offline. COB, get verbals from every station on the general net, and I'll work with the department heads on system status and recovery."

"Roger, XO," Edwards agreed.

Nathan took a deep breath. "Okay. CHENG, report. Did it work?"

He looked at the hull cameras even as she spoke. The spirals of damage were no longer growing and no more dust streamed away from the ship. Kris spoke up, her voice filled with static. "Yep. I think so. No more critters eating the hull anyway. I've got a lot of smoke and electrical damage back here, but we're still in the fight."

Nathan took a look at the battlespace, considering that. The Control Ship was gouged and blackened, quiescent for the moment as it apparently contemplated its own damage. Their warheads were all gone, either expended in the attack or blasted by the Deltan defenses. The nanotech beam was also gone, as well as several of its laser emplacements. For the moment, the battle was paused, both ships wounded, warily watching their foe.

"Nope," he said into the net. "We're done. There's no way we can stop them with what we have left, and we've given them pause with what we're able to do. It's time for retreat. They don't know that we're dry at the moment, and I want to get away from here before they can repair their systems enough to try to take us. Everybody back into your pods. Helm, give me flank acceleration for the horizon and let's see if we can make it home before they do."

"Roger that, sir," Weston answered. "Fifteen g's in ten seconds, everybody!"

"We're buttoned up down in Engineering," Kris yelled. "Let 'er rip."

Weston fired the thrusters, turning perpendicular to the Control Ship, and the propulsion hull lit up with flank thrust. The drive star began to roll by beneath them, putting distance and the burning horizon between themselves and the Deltans.

But the Control Ship—dormant while they had cruised by at a constant velocity—awoke now to full destructive fury, unwilling to accept a draw.

Six lasers shot out, all aimed for the same point at the weakest area of their hull, along the damaged radiator spine. Radiator panels burned straight through and came apart. Allocarbium bracing, made up of hardened alloys and nearly indestructible carbon nanotubes, vaporized under the thermal onslaught. Gantries, pipes, and shafts parted, and the spine of the ship cracked right down the middle.

Fluids and vapor shot out from the damage and the destroyer snapped in two.

The propulsion hull barreled past the mission hull at flank thrust, sending both halves tumbling away from one another before the drive shut down. Cut off from all power, the mission hull went dark, the data stream it had continually sent toward the re-trans pod now silent. The propulsion hull, never equipped with communication antennas, was robbed of a final voice as well.

The *Sword of Liberty* was no more.

February 8, 2047; White House Oval Office; Washington DC

Lydia Russ watched the destroyer's final moments in real time, six months after the fact. No one in the room said a word, every one of them shocked into silence as the transmission from the *Sword of Liberty* cut away and the retransmission pod unemotionally kept up its broadcast, unaware that it sent forth its masters' epitaph.

White faced and barely able to breathe, Lydia could not turn aside as the two halves of the destroyer spun uncontrolled around the Control Ship. Constructs emerged from the implacable vessel, each one forming up around the two halves of the *Sword of Liberty*. Bracketed by these alien devices, the destroyer sections were steadied up and then pulled into the interior of the Control Ship. The warped and damaged plates of the alien vessel, which had slid open to reveal a dark interior volume, slid shut once more, entombing her friends, denying them even the solace of a burial in space.

The re-trans pod dutifully recorded the Deltan formation as it once again began revolving about its drive sphere, but whatever was to be done about the destroyed Junkyard and the heavily damaged other vessels went unanswered. As soon as the Control Ship and the Deltan formation passed within close proximity of the pod, a flash of light lashed out and all transmissions ceased. The stream from half a light-year away fell to static.

Lydia slowly turned away from the wall-mounted screen and glared at Carl Sykes and President Tomlinson. Tomlinson looked as wan and in shock as Lydia had. Sykes seemed perturbed, but not dismayed.

Lydia pointed a finger at the screen. "They're gone, Carl. We just saw them give up their lives to stop those damned Deltans. They made a sacrifice, assured that it wouldn't be in vain. But when I go to sleep tonight, and they're there in my dreams, what the hell do I tell them? Do I lie and say that the information they died to give us will help us alter the defense we're building, that their example will help all the allied space navies be even more effective when the Deltans finally get here?

"Or do I tell them the truth, that there is no space navy, that the three ships we've been building still aren't finished yet, that all the backdoor politicking and contract disputes haven't allowed us to lay down any more hulls, that not one piece of the design has yet to be shared with our allies, even though we promised it to them right after the *Sword* launched? Huh, Carl? Which is it?"

Sykes flashed a brief look of shame, but squelched it in favor of indignation. "Lydia, none of that is my fault. These things take time, and delaying the completion of construction until after first contact was a strategic decision and the right one in my opinion. I'm sorry your team was killed, but this has shown us where the design flaws lie. When we complete the cruiser specs, we can build a truly effective warship. Now we don't have to waste production time on these flawed destroyers."

"Bullshit!" Lydia screamed. "The destroyer design isn't fundamentally flawed. They damn near took out the whole Deltan fleet with one ship! If we quit on this design in favor of another version that isn't even drafted yet, we're going to be left with nothing. It's too late for this DC Beltway crap! The Deltans are coming and their intentions are no longer academic. They are the enemy and it's up to us to build our defense as promised and planned."

Sykes' anger appeared in full force. Whatever shame he had felt at seeing the *Sword of Liberty* destroyed was now buried. "That's not your decision to make! We may indeed go on with the *Sword* class destroyers, or we might decide to proceed with the *Trenton* cruiser. Maybe we'll do both, with or without releasing the designs to foreign powers, but that's something that will have to follow the full analysis of this data by my office. And while you may be convinced of the implacable intent of these aliens, I'm not. I don't fully endorse the way Kelley handled things. I think he was way too hot-headed and trigger happy. He fired the first shot on these Deltans and he was the first one to destroy a ship. For all we know, he took out a ship full of refugees!"

"Damn you, Carl! Open up your eyes. We've dragged our feet too long." Lydia turned to face the President, seated behind her desk. "Madame President, it pains me to have to say this, but if this nation doesn't do what's necessary to defend this planet, I'm going to take Windward's designs and Windward's technologies to another world power who will listen and do what's needed, nationalized US property or not. I'm sure I can convince the EU or the Chinese to react."

Sykes smiled. "That's it. Go ahead and try, Lydia. It will be my personal pleasure to throw your ass into Leavenworth."

Tomlinson looked at Lydia's stern expression and then turned to the Defense Secretary. "Carl?"

Sykes faced her. "Yes, Madame President?"

"Shut the hell up and get out of my office. Your services are no longer required by my administration."

Sykes' features turned darker in outrage. "What?"

Tomlinson stood, glaring at him. "You said that 'her team' was killed. What you're forgetting is that every single one of them was a sworn volunteer of the United States Armed Forces. They were our soldiers, my soldiers. It wasn't her team on that ship, it was the US Aerospace Navy and the United States of America in proxy. *We* have been attacked by an alien threat, a threat which encompasses this entire planet, and as President I'm going to see their sacrifice made worthwhile."

Sykes held up his hands. "Madame President, they were drafted as a ploy. Surely—"

"No. You're done. If you value the bureaucracy you've built up more than the lives of the people in our military, then you're not the soldier you used to be." Tomlinson turned to Lydia. "Ms. Russ, you have my deepest apologies for the failure of my administration to keep up our end of the bargain, but you have my pledge that that all ends today.

"Our nation is from this moment on a war footing. We will immediately contact our allies and fulfill our agreements for technology transfer, as we should have done long ago. We will indeed analyze the battle and ensure that any necessary design changes are implemented in both the destroyer plans as well as the astrodynamic cruiser version. Also, tomorrow, we will begin completion of the *Swords of Justice*, *Independence*, and *Freedom*. Their crews will be fast-tracked to full readiness, and we will launch all three by year's end. I guarantee it.

"And in light of what has occurred, it is my intention before the week is out to lay down the hull of our next destroyer … DA-5, the *Sword of Vengeance*."

16: "PATRONS"

Date Unknown; USS Sword of Liberty (DA-1), location unknown; Mission Day ???

Nathan Kelley screamed.

Despite the anti-nausea meds, his stomach flopped about, churning with anxious bile, threatening to disgorge its bitter acid up his throat and into his helmet. Cocooned within his Charlie Station pod, he spun chaotically about with the forward half of the ship, but the sickness that prepared to overcome him was only partly due to the motion. There was instead something that concerned him far, far more.

He screamed again. "Kris!!"

She—and ten others—had been aft in the engineering spaces, spaces which were now cut free of the mission hull and whatever remained of the flayed apart radiator spine. He had no hope whatsoever that she could hear him on the general net, but it did not stop his anguished cries.

"Kris! Talk to me, Kris!"

Nathan's helmet telltales flickered without any sense of order. The battle VR was filled with static, intermittent status bars, and multiple "blue screens of death" from systems cut off from their power source, their networks, and any semblance of connectivity. He could tell nothing about anything. For all he knew, he was the only one left alive aboard either half of the destroyer.

"Damn it, someone answer me! Kris!!"

A piercing whine shot through his ears. He winced and then froze as he heard an acerbic voice reply. "Jesus, Nathan. Would you just shut the fuck up for one minute?"

Nathan smiled desperately. It was Edwards. "COB! It's damn good to hear your voice. Listen, have you got any data? I lost everything after that beam cut through the ship's spine. Do you know what's going on with Engineering?"

"No, Skipper, I don't, but if you don't mind me saying it, you need to chill the fuck out. When I got my comms back, all I could hear was your heart bleeding over the damn net, and while I understand it, it's the last friggin' thing any of us need right now."

Nathan said nothing, chastened into silence.

Edwards continued. "I know you're worried about Kris—and I'll give you the benefit of the doubt that you're worried about the rest of us too—but she and the other engineers are like concern number twenty-seven on the list I've got running through my head. I need you to start with concern one and work your way down it, not the other way around. So, are you gonna captain, Captain, or do I need to cut your air off and let our happy-go-lucky XO take over?"

Nathan opened his mouth to bite back, but he closed it again with an audible snap and allowed himself to think instead of simply reacting. A few moments later, he keyed his mike again. "No, COB, you can keep me breathing. I'm sorry."

"S'all right, Skipper. Next time we're half a light-year from home and aliens chop my ship in half, with my sweetie in the wrong half, it'll be my turn to freak out."

Nathan chuffed a laugh, despite everything. "Can I at least hope that your little counseling session was on a private channel?"

Edwards' voice was full of good humor. "Hey, who's the Master Chief around here? Of course it was. Fact is, all the nets are down. I only heard you after I opened a pod-to-pod channel."

Nathan nodded to himself. "Okay. I don't know what you had as concern one on that list, but my first proper concern is situational awareness. I've got nothing on my VR, and we need to know where we are and what's going on before we can even start handling things."

"Roger that, sir. I'm in the same boat."

"Fine. If the nets are down and pod-to-pod comms are the only thing up, then we need to work through that. Kill the circuit with me and try to raise the XO, have him raise Damage Control Central, then CIC, then Weps, and so on. Work out a phone tree between the pair of you and see who's still with us and if anything's still working."

"And what will you be doing, sir?"

"I'm going to crack my pod and see what's up firsthand."

"Whoa there, Cap'n Kirk. You need to let somebody else boldly go first. There's no telling if we're open to space, irradiated, or hip deep in nano-machines, not to mention this wicked spin we've got going on at the moment. All you can say right now is that your pod is safe, so that's where you should stay."

"Negative, COB. I wish this spin was gone too, but—"

whiteness pervaded
shining in incandescence
nathan moved his arms freely
no longer encumbered
no longer restrained
<discontinuity>

Nathan started and jerked, but now was held fast by the pod's gel once more. The momentary bright glow was gone as well. After images filled his vision, negatives of whatever the source of light had been, as if he had looked into a bank of spotlights or the sun.

A mike clicked in his ears and Edwards' voice spoke. "What … the hell … was that?"

Nathan shook his head. "I haven't got a clue, but we don't have time to keep arguing about it. Our visitors are still out there, doing whatever they want with us. Get started on contacting everyone. I'm leaving the pod to figure out what's going on."

"Aye aye, sir. Do you feel it, though?"

"Feel what?"

"The spin. It's gone. The Deltans steadied us up somehow during that weird … moment. Right after you wished for it."

Nathan grunted. "I doubt my wishes had anything to do with it. They probably steadied us up to examine us, if we're lucky."

Edwards finished his thought. "Or they steadied us up in order to flay us more precisely, if we're unlucky."

"Yep. I'm out." Nathan cut off the circuit and reached methodically through the force-dampening gel to the pod's emergency release. He pulled the lever and the whole pod vibrated. The gel cleared away, sucked back into its own reservoirs. The VR screen over his faceplate pulled away and the shell opened. His chair slid up and forward, returning to its usual position in the bridge. A thin layer of the alcohol-based gel that had clung to him boiled away in the near vacuum of the compartment.

Other than the lack of air, and the absence of the other acceleration couches, everything looked normal on the bridge. No aliens lay in wait for them. He reached over and drew his screens and control panels toward him. Unlike the ones they duplicated in the battle VR, these worked.

Every system was offline. Power was gone and both the screens and the space's lights ran on battery back-ups only. Along with the aft half of the ship, the reactor and propulsion were cut off. The weapon system and auxiliary propulsion capacitor banks were fully charged, though. Without the reactor, they were the only sources of power the mission hull had once the battery back-ups ran out in a few hours. Nathan considered the situation. If he shut down the systems they usually powered and isolated the banks, they could conceivably keep life support and the auxiliary systems running for a few days.

Nathan shook his head in dismay. A few days. There was little point to stretching their survival time to a few days when it would take years for the alien formation to reach Earth, but perhaps in that time, they might learn something about the Deltans, something they could still transmit back home.

He shut down the missile sub-systems, the railgun, and diode laser banks, then did the same for the photonic reaction thruster pylons, conserving their precious energy, Finally, he tripped the breakers to the banks themselves. To re-route the power, they would have to cut out some main bus diodes and reverse some connections. It was a task Kris would relish.

Or one she would have relished.

Nathan stopped himself from thinking down that path, and refocused on the tasks at hand. All sensors and comms were down as well, but while the radar needed a level of power that he did not have, and could not have afforded to waste anyway, he did have backup power on the passive sensor systems. He reset the hull cameras and took a look around.

The tactical computer was still offline, so his view lacked the smooth, easy sweep of their combined picture, as well as the false color vector data that usually helped make sense of the vastness around them, but he could see a few things. They drifted over the drive-star, with the Control Ship just visible above the star's horizon, pretty much where she had been during the final moments of the battle. Had they been just a bit fleeter, just slightly quicker, they could have escaped.

He shook his head and switched cameras. Many of the small, hull-mounted sensors were broken or still offline, but others were blocked. By what, he could not tell, but as he switched from camera to camera he finally found the engineering hull.

Tattered pieces of the radiator spine remained, fitfully spraying clouds of vapor and coolant from shorn lines and shafts. The reactor and the drive itself looked battle scarred but intact.

Nathan breathed a sigh of relief.

Kris's broken half of the ship drifted steadily several miles from the mission hull, its spin also halted. Bracketing the aft hull was a silvery cage or framework that had presumably been put together by the Deltans, perhaps sent out from the Control Ship or even constructed in place by the nano-machines fired by the silvery beam Kris had overcome. He had no idea what its purpose was, but a similar cage was probably what blocked several of his own cameras.

He reached for a communications icon, to try and call the aft hull or the re-trans pod when—

<discontinuity>
bright flash again
all is lost in a haze of white
sense of motion
nathan flails
<discontinuity>

His arms swung wildly and he smacked his forearm painfully on one of his screens. "Damn it!" he complained, cradling his forearm in sharp self-reproach. He took a look at the camera view again. The aft hull was gone.

Nathan frantically searched through the cameras until he found it again. It had jumped, now directly behind them and close. In addition, the Control Ship lay immediately in front of them, big enough and near enough to fill the views of several cameras at once. Whether it had moved or they had moved in that brief moment of bright nothingness, he could not say.

He considered putting the weapons back online, but the alien ship was so massive relative to their remaining firepower that it would do little good. However, as he watched in mounting horror, the overlapping plates of the lobster-like Control Ship began to slide apart and open up, revealing a dark interior, an interior into which they were undoubtedly about to be drawn.

Nathan reached for the lasers—

<discontinuity>
bright white again
nathan's fingers blindly grope
skitter across the panel
nothing happens
<discontinuity>

The Bridge returned to dim normality. Nathan struggled to understand. The glow that filled his vision during those terrifying moments of nothingness was not source-less. The glow's brightest spots were analogous to the actual recessed lights on the bridge. It was as if all their light became thousands of times more powerful, as if the photons had become physical things themselves, drifting around him like a fog of light.

That was significant somehow, but he had no idea what it meant. Nathan shook his head, and scrolled through the cameras. The scene had changed again. The aft hull was nowhere to be seen, and the mission hull was surrounded on all sides, locked into place by brackets, spars, and webs of material.

They were inside the Control Ship.

Nathan shifted panels and frantically closed the breakers to the laser capacitor banks, trying to bring the lasers back online. Where they had been operational but useless before, though, now all he saw were red status icons. During the moment of discontinuity, not only had the ship been captured and secured, but the lasers had been either physically disabled or removed.

Nathan checked the railgun, and found much the same story. He shook his head and secured their capacitor banks once more.

Following that, he reset the internal comms system and called Edwards' pod. "COB, Captain. I've got us stable for the moment, but we've got some work to do if we're going to last beyond a few hours. And the situation up here is ... unsettling."

Edwards' voice crackled back into his ear. "Roger that, Skipper. Hey, I had a couple more of those whiteout moments. Any idea what's going on with them?"

Nathan frowned. "Yeah, I've got an idea, but I don't like it. It plays into our situation up here. How many of the crew do we have?"

"The XO's still touching base with his half, but pod-to-pod works for everyone I called, and the general net came online right before you called me."

"Right," Nathan said. "I reset the comm system from my regular panel. Those are still working. In fact, why don't you have everyone crack their pods, and we'll go back to standard ops. Or as standard as it's going to get with the current situation."

"Aye aye. I'll see you in a second."

Nathan continued checking out the status of the ship, and scrolling through the cameras out to the interior of the alien vessel. No Deltans presented themselves, at least not in any sort of recognizable form. The amber-glowing interior of the Control Ship was made up of silvery braces, gossamer webs of fine wire, articulated cables, black humps, and strangely shaped protrusions of multicolored, glossy material, blinking lights, and a thousand other things of unknown function, purpose, or design. He shook his head in wonder, still fascinated with the idea of their first contact, even though the reality of it had proved less than ideal.

Pods began to open, returning everyone's acceleration couches to their usual positions. Nathan released his straps and pulled himself up and over to Christopher Wright, whose suit and helmet steamed with evaporating gel. He reached out and clasped hands with his XO.

Wright smiled tightly at him, his eyes full of concern. "Captain, any sign of the engineering hull?"

"Yes, I saw it. It looked intact, but where it is now, I have no idea. We seem to be inside the Control Ship, so I imagine Kris and the others are inside here somewhere as well."

"Inside? Have the aliens made any attempt at communicating with us?"

"No, not that I've been aware of. They put some sort of framework around the two halves of the ship, and then they moved us in during those weird breaks in reality, but I haven't seen or heard from anyone or anything."

Wright grimaced. "Yes, I'd noticed those, but I didn't know what to make of them."

Nathan was about to respond when he felt a hand on his shoulder. Edwards floated at his side, having returned from checking on the other Bridge watchstanders. Nathan smiled and shook his Master Chief's hand.

He turned back to Wright and then went on. "I think the Deltans can manipulate our sense of time somehow. When each of those discontinuities occurs, things change up or shift all of a sudden. I have no idea how it's done, but I think they're putting us into some sort of stasis, freezing us in place while they move us around. Maybe the light gets brighter because even though we're moving at a much slower rate, the light is still being emitted normally, so it looks brighter to us."

Wright frowned. "Or it's being slowed down as well, but we're seeing all the wavelengths at once, even the ones outside our normal visual spectrum. Blue shifting thermal radiation into our visible range?"

Edwards shook his head. "Hey, yeah, or maybe we're seeing all the dust sprinkled by the Sandman. Listen, those sorts of details aren't really our primary concern at the moment, sirs. What matters is, if what you're saying is right, the Deltans can freeze us and do whatever they want at their leisure. How do we defend against that?"

Nathan shrugged. "I haven't a clue, but I know the Deltans are mindful of our defenses." He told them about the disabled weapon systems, and what he planned to do with their capacitor banks in order to keep the ship running for a while.

Wright nodded. "All right, Captain. That could work. But, if we're going to have to rewire the power system and re-air the ship, we need to begin immediately, before our suit air runs out."

"And patch up any breaches from the battle," Edwards added. "Not only do we not want our atmo venting out, we don't want any of whatever the Deltan's breathe getting in."

Nathan frowned. "This would be a lot easier if we had the engineers with us." There was more to what he meant, but he did not bother saying it.

Neither of the other men needed to hear him say it. Edwards clasped him on the shoulder again. "I'm sure she and the others are okay, sir. They were just as protected as we were, and if the aft half survived like you said, then they're going to be fine."

Wright nodded. "Yes, sir. And they're going to need air just like we are. The Deltans have yet to show up after bringing us aboard, but keeping us alive is the best sign we've had so far. My guess is they're probably giving us a chance to stabilize ourselves, perhaps so they can bring the crew from the other half of the ship up here."

Nathan looked doubtful. "I have yet to see anything from these aliens that would lead me to believe they have such a benevolent intent."

Edwards grinned. "Well, they haven't broken out the anal probes yet. That's benevolent enough for the moment."

Nathan put Edwards in charge of rewiring the power system and Wright on buttoning up the hull. They divided up the four Bridge crew between them and then branched out into the ship, gathering up crewmembers and handing out tasks. Nathan set out by himself, assessing individual systems and battle damage, balancing what they had against the situation they found themselves in.

In terms of balance, there was none. One crewman had died during the battle, at the location of the Deltan laser burn-through. Another five had died after the ship had been cut in half, three due to malfunctioning air systems, and one due to a broken neck. The final death had been hard to explain, until he noticed the empty IV drug reservoirs in her pod. It had malfunctioned, overdosing her on a lethal cocktail of the normally balanced flows of stimulants and depressants used to keep her alive during the extended high acceleration.

Two hours after commencing repairs, the remaining thirteen

crewmembers of the *Sword of Liberty* gathered in the ship's single mess. Nathan looked around at the assembled spacers. In a space built to hold a crew of 35, and which had supported 30 for a year and a half, thirteen was a depressingly spare assembly. He hoped against forlorn hope that Kris and her engineers were alive, and would soon be with them all here again.

Nathan glanced back at Edwards, who manned the environmental control panel on the aft/dorsal bulkhead of the mess. Those areas of the mission hull that could be properly patched had been. Anyplace too far gone—from either the laser attack or the nanobeam—had been sealed off forever. Now they each felt the air pressure rise in the room, and with it came a rising sense of safety and hope, even though they all knew that the air and power were both depressingly finite.

Edwards finally looked over and nodded to his Captain. Nathan reached up and unsealed his helmet. He removed it and took a deep breath for all to see. Exhaling, he nodded to them all and they each removed their helmets. Edwards did as well, and then wrinkled up his nose. "Damn, you guys smell like shit."

Everyone laughed, just as he had intended. Nathan turned to regard them all. "Good work, everyone. And I mean that—both in the battle and now, with our repairs. You've achieved something very real and important here. Together, we have faced a superior, unknown, and completely alien force—and have shown not only that humankind can survive against such a force, but that we can persevere and win. The *Sword of Liberty* and each of you are a force to be reckoned with. I want each of you to know that what we've done, and what we've shown can be done to the folks back home, has assured Earth its survival."

They all nodded back to him, solemnly accepting his praise. Nathan saw in each pair of eyes, though, the truth of what he left unsaid—that whatever happened back home when the aliens reached it in a few years, they had at most a few days, even assuming the Deltans left them alone, and they had no guarantee of that. They had been brought aboard for some purpose, and whatever it turned out to be, it was likely to be counter to their continued survival.

Nathan turned to Wright. "XO, what's next on the schedule?"

Wright smiled. "Well, Captain—"

<discontinuity>

unbearable brightness

fluttering, jostling motion

shadows flitting about madly

insane shapes among them all
<discontinuity>

Stasis ended, and there were suddenly five more suited figures among them, still wearing helmets. They each floated above the deck, clawing at their sealing rings. Nathan spun around and searched the new faces. Seeing Kris, he dove forward, catching her up. He unsealed her helmet and pulled it free, tossing it behind him to bounce off the bulkhead.

She gasped and coughed, pulling in heaving gulps of air. Nathan smiled and hugged her close, squeezing her fiercely, his heart pounding in his ears. He whirled around and saw that the other engineers were also free of their helmets and being cared for. He turned back and refocused on Kris.

She had her breath again and looked around the mess, wide-eyed. He kissed her, but it took a moment for her to regain her bearings and kiss him back. They kissed again, and then she pushed him back, confused and slightly afraid. "Nathan," she said, her voice raspy, "what the hell is going on?"

He smiled. "You're back and you're alive, that's what's going on." He squeezed her again, breathing in the smell of her hair, covered by the unfortunate scent of hours spent in a vacuum suit, but still there.

Kris returned his embrace, also thankful to be alive and to see him again. Eventually she pulled away again. This time he allowed it, and neither of them said anything about the tears welled in their eyes, or about the contented smiles on both their faces. Kris asked again, "Nathan, what is going on?"

He shook his head. "Nope, you first. After the ship broke apart, what happened in Engineering?"

She shrugged. "Well, everything went offline, but not before the drive crashed us into the forward hull like a couple of billiard balls. We went spinning away, unbalanced, with no coolant for the reactor, and no energized helium for the drive, and no way to see where we were going, much less control our path. I tried to jury-rig some way to tap into the camera feed or use the auxiliary antennas, to see what was going on with you guys, when, somehow, we lost our spin. Once it was safe to move around, me and the others broke out of our pods and got to work on our repairs.

"That's when I found out it was just me, Viera, Maxwell, Tambourge, and Blake." Her eyes welled with tears again, such that she had to wipe them away as they would not fall. "The others were all dead. There were electrical fires, and the reactor was scrammed, and, damn it, nothing worked. The air was compromised—we were on suit reserves only and there was so much damage, we thought we'd never be able to re-air the hull. And we kept having these blackouts, or whiteouts, I guess, brought on by a lack of oxygen. We kept working though, up until we started choking out."

She looked back at him and smiled wanly. "Then we had another whiteout episode and I woke up here. With you."

He smiled back and kissed her. "That's pretty much what we experienced, except for two things. First, we seem to be somewhere inside the Control Ship, and second, those weren't whiteouts from a lack of oxygen. It appears to be a sort of stasis or suspended animation." Nathan went on to explain everything that had happened to them in the forward half of the hull.

Kris's eyes grew wider and wider as he went on. When he finished, she just stared. A smile began to tick up one corner of her mouth. "That … is … awesome!"

Nathan arched an eyebrow. "Not exactly the word I would use to describe being captured by hostile aliens, but sure, 'awesome' works, I guess."

"No, no, no!" She pushed off from him and turned around to capture the attention of everyone in the mess. "Don't you see? This explains so much."

Edwards regarded her from where he was talking with one of the other engineers. "What does what explain so much, CHENG?"

"The Deltan's stasis field—it's why they don't mind taking 80 some odd years to get from one star to another. To them it's not 80 years, or whatever it would be with relativity thrown in. To them, it's in the blink of an eye!"

Wright moved to the front of the crowd. "They're putting themselves in stasis? But they seem to move around with impunity when we're under the field."

Kris nodded. "Sure. If you've got stasis, why not anti-stasis? That's probably what those frameworks they put around us do—those generate the stasis field, and if they have to move around while we're frozen, they wear an anti-stasis doohickey on their belts, or whatever."

Nathan smiled at her. "All right, I grant you it's pretty neat, but I'm not as excited as you are about it. To me, that means we can't oppose them effectively unless we can get one of the anti-stasis devices for ourselves, and the chances of that are piss-poor."

She nodded. "Sure, if you wanted anti-stasis, but that's the last thing we need right now. We only have a few days of life support, right?"

Wright answered, "Seventy-two hours at the outside, unless you can improve our setup."

Kris grinned. "Seventy-two hours running continuously, but what about if they put us in stasis? There's no reason we can't survive for years on what we have left—long enough to get back home. We still have a chance of reaching Earth!"

The crew all looked at her now, with expressions ranging from joy, to shock, to worry. Nathan carried one of the worried looks. "Assuming they do put us in stasis to bring us back to Earth, why? Why have they captured us instead of letting us die out there? What do they need from us? I'm excited about the prospect of seeing Earth again, too, but not as the pawn or tool in some alien attack on our home planet."

She smiled at him, and this time her smile had a slightly evil cast to it, much as she had back when she first described the Excalibur missile to him. "We're only pawns if we allow ourselves to be pawns. Just because they took our weapons away doesn't mean we aren't armed. Were the auxiliary drives still intact when you isolated their capacitor banks?"

"Yes, but why ... ." Nathan's eyes grew wide. He pushed off from where he was and caught her up in an embrace. He leaned in and whispered to her. "Can I be in love with you and completely scared of you at the same time?"

She smiled and kissed his cheek. "It's not very healthy emotionally, but sure, why not?"

Edwards and Wright exchanged a look and a shrug, but that was all. The XO moved over to Nathan and Kris, who turned arm-in-arm to regard him. "Captain," he asked, "what are your orders?"

Nathan sobered. "We need to take stock on what we have thus far. Divide up the crew into maintenance teams—some for checking air integrity and supplies, the engineers and some of the twidget-types for getting whatever systems we can online, comms especially, another team to check out the SSTOS. We may need to use it as a final redoubt once the systems in the rest of the ship fail due to lack of power. The shuttle has its own reactor. We could potentially survive there for several weeks. And, lastly, we need to arm ourselves from the weapons locker—"

<discontinuity>
an infinity of white
crew reaching out blindly

something else
something among them
<discontinuity>

Stasis fell away and Nathan whirled around. He caught sight of it just as several of the crew gasped and cried out. Bodies surged back from the mess's open hatchway, crowding up against the furthest bulkhead. It took a moment for them to clear away and give him an unobstructed view, but soon he, Wright, Edwards, and Kris were at the forefront of the assembled crew.

An alien held its position steady in the hatch's frame. The creature they had long referred to as a Deltan was nothing that could be encapsulated by such a pedestrian, human name. This thing was the product of a different biology, a different environment, a different science. It was alien in all senses of the word.

Nathan's mind, recoiling from the sight of something so strange, struggled to classify it, to break it down into parts which would make sense to him. In the broadest sense, it looked like the impossible crossing of a wasp and a squid.

Its upper body was hard and segmented, though its segments were not differentiated as cleanly into head, thorax, and abdomen as a terrestrial insect would be. Instead, the glossy gray segments grew narrower and longer at the top, with the last segment covered in a mix of a dozen simple multicolored eyes and four black compound eyes, with slits of unknown purpose alongside upper and lower pairs of mouths, ringed in cilia.

The segments lower on the body grew wider and shorter, eventually breaking up into overlapping plates, between each of which emerged scaled, ringed tentacles. Nathan saw at least a dozen tentacles of varying thickness supporting the creature in its position at the hatchway. The tentacles themselves appeared quite complex, branching again and again into smaller limbs and cilia, such that each one would have been capable of either delicate work or heavy lifting.

The Deltan was wrapped in a dull blue, translucent shift, and either ornamentation or instrumentation of unknown purpose. The entire alien and its garment also appeared to be covered in a uniform layer of plastic, to which a square-ish pack was attached at its back. Nathan wondered whether it was an environment suit of some sort, or if it was part of the creature's anti-stasis generator, allowing it to move when they were frozen in place. Perhaps both?

He shook himself. Here was their first contact, the first chance they would have to perhaps avert the war over Earth that seemed inevitable now. Nathan pushed off from the crowd to approach the alien who had captured them.

He was grabbed at the last moment by the XO. Wright pulled him back to the rest of the crew and placed a hand on his chest. "No, sir. You're not going to be the first one to talk to that thing."

Nathan looked incredulous. "Pardon me, XO?"

Wright's features were firmly resolved. "Not a chance, sir. You're our captain, our leader. We live or die on your word, and you are first and foremost in charge, but you also planned this to happen a certain way."

Nathan frowned. "I don't know if you've noticed over the past year and a half, but our plans have had a depressing tendency to go by the wayside."

"Not this one, sir. True, originally we were supposed to have a US ambassador and a couple of xenologists along for this purpose, but stealing the ship made that a moot point. And though our roles have changed to better fit the actual mission, I was originally supposed to be their liaison to the crew. With my background and training, I'm the closest thing you have to an ambassador and a linguist."

"You're stretching things a bit, XO. The situation has changed."

"No, sir. Just as I led the first communiqués aboard ship, I need to lead these negotiations. You're the captain, Nathan, but first contact has been—and is going to remain—my game. Right, Master Chief?"

Nathan turned toward Edwards. "COB?"

Edwards looked at them both, then gave the Deltan by the hatchway a critical appraisal. He faced Nathan again. "I'm with the XO on this one, Skipper."

Nathan turned red at the seeming betrayal. "Damn it, Master Chief—"

Edwards interrupted him. "Need I remind you that last time you spoke directly to these guys, they started shooting?"

Nathan's jaw dropped. "That is a complete mis-representation of what happened out there."

Edwards shrugged. "It is what it is. Now, sir, please give your authorization for our XO and ambassadorial liaison to proceed with his damn job."

Nathan fumed, but—with a final glance at the Deltan waiting at the hatchway—nodded curtly to Wright after a few moments. Wright nodded back and then pushed off from the crew to close half the distance to the alien. He stopped his flight with a quick grasp at one of the overhead's handholds and then re-oriented himself to a more dignified standing position.

He inclined his head respectfully to the alien and smiled. "Hello. I am Lieutenant Commander Christopher Wright of the United States Aerospace Navy, and Executive Officer of the USS *Sword of Liberty*. In the interests of peace, and in order to settle the conflict that has arisen between our two species, I am authorized to communicate with you on behalf of the people of Earth."

He paused. The alien did nothing but stand there. "Do you understand me? Is there another language you are more familiar with?" He turned his head to look back at Edwards. "COB, can we get the linguistic program running on the computer here in the mess?"

Before Edwards could respond, the Deltan moved. It held forth a device in one tentacle, which scintillated in a rainbow of colors. Between it and the XO, a flat image appeared in mid-air. Wright turned back to look at the image and the alien, giving both his full attention.

He smiled. The images were a series of clips, replayed snippets of television programs caught up by the Deltans from the Earth's distant broadcasts, and now shown back to them as a form of communication, though none of them knew what the message might be.

City skylines and architecture were mixed in with sculptures, paintings, and plays. Soundless visions of singers, concerts, and comedians were cut in between biographies of famous artists and writers at work. Trailers from movies and news clips of ballet and opera openings were shown now and again. It went on for several minutes, widely varying and never repeating. It was possible the Deltans had hours upon hours of stored clips.

Wright nodded and laughed slightly. "This is art! Is that what this is all about? Have you seen our art and culture and that's why you're coming? What is so important about our works, that you would make such a long journey? Why haven't you simply contacted us and asked for some sort of exchange? Why the attacks and the hostility? Please make me understand what it is you want from us."

The alien's head analog tilted slightly, regarding the XO. The images vanished and it lowered the device in its tentacle. Another tentacle rose up, carrying a different instrument.

A silvered beam of suspended nanomachines lanced out from it, slicing into Wright at the abdomen. Nathan cried out in shock, along with a number of the crew, Kris included, who shrieked. They were all drowned out, though, by the screams of mindless agony from the XO himself.

The beam scanned up and down his body, spreading the nanomachines all over him. The particles flowed around his body like a silvered mist, flaying him apart microscopic layer by microscopic layer, fast enough to watch him vanish, but too slowly to be merciful. His vacuum suit and skin vanished, and then the flesh beneath, but not one drop of blood was cast off, converted instead into ashen dust and silvered particles.

After too long a time, the screams cut off and they could only watch as their XO was rendered and skeletonized. The crew had surged back and lined the opposite bulkhead, some crying, some comforting, and all afraid of what sort of hell they had fallen into. Nathan, Kris, and David Edwards alone stood apart, the pair of them holding their Captain in place from his instinctual attempt to go to his murdered compatriot's aid.

The beam stopped and the alien brought the device down. The cloud of nanoparticles kept up their work, though, and soon the XO's bones started showing holes, thinned out, and vanished into dust. Of Wright, there was nothing then but a dense, swirling cloud of particulates.

After a moment, purposeful motion could be seen within the cloud. Similar to a time-reversed strip of film showing a decaying body growing backwards toward life, gray and silver dust coalesced, building up a body from the bones outward. Flesh, skin, hair and features appeared, laid down layer by layer, like a line-by-line printout of a human being, differentiated by what had been there before only by coloring. A body was made up of reds and whites, and a dozen other subtle hues between them, but this pallet had only gray and silver.

At its end, the cloud was gone, its entirety now comprising a statue of Christopher Wright, nude and flawless, inexplicably standing on the deck in disregard to the absence of gravity. As they watched, the gray and silver coloring of the body faded and gained inhuman detail. Finally, the statue took on the cast of white marble, shot through with random veins of pink and amber.

As a piece of art, a memorial to Wright, it had worth, but not any worth that justified his murder. Nathan no longer struggled against Kris and Edwards. He simply glared at the statue and the alien with unmasked hatred.

That hatred shifted to shock and confusion, though, as the marble statue of Wright turned toward him fluidly and smiled. The statue glanced back at the alien blocking the hatchway and then walked—again in contravention of microgravity—to Nathan, Kris, and Edwards.

The thing that had been their XO, and which mirrored his appearance in exacting detail, nodded to them all and spoke, its voice similar enough to

Wright's to be unsettling, but stripped of all emotion and inflection, words without conscious thought or feeling. "Greetings. I am prepared to communicate with you in regards to our purpose and design. Will you speak with me?"

Nathan shuddered, listening to the thing speak, unable to reconcile its toneless copy of Wright's voice with the passionate, disciplined man who used to own that face. "What the hell are you?"

The statue gestured to itself, waving a hand over its body. "The man Wright was your ambassador. I, too, am an ambassador. This is our emissary, capable of communication in human terms, an avatar of the beings you know as the Deltans, though that designation is incorrect in every way worth considering."

Nathan shook his head, horrified and confused beyond all measure. In the back of his mind, he realized that it could have just as easily been himself who was converted into this entity, a thought that both shamed him and relieved him at the same time. He struggled to get his mind back on track. "What do you mean, the 'designation is incorrect'?"

"The beings en route to your planet are not from Delta Pavonis, nor any nearby star system. Their home and their place is quite distant from any place you would know, at least in any sense that you will understand. That star system was merely the sight of their last acquisition, a priceless treasure which you destroyed during your futile attack."

Nathan's eyes narrowed, and he looked back and forth between the alien and the statue of Wright through which it communicated. "Acquisition? Treasure? What are you talking about? Why are you coming to Earth?"

The avatar smiled. It might not have any emotion in its voice, but its expression demonstrated its condescension quite well. "Your people have openly displayed their magnificent cultural wealth for all within a hundred light-years to see, with selfless disregard for protecting its unique and singular worth. And we have taken notice. We are appreciative. We adore the works of Earth and we are devoted to its safety and guardianship. We do not seek enslavement. No, no. We only want to preserve and enshrine the greatness your species has wrought.

"We are your Patrons, and we bring you the galaxy, to the betterment of all."

17: "UNIVERSAL TRUTHS"

Date Unknown; USS Sword of Liberty (DA-1), location unknown; Mission Day ???

They all stared agape at the aliens' marble avatar, trying to process their thoughts and their pain, to reconcile its cold, mechanistic words with its face—the face of their own XO—which smiled at them in amused condescension. Nathan's mind and emotions whirled about, unable to settle on any one bit of the automaton's announcement. Patrons? The cultural works of Earth? The casual murder of Christopher Wright and his rebirth as this ... thing? Where did one start?

Dave Edwards, an eminently practical—if impudent—individual, recovered from this latest string of shocks first. He pulled himself forward to float slightly in front of Nathan, focusing the avatar's attention on him rather than his Captain. The Master Chief drew his face into an expression of contempt and distaste, the same look someone might give to a particularly large roach one has found in the sink. He shook his head and said, "Let me get this straight ... we're being invaded by art lovers?"

The marble avatar peaked an eyebrow over the blank, colorless hemispheres it had for eyes and glanced back to the alien—the Patron—holding station in the mess's main hatch. The alien flicked a tentacle tip and the automaton nodded and turned back to them. "That explanation is rather simplistic, but it suffices."

Edwards grinned with as much malice as he could muster, which at this point was a great deal. "Well, you'll have to forgive me, but that's about the stupidest damn thing I've ever heard in my entire life. No one crosses light-years of space and spends decades of time to go browsing over the artifacts of another planet like some sort of interstellar garage sale."

Nathan's eyes widened and his brain finally engaged. He reached out an arm and dragged Edwards behind him. Nathan scowled at the Master Chief and spun back toward the avatar. "Sorry about that, but I'll admit that it sounds a little implausible to me as well."

The avatar shrugged, its features quite expressive even though its voice remained toneless and uninflected. "However plausible it might seem, given your preconceived notions of value and worth, is irrelevant. I speak only the truth, and it is a truth which should make perfect sense if you only give it some thought."

Nathan allowed himself to drift closer to the moving statue of his XO. "My thoughts are a little jumbled here, but I'm not getting it. We've imagined any number of dire motivations for you ... Patrons to be coming to Earth—things like desire for our resources, or our biological diversity, or simply the desire to subjugate us as life different from your own. Art and culture weren't high on that list."

The avatar smiled. "Yes, all of those inimical motivations that your fictions have ascribed to invaders, but those invaders were always merely disguised copies of invaders in your own history. Very few were developed with any sort of nod toward actual universal truths."

"Universal truths?" Nathan asked.

"Yes." The avatar turned and walked upon the deck, as if it were under the full acceleration of gravity. It approached a painting on the bulkhead of the mess, a likeness of the *Sword of Liberty*, engines blazing against the backdrop of a nebula. The automaton lightly touched the canvas and then faced them again. "What makes something valuable, Captain?"

Nathan frowned. "I don't know. We value things for all sorts of reasons. Some for their intrinsic worth, for their value as a resource in order to fabricate something we need, or something we like. Some things are valuable because of the difficulty of obtaining them or creating them. Some are valuable because they belong to us, for sentimental reasons, or for their worth as personal property."

The avatar gestured with its hand for him to keep going, a gesture it had no doubt copied from the thousands of video signals it had cataloged. "Yes, yes. And what does each of those measures of worth have in common? What is the universal truth that defines worth and value, no matter your culture, your species, or your planet?"

Nathan thought about his answers and what each of them shared. He looked beseechingly toward Kris, but she only shook her head and shrugged. He returned to the avatar and answered tentatively, "Rarity?"

The avatar smiled broadly. "Precisely. That which is rare or unique or is difficult to obtain, is what has value—value enough to cross light-years for. And knowing this, how valuable are simple raw resources for any society capable of expending enough of them to reach another star system?"

Nathan nodded, excited and pleased by their interaction, in spite of the hatred and revulsion he still felt toward the aliens and this vessel through which they spoke. "Given the technology you've already demonstrated and the sheer quantities of energy you're expending to get to Earth, I'd imagine that raw resources are no big deal for you."

"Certainly not. Elements and minerals are of no difficulty to obtain. With nanotechnology and other means, an asteroid can be rendered into its component elements in days, and those elements can be recombined into whatever composition we desire, with an efficiency far exceeding chemical processing. And those molecules can then be formed into whatever we desire, with greater precision and speed than any other manufacturing method. Material wealth holds no special distinction for us—it can be obtained in nearly unlimited quantities from any single star system, not just a populated one. It is the same way with energy resources. Hydrogen and helium are abundant and available wherever we travel, and that is only considering fusion as a power source. There are other, more compact and energetic forms of power that are more difficult to obtain, but not overly difficult.

"So, if your material and energy resources themselves are not rare enough to make us travel light-years for them, why would your cultural works be?"

Nathan shook his head, straining to put himself in the alien's mind. He answered slowly, "If the only reason to travel to another star system is to obtain something rare and unique, something physical that can't be obtained elsewhere, then I suppose the answer's obvious: while the materials aren't truly rare, what we do with them is ... because ... there's only one human race?"

The avatar clapped its hands together. "And there you have it. Life, throughout the galaxy and perhaps the universe, is ubiquitous. It exists in most star systems in one form another, so common, yet so subtly different, that it has no intrinsic value as a biological resource for any species other than its own. Intelligent life is only slightly more unique, but again, it has no real value to any other species. Whatever discoveries it might make, whatever technology it could conceivably create is governed by universal laws common to all races. Science and technology are not unique and therefore have no value to a sufficiently advanced race, such as the Patrons.

"Art, however, has value—value beyond merely what it does or from what it is made. Every piece of art is a unique statement, a singular expression of a localized, transient idea, alone within the entirety of the universe. Each piece is shaped by any number of factors, all of which are semi-random and unlikely to be repeated exactly in any other place or time: the biology and environment of the species creating it, the mental processes of that species, the history and aesthetics that have developed within the individual culture. All of these make a race's art—as opposed to simple materials or biology—rare and unique, and therefore of value beyond merely the species creating it."

Edwards shook his head and sneered. "That doesn't make any sense. Art only has value beyond its materials if you understand it, if you understand the emotions and the sentiment behind making it. Hell, I don't give a damn for modern art, but some folks'll pay hundreds of thousands of dollars for it. If a barrier like that exists within our own culture, why would we expect an alien culture to understand, appreciate, or value our art? I mean, to you Patrons, there wouldn't seem to be any way to tell the relative value between a second grader's refrigerator finger painting and a one-of-a-kind Jackson Pollack."

The avatar glanced over at Edwards and appeared vaguely disappointed—an expression he had received from the actual Wright on many an occasion. The Master Chief bristled at the look, a look his antagonistic friend and superior would never give him again.

The statue spoke. "You assume that we are incapable of making the same distinction that you can. I will admit that an understanding of your culture and your development are necessary to properly classify your artifacts, but it is a task with which we are familiar. A child's crude attempt at expressing its thoughts and emotions in a work of art is fundamentally different from a master-work. As a snapshot in time of an artist at that level of capability it has value, but because of the likely abundance of these 'finger-paintings' and because of their simplicity and coarseness, that value will be limited. If these 'Jackson Pollacks' are indeed rare, and if their complexity and nuance are appreciated by a large portion of your culture, trust that we will soon discover that same value."

The avatar nodded at its own explanation, then gestured to the alien at the hatchway and stood aside. The alien brought out the imaging device it had shown them earlier, before it had killed Wright. They all moved back, away from the device, uncertain of what it was about to do.

Scintillating rainbows of light sprang out from the unit, coalescing in midair before them into a three-dimensional image. It was the Cathedral, lit from below by the drive-star, either before they had damaged it in their attack or repaired in the time since.

The avatar narrated as the image swooped in to examine the alien vessel's gothic arches and filigreed stonework more closely. "This is the

Patrons' largest and oldest collection, that of the Keltara. The Keltara were a species quite similar to your own—bipedal oxygen breathers, builders and artisans. Their level of technology when we discovered them was the equivalent of several centuries below your own. Their various sub-cultures were in a renaissance of sorts, but none had yet experienced an industrial revolution."

The image moved into the Cathedral. Strange sculptures and paintings of lizard-like creatures standing stooped upon their hind legs lined presentation halls and corridors. Garbled, raspy, unintelligible speech poured forth from a hologram within the alien ship, showing what they assumed to be some sort of play. The image swept on, to examine finely detailed wrought armor, ornate items of jewelry, and thousands of smaller works, from manuscripts and reliefs, to tapestries and musical instruments. The color schemes all seemed either too garish or oddly muted, designed for eyes and aesthetics accustomed to different wavelengths of visible light.

The image changed, now showing the Polyp, the organic-appearing vessel in the Patron fleet. "This collection is representative of the combined works of the Ixkillixis, a race of ammonia swimmers. They were quite advanced in terms of mathematics and philosophy, but as they existed in a liquid medium, they never discovered fire and were unable to progress beyond simple tool-making. However, they achieved some fascinating and beautiful things with hand-shaped tools and extruded objects. They experienced their environment through a mixture of vision, sonar, and chemical tags, like your dolphins, had they progressed beyond the intelligence of dogs."

Inside the Polyp, liquid-filled passages displayed gently curving loops and ridges of shaped coral and stone, glowing with bioluminescent greens, pinks, and yellows, all arrayed in mathematically complex, nonrandom patterns. Strange, haunting sounds like whale-song and the clicks and chirps of dolphins issued forth from the image. A hologram within the Polyp showed trilaterally symmetric creatures, best described as boney, plated octopi with immense, intelligent eyes, swimming around one another in what could only be described as a dance.

The image changed again, this time zooming in toward the Junkyard. To Nathan, it looked different than it had before they had destroyed it, though whether that was because it was an old image from a different aspect, or whether it was a new image of a re-constructed vessel, he had no idea. If it was a new Junkyard, how long had it taken to rebuild? How long had they been in stasis? How far from Earth were they now?

The avatar frowned. "This is what remains of our last collection, that of the Nnnnek, whom you *could* properly refer to as the Deltans, since their home star was our last destination, Delta Pavonis. Most of the artifacts are now reconstructions, the originals destroyed by your senseless assault. As a result, the collection is of limited value. Reconstructions simply do not have the same worth as originals, no matter how exacting their attention to detail.

"The Nnnnek, were a hive-minded, insectoid species. They were quite unique in that they had no identifiable sense of nostalgia. Since the individuals were just parts of a few, nearly eternal, whole minds, their works of art and culture were all perpetual works in progress. Each building, each sculpture was in a constant state of flux and alteration. Whatever they did not need at the moment was discarded with little care, and used again or not as the mood struck the over-minds down through the ages. This lead to the 'junky' appearance that none of your species were capable of understanding, but among the junk were individual articles of such exquisite refinement and complexity that a non-hive awareness could hardly appreciate them fully."

The avatar shook its head and narrowed its stone eyes. "And you blew it up."

The image switched to the interior of the reconstituted Junkyard, but before any of them could see these recreated masterworks of insectoid culture, the image blanked off, denying them a peek of the damage they had caused. The alien lowered the device and then stood still in the hatchway again, glaring at them with its many strange eyes.

The avatar walked back to the center of the room, standing where the images had floated, between the crew and the Patron. "And that is the purpose of this fleet. That is why the Patrons have devoted eight decades to traveling to Earth. Yours is a rich, vibrant culture, perhaps the richest ever encountered. You advance and create so rapidly, that it will take a display ship of staggering dimensions to do justice to the entirety of your history and culture. The works of Man will become the centerpiece of my masters' collection and humanity will be held in awe throughout the community of the galaxy."

Nathan tilted his head to one side, as if to gain a new perspective on the avatar. During the virtual tour of the Patron fleet, his head had finally gotten full control over his emotions and he thought analytically again, no longer just reacting to each successive shock. He smiled slightly, wondering if either the alien or the avatar could tell the difference between a friendly look and the hateful, calculating one Nathan sported now. "Well, it sounds like you Patrons are a bunch of selfless humanitarians, if you'll pardon the term. But what exactly do we—or the people of Earth—get for handing over all those Velvet Elvises? As a people, we value those works you're admiring even more than you do."

The avatar smiled, a smile so close to the one Christopher Wright had so rarely displayed—preferring to hide it beneath his usually serious demeanor—that Nathan nearly lost his new-found composure and tried to smash the living statue. "We are sorry for all the mistakes that have been made thus far—most of all for the regrettable necessity of the sacrifice that Mr. Wright made to form a bridge between us.

"Believe us when we say we hold no malice for the people of Earth, despite the confrontations and violent misunderstandings that have thus far defined our contact. We were, in fact, taken aback by your visitation all the way out here. When we first discovered you through your radio broadcasts, we never imagined you would develop the means to travel this distance in the short time you had available, but, as we have said, you are an imaginative, driven race. We had been prepared to present our case after we arrived in your local space, but now we have you.

"Our desire is that you and your crew will join us in negotiations with Earth, that you will calm the admittedly justifiable concern which has arisen regarding our arrival, and that you will ease the transfer of representative artifacts and original works from your planet to the display vessel we will build. In return, you will receive exact, nano-resolution copies, indistinguishable from the originals to your technology. And we ask that we be provided explanations for the artistic intent and history behind each piece, so that our galactic peers can understand what they are seeing—in return for which, we will be happy to pass along any information or resources which can aid your species in achieving your goals and desires. As we have said, materials and technologies have no intrinsic worth to us, but they do have value to you, and we have no wish to hold you back from your destiny."

Nathan's half smile was still frozen in cold hatred. He looked at the statue and at the alien behind it, and considered the offer. Was this all just a huge misunderstanding? Were the deaths and violence thus far tallied simply the clashing of two widely disparate cultures, grease upon the innocent, but callous, gears of progress.

It all led up to this. It all led up to now. Gordon Lee had devoted twenty years and his life to this moment. They had a built a ship that had changed the world, had fought and bled, and planned and re-planned, had endured literally astronomical obstacles to reach this point.

Nathan was no statesmen. He was no ambassador. He was only an officer of a single nation on the globe, and that only because of an act of political face-saving. Did he have the right to commit mankind to either destruction or salvation based upon what they now knew, what they had just been told?

He shook his head, considering his doubts, objectively looking at the situation and the avatar's explanation without prejudice or paranoia—or at least he tried to. For a long moment, he said nothing. He simply concentrated, listening to the nervous breathing of the crew behind him, and the absence of breath from the avatar before him.

Eventually, he turned his head and peaked an eyebrow, looking at Master Chief Edwards, his old, trusted shipmate. Edwards' own expression was blank. "I know that look, Nathan. You sure you want to kick on this? There ain't no goin' back once you do."

Nathan nodded. "I think it's better we know for sure now, rather than find out too late. So give it to me honestly. Don't hold back."

Edwards frowned and shook his head. He said simply, "Past tense, boss. Every one of 'em."

Nathan nodded and glanced over to Kris. Her eyes were still lined with red, though her tears for Christopher Wright and all the others had either dried or faded away. Her mouth was set in a firm line until she answered his unspoken question. "Universal truths, Nathan. The artist's paintings aren't worth diddly until after he's dead."

"Yep," Nathan answered, "I figured the same thing."

She smiled. "I love you."

He returned it. "I know you do. Me too."

Nathan turned back toward the avatar. "On behalf of the US government, and as a representative of all the rest of humanity … fuck you. You are hereby directed to alter course to skirt our solar system. If your intentions are benign, we can establish a dialog and an exchange after you come to a stable orbit well outside of our Kuiper Belt. However, if you insist on closing with our solar system, we will tear you apart. You will come up against the massed might of every nation on Earth, most notably that of my own country, the United States of America. We will release wave upon wave of hell on you, until not even the atoms of this ship remain. Your collections will be reduced to ash and plasma. You won't take so much as a single postcard from our world, and you by God won't harm a single person on the whole face of the planet."

The statue's eyes narrowed. "Why? Why would you be so belligerent and defiant after we have apologized and explained ourselves?"

Nathan smiled again, this time more broadly. "Because—We. Don't.

Believe. You. You just told us about three of your collections, the Keltara, Nnnnek, and the Ixki … whatever—but you spoke about every single one of the races in the past tense. Now maybe that was just an oversight, a translation error, but between damn near a century of our television and radio broadcasts and whatever you stole from my XO's brain when you cut him up, you've shown a pretty decent command of the language. What I don't think you quite got was nuance and subtlety, just like you don't quite get how we express emotion verbally. I think you used the past tense to describe those races because it was the correct thing to do—since they only exist in the past."

The statue was stock still, not reacting at all. Nathan continued. "You might take every work of art from our planet, every last trinket and use it however you use it in whatever economy or society there is out there in the greater galaxy—though how that interaction works on interstellar timescales, I have no idea—but you'll use it to gain power. That power, that wealth only retains its value if there are no other human artifacts. If anyone else drops by and picks some up—or if we start bartering for ourselves—your collection is devalued. The only way your collection keeps its worth is if there's no more human stuff being produced for other entities, other patrons to acquire.

"Maybe you'd act in good faith right up to the end, playing nice so we won't damage the goods fighting against you, but in the end you'll torch the planet. You'll make us 'past tense' because that's the only way that particular universal truth works out. Well, forget it. We're not going to help you sneak up on mankind unaware. And without us making the introductions, you can plan on every nasty trick our human culture can devise being thrown at you. You're not indestructible. We've proven that, and now we're going to make you pay for even *thinking* about raping our planet."

The avatar stood frozen, stone-faced. In the hatchway, the Patron itself entered the mess, maneuvering nimbly in microgravity with its mass of tentacles. Nathan and the others all stiffened as it came closer and raised the same device with which it had destroyed Wright.

Nathan forced himself to remain still, to not retreat as the creature pointed the weapon at him.

The avatar shook its head, its expression sincerely saddened, even if its voice was as articulate and monotone as ever.

"We thought it probable that you would defy us, but we had to make the attempt. There is always some damage incurred when a species resists. Plus, it is always difficult to catalog and describe the various works when the artisans and historians are dead, but we will deal with it. We always have.

"What will happen is this: when we arrive in your solar system, we will sweep aside whatever primitive resistance you have cobbled together, and then we will take station at one of your planet's LaGrange points. The drive will be turned upon your planet and the resulting disruption of your ionosphere and the cascades of radiation will, within a few days, sterilize the Earth. Humanity will be dead, and your works will remain, hardly the worse for wear. Do not doubt us. It is not the first time we have done it."

Nathan glared at the weapon in the Patron's tentacle, his jaw set in anger. "And what about us? Are you going to break us all down with that thing like you did our XO?"

The statue smiled. "No. You may yet have an opportunity to survive, to serve. A human perspective will be necessary to properly catalog and classify the collection. So you will go into stasis as others have. And when you emerge from the white field, your planet will be dead, your artifacts will be in a dazzling new collection, and the wider galaxy will be presented the whole exhibition to the accompaniment of the last humans' anguished cries—your own anguished, bitter cries."

Nathan snarled, and his wordless, angry command spoke to most of the crew. En mass, they all surged forward, hands stretched out like claws toward the alien—

<discontinuity>
a sea of white
filled the mess
nathan cried out
in frustration
at the vanished patron

18: "WELCOMING COMMITTEE"

December 10, 2055; Patron Collection Fleet, outside the orbit of Jupiter, 6.5 degrees below the ecliptic and approaching Earth

For nine uninterrupted years, CDR Nathan Kelly floated transfixed—caught mid-leap, his face frozen in a mask of hatred and rage, stuck like a fly in amber. He and the others were locked in place by dim golden light, the barest hint of illumination, awash in the glow of quantum fluctuations slowed and softened to visibility by the step-function transition of stasis, separating normal spacetime from the region where they lay, where time's arrow was stunted and light itself barely crawled along.

The *Sword*'s crew was trapped, impotent prisoners of a single moment, unable to affect the course of their captors in any way. Had thought and reflection been possible, Nathan would have seethed and put his mind and their collective will to thoughts of escape. But there was no thought. His mind was still fixed upon nothing but murder—hot, mindless revenge against the one nameless Patron they had seen, the Patron who had frozen them in time and then moved on without sparing them another thought.

They—and all humans, all other species—were but petty annoyances, minor obstacles to deal with en route to their latest acquisition.

Moving out from the captured captain and crew of the late *USS Sword of Liberty*, the living statue of Christopher Wright—avatar of the Patrons—stood motionless as well. In its case, however, it was as empty of volition and will as a mere statue. Even if it were not in stasis, it would not move. The alien that had given it life had gone on to other, more important things.

Outside the mess, the patched forward hull of the destroyer continued on, changeless within the hangar of the Control Ship. Temporary repairs that had been designed to last for days had been held in place for years now by the stasis field surrounding them—and that field itself was sustained by the curving spars of the stasis generator, the first hint of alien technology to be found as one moved outward from the long-trapped crew.

The spars bracketed and embraced the *Sword of Liberty*, blocking it away from the universe at large. Within their encircling arms, spacetime bent and dipped sharply, separating the dim region where duration was eternal from the brightly lit hangar in which time flowed straight and true. Elsewhere in the Patron vessel, other stasis fields also existed, allowing the aliens themselves to endure the long, unavoidable voyage between stars. For all intents and purposes, the Control Ship was eternal, implacable, a sleeping dragon content to allow its technology to carry it safely to its destination and its treasure.

Outside the restored, pristine hull of the Control Ship were the other ships of the Collection, most of them cruising about in stasis as well in order to preserve the shiny bits of now-dead alien cultures the Patrons had stolen for their own benefit.

These frozen, eternal ships spun slowly about the equator of the drive-star, whose roiling surface and brilliant, powerful exhaust were anything but frozen. However, even though it moved, and burned, and blasted forth with fusion fire and photonic thrust, it too was as static and eternal as the Sun, varying continuously over time, but truly changing only on the scale of eons.

Altogether, the Patron/Deltan fleet was unstoppable, a thing relentless and forever-lasting. For nine years since the last time it had been toyed with, it continued on toward Earth, unperturbed, unopposed, and beyond the reach and capability of the human race, who cowered upon their single planet before the approaching alien force.

That time was over.

░░░░░░░░░░░░░░░░░░░░

Stealth in space was impossible.

That simple tactical conclusion was the logical consequence of the laws of thermodynamics. For a weapon to operate, power must flow through it. For power to flow it must have a source. Since no source can be 100% efficient—another law of thermo-damn-namics, as many frustrated engineers referred to it—then every source must give up detectable heat to its environment, thus increasing universal entropy and shuttling everything one step closer to eventual heat death.

The *Sword of Liberty* had therefore been built with large, vulnerable radiators, simply because there was no other choice. They had been hidden and protected as well as the engineers could, but they still proved to be a tactical vulnerability. The Patrons themselves made no effort to hide their waste heat, having proclaimed their presence a good ten light-years from Earth. It was foolish to believe any weapon of any reasonable power could be hidden away in space from any and all observers.

But from one observer? From one specific direction of travel, along a trajectory capable of being predetermined years in advance? From an enemy as assured, secure, and complacent as the Patrons? In that one limited case, unlikely to occur except in the case of an enemy as tactically dominant as the Patrons themselves—in that case perhaps a few surprises could be set up.

LFM-10277 was cold. It did not feel that in any real sense—its own AI was too low-powered and dimwitted to interpret physical parameters as feelings. But it was actually cold, radiating only a few degrees above the cosmic background radiation, indistinguishable from a myriad of small rocks strewn through the vacuum of space, and which were somewhat denser in this area, not far below and out from the leading Trojan point of Jupiter. At this temperature, the amount of available power was on the order of milliwatts, hardly detectable and nothing of consequence to the approaching force.

As a rock, it held no particular danger. The Patrons had overcome the problem of the rare mid-space collision millennia ago. What the humans accomplished with layered whipple shields of varying density and a thick nosecone of lead and ice was resolved much more elegantly by the aliens. Invisible fields pushed out ahead of the drive-star, either pushing molecules and larger objects out of the path of the convoy entirely, or pulling them in to be swallowed in the fires of the drive itself. A torus of perfect vacuum surrounded the four Patron ships themselves.

But as something disguised as a cold rock, LFM-10277 was a good deal more threatening. First it was larger and far more massive than it appeared. While the leading face of it was rocky with a roughly spherical half-meter diameter, it actually extended back several meters. Its greater density meant that its path was less perturbed by the protective fields of the drive-star. And as the limited albedo of its stealthy, disguised surface reflected back a greater and greater amount of the drive-star's thermal radiance, it could begin to add its own heat to the mix, getting hotter and more energetic as the Patron fleet closed—all without alarming any of the alien AIs keeping watch for their masters in stasis.

When the secondary systems came to full power they began warming targeting circuits and cold-chemical vernier thrusters, then prepping the weapon's densely charged sacrificial capacitor banks for cascade breakdown. At that point, the Patron fleet was almost even with the solitary weapon. In milliseconds, the Lasing Fusion Mine's heat and power spiked to incredible levels, broadcasting its position and intent for anyone or anything to see, but by that point it was too late.

LFM-10277 burned with a light brighter than the sun as a slushy ball of metallic hydrogen was compressed to fusion densities by Kris's non-nuclear photonic initiator. The energy from the blast—much larger than any of the *Sword of Liberty*'s own warheads—was then confined, channeled, and ordered for a brief instant by coils of electromagnets and ablative mirrors. Before the whole assembly dissolved away in a fusion release on the order of tens of megatons, 24% of its energy shot forth at the speed of light in a single beam of coherent x-rays.

The laser struck a glancing blow on the Control Ship, but that glancing blow vaporized entire decks along a narrow cone through the alien vessel, then exploded outward in a fiery wave of transfer energy. As a single shot, it dealt an impressive degree of devastation, but it was by no means enough to put the Patron ship out of commission, not for a race which could reconstruct anything at the nanometer scale with relative ease.

However, LFM-10277 was numbered 10277 for a reason.

Even as the Control Ship rocked and reeled from the mine's laser, three more beams struck from three different directions. Two imparted glancing blows like that of 10277, but the third cored the alien vessel straight into its center of mass. The beam burned down through a quarter of the ship's depth, and every joule of x-ray energy was converted to an explosive thermal/kinetic punch. The Control Ship dipped in its orbit and the drive-star itself flared in response.

All over the Patron vessel, systems began to fail.

▰▰▰▰▰▰▰▰▰▰▰▰▰▰▰

> whiteness pervades
> hints of images flash and jump
> nathan screams
> raging but powerless
> what is happening
> <discontinuity>

The moment of stasis ended abruptly, as short and as interminable as any of them had been. Nathan's suicidal charge toward the door of the mess—toward the Patron who no longer stood there—continued unabated. He crashed into the door frame with nothing to expend his murderous rage upon.

He punched the bulkhead in frustration, and then was slammed against that same bulkhead as the rest of the crew behind him—who had all made the same charge at their one identified enemy—crashed into his back. Nathan pushed back and up, crying out, "Off! Get off! It's not here any more!"

They all surged off of him as fast as they could. Nathan looked around when they were clear and surveyed the situation in the mess. The Patron was nowhere to be seen, but its avatar still stood rooted to the deck behind them.

Nathan drifted over, approaching the statue warily, looking for any sudden movement from the marbled form. Nothing. He reached out a hand to touch its shoulder, but just before he made contact ... .

The mess room suddenly shook and shuddered. The avatar, which had been firmly planted upon the deck, came free and drifted up to bounce off the overhead and float uncontrolled through the room.

Nathan jerked his hand back and then looked around him again, his eyes seeking out Kris and Edwards. "What was that?"

They both, along with the others, looked around carefully. Kris reached upward, pulling herself into contact with the overhead and laid her ear against the metal surface. She looked back at them. "I hear a rumbling or a roaring transmitted through the hull."

Master Chief smiled. "I think our hosts might be having a bad day today."

There was another sharp blow, and a couple of the crew cried out. Nathan reached down to the deck and felt the unsteady vibration Kris had described. He nodded. "I think you're right. Either something's gone wrong on board ... ."

Kris grinned back. "Or something's been made to go wrong. I wonder how long we've been out?"

"Long enough for Earth to build at least one effective defense," Nathan answered. "Thank God. I was afraid Sykes and his cronies would keep a damper on the programs Lydia had going. I wonder how close to home we are now?"

Edwards grunted. "More importantly, how much time do we have before these art snobs get their acts together and decide to put us back in a still life?"

The ship shook again, this time severely enough for it to affect their own jury-rigged wiring. Compartment lights flickered and they could hear the groaning of the hull as the stresses the Control Ship endured were imparted on what remained of their destroyer.

Nathan grimaced. "Yeah. It would be just our luck to hitch a ride all the way back to local space and then get killed by friendly fire." He quickly locked eyes with his remaining crew, glancing swiftly from one to the next. "All right, everyone, we're going to get out of here and, if possible, join up with the home-team. And if we can do a little mayhem on the way out to help our brothers-in-arms, well, all the better."

Edwards quirked a brow. "Do you happen to have a plan for this effortless egress, Skipper?"

Nathan shook his head. "I don't, COB, but she does," he said, gesturing to Kris.

The ship shook again as it took another hit. Edwards glanced back and forth between Nathan and their Chief Engineer. "Oh. Really? I must have missed that particular meeting. Care to share, boss?"

Nathan moved closer to him and grasped him on the shoulder. "Afraid not. I don't want to inadvertently give away our plans to unfriendly ears," he said, waving a hand at the slowly drifting avatar. "Just do what she says."

Everyone turned expectant eyes upon Kris, who, despite everything that had happened to them, managed to blush slightly. "It's not a very safe plan."

Mike Simmons, their TAO and Ops Officer who had led them in decimating half the Patron fleet, grunted a laugh. "And waiting here doing nothing is so much safer."

Kris shrugged. "Okay. Andrew," she said, addressing the helmsman, Andrew Weston, "The remaining engineers and I are going to be jury-rigging some power. I need you to go to the bridge and set up a program for remote triggering ... ."

She went on, handing out assignments, providing little detail, but all of them had worked together for years, and for over a year and a half on the voyage itself. They listened to what she said as well as to what she did not say, filling in the blanks for themselves. A few pairs of eyes grew fearful, but most of the crew began to smile wickedly. They might all die in the attempt, but if it worked, it would be spectacular.

In pairs and groups of three, they all departed—some headed to the banks of batteries and capacitors where their only remaining power was still stored, while others headed to watchstations to set up automated programs to aid their escape, and still others hit the SSTOS Hangar and the weapons locker / armory.

Soon, Nathan was all alone in the mess, just himself and the quiescent avatar. The only sound breaking the tableau was the occasional repeated lightning crash of a strike upon the Control Ship surrounding the destroyer.

He approached tentatively, the fear, nerves, and anticipation built up during the talk of escape falling away to be replaced by renewed feelings of hate and devastation. The captain pushed off the overhead such that he could match the statue's drift, and he looked upon the frozen white face of his XO.

Nathan gazed into the flat, marbled eyes of the avatar, searching for any hint of awareness, any sign of life or humanity, but there was nothing there. This was simply an inert tool of alien design—a golem cleverly sculpted to mimic a friendly, trusted face.

Despite the resemblance, there was nothing about the avatar's form in homage to Christopher Wright. This marvel was, if anything, a repudiation of everything that Wright had been, an insult to his life and memory.

Nathan snarled, reached out to grasp the statue by the shoulders, and pushed it back violently. Since they both floated out of contact with the deck, his shove pushed him back in a spin exactly opposite to the one he had given the avatar, but where the statue spun stiffly—striking the bulkhead behind it with a loud crack—Nathan reacted smoothly—tucking in to spin faster, then kicking off the deck and the opposite bulkhead to drive his outstretched hands at the statue like a battering ram.

He slammed into the avatar and pinned it in the corner between the bulkhead and the deck with his momentum. There was a loud crack and the statue broke in half at the waist, casting stone dust out to hang motionless in the air.

Nathan grunted, grabbed the torso by the wrist, braced himself, and swung the upper half of the heavy avatar down onto the table. Another crack and the arm shattered. He shifted holds, swung again, and the torso was rendered armless, with long chips and cracks appearing on the statue's head.

Nathan breathed heavily, only briefly worrying about the nano-created stone dust he inhaled. He rested a foot upon the statue's head and glared down at the broken form. Wright's face was placid. Nathan shook his own head and whispered, "I'm sorry," as yet another attack thrummed through the hull.

Holding himself in place with the edge of the table, he kicked out with his free leg and snapped the head from the statue in another explosion of dust. It bounced up and rebounded from bulkhead to bulkhead until it eventually drifted slowly over the deck, bumping along as it spun around, uncontrolled.

Nathan surveyed the devastation one last time with a heavy feeling of regret and self-recrimination, and then pushed off toward the hatchway to join Kris.

There were nearly 18,000 lasing fusion mines distributed along the expected path of the Deltan/Patron convoy, but even with the alien's course well-predicted, it was unrealistic to expect more than a small percentage of them would actually be in a position to engage the enemy. Space was simply too large, and prudence dictated that the field be spread wide in case the aliens altered their path as they closed with the solar system.

Of the 9500 mines along the primary route, a still smaller percentage were actually within range to make an effective attack. Others were simply too far out or were arrayed elsewhere along the circumference of the drive-star, too far from one of the relatively small alien vessels to make an attack. And not all of those within striking distance were effective. Due to the limitations imposed by their "stealthy" low-power state, many simply reacted too slowly or inaccurately, wasting their one and only shot upon either empty vacuum or the burning hell of the drive.

Therefore, approximately 2000 mines of the remaining field with a decent probability of hit upon one of the actual Patron vessels were distributed uniformly along the fleet's projected course. This spread the mines out to increase the overall engagement time and to avoid calling attention to the massive field of weapons lying in wait. If the Patrons did nothing, each of these 2000 mines would have the opportunity to slice, burn, and pierce their way through the alien ships—and there was no way for the Patrons to survive, not when each and every shot was individually more powerful than 10 of the *Sword of Liberty's* warheads.

Of course, that assumed the aliens would do nothing to defend themselves. This was not the first time the Patrons had faced armed resistance, however. Perhaps it was the first effective opposition in centuries, but these conquerors were not without tricks of their own.

Beneath the embattled Control Ship, the drive-star suddenly fluoresced, radiance boiling out from the knot of energies gathered below the main alien vessel. The orange and purple ropes of light binding the drive-star's plasma tightened and shifted. In reaction, the photonic thrust blasting out from the pole flashed brighter and widened out, turning from a tight column of light to a broader and broader cone.

Propulsive photons lit up local space, trading thrust for searing reflections. Dust motes, particles, and each and every rock and mine within striking distance shone like a local cluster of microscopic stars. The smaller inanimate flecks were burned away or flung far from the fleet. The larger, more massive mines had their low reflectivity coatings burned off, each one becoming brighter and more noticeable.

As the carefully placed weapons melted and cracked from differential heating under the wide, indiscriminate onslaught, the weapons that had a chance of destroying the Patron ships triggered early, far out of range and position. Fusion explosions and invisible beams of x-rays dappled the vacuum around the fleet, spearing infinity with furious energies, but failing to connect with their true targets.

For the few remaining weapons still close enough to score a hit, the new brilliance of their positions gave their one real defense away. Lasers and nano-particle beams shot out from the Cathedral, the Polyp, and the Junkyard, defending themselves and the Control Ship from further attack. Lasing fusion mines, struggling to wake up and perform their duty, were annihilated before they could fire.

From 18,000, to 9500, to 2000 mines, Earth's second attempt at battle came to a mere 217 total strikes. The rest either never came into play, failed to fire, missed, or were destroyed before they could make their attempts. The damage dealt by this relatively low number of hits looked devastating, but for a culture capable of rapid nano-scale repairs, it was not catastrophic. By the time the Patron fleet met humanity's next line in the sand, they would be nearly unmarked, with little sign of the attack but for some missing mass and a higher ratio of replicas to originals in their collections. All mankind would have to show for the hours of battle as the fleet fought its way through the mine-field would be a little information and good deal less assurance that their other preparations might be any more effective.

Within the Control Ship, now safe from the assault of its latest quarry, the Patrons began to re-assert some sense of order. Systems came back online as damage was repaired. Atmosphere ceased to billow out from chasms cut and burned into the hull. Lights came back on and machinery hummed back to life.

And the stasis fields surrounding the *Sword of Liberty* snapped back into operation, suspending time, interrupting Nathan and the crew, and exposing their every careful preparation for the aliens' inspection.

The destroyer's mission hull was again awash in dim golden light, trapped in stasis, but something still moved, an alien form around which the golden radiance of time-almost-stopped shied away, replaced by a blue-white nimbus. The segmented, tentacled Patron moved slowly, remaining carefully within the tight boundary of the anti-stasis bubble conforming to it. If it moved too swiftly, the space-time counter-reaction would not have time to negotiate its motion within the wider stasis region. It would become frozen, or worse, beset by destructive atomic tidal stresses shredding it at the molecular level.

The Patron—the same one who had first made contact with the crew, not that there was individually much difference between the thousands of its species within the fleet—drifted through the human ship, noting with close analogs to interest and consternation that its prize humans were not where it had left them. It seemed that the troubling creatures had been in the midst of mischief-making.

The humans were everywhere, all dressed out in vacuum suits and frozen in place throughout the ship behind makeshift barriers and defenses. Weapons had been broken out from the armory and distributed amongst the crew, as if such simple chemical slug-throwers could ever be effective against an enemy that could cross stars, stop time, and even bend space.

The defenses seemed to center upon the ship's single shuttle, though how they expected to escape from within their own hull, and then from within the Control Ship itself was unknown. To even make an attempt, they would have to employ some significant ship-to-ship weaponry, but every missile had been expended, and the Patrons had ripped out the railgun and the laser emplacements themselves. Also, the reactor was gone, so they could not even have turned that into a weapon, were such a thing possible.

The alien recalled the fictions Earth had heedlessly and endlessly broadcast out into space, with their repeated themes of succeeding and surviving despite seemingly insurmountable odds against them. Had it been human, it would have grinned and shook its head. This was their last stand.

This … pitiful display actually seemed to indicate that the crew thought they had a chance of winning, of escaping. It surveyed the ship, but found nothing to indicate that this plan was anything but the most forlorn of hopes. It actually made the Patron think less of them, and of humanity as a whole. To think that they would endanger their precarious position on so feeble an attempt, it almost seemed to express a suicidal intent.

The Patron thought briefly of honoring their apparent wish. With them frozen like this, it would be no problem at all to end each of their lives, in any of a variety of ways. But that would almost seem to be a gift.

Better to take their hope from them entirely, to crush even their weak ability to oppose their captors, and then show them the price of their pride, the price of destroying so many irreplaceable treasures for their own selfish survival. The Patron went to work.

It and its remotes moved through the mission hull, disarming each of the defenders and destroying the weapons. The crew and the broken remains of the guns were then deposited back in the mess room amidst the shattered pieces of the avatar. After a time, the task was complete, with Nathan, Kris, Edwards, and the rest arranged in a circle facing one another.

When next the Patrons awoke them, they would return to normal time facing each other, powerless, and spared only by the cruel mercy of the aliens. And the next thing to which they would be forced to bear witness would be the murdered Earth, reaped of all its treasures, fated to be forgotten by the universe, except as an exhibit for their captors. Then, at last, these final few humans would know the futility of opposition.

The Patron departed, satisfied and at ease.

19: "FROM DARKNESS—LIGHT"

December 28, 2055; USS Trenton (CA-1), Flagship, CRUDESGRU One, within the Asteroid Belt on approach to Earth

Lydia Russ squinted at the wide screen in front of her in the *Trenton's* wardroom, silently cursing the slow assault of age that wore down her senses, despite the sci-fi future she found herself in. It was unfair that after all the pain she and the others had been through, all that she had compromised and wheedled to achieve, and all the impossible obstacles that had nevertheless been overcome—that her savoring of this moment would be diminished by something as pedestrian as an old lady's eyes.

On the wardroom screen, false color overlays pinpointed every significant rock and asteroid in their quadrant of the Belt. Years of movies and popular portrayals had convinced her inner expectations that the Asteroid Belt would be a jumble of tumbling mountains, filling the night black sky all around. The reality proved much more mundane. In terms of the wide vacuum of space, it was a busy mess, but only relative to the emptiness between planets.

Hundreds of kilometers and seconds of arc lay between even the closest of the independent, serenely rotating mountains of iron-nickel ore and silicates, shot through with veins of richer, heavier metals. Only upon a compressed, simulated view such as this one—from the main tactical screen aboard the bridge of the US task force flagship, where a major portion of the Belt could be displayed at once—did the belt seem as dense as common belief held it to be. Were the screen a window, however, she would be hard pressed to point out even a couple of dim rocks within view to lessen her isolation.

Some of those asteroids were practically crowded now, however. Along the projected path of the Deltan approach and behind the bulk of four semi-close behemoths—each unnamed mass many times the size of Mt. Everest—were the total assembled forces of the planet Earth. As an ambush site, it was as ideal as they could make it. Of course, it had to be.

This was the last stand, the line which could not be crossed, the best that mankind could collectively muster. Yet the numerous ships were

261

dwarfed by the asteroids they hid behind, asteroids which themselves were dwarfed by the enormity of the solar system and space itself. As sparse as the asteroid belt was in reality, the defenses of the human race seemed even sparser in the presence of this unstoppable enemy. And beyond this were only the pitiful fixed emplacements back on Earth.

Lydia forced her doubts away, convincing herself she felt nothing but fierce pride and determination. It was an act of will which was only sustainable because of where she found herself—here, where determination would be needed to see them through, rather than "safe" at home.

Her presence and the confidence it implied was not an asset embraced with equal enthusiasm by everyone. A searing, disapproving gaze bore down upon her from behind. She hardly needed to note his reflection in the screen to realize who it was. It was a look he had favored her with routinely, ever since she had announced her intention to remain aboard.

Lydia's eyebrow arched slightly and she spoke in a patient, amused tone, not bothering to turn around to confirm her guess at his identity. "Can I help you, Admiral?"

Rear Admiral Calvin Henson—former colonel in the US Air Force, original commanding officer of the *Sword of Liberty,* and current commanding officer of the US Aerospace Navy's Cruiser Destroyer Group One—smiled tightly. He pulled himself next to Lydia, the "mother" of the entire USAN, and tried to address her face to face at the very least. He would do anything if she would just listen to reason. "Ma'am, our last rescue cutter—*Nightingale*—is ready to cut free and head for cover. I'm holding her for you. Please, Ms. Russ, you need to get aboard."

She turned and looked at him, firm in her resolve, but compassionate for his position. "I'm sorry, Calvin, but you know I won't do that."

He pulled himself in closer, not in any attempt to intimidate, but as an opportunity to speak low and frankly in the presence of the few other personnel present in the wardroom, to save either of them embarrassment over what needed to be said. "Ma'am, this international fleet wouldn't be here without all that you've done. God knows every single squadron owes you for its existence, but that gratitude was only enough to get you this far.

"You simply have no place in my operational chain of command. You're not a tactician, strategist, or systems tech. Frankly, all you are is a VIP and a liability. There is a very good chance that you're going to be injured or killed when that fleet crests those asteroids, and all you are going to do then is draw resources and attention away from an injured or dying crewman. Not only that, but your loss would be devastating to the defense back home, and that's something none of us can afford."

She frowned, and her eyes narrowed slightly. "I don't know if I agree with the value you place on me, especially as far as that planet of sitting ducks back on Earth are concerned, but I'll concede that I have no place in your battle organization. What do you intend to do about it? Throw me off?"

His mouth tightened. "What I want you to do is see things from my perspective. Get on that cutter of your own free will."

The Admiral turned to glare at the handful of officers still populating the wardroom. Each of them realized his intent and quickly and quietly departed. Once they were alone, he turned back to Lydia, no longer glaring, but still intent on her concession or explanation. Neither of them said anything.

Eventually, Henson's face softened and he slumped in as much as anyone can in freefall. "I'm not going to throw you off, ma'am, but you at least owe me a reason why you have to be here. And not simply as a sign of your confidence in us, like you told *Trenton*'s CO, because everyone knows that's just some PR bullshit."

Lydia smiled at him. "Such a cynic, Calvin. I'm shocked, just terribly, terribly shocked." She turned back to the display screen with its false color representation of their ship, the *USS Trenton (CA 1)* and the five escorting *Sword* class destroyers that made up CRUDESGRU 1, tucked in behind a mountain of iron and silicates.

CRUDESGRU 2, similar in composition but headed up by *USS Lake Erie (CA 2)*, lay about 2000 km further on behind another rock, while two other asteroids were held by allied UK/CAN/AUS and EU squadrons, adapted *Sword* class destroyers all. Support ships, minelayers, and rescue cutters from a variety of countries—countries allied not only by the desire to aid in the defense of Earth, but also by the obligation to produce such vessels as the price of receiving the required technology and designs—fled from the planned ambush site to hide behind still other asteroids, deeper in the Belt. Each fleeing vessel was careful to remain within the shadows of the large asteroids shielding the four strike-groups, lest they give away the slim hope of a surprise attack against the Deltans.

Most, but not all of the tonnage out there was American—they had, of course, started first and were the original developers of the tech—but all the designs were Windward's, either directly or as a close adaptation. In a very real sense, Henson was right. This fleet would not have been here defending the Earth without all that she had done.

But the honor of parentage was not hers to claim. She was at best its stepmother, moving in to carry on when those who had toiled and worked and paid with their very lives could no longer complete the fight. The father of this fleet, Gordon Lee, had never seen a single one of his children fly. Its other progenitors had been lost to the unknown, and in so doing had gained them the information they all needed if they were to have even the smallest chance of survival.

Every other person who had led this battle for all their futures had made the ultimate sacrifice. Was she truly a part of its wondrous, miraculous ascendance if she felt unwilling to pay the same price?

Her eyes misted as she stared through the screen, hardly seeing the icons of the ships any more. How much of what she felt could even be put into words? How much would someone like the Admiral ever believe? "I have always been here, Calvin. But I have not always been part of the solution. I've been referred to as the mother of this fleet. You just said much the same, yet,—in the beginning—I tried to abort the whole affair. What if I had not? What if I had done as Lee begged me to do and thrown the full measure of the government behind his project? What if I had contained that bastard Sykes earlier? Would we be where we are today? Could we have gone further? Could we be better prepared?

"The Deltans have stolen the lives of all the people who ever meant anything to me, and I owe them a reckoning for that. But I also owe the people—my friends—who have come before me, who faced this foe with a level of faith I was late in achieving. It's a special sort of hell to be the one left behind. I'm certain you've been in that same position, given your career. You understand. I have to see this through. I have to face down the Deltans here. I have to stand shoulder to shoulder with my family and see this through to the end—here on the front line, facing the same threat they faced, not hidden away on Earth or cowering behind some asteroid. Admiral, I have to be here, because here is where I've always been, here beside the crew of the *Sword of Liberty*."

Henson locked eyes with her, trying to ascertain her true feelings, her actual intent. To his shock, he saw a sincerity so true, a resolve so intense, that he had to look away from the fierceness of it.

Lydia followed his gaze down and touched his temple gently, drawing him back to her. This time she appeared softer, more vulnerable. "Please, Admiral, don't force me onto the sidelines. Let me finish this."

He glanced over at the screen, then back to her. He shook his head and raised his comm suite. Pressing a single button, he said, "Bridge, this is the Admiral. Cast off *Nightingale* and send them to the reserve point. There are no further passengers." With that, he nodded to Lydia and turned to pull himself away.

She reached out an arm and stopped him with a gentle grasp. He looked back and saw her smile slightly, tears of gratitude welling un-fallen in the corners of her eyes. "Thank you, Calvin. You'll never know how much this means to me."

He grunted. "Ms. Russ, I'm not quite as sentimental as all that. I said you served no purpose on this ship, and it turned out I was wrong. It's as simple as that."

Lydia grinned more fully. "Oh, really? And what purpose is that?"

"Ma'am, you seem to have a faith and a will stronger than any single warhead, and everyone on this ship has seen that and been inspired by it. You are not a shooter—that's true—and your value may only be symbolic, but the strength of that symbol may prove critical in the end. If this battle is as close a thing as I fear it may be, your spirit could be all that sustains us. I had forgotten, and for that I am sorry. Your place is here."

With that, the commander of CRUDESGRU 1 turned and left, leaving Lydia alone in the *Trenton*'s wardroom, alone with her thoughts, her fears, her hopes, and with the converging icons on the tactical screen.

The battle was about to begin.

◆◆◆◆◆◆◆◆◆◆◆◆◆◆

A tragically beautiful dawn came to the asteroid belt.

These inelegant remnants of the ordered solar system had never known any illumination beyond the meager sunlight of Sol, far, far beyond the orbit of Mars. And all that cold light had ever revealed were stark shadows dappled across slate gray ore and faded brown rock. The Belt may have held incalculable wealth as a resource, but it had never been exactly attractive.

That assessment changed with the arrival of the Patrons, though. The drive star still sprayed its photonic thrust wide, and the convoy continued to decelerate, still normalizing and circularizing its orbit over these long months and years of thrust. Even though they were well and truly captured by the gravity of the distant sun, they were not yet at their intended destination, wherever that might prove to be.

For both defense and maneuver, the drive star blazed on, burning and illuminating sections of rock that had never before seen light of any kind. Crystals and pure un-oxidized metals fumed and shone brilliantly from deep crevices. Striations of heterogeneous minerals stood out for the first time like the lines and whorls of some demented abstract canvas.

Dawn came to the asteroid belt, but vastly brighter, more revealing, and in direct opposition to the only light that had ever really touched them since the moment of creation. Here was beauty, but a terrible beauty wrought only by destruction.

The Patrons paid this truly unique spectacle no heed, however. They simply cruised on, either unaware or uncaring. Their four ships—the Polyp, the Cathedral, the reconstituted Junkyard, and the slightly smaller, yet more forbidding Control Ship—all orbited serenely around the drive star, protected by its thrust and unmolested by any mines or attackers for the last few weeks. The ships had all returned to their quasi-Lagrange positions, seemingly unworried about a different, more defensive configuration.

The convoy came upon a loose, arbitrary grouping of four asteroids separated by thousands of kilometers, seemingly no different from any other set of rocks in the Belt. It passed blithely through the center of the group, content to allow the proven effectiveness of the drive star's radiance to defend it from any potential attack.

But a static, single layered defense was a weak one, no matter how effective it might originally have been.

The searing cone of light swept over the asteroids' rocky surfaces, leaving behind fields of pitted, half-melted stone which ended abruptly at the mutual horizons on all four masses. The defensive radiance then passed on, leaving the shadow zones behind each untouched. From those shadows, the coordinated first strike flashed out.

Twenty-two warships each unleashed initial salvoes of thirty missiles— nearly a third of the load-out for the destroyers, but just a ninth the complement of the two larger cruisers. The 660 missiles which streaked out from the four asteroids toward their convoy targets were not the still, stealthy threats of the mines. This wave of devastation was like the *Sword of Liberty*'s attack: swift, directed, and erratic, but dozens of times larger and more deadly.

Missile trajectories blossomed into hundreds of disparate tracks, only converging upon one of the four possible targets at the last moment. One fifth of the wave exploded into fusion brilliance along a direct line between the targets and the shielding asteroids in an effort to obscure direct targeting of the warships now emerging from their hiding places. For a moment, the drive-star's luminance was overcome by a halo of nuclear glory, and only then did the offensive wave truly take effect.

Fully half of the remaining missiles made their objective the Control Ship, with the remaining split between the other three lesser targets. 264 missiles corkscrewed in toward the lead vessel, becoming over 1500 individual warheads, each one a step in a fiery spiral ending in immolation. The space above each target began to froth with the white globes of nuclear flame and the lobed spears of coherent x-rays as the warheads worked their way down toward the endgame.

The first few hundred beams flayed into the Control Ship and the museum vessels without opposition and very nearly ended things there. The critical weakness of the Patrons was also one of their greatest tools: stasis. The game-changing nature of the alien technology meant that the Patrons and their equipment could survive any shock, thermal load, or duration that the stasis machinery itself could survive. Short of a direct hit or the indiscriminate battering ram of transfer energy, the invading force would survive even this onslaught—provided they could stop the attack before those direct and indirect assaults pulverized or vaporized even the hardened areas of the fleet.

And that was the Achilles Heel of the device that enabled the Patrons to survive the vast distances between stars. Stasis made them slow. It introduced an unavoidable pause in whatever reaction they might take, and as mankind had exploited it twice before, they did so again.

The Control Ship erupted in apocalyptic fissures of light as beam after beam flayed it or stabbed deep, rending deck after deck, layer after layer of alien technology. Entire sections of the vessel were cut free to spin wildly away from the pseudogravity around the drive star. Patrons died by the dozens as the warheads worked their way ever closer.

Rear Admiral Calvin Henson smiled slightly, deeply satisfied but cautiously optimistic. He keyed his mike to the flag battle net, his link to his group's commanding officers, as well as CRUDESGRU Two and the two allied destroyer squadrons. "All stations, CRUDESGRU One will remain on a southern approach, centered on the Control Ship. Group Two, detach and proceed at best speed to the opposite side of the drive star, make your approach out of the magnetic knot to the north. Your objective remains the Control Ship. Recommend detaching *Sword of Industry* as command and control relay to coordinate additional salvoes after you pass the limn of the star. DESRON Alpha, break east and engage the Polyp and the Junkyard. DESRON Bravo, make for the Cathedral and continue."

Commodore Dan Torrance, his old XO from their mutually stolen bid for command of the *Sword of Liberty*, responded first. "Roger, Admiral. We're headed for the backside and we'll meet you again up front, hopefully with nothing but a debris field between us."

"DESRON Alpha, aye." A clipped British voice—Commodore Lawrence aboard *HMS Conqueror.*

"DESRON Bravo, will comply." And this, a slight German accent—Flotillenadmiral Krueger of *NAE Bismarck.*

From within the confines of his acceleration coffin, Henson nodded as best he could. Almost all the first wave's missiles were committed, with outstandingly destructive results and virtually no reaction from the enemy vessels. Yes, optimistic, but cautiously so. "Tactical teams, release second wave per the op plan and prepare for direct fire when within range, at ships' discretion."

All his subordinates' voices together. "Aye aye, sir!"

Uncomfortably cocooned within her own "coffin" inside her stateroom aboard the *Trenton,* Lydia Russ fretted with the wealth of information she'd been offered by Calvin Henson. Despite her lack of a place within his tactical organization, he had seen fit to provide her with a direct view of the action, just as his tactical watchstanders saw it. The veering icons, lines, and splashes of color proved to be a three-dimensional mess, however. She silently complimented whatever training program enabled the tacticians and technicians of the aerospace navy to make any sense of the gobbledygook she had become privy to.

After a short while, though, she began to get the gist despite herself. All the available information appeared overwhelmingly lopsided toward man's victory. And as she felt her body vibrate with the multiple ejections of the second wave of missiles, it only seemed as if it would shift even more in humanity's favor.

She could not help thinking, however, that were she in gravity, she'd be listening for the other shoe to drop.

preparations undone
shift and jostle, whirl about
back where we started
are secrets revealed
<discontinuity>

Stasis vanished abruptly once more, and every remaining crewmember of the *Sword of Liberty* comically whirled their arms about as they adjusted to their new locations. Where before they had been armed and arrayed in defensive positions throughout the remains of the ship, now they were all back in the wardroom, in a circle, surrounding the broken pieces of their small arm weapons.

Nathan looked at his crew, silently checking their names off an internal truncated list, ensuring they were all there. His eyes lingered on Kris, across from him in the circle, until she locked gazes with him and he could see and feel that she was all right. He looked at the pile of guns and then turned to Dave Edwards. "They took the low-hanging fruit. Did they wreck all our preps though?"

Edwards shrugged, then pushed off from the bodies next to him and flew over to the ops console there in the wardroom. "Dunno, Boss. Let me check."

Before he could query the system though, the entire hull jerked and flexed violently, scattering people and gun parts through the air. The debris filled the weightless room, sowing even more confusion and pain as the pieces collided and rebounded painfully off both person and bulkhead without discrimination.

Kris grinned even as she rubbed a fresh bruise upon her forehead. "Well, at least we woke up during another round of action rather than coming in after humanity was toast."

LT Simmons steadied himself and responded, "Yeah, but that action seemed a little close and a little too strong. I'm glad our people are still giving the Patrons some effective resistance, but I'm less keen to wind up toast myself."

Nathan grinned. "Mike, we've been on borrowed time for who knows how long. All I want is a chance to get out of here. Whether we make or not is in the hands of whatever higher power's been watching over us up until now."

Kris drifted near and she and Nathan snagged one another out of the air and held on tight and close. "Never knew you were quite so religious, Captain-my-love."

"Hey, there are no atheists in foxholes. Or in this case, probably none captured by implacable aliens and thrown into stasis at will."

Kris frowned. "Stick with the foxhole analogy. It's pithier."

Edwards turned away from the console and gestured to gain all their attention. "Well, whether angels or the incompetence of our captors is responsible, our preps are still good. They satisfied themselves with wrecking our obvious weapons. Auxiliary capacitors are still charged, maneuvering jets are still good, and the shuttle shows five by five. Plus, get this: I'm picking up encrypted comm chatter. I can't decipher it without a key, but it means it's not just missiles or mines out there. There are people."

Nathan nodded. "That tears it. We make our attempt now. Everybody, we're abandoning our defensive stations and leaving. These aliens thought they'd taken away all our weapons, removed every means we had of opposing them. But they didn't count on our ingenuity, our resolve," he looked over at Kris lovingly and continued, "or our sheer stupidity. Let's do something stupid and suicidal and show our Patrons what it means to underestimate Earth."

████████████████████

As the last half of the first wave's warheads committed themselves, and as the second wave of missiles launched from the rapidly maneuvering Earth fleet, the invading Patrons finally reacted. And this reaction was the last thing anyone had expected.

For the first time in over 80 years, the drive star's radiance shut off. The blue-white beam—which had propelled the Patrons all the way from Delta Pavonis to Sol system, and which had in turn ushered on the technological leaps enabling mankind to meet them on something approaching an equal footing—vanished.

Aboard the *Trenton*, Rear Admiral Henson would have bolted upright if his restraints had allowed it. His feelings wavered between hope and dread, and he held his breath to see if this meant the end of the battle, or just that it was only now about to truly be joined.

His answer came—again—in an unexpected fashion. Below the battered Control Ship, the tortured lines of color constraining the drive star flexed and writhed. Their confining limbs now curled and looped, gathering the brilliant fusion plasma of the drive star into waves and arcs, not to direct an enhanced photon beam for thrust, but to propel the plasma itself outward.

Sheets of plasma jetted off the drive star to arc over the Control Ship and the museum vessels, coordinated prominences and mass ejections who's electrically charged sprays of matter attenuated warhead beams, burned missile bodies, and engulfed both laser and railgun fire. Where the vessels of the Patron fleet had been exposed to space and both direct and indirect assault, they were now shielded by atomic flame.

The flares of the drive star swatted the remainder of the first missile wave out of the sky, then broke free to send an intense wave of energy out to scorch both the second wave and the attacking ships. The plasma blasts cooled and dissipated rapidly as they left the confining energies directed by the battered Control Ship, such that they disabled only a tithe of the second wave and had even less effect on the larger, more distant warships. However, the sheets of star matter proved completely effective in shielding the Patron vessels. Worse still, as the level of assault slackened, clouds of nano-assemblers poured out to begin in-battle repairs.

With a command, Henson adjusted his plan, and all the ships of his fleet broke free of their original objectives to instead converge on the Control Ship. Where a distributed attack no longer worked, concentration and mass of fire might still carry the day.

The second wave, now given up for lost due to the mutating nature of the battle, was joined by a third missile assault, a continuous stream of missiles aimed past the Control Ship at the surface of the drive star itself, directed at the continually shifting upwellings which gave birth to the plasma sheets. Nuclear blasts pummeled the immense surface of the star, an attempt to use brute force to disrupt the fiery shields. At first, it seemed like trying to extinguish a blow torch as one would a candle, but after many, many poorly placed explosions, the series of relatively small puffs achieved in aggregate what no one individual blast could.

The shield thinned and faltered, opening clear patches over and around the Control Ship. Into these patches, lasers and railgun fire poured forth from the human warships. Each hit was small and dealt nowhere near the damage even one of the dwindling number of missiles could accomplish, but at the very least it disrupted the nanotech repair effort. At best they achieved a stalemate, but it was a tenuous draw, limited by the relative size of each force's magazines: missiles and railgun rounds versus the unimaginable mass of a dwarf star. And once their missiles were used up and their magazines had gone dry, the Patrons would pour forth an onslaught of laser and nanobeam fire that would decimate the Earth forces, not to mention the damage the drive star's propulsion beam could presumably deliver.

Despite the best that humanity could bring to bear, they were still going to lose.

"SITREP, people." Henson's voice on the net was grim.

Dan Torrance came back angry. "We're in position but nothing's making it past that goddamn plasma shield. Who the fuck uses a solar flare to guard their ships? How is it not burning them up?"

Lawrence, the British DESRON commander, spoke up. "Our lads

have analyzed a cross section of the shield. It's actually quite distant from the ships themselves. Our entire force could easily fit inside that volume."

Henson jumped on that quickly. "This goes back in our favor if we remove the interference of that shield. If we can't disrupt it, can we at the very least get inside it?"

Torrance blew a low whistle. "It's a wall of fusion plasma, Calvin. The only reason it didn't burn right through our ships when they started throwing solar flares at us was that it dissipates and cools rapidly once it's away from whatever's keeping the plasma confined. If we go down there, though, what's happening to our missiles and railgun rounds will happen to us. Up till now we've had virtually no casualties."

"You think that's going to stand, Dan? The Deltans haven't really fired at us yet. The offense has been entirely on our side. As soon as we shoot our last missile, they're going to drop those shields and skewer us with every last damn megajoule of laser energy they can bring to bear. And we don't have enough time to retreat, resupply, and re-attack. They'll be in orbit of the damn planet before we can attack again. No. We have to finish this assault here and now, even if it means ramming the goddamn thing and blowing all our drives. Now then, any bright ideas on how to get past the plasma shield when it's at its strongest?"

Krueger, the German DESRON commander, then mentioned reluctantly, "We have an idea, but none of you are going to like it."

The ships of the combined fleet ceased firing missiles and shifted positions, drawing closer and closer to one another until Group One and the UK squadron formed one wedge-like phalanx approaching from the south and Group Two and the EU squadron formed another wedge from the north. The *Sword* class destroyers arrayed themselves in front of and around the two cruisers, with the bulk of each formation opposite the direction of the plasma flow surrounding the Control Ship. The prominences of their drives blazed so closely to one another, that there was a very real danger of fratricide—destroying their fellow ship's hulls before the Patrons even fired a shot.

The two formations each went to maximum group acceleration, nearly crushing their crews within, but gaining the vital speed they needed to make it through the wall of plasma and to their quarry. Missiles, lasers, and railguns all ceased firing, as combined fleet tactics turned toward formation and maneuver. Closer and closer, the brilliant ramparts of dense, ionized matter loomed, while within each ship, every servicemember grew silent with the knowledge that finality was upon them.

Just before breaching the curving wall of plasma, missile hatches rippled open, disgorging dozens of missiles, but these did not dive for the plasma sources upon the drive star or scream toward any of the Patron vessels. Instead they flew out a short distance and formed a second wedge leading the first defensive layer of destroyers before the plasma sheath blocking them from the Control Ship. As each missile touched the fringes of the prominence, all six warheads aboard them detonated in maximal fusion glory. Nuclear shockwaves and pulses of radiation battered the destroyers which fired them, but—more importantly—also blew back the plasma of the Patron shield for the briefest of moments.

The destroyers passed through the thinned region of shield plasma, and absorbed or blocked what remained, casting a shadow of safety upon the cruiser at the heart of each of the two wedges. *Trenton* and *Lake Erie* followed close behind and breached the Control Ship's shield in turn, but it was not without cost. A momentary weakening of stellar plasma did not mean that the plasma was not still capable of causing damage, nor that it remained in that weakened state.

The first destroyer to breach of either group, *Sword of Freedom* of Group One, proved slightly too far ahead of the missiles' explosive shock front. Stellar plasma cut deep within her, vaporizing the destroyer from the bow back as momentum fed her into the fire. She simply ceased to be, the flames of her demise still nothing next to the luminous energy of the plasma itself.

Flanking her and slightly astern, *Intractable* and *Sword of Vengeance* hit the pause imposed by the missile shockwave. That pause was still energetic enough to raze both vessels. Armored hull plates blackened and popped, springing free to allow the energized gasses of the plasma shield to stab deep into each ship. Crew died and weapons burned, but the hulks of both ships made it through. The next rank, with four destroyers and *Trenton* herself, pushed through with survivable damage, but every last radiator on each ships' amidships spine was blown—still the greatest weakness of the human warships. However, the cruiser design mitigated this obvious flaw, and from her spine *Trenton* extended a full set of auxiliary radiators from within armored sleeves along her central spine. Heat management would cripple the remaining destroyers, but *Trenton* would soldier on.

Group 2 breached the plasma shield with a similar butcher bill, and Admiral Henson had to take a moment to allow the shock to dissipate as he saw all the damage that had been wrought on the fleet. Out of two cruisers and eighteen destroyers, only the two cruisers had made it past the shield relatively mission capable. Of the 17 surviving destroyers, five were all but blackened frames to which a few dismal lifepods clung, ten more were in various states of distress, and two—*Sword of Independence* and the *NAE Paul Teste*—appeared virtually undamaged aside from their damaged radiators, but their lack of cooling capability still rendered them almost immobile and with a very brief attack window before their systems overheated.

It horrified the admiral.

He could not dwell upon it yet, however, because the now exposed Control Ship—which already looked less distressed under the silver clouds of repairing nanotech—opened fire with multiple lasers and assemblor beams. The battle had only just begun, and though they had wounded the enemy severely and survived his surprising defense, their victory was by no means a foregone conclusion.

Calvin Henson glared at his tactical screen and snarled, "All vessels, FIRE!"

━━━━━━━━━━━━━━━━━

"Move faster, damn it!" Nathan yelled. The crew streamed up the corridor before him, just short of panic.

Their initial attempt to escape the wardroom had been stymied for a time when the violent shaking of the *Sword of Liberty* and the Control Ship that surrounded it had jammed the doors between them and their destination and made opening them next to impossible. Then the shuddering largely stopped, and they all worked with nervous intensity, worried they had missed their opportunity to join with their compatriots from Earth, worried that now when they had committed themselves and there was no way to hide what they were up to, the stasis would return and all would be lost.

Nathan and Dave Edwards, channeling the spirit of Christopher Wright proceeded to yell and berate the fragile crew until they began working again, struggling to open each and every pressure door, step by step closer to their objective. Now, as they finally set to work opening the last door, the wide loading doors leading into the hangar, the concussions and shaking of the Control Ship being subject to pitched battle began anew.

Kris looked to Nathan. "Second wind? Think our side took a little breather and now they're back to fight?"

Nathan shrugged. "I have no idea, babe. But if the Navy brought enough firepower to re-engage after being repelled once, then they may well have enough to finally crack this ship down to whatever protected core we're in. And that's good and bad for us."

"Yeah. Good that maybe we'll have a clearer path out of the belly of this monster."

Edwards chimed in after her. "Yeah, and bad because they ain't gonna be likely to hold fire if and when we bust out. Hate to go all this way to end up a victim of friendly fire."

Nathan looked around them. "I don't know. I'm not feeling the big hits like the missiles would make. These are taps like kinetic rounds. Maybe the battle isn't going as well as we could hope after all."

Edwards grinned. "Then maybe our boys need a little help. Your girly's got a prescription for some heavy duty mayhem against these bastards. I say we let it loose and deal with whatever comes." The Master Chief turned to the techs working on cranking the powerless door open. "Or I would if you idiots could just open a goddamn door!"

With that, the door sprang open and people began to rush through toward the SSTOS. Edwards pushed off the overhead and pulled himself through the doorway. "It's about friggin' time! Well, don't wait on me, boys and girls, get aboard! Because I promise I will kick your ever-lovin' asses—legs or no legs—if you let me board that shuttle before you do."

The crew flew aboard the shuttle, unencumbered by any luggage or supplies. Kristene and Andrew Weston shoved their way to the front of the boarding throng so they could finish the preps for launching and initiating her plan. Edwards went aboard as the last crewman to enter, leaving only Nathan aboard the *Sword of Liberty*, the captain about to abandon his post.

Nathan stood half in, half out of the shuttle, braced in the frame and looking back at what he had worked so long to build, at what had sustained them and protected them for so long. The *Sword of Liberty* was not just a ship. It was a part of him, a part of them all, and the final part that he could touch of Gordon Lee, his last link to the great man and his friend. After this, live or die, the past would be gone, laid to rest. Did they have a future? And if so, what did it hold?

"Stop the sentimentality and get your overpaid ass on the bus, sir." Edwards clasped his hand, drawing Nathan in. Nathan nodded and swam into the shuttle, turned and shut the hatch. He checked the seals, glanced around to assure to himself that everyone else had strapped in, Edwards included, and pulled himself to the cockpit.

Weston had brought the reactor online and the engines were warmed already. Kris had negotiated a link to *Liberty*'s bridge and monitored the conditions aboard her. Nathan drifted behind her. He felt the vibration of the shuttle through his palms as he held himself in place, followed by a sharp shudder, transmitted through the SSTOS, through the ship, and presumably through the alien vessel. "I'm feeling missile strikes, Kris. It's time."

Her fingers hovered over her screen's connection with the *Liberty*. "Nathan, you know this whole scheme is nuts. I got the damn idea from a freakin' Niven story I read as a kid. We're probably either going to be blown up, or else it won't do enough and we'll still be stuck in the middle of this Patron prison. This is a huge gamble."

"Kris, I'm CO, so it's my gamble and I choose to gamble on you. Do it."

Without another word or hesitation, Kris stabbed down on the button, initiating the *Sword of Liberty*'s final program. All the power cells, batteries, and capacitor banks for the power conditioning system, the empty missile modules, and missing railgun and laser emplacements suddenly reversed their flow of energy and fed electrons back into the destroyer's grid. This energy circulated about, bypassing shutdown system after shutdown system, seeking a lower potential and somewhere to expend itself. Finally it found an objective and flooded in, energizing the twelve enhanced photon drives of the auxiliary propulsion and maneuvering system.

Despite merely being the actuators for the forward half of the hull, they were still powerful photonic rockets on their own. All twelve fired at beyond full power—their safeties removed—and their radiance punched outward into the atmosphere surrounding the bay enveloping the wrecked forward half of their ship. Just like with their initial launch and that of the Promise, each thruster fired like a continuous stream of nuclear firecrackers. Twelve blowtorches lit with a fire that only existed at the heart of quasars poured energy into nearly every outward direction, and just like the nuclear missiles attacking from outside, their transfer energy propagated outward from the point of application.

Here within the protected inner shell of the Control Ship, where no attack had ever reached, the Patrons had left their hostages one of their most powerfully destructive tools to act as a weapon.

▰▰▰▰▰▰▰▰▰▰▰▰▰▰▰

Calvin Henson winced as another laser bit deep into *Trenton* and more lifesigns flashed red. "Captain Everest, your men have GOT to get those missile cells back online. This little trickle of an attack we're putting out isn't doing enough. I need more than one missile at a time and two railguns!"

"Admiral, my men are doing what they can, but the shield plasma fused together too many of the VLS hatches, and hardly any of the missiles in those cells are communicating with the weapon control system. Even if I send someone EVA, the birds won't work!"

"Captain, if we don't have any missiles then our only option is to become a missile. I will order this group to ramming spee—"

"Admiral!" a new voice cried out on the battle net. Henson thought he recognized it as his Flag Captain's Weapons Officer. "The Control Ship is starting to swell! We're seeing a massive thermal bloom at her core and she's ceased firing."

Henson flipped his screen back to the data in question. Sure enough, the smooth, hard core at the center of the crustacean-like ship of overlapping plates, which they had thus far been unable to scratch, swelled and cracked. Molten metal and flame gushed outward from spot after spot.

He did not know what was happening to it, but he dare not let the opportunity get by. "All remaining units: Fire for effect! Everything you have left, overheating or not."

The shuttle bay of the *Sword of Liberty* disintegrated around them. Their SSTOS flipped end over end, banging into flaming, flying debris, a leaf in a hurricane of furnace light. Nothing, not even the auxiliary drives themselves, could hold together in this maelstrom. Abruptly the brilliance of the photonic drives cut out and all that could be seen was the burning, collapsing bay where their ship had been held captive.

Weston deftly stabilized the battered SSTOS and spun the shuttle slowly about. All three sets of eyes in the cockpit darted about, each of them trying to find a way out. Nathan soon jabbed a hand forward, pointing past Weston's shoulder toward a fissure through which debris streamed, beyond which was the deepest, blackest night. "Andrew, can you get us through that crack?"

"Skipper, I damn well will get us through. Can's got nothing to do with it." Weston punched up maximum thrust, rocketing the SSTOS forward and turning the shuttle to align their frame with the fissure. The spaceplane crashed through, ripping free their wings and tail, and causing a terrible cacophony of alarms and screaming passengers.

Nathan and Kris screamed too, but for entirely different reasons. "Hell, yes!! Andrew! We're free! We made it!"

███████████████████

"Admiral! The Control Ship is breaking up and the plasma shield is dissipating. We have chunks of debris ejecting from the core, but we have no way of knowing what's just damage and what might be a Deltan escape pod."

Henson thought about the status of the fleet, about all the people they had all lost. "We're in no shape right now to worry about prisoners or to allow their leadership caste to get free to threaten us again. Take all escaping debris under fire."

███████████████████

Lydia felt at peace for the very first time since Gordon's death. She took in the rapidly disintegrating wreck of the Deltan's most heinous vessel and allowed herself to feel satisfaction, allowed herself to embrace the hatred, to acknowledge it so she could then discard it and move on. The Deltans had deserved everything they had gotten, but they were over now. She could move on from being the mother of the fleet to being what she had last been happy being: a scientist and an observer of all things.

Lydia looked over the tactical display, at the debris now being targeted since that put the most accurate, highest resolution sensors on them. It was a pity all the pieces she looked at would be destroyed. Who knew what sort of technical marvels could be extracted—

What is that, she wondered. No, it can't be, it doesn't look right … maybe some technological convergence … no, it is their shuttle! It has their crest, but it looks so damaged …

Lydia rapidly scrolled through menus, until she came to the comms screen and checked incoming transmissions from the area where that one piece of debris flew. Her eyes grew wide.

███████████████████

"Calvin! You have to cease fire!" Lydia cried frantically over the net.

Henson wasted an annoyed expression within his acceleration coffin. "Lydia, why are you on this circuit? Shut down and stop interfering."

"No, no, you don't understand. It can't possibly be a real miracle, but it might as well be. Calvin, they're alive!"

"Who's alive, Lydia? What do you mean?" A tactical close-up of one piece of debris appeared in three dimensions before him. This piece appeared to be marked with a navy crest and seemed to be maneuvering slightly, but it also had a comm log attached to it. Henson expanded it, and his eyes grew as big as saucers. He threw the "hold-fire interrupt" for the entire group.

Lydia kept talking, excited. "It's really them. I don't know how, but it's them. The *Sword of Liberty*'s crew survived!"

EPILOGUE: "UNSHEATHED"

December 30, 2055; USCG Nightingale (SRC-7), Rescue Cutter on detached duty as survey vessel; Patron Quarantine Site; Asteroid Belt

Nathan did not react when Kris pulled herself into the cutter's now empty wardroom to join him. He remained intent on the view taking up half the tiny common area's wall, a screen showing the Patron drive star and the lumpy ring of debris that now surrounded it. The drive star was finally quiescent—the last of the angry red and purple coils of energy that had constrained and controlled it had faded away that morning. It now appeared to be a moon-sized dwarf star, an impossibility of nature that nonetheless existed as a new companion in the solar system. In the debris field, teams of Marines in armored vacuum gear supported by dozens of armed SSTOS, went from location to location, identifying tech, isolating and capturing Patrons who had survived the battle, and doing whatever they could to gather and catalog the artifacts and records of all the species the Patrons had "procured."

It promised to be a fascinating endeavor, and all of the old crew had been interested in seeing what they would all learn, but not nearly interested enough to stay even one more day away from the relieved, celebrating Earth. Every other member of the *Sword of Liberty*'s surviving crew had headed home to reconnect with their planet and their joyous loved ones—all except Nathan and Kris. They were all heroes and had been slated to receive heroes' welcomes, Nathan and Kris especially. But her lover and Captain could not pull himself away, despite every argument Dave Edwards made. And Kris would not even think of going without him.

Kris slid in next to Nathan and pulled his face away from contemplation of the screen. She closed in and they kissed, long and longingly. Eventually she pulled back, glad that his eyes stayed with her and did not return to the screen. "I'm worried about you, hon."

Nathan smiled. "Worried? Why?"

"Your parents and my mom, and all our friends, and some no doubt absolutely EPIC parties are all waiting for us back on Earth, but you won't go. You can't leave all that Patron junk behind."

His smile became tempered, more thoughtful, wistful. "I do want to go home."

Kris grinned wide. "Then let's go! We have our own stolen cutter, so we can do whatever we damn well please."

"It's not stolen. It was officially requisitioned and assigned."

"Same difference, but my way is more fun and more in keeping with our track record. C'mon. Let's go. Your parents want to see their son, freshly resurrected back into the land of the living and years younger than he has any right being."

Nathan nodded and looked briefly back toward the now quiescent drive star and its ring of broken wonders. "How can you leave it behind so soon?"

"How could I not, Nathan? I'm as big a space geek as there ever was, but we've done the deed now. I've seen it all! We went further, traveled faster, discovered more, and accomplished things beyond what we ever expected to in our wildest imaginings. And we survived against the greatest odds. After all that, I'm *tired*. Even I am willing to let somebody else ask the new questions while I take a damn break. What about you? Why can't you let it go?"

Nathan looked back at her, turning sober, serious, and anguished. "Because I still don't understand it. None of what they told us makes any sense."

"How so?"

"They said they collected the art of all these species, for prestige or for currency as the only truly unique and thus rare and valuable commodity in the universe. Everything else is just resources, easily obtained with nanotech. But the expression of perception, that somehow had value to them and—here's what's key—the larger society they dealt with."

Kris looked confused.

"So what? They collected art and showed it off to all their buddies for credit or respect or whatever. Big deal."

"It is a big deal, Babe, because it doesn't make any logical sense. It took them 80 damn years to get here. What kind of society and commerce could possibly exist when it takes 80 years to reach the next station?"

Kris paused and looked at the screen herself, while this time Nathan watched her. "Well, they do have stasis."

Nathan shook his head. "No, that's not enough. I don't accept it. There has to be something more, something that allowed them to have commerce and society as we know it, with regular interactions between sentients, not something mediated by nearly a century of travel and a lifetime in stasis. Sure, I can see them pulling out of this society for 80 years or 160 years to open new markets and artificially increase demand for the products you're pulling out of circulation, but not as an every day thing, not when you could live your whole life between interactions. Otherwise, why bother trying to have a society at all?"

Kris pulled him into a long hug, facing him away from the screen that taunted him so. "Honey, staying out here isn't going to net you those answers. You've asked an unsolvable question, until we can get the surviving Patrons to talk to us. But, I really doubt you're going to gain any greater insight here and now rather than after a well-deserved trip ho—"

Nathan felt her stiffen in his arms as her voice cut off. "Baby?"

Kristene spoke again, but her voice sounded odd, like a little girl in shock. "There's another mystery we didn't know the answer to. Why did they go so slow, dragging that unnecessarily heavy drive star around with them?"

"Huh?" Nathan pulled away from the now limp Kris and looked back at the screen. Upon it, the drive star had changed. Instead of the miniature white dwarf, the inner portion had turned black. The outer edge became a silver swirling radiance, that spun faster and faster, extending tendrils of silver and gold light into the obsidian interior, an interior that now seemed not merely black, but *distant*, its shape having transformed from a sphere to a funnel that somehow receded from all directions at once into a new space.

Nathan's jaw dropped.

Kristene sounded entranced again. "Maybe, the answer to both our questions is that the Patrons dragged a freakin' wormhole mouth with them the whole way, and that setting up shop in that greater society doesn't take 80 years … it just takes seconds."

"Holy crap."

They both stared at the newly transformed wormhole and wondered what lay beyond it. Would this be their entry point to a greater galactic society, a way into the limitless experiences of the universe at large? Or was this a Patron beachhead right in the heart of their solar system, a new front in a war only just begun? Nathan and Kris each sought the other's hand and held tightly to one another.

Nathan turned concerned eyes upon Kris, and he felt both unsurprised and immensely relieved to see that she was smiling broadly. She, for one, refused to be cowed by the darker possibilities the wormhole mouth represented, preferring to embrace the wonder rather than the worry.

Her cheeks dimpled as possibilities and potentials multiplied within her thoughts. The jaded, tired scientist who only wanted to follow the rest of the crew home had vanished. Kris leaned in close. "You know, maybe there's still something new out here to see after all."

And Nathan knew then that everything would be all right.

THE END

ABOUT THE AUTHOR

Thomas A. Mays (Tom) is an 18-years-and-counting veteran of the US Navy, working as an officer in the surface fleet aboard destroyers and amphibious ships, as well as assisting with research into ballistic missile defense. He has two degrees in physics, but his passion is writing. He tries not to let what he actually knows get in the way of telling a good story. The author of several short stories in both print and online magazines, this is his first published novel. Tom usually lives wherever the Navy tells him to (currently North Carolina), making a home with his lovely wife, three beautiful kids, and an insane Hawaiian mutt.

Tom's blog, The Improbable Author, can be found at:

www.improbableauthor.com

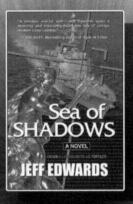
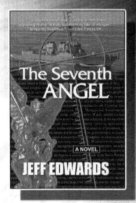
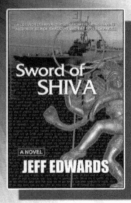

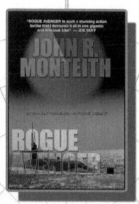

Award-Winning Novelist
JOHN R. MONTEITH

Made in the USA
San Bernardino, CA
04 May 2015